Staccato Publishing
Zimmerman, MN

First US Edition: March 2013

Author: C.S. Yelle
Editors: Sara Johnson
Karen Reckard
Cover: Terra Koster of KMS Design

ISBN: 978-0-9839341-5-8

Printed in the USA

Taking Angels

The Angel Crusades

C. S. Yelle

For Allen,
Thank you for your support
CS Yelle

Chapter 1

Eighteen and dying. My reality *sucked the big one* and I'd had enough.

The movement of the canoe hypnotized me while I lay in the bottom of the aluminum craft, the waves creating a hollow pinging sound as we cut across the lake. I kept my eyes closed against the bright sun baking my face, the light breeze keeping me from feeling the burn.

Spending most of my time in hospitals under the dull fluorescent lighting with its incessant hum had left my skin pale and white. I'd rather be out here instead of taking chemo or radiation, anyone would. This felt like heaven; a place I'd spent far too much time thinking about lately.

"Britt, you're getting sunburned," Mom scolded as she paused in her paddling to stare back at me. "Put your chin down so your hat can block the sun."

"Let her be, Mary," Dad sighed.

"She's going to get burnt. It isn't good for her skin, Jim."

"What will it do besides make her uncomfortable?" Dad argued.

He paused now and again to drag the paddle in the water, steering us towards his goal across the lake. I didn't remember which lake we were on; only that it was part of the pristine Boundary Waters Canoe Area in Northern Minnesota.

I pulled the large-brimmed hat down over my eyes and went back to listening to the rhythmic waves. I moved my bony butt on the metal support of the canoe, trying to get comfortable. Without any padding, it wasn't happening. Still, it beat the hospital beds and the sterile linens.

Shifting again and looking to where we headed: tall pines reaching for the blue sky, little white clouds floating overhead; I remembered the place. It was a nice campsite with good fishing and a waterfall leading into the next lake. The mosquitoes were murder on that trip six years ago. I hoped they didn't like the taste of my blood as much this time. Maybe the chemo could stop *something*.

"Not much further, Britt," Dad said. "Getting stiff?"

"Yeah." I nodded, shifting a little more.

My parents kept paddling, steady and strong. I closed my eyes again, recalling how Mom and I used to take turns paddling up front. Now I couldn't lift a paddle, much less use one. Soon sand and rock crunched against the bottom of the canoe bringing us to a sudden stop, jolting me hard against the metal frame.

"Land ho," I cried as loud as my chemo ruined lungs allowed. I breathed like a severe asthmatic or someone who'd smoked all her life.

Mom began unpacking our supplies while Dad pulled the canoe further onto shore and I went along for the ride. The smell of pine hit me and the sound of the waterfalls reached my ears.

"I want to go in the water." I forced a grin from under my absurdly large brim.

Dad nodded as he lifted me in his arms and carried me to shore. "You need to get your suit on and we have to set up camp first."

"I have my suit on." I showed him, pulling my shirt up with a thin hand.

He chuckled. "We have to get things set up before it gets too dark though, Britt."

"Can I just sit in it up to my waist?" I pleaded, glancing at the outlet and the water flowing over some nearby rocks.

He stopped and turned to Mom who stood with her arms crossed, listening to our conversation. She opened her mouth to object but looked at my face and her expression faltered. She gave a resigned nod.

"Yay." I clapped as Dad set me down.

Mom helped take off my shorts and top leaving the baggy one-piece to cover nothing anyone would want to see. Dad picked me up again, walked down the bank, and began to set me in before I stopped him.

"Hey, I want to have some current flowing over me," I protested. "Closer."

He glanced at me and then back to Mom. Sighing, he took another dozen steps or so closer to the small waterfalls. A light rumble reached my ears as the water struck rocks out of sight and felt the mist drift over us. A bigger fall lay just beyond these.

The cold, fresh water made me shiver as he put me into a spot between two large rocks, worn smooth from centuries of moving water. I gasped and tensed until my body began to relax, acclimating to the temperature.

He looked down, impatient, as I grinned up at him.

"What?"

"Is that enough?"

"No, I want to sit a while."

7

"Britt, I need to set up camp."

"Who's stopping you?"

"I can't leave you alone." His eyes were wide and anxious.

"I won't be. You and Mom are only a few feet away, I'll be fine."

He stared at me, cocking an eyebrow and crossing his arms over his chest.

"Go on, I'll be fine," I reassured him.

His eyes narrowed as he leaned his head to one side and frowned. Without another word he walked back to camp, looking over his shoulder every few steps, making sure I wasn't going to slip off somewhere.

The funny thing is…that's exactly what I planned. The four years of treatment, the endless hours in a hospital bed; I wouldn't allow any more. I would slide myself into the current and let the water take me away from here, from this world filled with nothing but pain and suffering. The decision didn't come easy. My parents were wonderful, my friends, the ones that stuck by me, very supportive. I would miss them all, but to watch their eyes cloud with sympathy and sorrow as I became a hollow shell was something I didn't want to put any of us through. Not anymore.

I glanced over my shoulder at the camp. Mom was setting up the tent with Dad. I waved at her, putting on the smile I learned to use when she needed to feel better. If they knew my plan, of course they'd try to stop me. What parent wouldn't?

She waved and turned back to the tent and my smile melted away.

Inching my butt forward, closer to the current tickling at my toes and ankles, I slid down further, pushing off from the smooth boulders. My suit hitched up, but I didn't care about a wedgy before floating to my death. I grinned at the thought. After all those months in a hospital bed, sliding down as my underwear crept up wasn't even a worry. It ended today, now.

Stealing another look at the campsite revealed them collecting firewood around the edge of the camp's clearing. Their backs to me, I took my chance.

I thought it would feel different, somehow, when my body floated off the rock. The panic I feared would seize me at that moment didn't come. The urgency to reach this point melted away. I leaned back, my head rested in the water. An eagle drifted above me gliding on air currents while it searched the water for fish, captivating me with its elegance and majesty. I'd forgotten the beauty of this place. For the first time in over a year, I felt my world around me, caressing me, stimulating my senses which had gone stale and making me feel...alive.

A rush of fear gripped me. What was I thinking? I wanted to live, I wasn't a quitter. I wanted to fight until I couldn't fight anymore. But the realization that my choice in the matter was gone hit me as I slid into the current, my head above water for a split second before the sounds went muffled. My silly hat with the big brim pulled away from my hairless head.

I expected them to try and reach me, hoping they would be too late. Now, I prayed that they would come. Paddling with all the strength in my atrophied muscles, I fought the current. It tugged, hard, and carried me away.

Mom screamed and Dad shouted right as a loud splash hit the water upstream.

I opened my eyes in the hazy water as a dark shape darted past, too late to catch me. I hit something hard and was airborne, the sound of the falls rumbling in my ears. The feeling was like nothing I'd experienced before. The air and the water mixed to frothy foam and then I plunged underwater again, the sounds going muffled. My body hit the rocks and debris at the bottom of the falls, jarring me and forcing the warm air from my lungs to be replaced by cold, crisp lake water. Spinning over and over I lost my sense of up and down as the churning water kept me lurching from side to side. My head throbbed and my lungs bucked. The water pulled me along and soon black spots filled my vision. The spots spread until the blackness enveloped everything. Then, the pain was over and the next stage of my existence, if any, began.

I heard a voice. Melodic and sweet; female I thought, but couldn't tell for certain. The words indiscernible, the voice sounded urgent then stern; something I didn't want to hear upon my arrival in heaven. I cringed.

Then another voice came, deeper but no less sweet. Calm and soothing it flowed on, pulling me with it. I longed for it to keep speaking, to fill my ears with its infectious happiness and joy. The voice I needed to hear in heaven. A much better welcome, I concluded.

I pried my eyes open but my vision blurred, showing me nothing but light and shadows. Blinking to clear them only made it worse. The voice touched my ears again, the deeper one. I took a deep breath, surprised by the wonderful odors of pine and lilac, the enveloping happiness consuming me.

I blinked again, beginning to see them as more than just shapes. Halos of blonde hair against the sun and a faint glow about them. They were angels, both of them. Even though my sight remained cloudy I could discern one female and one male as they stood before me; the collage of green starting to take the shapes of trees behind them. The familiar sound of the waterfalls and a rushing river drifted to my ears and mist wet my skin. How could that be?

"What have you done?" the female's voice accused, her words finally clear.

"I don't know," the deeper voice said.

"You did something different," she pointed out.

I frowned. What did he do?

"I touched her, but it didn't work the same."

"This is not good," the female warned. "You touched her too late."

"What are we going to do?" he asked.

"We? There is no 'we.' You touched her, I didn't."

Both faces turned to me again. The shapes became clearer as the two heads of hair came into focus.

"Don't tell anyone, you have to promise," the deeper voice pleaded.

"Fine, but if they find out, you're on your own."

I closed my eyes and everything began to jerk and twist as sirens sounded in my ears and the smell of antiseptic filled my nose, pulling me out of my peaceful

11

dream. Opening my eyes, my parent's faces lurched into my field of vision.

"She's awake," Dad shouted.

"Oh my God," Mom cried. "Britt, can you hear us? Britt?"

I tried to sit up, but found my body strapped down making it impossible to move.

My parents vanished. A woman and a man stuck their heads over mine, one with a light attached to his head shining in my eyes, blinding everything else.

"Britt, you're okay, but we've got you on a backboard so you won't be able to move," the man said, definitely not the musical voice from earlier.

"You're in an ambulance in route to the Ely Hospital," the woman explained.

"Can you remember what happened?" the man asked, lifting an eyelid and looking at my pupil.

"I drowned?"

"You *nearly* drowned," the man corrected.

"Do you know where you nearly drowned?" the woman asked.

"The BWCA?"

"Good, good Britt." The man smiled down at me.

I heard my mother crying and wished I hadn't. Tears welled up and began to spill from the corners of my eyes.

"Britt, it'll be okay." Dad squeezed my hand lightly. "Everything will be okay."

I'd survived but now the cancer would win, taking away my choice. My one chance to take control back and I'd chickened out.

"Don't cry, Britt." Mom comforted me. "You're going to make it."

I cried harder; the thought of lying in a hospital bed, nothing more than a husk of myself and withering to nothingness filled my mind.

We pulled into the emergency room entrance, the automatic doors whirring open as they wheeled me in. The two paramedics were on either side with Mom and Dad following close behind. The fluorescent lights beat down from overhead as we sped past.

"Oh great," I sighed. "I'm home."

We went into a room with two nurses and a doctor rushing in behind us, calling out directions to the paramedics. The doctor examined me while the nurses put an IV in one arm and a blood pressure cuff on the other. They attached electrodes to my chest and began switching on all the standard equipment until the room beeped and chirped, just like old times.

The doctor straightened from listening to my heart and lungs, his brows furrowed.

I looked up at him and he smiled.

Noticing my inquiring look, he nodded. "Sounds fine. Lungs clear, heart strong. Do you feel pain anywhere?" He continued to press his hands along my body, searching for breaks along my rib cage and then moving to my arms and legs. He pulled back the warm blankets the ambulance crew wrapped me in.

"No, I feel …" the thought trailed off. I didn't feel any pain. None. Not the continuous aching of my muscles, joints, and bones from the cancer. Even more surprising, nothing hurt from the trip over the falls and the landing on the rocks below. I had to be in shock.

"She's stable. Let's get her to x-ray and see if anything is broken," the doctor ordered. "If those come back clear, we can take you off the backboard and check you out further."

They wheeled me out of the room with the monitors and IVs attached to hooks on the bed, the cords and tubes tapping against the side rails of the bed. I lay under the x-ray machine as it hummed above me, taking pictures and possibly reducing my chances of having children in the future, although the cancer would pretty much have seen to that already.

We returned to the room, passing the concerned faces of my parents as we rolled in. Seeing them reminded me of the worst part: the pain they continued to endure every day my future hung in the balance.

The bed jerked to a stop and the nurse clicked the brake on the wheels. The doctor stood over the top of me before the bed stilled and unbuckled the straps fastening me to the back board. With the help of the nurses they slid the device out from beneath me and eased me onto the soft mattress.

"Nothing's broken," he said with a smile. "How you managed that one is a miracle." He stepped away to write something in my charts.
I lifted my head and looked at my body for the first time since going over the falls. My arms and legs, stomach and chest, looked … normal.

My mouth and eyes shot open. My body looked *normal*. Not sickly, not post chemo, post radiation, but normal, not in the process of dying. My muscles were full and firm. My bones didn't stick out like before, but were covered smoothly by healthy looking skin, not the pale white, almost yellow skin I'd come to expect.

"Mom, Dad," I shouted, my voice on the edge of hysteria.

They rushed in from just outside the door, their eyes on mine, searching for my anguish, my fear. Their concern turned to confusion.

"Look at me," I cried.

"We are," Dad said, still concentrating on my eyes and face as his mind tried to justify what he saw and what he *should* see.

"Mary," he said. "Look at Britt." He placed a hand on her chin, moving it to look at my body.

Mom's face first went white and then flushed red.

"Oh, Britt," she gasped, rushing to me, sending one of the nurses sprawling. She put a hand to my head as she pulled me to her chest.

"I think your hair is growing." She leaned back, her eyes wide, looking at my head.

I raised a hand to my scalp and, sure enough, the beginnings of new growth tickled my fingertips. Closing my eyes to my parents and their joy, the fading vision of the two angels floated in my thoughts. Why did they send me back? Was I not worthy? The way the angels discussed "touching" me made me feel uneasy, uncertain.

What did they do to me?

Chapter 2

The doctor ran some more tests to assure my stability after the ride over the waterfalls. He scratched his head as he signed the discharge papers, a crooked smile on his face.

"Looks like someone was watching out for you today, young lady," he said as my parents grinned at me over his shoulder.

"Uh, I guess." I shrugged.

"I can't check your cancer without sending blood and tissue samples out to a lab. I've been in contact with your specialists at Mayo and they want you to head down there for a look-see." He glanced back at Mom and Dad who nodded their agreement. The Mayo Clinic in Rochester was our second home and the best medical facility around.

"She looks different from before," Mom said and all eyes turned to her.

"Different how?" the doctor asked.

"Well, she was a lot thinner this morning," Mom began.

"That can be due to some swelling from the tumble she took," the doctor explained.

"And her hair is growing again," Mom continued.

"We don't know a lot about how the body reacts to the radiation and chemo. I've seen patients who haven't had hair for years. They begin growing hair again out of the blue."

"But her eyes," Mom whispered.

"My eyes?" I said as the doctor and Dad echoed, "Her eyes?"

"Yes, they were brown. Now they're…" she hesitated as the men turned to me.

"Blue." Dad stared at me, surprised, and turned back to Mom.

"Let me see," I demanded.

The doctor reached in the drawer of my side table and pulled out a small mirror. He handed it to me and stepped back beside my parents.

Lifting the mirror I looked at a stranger. Light colored fuzz covered my head, softening the appearance of the purple scar from the most recent surgery and deep blue eyes met my gaze. I stared for a long time as the room remained silent except for the steady breathing from the other occupants. My breathing, on the other hand, came in uneven rasps as my mind tried to wrap around all of this. The waterfall, the angels, my changed appearance; they must be connected, but how?

"There are known cases of accidents where head trauma has altered the person's eye color, although it is very rare. Britt doesn't show any signs of head trauma. She doesn't show any signs of trauma from going over the falls at all." The doctor shrugged, clearly bewildered. He handed me my discharge papers, placed a hand on my shoulder, and gave me a comforting smile as I lowered the mirror and looked at him, also at a loss.

"Good luck, Britt. I hope your good fortune continues." He turned and walked away as my eyes followed his white lab coat out the door.

We left the hospital, rushed back to Grand Rapids, packed up some things, and headed to the Rochester Mayo Clinic to see my specialists. The entire ride to Rochester, Mom kept peering back at me as if I would grow another head or something. The fact was I didn't know for sure I wouldn't. I couldn't even rule that out for sure. Staring out the window, trying to ignore her, I thought about the encounter with the angels. Why did this happen to me? It felt as though someone had interceded in my life, giving me another chance. But why? What made me special?

We reached the Mayo Clinic early the next the morning and they admitted me. I slipped into the too familiar hospital gown and climbed between the not-quite-soft sterilized linens I'd vowed to avoid a mere twelve hours ago while floating in the cold lake.

"Hey Britt." A red-headed nurse greeted me as she entered the room.

"Hey Sandy," I sighed.

"You missed us so much you had to visit early?" she teased.

"Guess so." I shrugged, not amused.

"Little miss sunshine." A large man with a long blonde pony-tail and a big grin on his face chimed in as he walked in.

"Hi Roger." I sat up, smiling.

"The Doc says you need to give us some blood to check out." He placed the kit complete with test tubes and vials sticking out of the compartments on the stand next to the bed.

"You guys are like vampires," I groaned, extending an arm.

"The life of a lab tech," he chuckled.

Sandy hooked up the standard equipment and started an IV in the other arm as Roger drew some blood.

None of it fazed me anymore and I sat looking at them in silence until they finished.

"There you go." Roger opened a Band-Aid to cover the fresh puncture mark. "Hopefully we won't need anymore."

"I've heard that before. You'll know where to find me if you do."

"Hey, where did it go?" Roger said, moving my arm and looking at it from different angles.

"Where'd what go?" Sandy asked, walking over next to him.

"The needle mark." Roger motioned to my arm. "I can't see it."

We stared at my arm as Roger lifted it to look closer, but none of us could see the mark.

"That's odd." Sandy shrugged at Roger.

Roger tossed the opened Band-Aid in the trash, got up, and walked out shaking his head.

"Just give me a buzz if you need anything, alright?" Sandy said to me as Roger left.

"Yeah," I acknowledged, looking past her to my parents as they visited quietly. This all seemed routine, yet hope tingled in the back of my mind that it didn't have to be, not anymore. Lifting my arm closer to my face, I studied the perfect skin. Drawing blood usually made me bleed a lot. This wasn't normal. My breath caught in my throat as my eyes widened.

When I was eight, I wiped out on my bike and broke my arm leaving a long scar where the bone punctured the skin. The scar was gone. Lifting my other arm, the scar from getting burned on a hot poker stick at the campfire was missing as well. Staring at Mom and Dad for a moment to assure they weren't watching, I shifted in my bed and pulled the open back of the hospital gown around to look at my right side. Smooth skin replaced the four inch appendix scar.

Did the angel's touch do this? Lying back, I wondered what other changes might come. I pondered this until I fell asleep, ending the craziest day of my life…so far.

I woke the next morning to see Doctor Morgan, my epidemiologist, smiling at me. My parents rubbed the sleep out of their eyes and straightened their clothes as they sat on the two small couches in the room; their beds last night.

"Good Morning, Britt," Doctor Morgan greeted me. "I understand you decided to take a water ride without the water park."

"I guess you could say that," I said, embarrassed.

"The blood work came back and the results are quite surprising."

Mom gasped and Doctor Morgan turned to her. "Nothing bad, just surprising," he assured her and then looked back to me. "The preliminary tests show your cancer is gone."

My parent's cries of joy filled the room as I stared at the wall. A tickle in the back of my mind kept me from feeling the happiness my parents felt. Something about the way the angels spoke of 'touching' me came back, giving me pause. Like something wasn't right about what they'd done.

"I'd like some other specialists to take a look and see if we can figure out what happened," Doctor Morgan said.

"What kind of specialists?" I asked.

"Another epidemiologist and a neurosurgeon," he said calmly.

"Neurosurgeon?" Mom spoke up.

"Doctor Kramer from Ely mentioned your eyes changed from brown to blue." He leaned closer, verifying my eye color and leaned back nodding. "We have to make certain you didn't sustain any sort of head trauma. We should have you out of here by the end of the week."

"A week?" I moaned.

"We don't want to miss anything," he said pressing his lips tight together. "Let me examine you before we start the next round of tests." He stepped over and began to run his hands along my arms, watching my reaction as he pressed in the joints, the muscles, and along the bones. "Does that hurt?"

"No."

"Let's take a look at your incision from your last surgery," he said, as I leaned my head forward and he ran a hand through the new growth of fuzz. "When did this start coming back?"

"After the accident," I said, stumbling over the word, 'accident.'

"This is odd." Doctor Morgan reached over, clicking on the exam light and pulling the extending arm over my head.

"What?" I said.

"What is?" Mom said, as she came over to stand next to the doctor.

"Her scar is gone," Doctor Morgan said.

"No way." I lifted my head only to have him push it back down again.

"Oh my lord," Mom gasped.

Dad shuffled over and his feet joined Mom's and Doctor Morgan's in front of me.

"I'll be damned," Dad sighed.

"Really?" I asked, forcing my head up against the doctor's hands until he let me look up.

"No scar." Mom nodded.

"We all saw it at the hospital in Ely," Dad murmured.

"But it isn't there now," Doctor Morgan said.

"Cool," I grinned.

"Yeah, cool, but strange. We need to get those tests going and the other specialists in here. We'll have them in to see you right away." He looked at me and then my parents. "Alright, talk to you later." He nodded and walked out.

Mom leaned over and gave me a hug. "I'm so happy," she whispered.

Dad looked at me, a blank expression. A slight smile curled his lips as he stared in a daze. This was much better than having them watch me die and me watching them watch me die. A slow smile spread across my face at the thought of having a normal life, for once.

"Morning Britt." A woman broke in as she pushed a wheelchair into the room.

"Morning Courtney."

"Ready to take a ride to the MRI?"

"Do I have a choice?"

"Not really," Courtney joked as she took the IV tubing from the shunt in my arm and hung it over the monitor.

I climbed out of bed and into the chair, glancing over at Mom and Dad. "Be back in a flash."

"Well, more than a flash, probably a couple of hours. Plenty of time to go to the cafeteria," Courtney said.

"See you later," Dad said, standing and coming over to give me a kiss on the top of the head.

"We'll be here when you get back." Mom joined Dad by my side and placed a hand on my shoulder.

"No worries," I said. "It's not my first time around the block."

Courtney wheeled me out of the room and down the hall into an elevator. As the doors closed, she stepped around me to tap a button on the panel.

"Waterfall?" she asked, turning to stare at me in disbelief.

"What?"

"You went over a waterfall?"

"Yeah."

"Now I've heard it all." She shook her head.

Guess everyone had heard it by now. News travelled fast in these halls.

I lay in the MRI for over an hour, trying to stay still, until Courtney wheeled me back to my room and my waiting parents. I climbed into bed and fell asleep, exhausted by the morning's activities. It takes a lot of effort to stay still.

I dreamt of the voices, the sensations surrounding me in my moment spent in heaven. They spoke uneasy, not certain about what they'd done. What had they done? I woke with a heavy feeling of uncertainty, but was determined to keep a positive attitude. Doctor Morgan sat visiting with my parents. When he saw me awake, he stood and came over to the bed and sat down on the edge.

"The MRI was inconclusive," he began. "We would like to do some injections and then run it again."

"Inconclusive?"

"We couldn't see anything out of the ordinary and that concerns us."

"So if there is nothing out of the ordinary, does that mean the tumor is gone?" I asked, already knowing in my heart it was.

"We aren't sure. A tumor like that doesn't just go away. We need to discover what happened. We'll run another MRI tomorrow and then do a CT the next day."

"What else?" I asked, reading his hesitancy.

"We need to take some bone marrow from you and check that as well."

"No, not that, any of the other tests, but not bone marrow."

"Britt, I know it's unpleasant…"

"Unpleasant? Have you ever had it done to you?" Doctor Morgan shook his head.

"Exactly. If you had, you'd know it's a lot more than unpleasant. Next you're going to tell me that I need a spinal tap too." My jaw dropped at his blank expression.

"Britt, we need to be certain the cancer hasn't relocated. We have to check every possibility."

Tears filled my eyes as I looked to my parents. Their faces told me they weren't going to be any help. I turned back to the doctor.

"I'm sorry, but we're hopeful there'll be nothing to find." He stood, gave a nod to my parents, and walked out.

"This really sucks," I said, rolling away from my parents and pulling the covers up to my neck.

Lab techs came in two more times to draw blood, making it impossible to get to sleep until after dinner. The dreams of my angels came again. Only the good parts as the voices reassured me everything would be alright. The soothing, melodic way they spoke sent waves of comfort through me, giving me a fresh attitude before waking up to more tests.

The next morning, true to his word, Doctor Morgan had them take me back to the MRI after injecting me with some sort of dye. I struggled to hold still as they searched, and searched, and searched.

The CT scan was next and I didn't get back to my room until just before dinner. Sliding into bed, completely exhausted, Mom handed me her cell phone. Staring at her questioningly, she motioned for me to talk.

"Hello?"

"Britt, is it true?" A familiar voice said.

"Hey Trish," I grinned into the phone. "So far, so good."

"That's crazy," a different person said.

"Elisa?"

"Hey Britt," Elisa said.

"Where is…"I began.

"I'm here too," a third voice spoke up.

"Cassie," I laughed.

Cassie, Trish, and Elisa were my three best friends in the whole world. "The three amigos" I called them, well, Dad started calling them that first because they were inseparable. They always came around to lift my spirits after tough chemo bouts and kept me up to speed with the high school gossip.

"Your Mom got us on a conference call and filled us in," Trish said.

"Your cancer is gone?" Cassie asked.

"She'll tell us if we let her talk," Elisa moaned.

"So far all the tests show no signs of cancer anymore," I explained.

"How many more tests do you have before you can come home?"

"Only the two crappiest ones, bone marrow and spinal," I sighed.

"Just think about all the fun we're going to have once you get back," Elisa encouraged.

"We miss you, girl," Cassie added.

"Hang in there, Britt, we love you," Trish said.

"I love you guys too. Thanks and see you soon. Bye." Hitting 'end' on the phone, I handed it back to Mom as she stood with tears in her eyes.

"What?"

"I'm so happy you can share your life with friends like them," Mom sniffled.

"Me too, they're the best."

Dad sat quietly in the corner, smiling. That was enough for me.

*A different dream came that night, replacing the
happy ones. Blurry images at first, it gained clarity as it
went. A woman screaming in terror ran from something
unseen, unable to escape. Pain gripped me, threatening
to tear the heart from my chest as her life was ripped
from her.*

The guilt of being alive washed over me as I woke
with a feeling of dread. The woman's death felt so real it
weighed heavily on me. The thought of seeing each
morbid detail of her demise terrified me. Her last
moments played out before my eyes; something not
meant for my eyes, the feeling of intruding almost as
strong as the horror of witnessing her final breaths. The
strange odor of lilac permeated my senses. Gasping for
air, I looked around the room for its origin, but the room
was empty of any kind of flower. With a hand to my
breast, my heart finally slowed enough that I wasn't
afraid it might pound from my chest. I slid back against
the pillows and stared out the window at the pre-dawn
blackness. How could a dream feel so real?

Depression threatened to win when they wheeled
me down to the bone marrow procedure. Lying as still as
possible while they drilled a needle into my bone, I
fought to keep the image of the dying woman from
washing over me, consuming me. Pressing hard, I
brought forth the images and voices of the angels. As they
came into focus it gave me something happy and
promising to concentrate on.

Arriving back at my room, my strength drained
from me, I slid into bed in a heap. It was late evening
when I woke, having slept the entire day.

"Welcome back," Dad said, sitting off to one side in an overstuffed chair.

"How long have I been asleep?"

"Nearly eight hours. You obviously needed it."

"Where's Mom?" I looked around the room.

"She went to get something to eat."

"You could have gone with her. I'm a big girl."

"You'll always be my little girl, no matter how old you are." Dad smiled as tears glistened in his eyes. "I hate sitting by and watching them hurt you."

"Doctor Morgan said I needed to do it."

"Knowing you need to do it doesn't make it any easier, does it?"

"No, not really. Does it for you?" I asked.

"Not in the least." Dad shook his head. "What the hell happened up there, Britt?"

The question caught me so off-guard that I gasped and held my breath as my mind raced to figure out how to answer him. Exhaling, I shrugged.

"I don't know. One minute I was going over the falls, and the next I was in an ambulance." I couldn't tell him the truth. Even Dad would think me certifiable if I started talking angels.

"I'm so sorry I couldn't get to you." He choked up and the words came out in a weak rush.

"I know, Dad. It isn't your fault. I shouldn't have insisted on going in the water so close to the falls. It's my fault."

Our eyes met and in that split second, he reconciled his uncertainty about the truth of what happened. A spark of realization twinkled in his eyes and he knew. He knew I did it on purpose. His face lost all expression and he gave me a curt nod as he stood. Walking over, he bent down to kiss me on the forehead. He backed away just far enough for our eyes to meet again.

"I will never, ever, stop loving you until the day I die. And I will do everything in my power to keep you safe."

"I love…" I began, but he interrupted me.

"Don't you ever, I mean ever, try something like that again. Do you hear me?" The tone of his voice and the intensity in eyes left no doubt how deeply he meant it. "Not on my watch." He straightened and walked from the room as I gave an uncontrollable shiver. I'd never seen him like that before. It was the closest he had ever come to losing control with me. Note to self: never get him any closer.

After eating a late dinner I fell asleep again, completely forgetting about the nightmare from the night before until the next nightmare had me.

A man sat in his recliner watching the Twins when he came into focus. He dosed lightly and turned in my direction just as his eyes shot wide. He opened his mouth as if to speak, but only cries of pain came out. The pain in his eyes turned to distant a stare as his lungs heaved once more and then went still.

I woke with a gasp, sitting up straight, looking around the small room. My parents slept on the two couches, undisturbed by my abrupt movement. Leaning back I felt the sweat, cold and wet against my back, had soaked the sheets and made me shiver. My nose crinkled at the residual smell of lilacs. Moving the bed to a sitting position, I searched the room for the lilacs but again, they weren't there. I sat staring at the sun coming up through the window, another day of testing and another life taken with me as witness.

Later, lying on my stomach as they drew spinal cord fluid from me, I cried uncontrollably. Unable to draw on the strength of my happy dreams, the nightmares took control and flooded me with sorrow. The surgical team thought I cried from the pain and gave me morphine, but it only made me loopy and more fearful that the dreams were actually real. I didn't remember getting back to my room, too drugged up on the morphine, but woke later that evening. I had to stop losing days like this; I needed to get out of here and on with my life, whatever that entailed.

As if reading my mind, Doctor Morgan walked in, pulling up a chair between the couch my parents sat on and my bed so we all could see him. He held a thick manila folder and flipped it open as he crossed his legs.

"Good evening." He looked from my parents to me.

"Isn't it a little late for you, Doc?" I asked, never recalling him being in to see me so late.

"I thought we could speak tonight and get you on the road early tomorrow."

I smiled, staring excitedly at my parents who mirrored my happiness.

Nodding to Doctor Morgan, I waited for him to continue.

"We're at a loss. The doctors going over the test results, as well as the techs administering the tests, have never witnessed anything like this before."

"What is it?" Mom asked, leaning closer.

"Britt, you are the healthiest we've ever seen you. Your lungs are now the lungs of a healthy eighteen year old. Your liver, shutting down before the near drowning, is healthy. Your brain tumor is gone. Not only is the cancer gone, but every evasive procedure we did on you is already healed completely with no signs of it ever being done. It usually takes weeks to heal from the insertion points for the bone marrow and the spinal tests, but it's like you healed as soon as the needles were withdrawn. There was no bleeding, no seeping; nothing. The techs reported they couldn't even see where they had pulled the needles from seconds after the fact."

We sat in silence, staring dumbfounded as the doctor expressed his surprise and shock.

"The most confusing thing is there are no signs of any kind of trauma to your body at all. Even past surgeries, injuries, everything that was well documented; you no longer show any signs of damage. As a matter of fact, your appendix is back and healthier than ever." He threw up his hand in exasperation and the documents flew into the air, cascading to the floor.

"What do I do now?" I asked.

"You live. Go live your life and take it where it leads you. I don't get to say that often, but I want you to experience everything this life has to offer, Britt. Somehow, for some reason, you have been given a new lease on life, and you need to grasp it with both hands and hold on tight." He stood, leaned down to give me a hug.

He shook Dad's hand and gave Mom a hug. "Have a good life," he said with smile and walked out the door, leaving the file of my past life lying on the floor.

Chapter 3

We pulled into our garage late one evening two weeks after leaving for the BWCA, exhausted but optimistic by the prospect of a future, something I had long given up on.

"I'm so tired," I sighed.

"Get to bed," Mom told me as we hauled ourselves from the vehicle.

Pulling my backpack from the rear seat I headed upstairs. Swinging the door open, I flicked on the light. The room was the way I left it, everything in its place, except for some flowers and balloons on my desk by the window.

I dropped my backpack to the floor, walked over, and opened the card grinning.

Welcome home. We're happy for you.
Elisa, Cassie, and Trish.

My 'three amigos' never let me down. I set the card on the desk, flopped onto the bed still in my clothes, and fell asleep in seconds.

The dream came with horrifying vividness. This time I chased someone running, trying to get away from me. Of that I had no doubt. He came to a dead-end, brick walls surrounding him and only one way out. Looking back into my eyes, he reeled in fear. Someone stepped between us, someone light and airy, almost not there at all. He put a hand up to stop me. I laughed, but it wasn't my laugh. A stranger's hand reached out from my body,

grasping the airy person by the neck. He screamed in
pain as the person against the wall behind him cried out
in agony. Both fell silent, the airy body hanging limp in
the outstretched hand. It flowed into the hand, losing its
shape; its identity. I looked back at the person leaning
motionless against the brick wall, his eyes open wide,
terror still stretching across his face.

I woke with a scream, Mom holding me, pulling
me against her chest.

"Britt, Britt, it's alright, it's going to be alright,"
she soothed, caressing my head, rocking me back and
forth.

My nose crinkled as the tell-tale smell of lilac
intruded on my senses again.

At eighteen, it should have felt uncomfortable;
embarrassing, but the terror racing through me kept me
grasping her, pulling her closer, needing her comfort and
protection. It took over an hour for the shaking to stop. I
sat wrapped in my comforter, legs crossed under me,
determined to get control back before turning off the
light. Mom sat with me until I nodded at her questioning
look and she stepped out, closing the door behind her
with one last worried glance, the lights still on.

The dream felt so real. I didn't understand at first,
but comprehension eventually percolated to the surface.
Maybe it *was* real. I pulled the covers closer as the
shivering started again; the vision of the man in the alley,
his eyes focused on mine, coming back to me. The horror
in those eyes were burned into my memory, etched there
for all time. And that smell of lilac. Ever since it came to

34

me at the waterfall it wafted to me after every bad dream. Why?

The sun shone through the window across my face, waking me as I leaned against my headboard, still sitting up. I straightened my legs, cringing as the tingles felt like needles across my shins and through my feet. A dream, that's all, I kept telling myself trying to rationalize, to convince myself. But this dream freaked me out. The chill running up and down my spine coupled with the tingling in my legs made my skin burn as if on fire.

The clock on the nightstand showed ten and I slid out of bed staggering over to the window to look out at the large oak tree to one side of the house and the quiet side street. I grasped at their normalcy needing them to anchor me, ground me from the craziness of the dream; much like I did many times after therapy pushed me down threatening to take control. The tree and street brought me back to my reality like beacons showing me the way home, giving me comfort.

I closed my eyes and pulled the most exciting thought I could to the front of my mind. School started in a week. I felt amazed to have the opportunity to be there for my senior year. After so many years of sporadic attendance, along with private tutors when the chemo and other treatments became too overwhelming, the idea of attending school brought me joy. Though the thought of spending my days in school with my friends, doing the kinds of things every senior in high school did, felt bittersweet if it meant my nights were going to be filled with terror.

I hobbled over to the long mirror on the back of my bedroom door as feeling eased back to my sleeping legs. I stared at myself with continued disbelief. My hair was growing like crazy. In the past two weeks it went from nothing to shoulder length. And where it used to be dark brown, hearly black, it was now golden brown.

My breath caught in my chest as my happy dream came to mind. My hair matched the color of the angels'. I ran a hand through the silky locks and smiled. My skin, still slightly pale in the sunlight streaming through the window, was the only remnant of the sickness that racked my body for almost four years. The rays shone on my handful of the now golden, thick hair. And my eyes stared back at me, bright blue. That still freaked me out, almost as much as it did Mom. Well, not that much. She never mentioned it, but I often caught her glancing at me, just before she turned away with a shudder.

Touching my cheek, it felt smooth and soft. If this was a dream, I never wanted to wake up. A tap sounded on the door and I walked over to my bed and sat down. "Come in."

The door burst open and the "three amigos" came rushing in, tackling me on my bed.

My mother peered over their shoulders, worry spread across her face. "Girls, you need to be careful."

"That's okay, Mom," I laughed as we rolled on the bed.

"The weak link has returned," Cassie cried, barreling over the top of me.

"Where've you been, girl?" Elisa laughed.

"We know where she's been, but now we need to know: where's she going?" Trish smiled, standing up and pulling me into a sitting position as the other girls sat up and crossed their legs.

"OMG," Cassie shouted. "What is happening with your hair?"

"It's gorgeous," Trish said, running a hand through it.

"Didn't you have black hair?" Elisa asked.

"Yeah, sort of," I said. "It's been so long since I've had hair it's hard to remember."

"I love it," they said in unison.

We looked at each other and burst into laughter, Elisa and Cassie falling back onto the bed and Trish dropping to a knee on the floor in hysteria. When we finally wiped the tears of laughter from our eyes, the girls looked at each other and then turned their gaze on me.

"What?" I asked, a little concerned with the way they smiled at me.

"Shopping," Trish cried out.

"You need to go shopping," Elisa agreed.

"Most definitely." Cassie grinned.

I looked to Mom as she stood in the doorway.

"You do need some clothes and it will be good for you to get out with your friends." She smiled.

"Yeah," the girls cheered.

"Jump in the shower and we'll do an inventory on your closet to see what you need," Trish said, walking over and sliding my closet door open.

"Fine, but you need to be gentle," I said, extracting myself from Cassie and Elisa to join Trish by my closet. "It's been a long time since I've power shopped."

"Like riding a bike," Cassie said.

"Once you've done it, you never forget," Elisa added.

"And by look of this closet," Trish said with a hand on her chin, "you need to get rid of the training wheels… and training bra." She grinned and reached into the closet, took an old bra on one finger and twirled it around.

"Hey," I shouted, trying to grab the bra as she deftly kept it away.

"Go shower, we have work to do." Trish smiled, flinging the bra back into the closet.

I rushed to the shower and got ready. Mom stuck her head in the bathroom as I stood, wrapped in my towel brushing my hair, trying to decide what to do with it.

"I don't know how I want my hair," I sighed.

"I would say it looks great the way it is," Mom pointed out.

Looking back in the mirror I shrugged. Guess she was right.

"I wanted to check and see if you needed some help with makeup since you never wore any before, but I can see you don't need any." Her eyes met mine in the mirror's reflection, holding my gaze for a moment and then she turned away.

Nodding to my reflection, a stranger's blue eyes stared back. The eyes; she had the hardest time looking at my eyes. Out of all of things that changed, my eyes bothered her the most.

"Britt, let's go," the girls cried from my room.

Spinning, I gave her a peck on the cheek, and then raced to the bedroom where Trish had salvaged some clothes for me to wear on a 'temporary' basis.

After slipping into a tank top, light green button up shirt, and some faded blue jeans we were out the door. We jumped into Trish's Jeep Wrangler with the top down and raced into town. There weren't a lot of choices in Grand Rapids but we headed for the one mall. 'The small' the girls called it. It had a few clothing stores along with a book store, drug store, and beauty boutique.

When the amigos power shopped, they really power shopped. We nearly melted Mom's credit card at the rate we spent. I tried slowing them down, suggesting we get something to eat before they could do more damage, but it did little good as they pushed me into another store with the united cry, "later".

I have to admit, the excitement of buying clothes in the woman's section instead of the children's section appealed to me. Walking out of the changing room where the girls waited to give their approval, I watched their mouths drop open.

"What?" I asked.

"Britt, you're gorgeous," Elisa gasped.

"Oh, come on."

"No, seriously; Elisa's right," Cassie agreed.

"Britt, you are one hot woman," Trish added as she walked up to me, took me by my shoulders, and turned me to the mirror.

The image in the mirror made me gasp. I stared in shock. The person in the mirror belied the little girl memory of me. A woman stared back at me; the new clothing accentuating the shapely figure I now possessed.

Trish stood smiling next to me. I always thought her the most attractive of the bunch, but her long dark hair, deep brown eyes paled next to my vibrant blue eyes, shimmering hair, and glowing skin.

Cassie came to stand on my other side, grinning as she wrapped an arm around me and gave me a supportive squeeze. Her bleached blonde hair, tiny waist, and blue eyes were beautiful. I felt arrogant realizing myself prettier.

Elisa's reflection in the mirror as she sat behind us revealed her smiling face. Tears welled up in her green eyes and she turned her red head away, embarrassed, hoping we wouldn't notice.

These were the girls the guys chased. It never happened to me. I never felt like a woman what with the cancer stuff going on. Until now. Elisa joined us as the girls swarmed me in front of the mirror, giving me a group-hug as I stared at our reflection, BFFs.

We swung by Sammy's Pizza, our favorite pizzeria, and I called Mom to let her know. We sat in a booth, the backs so high you couldn't see the people on either side. Ordering a pizza, we caught up on all the gossip I'd missed the last two weeks.

Reluctantly I told them about our canoe trip. Telling them I had a spell and we went to the Mayo Clinic to check it out, I decided not to share the details about trying to kill myself. Actually, Mom never asked if I did it on purpose, though after my conversation with Dad at the Mayo, I knew he understood. He went along with Mom's opinion that the current swept me away and I was too weak to cry for help. Besides, I did change my mind, I rationalized.

Elisa told me about Tommy Newman, the starting quarterback on the football team, and her latest. "The

Thunderhawks are going to be awesome this year." She beamed.

"You're biased," argued Trish.

"Yeah, so?" Elisa grinned as we erupted into laughter.

"Just because you're dating Jeb Strand who doesn't have an athletic bone in his body," Cassie started.

"He has other talents," Trish defended.

"Like what?" I asked.

"Jeb's a musician," Trish explained. "Lead singer and guitar player for the band, Apocalypse Now. They're playing at the first school dance."

I raised an eyebrow.

"What?" Trish asked.

"I never pegged you to be into the moody artistic type." I grinned.

"If you think Jeb doesn't fit me, you should see Carl," Trish laughed.

"Carl?"

"You leave Carl alone," Cassie moaned.

"Carl; chess club, valedictorian, yawn," Elisa said with a laugh.

"He's nice," Cassie argued.

"Carl Vladerman?" I looked at Cassie, shocked.

"He's really changed," Cassie said.

"Yeah, no more out-of-style clothes and thick glasses," Elisa said.

"Contacts and my fashion sense have helped a lot." Cassie nodded.

Things changed fast in Grand Rapids. Elisa always had a boyfriend, dating one popular guy after another, but Cassie and Trish didn't like to risk getting hurt.

"When did all this happen?" I asked.

"We didn't think it was right to tell you about our lives while you went through all that cancer stuff," Trish said.

"Now we have to get someone for you." Elisa smiled.

"Uh, not interested." I raised my hand shaking my head.

"Oh, come on," Trish protested. "There has to be someone in town you could fall for."

"Not that I know of." I shrugged.

"Did you hear about the new family who moved into the old Miller house?" Cassie said.

"No, who are they?" I asked. The Miller house was the oldest, most elegant house in town. The last owner, the president of the local paper mill, sold out to some company from Finland and left town.

"Their name is Parks," Cassie continued. "Victor Parks just bought the paper mill."

"They have any kids?" Trish asked.

"Seniors; a boy and girl, they're twins." Cassie knew everything. Her mother worked at the school and any new family moving to town needed to register their children with her.

"Is he cute?" Elisa raised her eyebrows, rubbing her hands together in excitement.

"Hey, you're dating Tommy," Trish said.

"I may have to throw him back if he's too small." Elisa winked.

We all began to laugh again.

That's when I heard them. The voices were low yet I picked them out as if they sat next to me. Melodic and sweet, the sound enveloped me, surrounding me as I sat motionless, my mouth open and eyes wide.

"What's the matter Britt?" Trish asked, concern wrinkling her forehead.

"Britt, you look like you've seen a ghost." Cassie placed a comforting hand on my arm.

"I, I…" I stuttered, listening to the sound still wafting to my ears. "Can't you hear that?" I looked to each of them.

"People talking?" Elisa asked.

"Yeah," I said, thankful they heard it too and wasn't losing my mind.

"What about it?" Cassie questioned.

"Where is it coming from?" I asked in a daze.

"The next booth, do you want me to tell them to quiet down?" Trish suggested.

"I'll do it," Elisa said, jumping to her feet and ducking out of sight to the next booth.

"Wait," I cried, reaching for her too late.

"Uh, hi, I … thought you were someone else," Elisa said and then the soft singing reply. I couldn't make out the words, but the murmuring resonated through the booth.

Elisa slid back into her seat across from me, a stiff smile on her flushed face.

"What's the matter, who is it?" I asked taking her hands and squeezing them as they rested on the table.

She turned deep red and grimaced, pressing her eyes shut.

"What?" Cassie asked.

Trish and I leaned closer.

"I can say for certain the Parks boy is cute and his sister is gorgeous," Elisa whispered, her head down.

"How do you know...?" Trish began, but then turned red as well. "They're in the next booth?"

Elisa nodded. Her eyes sprang open, looking at our hands still clasped in front of her on the table.

We huddled closer, lowering our voices to excited whispers, trying to control ourselves.

"OMG," Cassie gasped.

Elisa nodded, her face turning even redder, if that were possible.

"What does he look like?" Trish whispered.

"What does she look like?" Cassie added.

Elisa looked at Trish and then Cassie before turning to me. "Golden blonde hair, bright blue eyes, gorgeous," she whispered. "Kind of like Britt."

All eyes swung to me as my face got warm. "What?"

"Their hair and eyes look like yours. She's incredible and he's quite the hunk." She grinned as Trish and Cassie giggled.

I stared at Elisa, dazed as thoughts whirled in my mind. Could they be the angels from the river? Here in Grand Rapids?

Chapter 4

I eased myself from the booth, unsure what to say when I saw their faces clearly for the first time. Elisa, Cassie, and Trish looked on, curious. Ignoring their questioning stares, I took a cautious step to the next booth. Empty.

I gazed at the red vinyl seats. The half-eaten pizza still steamed on the serving tray, the drinks fizzed in the glasses; the straws bobbing at the surface hung precariously on the edge. Trish moved up beside me blinking at the empty seats. Cassie and Elisa joined us as we stood staring at the vacant booth.

"They were here a minute ago," Elisa sighed.

"That's odd." Trish shook her head.

"Why would they do that?" Cassie added.

Our attention turned to the electronic ping of the restaurant door swinging shut and I raced towards it, the girls at my heels. I stepped out onto the sidewalk as a dark sports car sped past, a wisp of golden hair blowing out the open passenger window the only glimpse of the occupants. The girls pressed up behind me.

"What are you doing?" Trish asked, her face flushed.

"I think I know them," I answered, watching the car rush into the distance.

"How would you know them?" Cassie asked. "They moved in yesterday and you were in Rochester."

I saw the doubt in her eyes mirrored in Trish's and Elisa's, yet couldn't explain it. How could they believe me if I found it hard to believe myself?

"Guess I'm wrong." I shrugged. "I thought I recognized their voices, that's all."

Elisa shook her head. "Weird."

"We should go. I promised Mom not to be too late," I changed the subject.

They nodded and we went back inside to pay the bill and head home.

I waved as they drove away, my shopping spree bounty sitting in the entry of our house. I closed the door with a sigh.

"Britt?" Dad's voice came from the living room.

"Yeah." I stuck my head in.

"Everything go okay?" Mom asked, looking up from her book.

"Fine, but I'm beat. I think I'll head to bed." I walked over, giving Dad a kiss and hug and then reached over to do the same to Mom. Gathering my shopping bags I trudged upstairs, piled the bags up on my bed, and flopped down next to them.

What should I do? I didn't expect my angels to be in high school with me. Would they have any classes with me? If so, what would I say? My heart raced as the stress of such a meeting played out in my head.

I changed into a big t-shirt, pushed the bags off the bed and climbed under the covers. A light tap came at the door just as I reached to turn off my light on the nightstand. "Come in."

Mom stuck her head in. "Do you want to come with me to the hospital tomorrow? I'm going to stop in and see how the other long-term care patients are doing."

"I'm not a long-term patient anymore, Mom. They aren't *other* long-term patients, just long-term patients," I corrected.

"Oh, yeah, right, but I want to visit. They've been so supportive of us and I don't want them to feel we forgot about them just because you're better."

I stared at her for a moment. The ghosts of hospital disinfectants and cleaners haunted my nose and the dull humming and beeping of all the monitoring equipment filled my ears. I pressed my eyes shut against the memories, trying to squeeze them out of my head by pinching my eyelids together. It was the last place I ever wanted to be again. Then the memories of the people who took care of me and the other patients who constantly encouraged me filled my head. Did I want to forget those times? I became this person because of those experiences. Did I just want to forget all about it? No, I needed to take the bad with the good. My head nodded slowly with my thought, quickening as I came to my conclusion and my eyes opened to look up at Mom. "Sure, it's the right thing to do."

"Good. Sleep well." She grinned, closing the door.

I smiled and slid down further under the covers. This was a good thing, but it wouldn't be easy. I reached over and switched off the light.

The dream felt so real. I swore I was awake walking along a sidewalk in a park, strangely familiar. The smell of the grass and flowers drifted to me, giving me pause when lilacs made themselves known. Could I smell in my dreams? Approaching a couple on a bench kissing passionately, not paying me any mind, I stopped and stood watching for a while until they noticed my presence. I moved closer to them, saying nothing, the only sound coming from the scuffing of my feet against the pavement. I got close enough to reach out and place a hand on each of their shoulders. Their eyes flew open in surprise, fear spreading across each face as they struggled to move, to run, to escape. I held them fast. They searched my face for answers, but by their confused expressions, they found nothing. I didn't waiver as screams erupted from their bodies, didn't loosen my grip. Suddenly, the cries stopped. Eyes stared empty at me, their questions unanswered forever. Wispy vapors flowed up my arms out of each and I finally released my hold leaving empty shells sitting, holding each other for eternity.

I woke panting and soaked with sweat. My arms and legs began to shake from images of a clarity no dream should possess. I angrily rubbed at my nose, trying to wipe away the smell of lilac that assaulted my senses and felt the guilt running through me as the death of these people filled me with regret and sorrow. I never cried out during the dream this time, finding it odd, my becoming callous. Or was I just numbed by the dream's horror? Lying with the covers thrown back, I allowed the air to cool my sweaty body, I'm not sure when I fell asleep, but no other dreams came to me.

The next morning during the drive to the hospital, memories bombarded me. The fear of taking this road and not coming home for months at a time, gripped me tight. I shivered as we pulled up to the brown brick building where I spent what seemed like an eternity, helpless within its walls. We parked in general parking, something foreign to me. My normal point of entrance usually consisted of going through the emergency room after a nasty spell or a reaction to the treatment.

Walking into the long-term care unit, a place few people leave, memories I'd just as soon forget came to mind. I escaped this place; convincing my parents to bring me one last time to the BWCA canoeing. After the trip, my choices would have consisted of either coming back to the hospital or dishing out tons of money for home hospice; something my parents couldn't afford.

As we walked down the hall, the hum of the lighting reached my ears and the smell of disinfectant filled my nostrils. I noticed a strange glow around people as they passed by. Mom, the nurses, and doctors had a bright glow about them. Some patients we passed in the hall had duller glows. I chocked it up as an illusion from the fluorescent lights. My eyes needed to get used to them again.

I stepped into my old room to see sixteen-year old Jessica, my roommate for two months before the canoe trip, lying in bed. Seeing Jessica I knew the glow came from her, not the lighting. From head to toe she gave off a dull gray light, like a flashlight whose batteries were going dead.

I stopped in the doorway as Mom went in and greeted Jessica's mom and grandma, sitting in the room. The three women had a bright glow about them. Looking back to Jessica as she turned her head to me, I noticed her glow stayed a dull gray. Moving over next to her, uncertain, I stared at her face, noticing the yellow color creeping into her eyes and skin.

Jessica lay dying of bone cancer and she didn't have much more time than me. More time than I used to have, I corrected. My gaze wandered from her weak smile down her skinny body as she lay in her gown, the covers cast to one side.

I remembered those hot flashes. One minute cold, bundle up and you still shiver, and the next you're a furnace and can't get the layers off fast enough. Sweat beaded on her bald head and she panted a little looking up at me as I searched for the words. Then I saw something I'd never noticed before. The skin on Jessica's hand and arm nearest me appeared to become translucent and her diseased bones underneath showed clearly.

"What's wrong Britt?" my Mother asked, turning from the other women as they all focused on me.

"Nothing," I said tightly.

I looked their way but never really saw them, turning back to Jessica again. Her face pleaded, wanting to end the pain, to end the agony gripping her. Forced to take so much medicine, she could only lie in bed and wait for the end. In those eyes I saw myself only two weeks ago, ready for it to be over, willing to do anything to end it. I stood here now with a second chance. Why couldn't she get a second chance?

The women turned back to their visiting, paying us no mind.

I don't know why, but I reached for Jessica's hand still staring into her eyes. Something surged from deep inside me and pulsed through my arm, my hand, and into her. Jessica's eyes went wide and her mouth formed an 'o.' The pulsing lasted maybe a couple seconds at the most and then vanished. Our eyes never strayed or

50

blinked as we held each other's hand, oblivious to anyone else in the room; only the two of us mattered. She smiled as she stared up at me and I gave her a wink, somehow knowing, I don't know how, but knowing, she no longer had cancer. I sat on the bed next to her, holding her hand, exhausted. She pulled me down to her, embracing me.

"Thank you," she whispered.

Unable speak, I pulled away, my eyes still locked on hers. Our understanding needed no words.

The women, still involved in their visit, were none the wiser and judging from Jessica's look, they wouldn't be. She understood no one could know.

"I need to check on some of the others." I got to my feet, nearly falling back onto the bed before catching myself.

Somehow I knew what I could do. Felt it. It must have been the angel's touch. I planned to pass that touch to everyone I could. It took a lot out of me, but I couldn't let other people die when they didn't have to.

Gathering my strength, I got to my feet and headed down the hall. A ten year old boy, Billy, lay in his bed with leukemia. He took my hand and the surge from me made him giggle. His parents turned to us with a questioning stare.

"Britt told me a funny joke," he grinned, looking up at me.

I smiled, giving him a nod and walked out. Outside his room, I paused to catch my breath, leaning heavily against the hand rail along the wall. Taking a deep breath, I straightened and pushed myself forward.

Moving on to a fifty year old dying of pancreatic cancer, her glow the dimmest of all thus far, I placed my hand upon her arm as she lay sleeping. She opened her eyes and turned her head to face me as she felt the healing creep into her. My eyes wandered down her body trying to focus on her cancer. A soft touch brushed my arm and I lifted my head to see the woman, concern stretched across her face, staring at me.

"What are you doing?" she asked.

"Don't worry, I won't hurt you. I'm here to help," I said and began to look away.

"No," the woman said, squeezing my arm ever so slightly. "It's you I'm worried for. You mustn't exert yourself so much. You look exhausted."

I stopped, raising a hand to my face and looked to my left at a mirror hanging over a sink. Deep circles under my eyes made the bright blue look dimmer and sunken in their sockets. I took a deep breath and pushed my shoulders back.

"I can do this," I assured her. My voice cracked, betraying my weakness.

"It's too much," the woman argued. "Come back another day when you have rested."

Taking in the woman's dimmed glow again I shook my head. "I have to do it now." I didn't finish the rest. The woman understood how close she was to the end. She might not last until tomorrow and needed to be healed now. I surged energy into her for the longest of the three. She closed her eyes and let a small moan escape her lips.

When I finished the woman looked up at me, a smile on her lips, but worry showed in her eyes. She made me agree not to try to help anyone else today. "Okay, fine. I'll stop for the day," I told her.

She closed her eyes with a contented smile on her face as I slipped out of the room.

Standing in the hallway, the woman's words of caution hit home. I needed my strength to do this and the dimmer the light, the more strength it required. I couldn't heal anyone else without resting so I crept down the hallway, exhausted.

Resolve to stick to that plan came easily until I passed the next room and glanced at the bed. The glow shone so dim I gasped. Pushing the door open, I walked over next to the bed. The woman's breathing came shallow and labored, pulling hard for each breath, a major effort for her failing body. She couldn't have been more than twenty five, but her body lay beaten and battered. The machines whirred and beeped as a man slept in the corner of the room curled up in a chair.

I concentrated on her broken and bandaged body, the orange glow of internal damage meeting my gaze. Gently taking her hand, cradling it in mine, the warmth of her body felt indiscernible against my skin. As the surge began something inside warned me, told me to pull away and not do this, but the desire to help her pressed hard making it impossible to withdraw as the energy from within me surged forth. My internal urgency to stop railed at me, still I held on, ignoring the pain as it ripped at me trying to break my grasp. Fighting with every bit of strength and stubbornness within me, I held on and wouldn't let go.

That was when everything began to blur and the edges of my vision turned black. I staggered and a firm hand caught my elbow and strong arms wrapped around me, holding me up.

"I can't stop…" I tried to explain.

"You have done what you can," a soft, deep voice full of understanding and sorrow said.

We turned away from the bed and everything went to black.

I opened my eyes to Mom leaning close as I sat in a chair across from her. Her concerned expression ebbed away as my eyes met hers.

"Britt, you scared me to death," she sighed, a hand over her heart.

"Sorry, I must have fainted. It's a bit overwhelming coming back here," I explained. "A lot of memories."

She pulled me into a hug, squeezing too tight as I grunted in her arms.

"I'm fine," I said, out of breath.

"Do you need anything; a drink of water or something?"

"Yeah, thanks." I smiled when she let me go and sat back again. "Where are we?"

"In the waiting room. I found you sitting here, unconscious. It nearly gave me a heart attack."

"Sorry about that." I reached for the water and the plastic glass slipped from my hand as I saw the scar. "Oh, Britt, are you alright?" Mom asked as she bent to pick up the cup and then rush to get some paper towels by the sink.

My eyes widened with shock as I lifted my arm to see the scar from my childhood bicycle accident stretching down my arm. I stared in disbelief at its sudden reappearance. How?

Then it became clear. Pushing too hard had a price. The need to be more careful and selective became apparent. But how could I select which person to save and which person to let die?

"Are you ready to go?" she asked after wiping the floor and dropping the paper towels into the garbage along with the cup.

I wanted to say no, feeling the desire to visit everyone in this wing, but I knew upon seeing them it would be impossible to keep from trying to help them. Knowing I couldn't do any more today, I nodded.

"Can we say goodbye first?" I asked.

"Sure, if you feel up to it."

"I do now," I said getting to my feet.

We walked, holding hands, into Billy's room. He smiled knowingly at me. His pain now gone.

"Take care, Billy," I grinned.

"I will, Britt," he said, his glow shining strong and bright.

Jessica and the woman with pancreatic cancer glowed brightly as well and I felt confident they were now cancer free.

As we walked past the last room sounds of sorrow wafted into the hall. A nurse, her eyes red and teary, brushed past as the door swung open. The man who slept in the chair leaned over the bed, his head bowed as his hair hung across his face. He turned to look at me as I stood in the doorway, awash with anguish.

I didn't save her. I tried, but I couldn't save her.

It was impossible not to see accusation in his eyes as he stared at me. He turned away and tears blurred my vision as my mom put her arm across my shoulders, ushering me past the door and leaving the man to grieve in private.

"You look tired Britt," Mom said on the way home.

"Like I said, a lot of memories."

"Not everyone gets a miracle like we did," she sighed.

"No, not everyone," I agreed, but knew as long as I could, I would try.

Chapter 5

Lying in bed staring at the dark ceiling as the events of the day played out in my mind, I couldn't help but feel joy over healing those patients today. I possessed the ability to heal people. Even as the thought of killing people in my dreams pressed to outweigh the good I've now discovered possible, I smiled at the pleasure I felt at counteracting such evil with such good. But I needed to be smart about this. I needed to be careful not to push myself too far. I stared at the scar on my arm. Really careful.

The next morning I hurried down the stairs running on pure adrenaline after not sleeping a minute last night, but having a solid grasp at what I needed to do. Sliding to stop in my stocking feet and oversized t-shirt as mom sat at the island drinking coffee and reading the morning paper, she looked up at me curiously and smiled.

"What's gotten into you today?"

"I know what I want to do for the rest of the summer," I announced.

"Hang out with your friends and shop?"

"No, volunteer at the hospital." I stretched out my arms gesturing grandly.

"After yesterday I thought the hospital was the last place you wanted to spend time."

"Yeah, well, I've been giving it a lot of thought…"

"You've spent so much of your life there already," Mom cut me off. "Maybe you should think about it some more."

I nodded at her reasoning. It would make sense to someone who didn't know what I could do. I lowered my eyes, glancing at the front page of the paper as it lay on the island and read the headline.

Councilman Found Dead in Alley
Apparent Heart Attack

The picture below the headline stopped my heart as the eyes of the man from the alley in my dream the night before gazed back at me. My heart started up again and raced, threatening to leap from my chest.

A killer. I was a killer. Not just in my dreams, but for real.

"Britt, what is it dear?" Mom reached over and touched my arm.

I recoiled from as if her touch burnt my flesh, my eyes unable to pull away from the accusing eyes of my victim.

"What's wrong with you?"

I looked up to see worry fill her eyes and line her forehead.

"No, I don't want to think about it," I said my voice soft but determined. "I want to volunteer at the hospital today."

"Okay," she said with a nod. "I'll make some calls."

She stood and walked out as I turned back to the paper, scanning the article and sighing with relief at no mention of murder or an assailant. At least no one knew about me. Was that good? Maybe I should turn myself in? Maybe that was the only way to stop me from killing.

"Yeah, right," I said with a laugh. They wouldn't believe me anyway. How could a girl give a guy a heart attack?

Mom came back into the kitchen and sat down, reaching over to take her cup and draw a long drink of coffee.

"You can check in at the main desk later today and they'll get you into their volunteer rotation," she said a bit hesitantly. "I suppose you won't ask to be in the pediatric department?" She looked at me without much hope of the answer she would like.

"Not a chance," I said with a shrug and walked out to get ready for my new life of helping people instead of killing them.

Did God see things as tradeoffs? If I saved more than I killed, maybe twice as many, would he see that as enough to save my soul? I sure hoped so, because as far I knew, I couldn't control the killing in my dreams.

By late morning I stood at the front desk as an elderly lady with short grey hair and a big smile helped me into the blue smock that identified me as a volunteer. If the smock wasn't obvious enough, the big bold black letters across the back announcing me as a volunteer cleared up any doubt.

"There you are," she said with pride. "Report to the nurses' station in the long-term care unit. They'll be tickled to have a young vibrant volunteer. Most kids don't like to be around people who have no hope of getting better." She pressed her lips together in resignation.

"I will," I said, hurrying away to the wing I knew too well.

I stopped in front of the desk where a large, dark-skinned woman sat studying something on her computer screen. Waiting patiently for what seemed forever I finally cleared my throat.

"Humph."

The nurse jumped with surprise and stared at me curiously.

"May I help you?"

"Actually, that's what I'm here to do for you." I smiled pointing to my nametag with volunteer embossed under my horrible picture taken at the front desk only moments earlier.

"Really…" the nurse began and then stopped as her eyes grew wide looking me up and down. "Britt? Britt Anderson? Honey, they told me what happened with you, but they didn't do you justice. You look wonderful."

"I missed you the other day Nurse Hardy." I could feel my face warm in embarrassment.

"You are truly a saint, wanting to come back and help those who are suffering like you were. You do know that miracles like yours are rare though."

"Yes, but I'm hoping some of my luck rubs off on a few of the patients." I fidgeted with the concealed knowledge of my plan.

"Funny you should say that. Yesterday, three patients seem to have had astounding turnarounds. Your roommate is one of them. She will be checking out later today."

"Jessica is getting out today?" I smiled.

"She sure is, but the doctor wanted a few more tests before she left. You should pop in and say hi. There is a nurse's assistant in with her right now, but I'm sure it will be okay."

The phone beeped on the counter and Nurse Hardy answered, motioning for me to go. I hurried down the hallway and hesitated at the door to gather my thoughts. But they felt scrambled and chaotic as I stood leaning against the door frame. My head spun and my breath came in short rasps.

I eased the door open to find a chair and sit down. As I stepped into the room, the spinning in my head intensified and my vision lost focus, causing me to stagger into the stand sitting beside the door, knocking the food tray crashing to the ground.

Squinting in pain, I focused on the bed with Jessica lying prone on it; a man loomed over her. Something didn't seem right. A glow filled the space between Jessica and the man's hand as it hovered a foot over her body. Jessica's face came into focus as her terrified eyes stared back at me, beseeching me for help. Her mouth spread wide in a silent scream.

I tried righting myself only to tumble forward, reaching for her attacker. "Stop," I squeezed out before falling to the floor semiconscious. I knew what the nurse's assistant was doing to Jessica and couldn't do anything about it. It was just like in my nightmares, but right here in real life. Tears welled up and dripped from my eyes as the white tennis shoes turned towards me. I didn't have any strength to lift my head or raise my eyes.

A hand rested on the floor in front of my face as he leaned over me. I felt the weight of his body press against mine and he took a deep breath that rustled my hair.

61

"Oh, you are delicious, aren't you? Maybe some other time." His voice sounded amused; playful.

My head throbbed as he pressed his lips against my cheek and then everything went black.

I woke up on a gurney in the hallway just outside Jessica's room. People hurried in and out of the room, not noticing me as I sat up and watched the commotion. I looked around, trying to pair a face with the man who killed Jessica. Realizing I never saw his face, I turned my attention to their shoes. That approach proved useless as they all wore the same white tennis shoes.

I didn't bother getting up to check on Jessica, knowing he never left anyone to tell a tale. Yet, what about me? It really sucked to be the exception in this case.

Nurse Hardy stopped in front of me as I stared off in contemplation. "Are you alright honey?" she asked, taking a hold of my hand.

"I guess," I shrugged.

"You must have passed out when you walked in on the nurse's assistant trying to revive Jessica. He sounded the code blue, but there was nothing we could do. Poor girl's body lost the battle with her cancer."

"But I thought her cancer was gone?" I said.

"So did we, but we must have missed some." She shook her head. "Her heart just gave out, poor thing," she said with a sigh and went back into the room.

I sat for a while longer and glanced up at the clock. With a few more hours on my shift I decided to go down and take a break in the cafeteria to grab a pop. I slid from the gurney and staggered for a moment, grasping the gurney for support. Once confident my legs would support me, I shuffled down the hallway, my legs regaining their strength as I went. Soon I was walking normally as I turned the corner to the cafeteria.

I pulled my phone from my pocket and dialed Trish, then changed my mind and ended the call before it went through. Slipping the phone back in my pocket, I stepped up to the vending machine confident Trish wouldn't understand. I sat down at a table and glanced at the scattered occupants and then stared at the silver Diet Coke can, running a finger over the condensation forming along the metal surface.

"Interesting can?" a voice spoke close beside me, jarring me from my thoughts.

I looked up at a boy my age; bright blue eyes and shining white teething smiling down at me. He ran a hand through his golden hair, brushing it out of his face and his eyes filled with concern as they met mine. The image of my angel from the river flashed in my mind.

"I didn't mean to startle you," he said and then gestured with his hand for permission to sit down.

I nodded and stared at him as he eased into the chair next to me. Was this my angel who saved me in the Boundary Waters? A strong hint at his connection tugged deep inside.

"I'm Allister Parks." He extended his hand.

Reaching out I clasped it, holding on tight and making sure he wasn't a dream. That he wasn't going to disappear in a flash like that night at Sammy's Pizzeria. "Britt Anderson."

"Are you all right?" he asked when I finally released his hand.

"Yeah, just sorting some things out," I said.

"If you don't mind me asking," he said running a nervous hand through his hair, "what are you doing here?"

"I'm a volunteer." I gestured to my fashion faux pas smock.

"Oh yes, how could I have missed that?" he laughed.

"I want you to know I wouldn't wear this by choice." I grinned.

"I should hope not," he agreed and we both laughed.

"What are you doing here?" I asked, then wished I hadn't as he stopped laughing and his eyes turned hard. "I'm sorry. We don't know each other. It's none of my business."

He raised his hand, halting my apology and shook his head. "I asked you the same thing. I'm looking for someone but just missed them."

"So... no one admitted to the hospital... an employee?"

"I'm not sure. I found out he was here and arrived a little too late. That seems to be happening to me a lot lately." He shrugged and then his features softened again as he stared at me. "Have you been volunteering long?"

"Started today."

His eyebrows went up in curiosity. "Really, you seem so relaxed. Most people are tense around sick people."

64

"That's because I was one of them until a few weeks ago," I said reflexively and wanted to take it back.

"Interesting...do tell," he said leaning on the table and sliding closer.

"Uh, I ..." pulling my phone from my pocket, I stalled for a moment. "I have to get back to work." I stood and he stood up with me.

"Maybe you could tell me some other time?" he asked.

"Sure," I said, hesitating for an awkward moment, and then spun on my heels and walked away.

"Bye." He waved when I turned to look back at him over my shoulder.

"Bye," I said and scurried around the corner, out of sight, before giggling to myself.

So that was Allister Parks. My angel. Until he admitted his involvement with creating the new me, I needed to play it cool. Right now I had some work to do: keep a look out for that nurse's assistant who killed Jessica, and heal some people. A lot of people. The scale weighing my soul's content now tipped to the bad side and I needed to shift it to the good side, fast.

Stopping to talk to Nurse Hardy, I asked her who I could sit with for a while.

"Tammy in room 109 has leukemia and is really struggling," she said. "She has five younger brothers and sisters and her folks can't be here during the day since they both work. She gets real lonely."

"I'll go see what I can do," I said with a smile and marched down to room 109. Taking a deep breath, I pushed the door open to see the twelve-year-old propped up in bed watching some lame soap opera.

She turned to me as the door swung in and a smile touched her face as if she knew why I was there. The dull glow around her proclaimed to me a limited time left here on earth. I stepped inside and let the door ease shut behind me.

"Hey Tammy, I'm here to help," I said and her smile widened.

Chapter 6

The next few weeks I spent hanging with the girls in the evenings and volunteering at the hospital during the day. I wanted to volunteer in the evening, but was relegated to the daytime hours. A busier time for staff, it was a bit tricky healing people without being interrupted though soon I became accustomed to the routines and adept at avoiding the near misses I suffered in the beginning.

My plan was to heal one person a day to avoid overextending myself and causing the scars from my old injuries to come back. With few new cases coming in, I turned my attention to the emergency room and anywhere patients had precariously dull glows about them. So, splitting my volunteering time between the ER and the long-term care unit, the healing dropped down to a person every other day.

As I pulled into the parking lot one morning, a television van from a Duluth news station was parked out front. I walked in through the ER doors on my way to my locker as a film crew interviewed one of the doctors.

"What's the big change that caused the fatalities in this hospital to drop off so significantly in the last few weeks?" the reporter asked.

"We feel that things run in cycles, and we must be in the good part of that cycle right now," the doctor reasoned.

This didn't satisfy the reporter and he put a hand to his square chin, furrowing his brow over his dark brown eyes.

"Has anything changed in the past few weeks to explain this?" the reporter pressed.

"No, I don't believe so," the doctor said catching my eye as I skirted behind the news crew and gave me a smile. "Unless you count some outstanding volunteers joining us," he chuckled.

"Who would that be?" the reporter said taking hold of the idea and running with it.

"No, I'm just joking. I stand by the idea that it is just a good place to be right now."

I hurried past the scene before someone saw that I was a volunteer and started asking me questions. After gathering my volunteer vest and not wanting go back to the ER while the news crew still mulled around, I headed up to the long-term care unit to find it empty. No patients today had me going to the cafeteria to grab an early Diet Coke before trying to get back into the ER.

I sat at a table looking out the large windows at the manicured lawn as it stretched out before the wooded lot surrounding the hospital. I thought back to the first day my nightmare killer took Jessica and how he hadn't come to my dreams since. What was the connection between him and me?

The chair beside me slid out and Allister sat down beside me.

"Hi," I said, surprised.

"You've been a busy girl," Allister said, his tone low and disapproving.

"What do you mean?" I asked, hoping he wasn't taking about the murders.

"You need to be more discriminating of who you heal, and you definitely need to stay away from places like hospitals."

"What are you talking about?" I feigned ignorance.

"Britt, I know you're healing patients That will bring unwanted attention and could cost people their lives." He reached over and took hold of my arm, forcing me to look him in the eye.

"I, I…I didn't know."

"I know. I take full responsibility, but you need to stop coming here and doing this…at least for a while until the attention settles down."

"If you'd tell me what's going on I could avoid doing something like this again and…" I trailed off as he shook his head.

"All I can tell you is I can't tell you anything, not now," Allister said flatly. He stood and stormed off.

I watched him weave through the tables and hurry out the door. I needed some answers, but the person who held those answers wasn't talking. I stood, took off my volunteer vest, and slunk to the lobby where I dropped it off at the front counter on my way out; thankful the elderly woman wasn't there to guilt me into staying.

The rest of that last week before school started, I spent hanging with the girls and trying to ignore the glows I saw around people. I got good at staring past them except when I saw a dull glow surrounding someone. Jotting down their names, if I knew them, or descriptions in a notebook I kept under my mattress, hoping to see them again when Allister gave me the okay.

Eventually, I could turn the appearance of the glow off like a switch in my head.

The bad dreams were absent for that entire week. I prayed my good luck continued, looking forward to more positive days, and nights, ahead.

The three amigos and I cruised past the old Miller house all week, trying to catch a glimpse of the new owners. The house appeared lived in, the flowers bloomed on the large porch, but we never saw anyone tending them.

The first day of school I stood in front of a small oak tree in our backyard, the one I planted from an acorn, posing for the obligatory 'first day of school picture.' I rolled my eyes as Mom ushered me out to fulfill this yearly tradition.

"I'm going to be late," I complained.

"No, you're not," she assured, snapping another picture.

"The girls will be by any minute," I told her.

The familiar honk of the Wrangler's horn alerted us to the arrival of my ride and I rushed past Mom as she checked to see how her latest memory saved on her camera.

I ran into the house, grabbed my backpack, and hurried to the Jeep in the driveway, mortified to see Mom taking pictures of the girls out front.

"Mom, you're kidding, right?" I sighed.

"It's not every day your only daughter begins her senior year of high school." She choked up.

I reached out, pausing to give her a hug and kiss on the cheek before tossing my backpack to Elisa in the back and hopping in the front.

"I'll be home after school," I said.

We sped away and I glanced back to see Mom wiping away tears. I wiped a few of my own from my cheek and looked sheepishly to Trish in the driver's seat.

"Don't worry, Cassie cried like a baby before we got her away from her mom and they'll see each other at school," Trish smirked.

I looked back at Cassie sitting behind Trish as she gave me a hopeless shrug and we broke into laughter. We pulled into a parking spot at the same time a black Camaro slid into the spot opposite us. As Allister looked over at me our eyes locked and I felt the same connection as when we first met in the hospital cafeteria. Excitement at seeing him again mixed with the fear of his disapproval, paralyzing me in my seat. The girls gasped as they caught the direction of his gaze.

No one moved for a long moment and then the passenger in the Camaro, who I hadn't noticed until then, got out of the car.

Her long golden hair nearly touched her waist and she glared at me with vivid blue eyes. She slammed the door and stormed away, shaking the rest of us from our stupor.

Allister quickly got out and rushed after the girl.

I turned to find the amigos looking at me, shocked.

"What the hell was that?" Trish asked.

"What was what?" I stammered.

"Don't give us that," Elisa laughed. "The electricity between you nearly zapped us. He definitely likes you."

"Oh, does he?"

"Come on, Britt. You two connected and connected hard," Cassie said.

"He's just interesting. You know, the new kid."

"Bullshit." Trish put her hand on my shoulder and gave me a shove, nearly toppling me from the Jeep.

I grabbed the side of the vehicle to steady myself and then eased out onto the blacktop of the parking lot. How could I tell them I believed he was the angel who saved my life? I didn't have any proof...just a feeling, and one I couldn't be certain of. If he really saved me at the river, did that mean the girl with him was the other angel. She still seemed to be angry with me...but why?

The girls jumped out of the Jeep and we headed into school, me lost in thought, and them staring at me uncertainly. I tried not to notice, but I did.

I felt relieved to have my girls with me as I walked into school for the first time in over a year. Using tutors during my absence helped keep me on track to graduate though the social part of school was overwhelming, even with their support.

The looks the other students gave us were priceless. It felt like everyone stopped to stare as we passed. I was so happy to be back, I fought back tears as we reached Elisa's locker.

"I'm going to drop my stuff at my locker and head to class," I told them as Elisa pushed her books into the tiny space.

"See you at lunch," Cassie said as I turned to leave.

"Yeah, save me a seat." I smiled as I walked away.

I found my locker, took the books I didn't need until after lunch, shoved them in and headed to first period. I tried to ignore the looks, yet found it hard not to notice. I didn't even care why they stared at me; because the cancer was gone or I looked so different, it just felt good to be noticed for a reason other than being bald or sick.

I slid into my seat for first period and worked at pushing the glows around each person out of my mind. When I saw Mr. Kinsley, my first period math teacher, my breath caught in my chest. He glowed so dull he needed to be in the hospital. I stared. I couldn't help myself. Turning away as much as possible as he lectured, I doodled in my notebook to keep my mind busy.

So caught up in the glow, or lack thereof, around Mr. Kinsley and trying to escape it as soon as the bell rang, I rushed from the room into the hallway, never noticing the person walking in front of me until colliding with him. We fell into a pile of tangled legs and arms.

Strong hands took hold of my upper arms and helped me to my feet. I looked up into the eyes of Allister Parks. He bent to retrieve my books strewn across the floor before the other students could trample them and handed them to me grinning, his blue eyes sparkling. I gazed, dumbfounded at him, and he visibly fought back a laugh.

"Hello," he said first.

"Hi," I said, a frog in my throat, then turned away, blushed, and cleared my throat.

"Haven't been visiting the hospital anymore I hope?"

"No!" I shouted and then looked around as everyone stared at my outburst.

He handed back my books. "Good. I think things will settle down if we don't do anything else to draw attention."

"Whose attention are you afraid of drawing?" I took them quickly, waiting to be enlightened.

"We need to talk, but not here, not now," Allister said abruptly.

"That's such a convenient answer when you don't want to tell me something." I glared at him as we walked.

He looked up at the room number over the next classroom and stopped. I walked another step and paused, looking back at him.

"This is me." He motioned with his head to the classroom. "Talk to you later?"

"Yeah, later." I sighed and rolled my eyes before continuing down the hall to my next class.

The remainder of the morning flew by. Thankfully I didn't see any more people like Mr. Kingsley before lunch, but Allister worried me more than any glow could.

I sat down next to Cassie after she waved me over in the crowded lunchroom. Elisa and Trish weren't there yet so we waited, watching for their arrival.

"How'd it go?" Cassie asked, searching the crowd for the girls.

"So far, so good," I shrugged.

Twelve hundred students and four lunch periods made it easy miss someone if you weren't looking for them. As we searched, Cassie gasped and I turned to follow her gaze to the far side of the lunch room. When my eyes saw her I froze, unable to blink or move. Seeing her more clearly than this morning, my reaction was ten times stronger.

She looked so perfect, I felt ugly. Her eyes were ravishing, piercing blue. Her long golden hair flowed around her shoulders down her back. She turned to me as she walked past and I realized I'd stopped breathing. I gasped, lungs spasming uncontrollably causing the air to rush into my lungs noisily as she sat down at a nearby table by herself.

A figure passed between us, breaking my focus, and then sat down right next to her. My lips thinned and sweat beaded on my forehead when our eyes met again. I couldn't put my finger on it; he gave me this foreign, indescribable tingly feeling when I saw him.

He held my eyes with his and smiled, turning back to the girl next to him. I glanced at her again. She stared at me and then leaned close to him, saying something. They both looked back to me, her look disapproving, and his curious.

The lunchroom began to fill up and soon several students sat down with Allister and his sister, started a conversation with them. I wanted to go over and talk to him again, except his sister looked at me with such anger. I couldn't build up the courage so I sat eating my chicken sandwich in defeat.

I noticed something about the glow around them I never noticed about Allister in our other encounters. They didn't have one. Not a shimmer, a glimmer, nothing. I frowned, confused.

"OMG," Elisa said sitting down next to me, following my stare to the table across the room.

"The Parks," Cassie confirmed. "Angelina and Allister."

"So, do you know them?" Trish asked sitting across from us.

"Not from before," I sighed, "I ran into him a few times volunteering at the hospital and today, literally."

"Really? How embarrassing," Cassie commiserated with me.

"Tell me about it," I said, grimacing.

"You should introduce us," Trish went on boldly.

"I can't." I panicked, looking back at her, terror threatening to erupt.

"Easy." Trish put a comforting hand on my arm. "I didn't mean right now."

"You're really into him, aren't you?" Elisa asked, serious.

"I don't know." I frowned in thought. Was I? I wasn't too sure. The prospect of what he'd done to me and what I was doing now; what it meant made me uncertain how to act.

"That's pretty fast." Elisa raised an eyebrow.

"Wow, if Elisa thinks it's fast, it must be," Trish laughed. "She gives a cheetah whiplash the way she jumps from one guy to another."

"Hey, don't mock the system." Elisa glared.

I pulled my gaze from Allister, with difficulty, to look at Trish and Elisa. "What system?"

"Oh, Elisa uses a system to read when it's time to move on," Trish sighed.

"I developed it over the years and it works very well." Elisa shot Trish a glare. Her face softened as she turned back to me. "You see, Britt, all relationships have stages. During these stages, the connection between two people is at different levels."

I took a bite of my sandwich and shook my head. "I don't follow."

"The first stage is the honeymoon stage. Both people trying to please each other. The next stage, I call the transitional stage. If it's good, both people will be fighting to hang on to the honeymoon stage for all their worth. The next stage…"

"The dump-them-stage, Cassie and I call it," Trish interrupted, getting a daggered look from Elisa and a nod of agreement from Cassie.

"The couple stage," Elisa emphasized, "is too comfortable for me. When two people start to take each other for granted. And as you know, I should never be taken for granted." She pushed out her chest and flicked her auburn hair with a flourish.

"So how long do you stay with a guy?" I asked.

"Each guy goes through the stages at a different rate. So far, Tommy is still in the honeymoon stage. But Billy Jasper went through the honeymoon stage in a week and the transitional stage in a day, so…"

"You only went out a week?" I gaped.

"Hey, you have to know when to get out." She shrugged, taking a drink of juice.

I took another bite and turned back towards Allister and his sister. I felt a connection to these two strangers. I looked at them, pushing the idea they were the angels from my mind and considered them as people. It didn't make them less fascinating. Allister Parks held some inherent mystery I wanted to figure out. But a part of me wasn't sure I would like what I discovered.

I stared at them throughout lunch, scolded many times by the girls for being so obvious. Angelina and

Allister didn't appear to notice, only looking our way once more as they stood to leave.

I shook my head, clearing the crazy feelings from my mind. Get a grip, I told myself, he's just a boy. Still, I had a hard time convincing myself the truth of it. He and Angelina were something more...but what?

We went to the rest of our classes and then home after school, disappointed to find the Camaro already gone from the parking lot when we left. I expected to see him as we drove past their house, but again, the house appeared lifeless.

With a mountain of homework after the first day, I toiled away at it until late that night. Subconsciously I wanted to stay awake as long as possible and maybe be too fatigued to dream. When I finally clicked the light off, my heavy eyelids unveiled my dream like the opening curtain to a play as they lumbered shut.

I stood in a house, a kitchen to be precise, looking into a family room from the darkness. I saw the back of a woman's head as she sat on the couch, wrapped up in a blanket watching TV. I moved, unnoticed, creeping closer and reaching a hand, extended by the now too familiar hairy arm towards her. The hand contacted her shoulder and she turned with a start, the pull of vapors from her form already visible, as she screamed for a split second then went silent. Her eyes glazed and mouth fell open; her final scream silenced forever.

I woke with a shake as the bed still moved under me and felt my heart racing in my chest. When would this stop? How could I make these visions end? That's what they were; visions, not dreams. Dreams weren't real. These were real. Not knowing how much longer I could withstand the mental anguish, I questioned if surviving the waterfall was truly the better of my two options. Live with the horrific visions and guilt of being involved in countless deaths or ending it all at the waterfall. My idea that saving a life could somehow counteract the taking of a life didn't line up with anything I learned about Christianity growing up. Even my rationalization about keeping the balance wasn't working. That I was connected to the nurse's assistant, seeing him kill while doing nothing to stop him, weighed on me.

I lay back, my bed damp with sweat. Maybe Allister had some answers for me, at least some advice for how to stop them. How would I ask him, even if he did? Hey Allister, are you the cause of my nasty visions? Did you save me so I could take the fall for this guy? Yeah, that sounded like the perfect way to send him running and screaming in the opposite direction. I'd better rethink that.

I closed my eyes, focusing on the image of Allister with a smile and then grimaced as Angelina's glare came to mind. What did she have against me?

Chapter 7

The girls and I bundled up in our orange and black school sweatshirts and jackets to root for the Thunderhawks at the first football game of the season that Friday night. The disappointment of not speaking to Allister again that week overshadowed the excitement of the home game. I did my best to push it aside. Our meetings were restricted to passing in the hallway. Even though he smiled as he walked by, we didn't have another conversation.

We went to the game and cheered our team on to a 17-10 victory, then rushed to the dance afterward at the school gym, crowding into the bathroom at the school to redo makeup and get ready.

I stood back, watching as the others put on lipstick and touch up eye shadow. Since coming back from Rochester I didn't need to wear makeup.

Trish prepped frantically, her nerves at the prospect of watching Jeb and his band play at the dance getting the better of her. I'd never seen her like this before. Usually very calm and confident, she fluttered around like a bird caught in a tornado, her emotions all over the place.

Tommy planned to meet Elisa at the dance when he and his teammates finished celebrating. Elisa, calm and collected as ever, touched up her makeup in the mirror giving me a knowing wink as excited voices echoed off the porcelain walls of the bathroom.

Cassie brushed her hair and applied lip gloss, smiling at me through the mirror. Carl waited for her in the gym.

They took forever so I wandered out of the bathroom and stepped out a side door into the parking lot to get some fresh air. A bunch of guys leaned against some parked cars, smoking. They flashed a wary look as I came through the door, hiding their glowing butts at their sides in case I was a chaperone or security.

I turned away, trying to assure them I wasn't going to rat them out. They moved in closer, surrounding me on three sides. I looked at the closest and smiled, trying to push my nerves down.

"Hey," he said, giving me a smile.

"Hi." I looked around as if waiting for someone. I felt confident the girls would rush to the dance floor, never expecting me to be out here.

"You're Britt Anderson, right?" the guy asked, "The cancer girl?"

"That's me." I gave him a sideways glance while continuing to scan the lot.

"You sure don't look like you had cancer," another guy piped up.

"How am I supposed to look?" My glaring eyes met his boldly.

"Uh, I don't know, maybe skinny," he stuttered.

"She don't look too sick or skinny to me," a third boy said, "but how can you be sure with all those clothes on?"

"I'll check." The voice came from behind me as an arm wrapped around my waist and a hand reached up under my shirt.

I gasped and struggled to move away. The guys on either side of me each took an arm and held me tight. The hand crept further up my shirt, searching for a prize. I started to scream, but the hand around my waist moved and clamped heavily over my mouth, muffling my attempt.

"You need to let her go. Now," a smooth voice said from my left.

I looked up and Allister stood tall and solid, his perfect eyes so intense it sent a shiver down my back.

"If it isn't the new pretty boy trying to be a hero," the boy holding me with his hand up my shirt growled in my ear.

"I won't tell you again. Let her go," Allister repeated.

Two of the guys rushed Allister as he stood motionless. It happened so quickly. One minute they charged him and the next they lay on the ground, Allister standing over them. I didn't see him move.

The others flung me face first to the ground and attacked Allister. I pushed myself off the ground and looked up as Allister reached down and helped me to my feet.

He smiled, his eyes filled with assurance. "Are you alright?" he asked.

"Yeah, fine," I whispered.

"You shouldn't be out here alone."

"I'm not, you're with me."

"I shouldn't be with you after what's happened," he said, his smile now gone.

"What?" Crap, he knew. He knew about those people in my dreams. My heart raced and I began to panic.

"You had better get back inside," he suggested.

"Wait, I can explain," I pleaded, taking a step towards him as he turned to leave. I stumbled and he spun, catching me in his arms.

He stared into my eyes. His were so deep and clear I could see my reflection. He leaned closer, his breath against my face.

I don't know why, but I felt the urge to kiss him, leaning in, forgetting everything but the need to kiss him. His lips brushed mine, their soft skin caressing me softly. The connection drew me in as my lips parted and yearned for more. I gasped as he suddenly pulled away.

The doors burst open and the three amigos rushed out.

He gave me a smile, turned, and disappeared into the darkness.

"Oh my God, Britt," Elisa cried. "This is where you've been hiding? What happened to these guys?" She added looking at the unconscious boys scattered around me.

"They tried to get to know me better and Allister stopped them," I said.

"Making out with Mr. Gorgeous," Cassie squealed.

"You should have told us where you were going." Trish was not pleased. "Grand Rapids might be small, but not everyone is nice." She looked down at the boys beginning to stir, giving the one nearest her a little kick in the side.

"Sorry, I didn't plan it that way," I tried to explain.

"Too late now." Trish crossed her arms, giving me an angry look. "So tell us all about it." She grinned suddenly, sending me stumbling with a hip check. "Is he a good kisser?"

"I only have Jimmy Reynolds in the fourth grade to compare him to," I reminded her. "It wasn't actually a kiss, but close." I shrugged.

"Sleepover at my house," Elisa cried and we nodded our agreement. "I want every detail." She took me by the arm, gave the boys on the ground one last glance, and pulled me into the dance. Trish and Cassie followed close behind.

We danced every dance together, Carl and Tommy joining in, until Jeb ended the night with a song dedicated to Trish. Trish blushed and stood swaying in front of the stage the entire song.

We stayed around until Jeb finished packing up the equipment. Trish and Jeb then spent about a half hour making out in her Jeep while we waited for them. Elisa and Tommy steamed up the windows in his car and Cassie, Carl and me, sat awkwardly in Carl's car. Carl looked at his watch every few minutes, afraid of staying out too late and getting in trouble with his parents. Trish finally opened the door to the Jeep as Jeb stumbled out his side, reluctantly ending a lip lock with her. He gave us a smirk and hurried to his waiting band mates. Elisa and Cassie said goodbye to their boyfriends and I wandered over to the Jeep, feeling more than a little left out.

We stopped by Sammy's to pick up some pizza and then headed over to Elisa's house for a sleepover. We talked into the early morning. I explained the 'kind of' kiss with Allister at least a dozen times before the girls finally drifted off to sleep.

I knew he'd saved me twice now, but still didn't know why. He didn't act like anyone I ever knew. What would he do when he found out about my dreams? What if he knew? My hand slid to my lips, thinking of what almost was.

I fell asleep on the couch, my hand still to my lips.

My dream came slowly, easing into clarity as a window slid open. Why would anyone leave their window unlocked? Standing on a fire escape with looming buildings all around, the sound of traffic came to my ears as I turned and looked to the highway close by before stepping into the room. It was a bedroom, small and cramped, and cluttered with too much furniture. A young woman lay in her bed, sleeping peacefully as music played from a tiny stereo in the corner.

As I moved closer a wispy image surged towards me, confident, defiant. It resembled the woman sleeping, but more ghostly, spirit-like, her face stern.

"You don't belong here," she scolded, her lips not moving. "Be gone with you."

"I don't come for her," I said in a deep voice.

"Your kind is responsible for these deaths," the spirit accused. "I know it."

"Being aware of it and being safe from it are two entirely different things," I laughed.

My hand reached out quickly, gripping the ghost's neck, not realizing what happened until I heard the gasping.

"How is this possible?" It strained to speak.

"All is possible for us," I said as the spirit went limp. Then the wispy body was drawn into my own, absorbed.

I woke up screaming, sitting up on the couch where I'd fallen asleep. Elisa, Trish, and Cassie gathered close, their arms around me trying to comfort me. I cried so hard my blanket was soaked with my tears.

"It's okay, Britt, it's just a bad dream." Elisa tried to soothe me.

I looked to each of them, their eyes filled with worry.

"But what if it isn't?" I cried.

I rushed to the bathroom, closing the door behind me feeling their eyes on my back. Leaning on the sink I stared into the mirror. Foreign blue eyes, red from the tears, were reflected back at me. It was as if a stranger stared back, someone I didn't know anymore.

I splashed cold water on my face and wiped it away with a towel, leaving my face perfect. Perfect like them; Allister and Angelina. They knew something.

Allister and his sister held the key to this mystery. I needed to find out what they knew. No more delays. I raced out of the bathroom, grabbing my clothes and stripping off the t-shirt I wore to sleep. I quickly pulled my shirt over my head and yanked my jeans up, fastening them. I glanced up and Elisa, Trish, and Cassie watched me, motionless, their faces a mix of confusion and fear.

"What?" I asked, looking around the room for my shoes.

"What? That's all you have to say. You wake us up screaming to death, nearly giving us a heart attack and all you can say is 'what'?" Trish had the edge in her voice I knew wavered on the verge of a blowup.

"What do you want me to say?"

"Try explaining," Cassie spoke up.

"Fill us in," Elisa urged.

"I don't think I can," I sighed, pausing to look at them for a moment and then renewed the search for my shoes.

"Great." Trish threw her blanket back from her legs and stood up. "Just keep it to yourself. That usually works for you. Like when they diagnosed your cancer. It took you six months to tell any of us. You'd rather keep it all inside and then drop the bombshell on us. I for one am not going to sit around and let you rip me up like that again." She turned and stormed into the bathroom, slamming the door behind her.

"Is that what this is about, are you dying again?" Cassie asked, tears filling her eyes.

"No," I cried. "Not that." At least not from cancer.

"Then what?" Elisa asked.

"I'm not sure and don't want to tell you anything that might complicate things," I said, trying to explain. How could I share something I couldn't understand myself?

"Did anyone *tell* you not to share this with us?" Elisa pressed.

"No, but if I don't believe it, how could *you* believe it?" I asked.

"Have we ever *not* believed you Britt?" Cassie asked.

No. They were always there for me. Since first grade, they were there for me. Why did I need to shut them out? Allister told me to stop healing people, he never said I couldn't tell anyone.

"Get Trish," I whispered. "I doubt you'll believe it because I don't believe it myself."

Elisa ran to the bathroom and dragged Trish back into the room. Trish had her arms crossed in front of her, not a good sign, as she stared at me with doubt filling her eyes.

"I think it's time you knew the whole story of what happened to me, my cancer and ... the dreams," I started.

Trish sat down in a chair across from me as Elisa sat on one side of me and Cassie slid in closer to place a comforting hand on my knee. Good, I had their attention. Now, if I could only make them believe.

"You know we went canoeing at the BWCA a month ago," I began as they nodded. "When we were there something happened, something that changed everything about my life. Something totally out there, but I need you to listen and try not to judge." I looked to each face, relieved no skepticism showed. Hoping it would stay that way.

Taking a deep breath I rushed into the story, beginning with me sitting on the rocks in the river, the thoughts of suicide, and the change of heart which came too late. I raced through the part with the angels, not looking up, instead staring at my hands in my lap. I went through all the testing, the dreams that I now knew were visions, the hospital, and finally, my belief that Allister and Angelina were the angels from the waterfall.

When I stopped I still looked down, waiting for the doubting accusations or their laughter at my delirium.

When the room remained silent, I cautiously lifted my eyes.

Trish met my gaze first, her face awash with fear, her eyes, full of tears.

I turned to Cassie and she leaned into me, throwing her arms around my neck and crying on my shoulder.

Elisa stared back at me, no expression, not anything. Her face so void of emotion, she might have been a porcelain doll.

"Say something," I urged.

"That explains a whole lot," Trish spoke softly.

"Why all of a sudden you got better. Why you've been acting so weird and enthralled with Allister and Angelina Parks. Everything."

"You really think they're angels?" Cassie asked, seeming to agree with Trish's synopsis.

"I don't know." I shook my head.

"So what are you going to do?" Cassie brushed my hair off my neck where her tears had plastered it.

"She's going to confront Allister and find out," Elisa finally spoke.

"What if he won't tell me anything?"

"You don't think he would hurt Britt, do you?" Cassie's concern was evident.

"I don't know how he'll react when I tell him about the dreams." I rolled my shoulders.

"But if he has the power to save you, he has the power to..." Trish started, unable to finish the thought. To kill me. We all understood without her saying it. We stared at her, our combined fear filling the room at the prospect.

"We need to go over there," Elisa insisted.

"I can't ask you to put yourselves in danger like that," I protested.

"It's the only way," Trish agreed.

"We won't let you go there alone," Cassie added.

"If we go in the day it should be safer, more chances to be caught if he does try something," Trish pointed out.

I nodded my agreement. It made sense.

The girls scurried, getting ready as I sat watching them flit around me. It felt good to have them on my side. I didn't feel so alone anymore.

Chapter 8

We sat in front of Allister's house in Trish's Jeep, the top down, the wind blowing our hair in our faces in the early Saturday morning hour.

"Here's the deal." Trish glanced at me then turned to look at Elisa and Cassie in the back seat. "We can't tell anyone else about this. It's too unbelievable and it could be dangerous if we let the Parks think we'll out them on a whim. It might force them to get rid of us to feel safe. We need them to realize we're here to protect our girl Britt, that's all. Now put your hands in here and swear." She stretched her right hand out so it hung suspended between the seats. Elisa put her hand in, then Cassie and, finally, I set mine on top of theirs.

"We all swear we won't tell a soul about what Britt told us and we'll keep Allister's secret no matter what it is." She moved her gaze to each as she spoke and finished with a nod. "This I swear," she added.

"This I swear," we said in unison.

"Now we have a pact that can't be broken." Trish smiled.

We marched up to the front door, standing on the large porch with white railings and a porch swing on one side. I reached up and swung the large metal knocker to strike the door. The impact echoed inside the large house and we waited impatiently before the closed door.

"Well, I guess they're not home," I said, losing my nerve and turned, starting to leave.

Elisa snagged me by my collar, pulling me back just as the door opened inward and Angelina stood staring at us, her head cocked to one side like a dog listening to a high-pitched note no one else can detect. Her right eyebrow lifted and her lips puckered as if she just tasted something very unpleasant. She looked perfect as always, not a hair out of place.

"May I help you?" she asked, her voice light and soothing yet tinged with disapproval.

"Is Allister here?" I barely heard my own whispered words.

She opened the door wider to usher us into the foyer.

"Please come in."

The ceilings stretched so high it reminded me of a gymnasium. The stone floors shone sending our reflection back at us, the dark surface like a deep, cool pond.

"Would you please wait in the study?" Angelina pointed to the doorway on our right.

We nodded and moved into the room lined with cases filled with books. The shelving rose to meet the high ceilings. A ladder, slid to one side, allowed access to the far reaches of the highest shelves.

Angelina closed the door behind us and we moved around the room, staring in awe. A large cherry wood desk took up the entire end of the room in front of the big bay windows facing the street. Overstuffed leather furniture filled the room on the other side of the desk. The chairs and couches showed wear from years, maybe centuries, of use while reading the infinite volumes of text lining the shelving. Their deep, rich brown leather exuding a welcoming smell of worn leather beckoned us to sit.

Trish tentatively sat down in a huge chair while I eased onto a couch, the squeaking of the leather against our jeans echoed around the room. Elisa and Cassie moved behind the desk to stare out the window at the street. The same street we'd driven down countless times in our lives holding new interest from this rare vantage point.

"What are you doing here?" Allister asked, entering unheard with Angelina by his side.

I stood and walked over to stand in front of him. "I needed to speak with you."

"Why are *they* with you?" his displeasure lay heavy in his voice.

"They're my friends. They're here because they'll always stand beside me in tough times." I nodded to them as I spoke.

"What do you want?" he pressed, unmoved by my declaration.

"Some answers."

"About what?" Allister raised an eyebrow.

"What did you do to me at the river?"

"Not following," he said with a confused expression.

"You and Angelina were at the river below the waterfall," I continued. Even as I did, uncertainty crept up, giving me an uneasy feeling.

"I think you may have been so traumatized last night when I stopped those boys from harming you, you're projecting something more onto me. Something from another traumatic event." Allister patronized.

"I'm not making this up," I argued.

"She says you saved her life." Trish stepped up beside me.

Allister twitched, turning to Angelina but said nothing.

"I'm not lying about this," I pleaded, needing him to validate my sanity.

"When did this happen?" Angelina asked.

"A month or so ago," Cassie said from behind the large desk.

"We were still in New York." Allister met her eyes.

"Do you need to see our ticket stubs from the airline?" Angelina added.

"No, that won't be necessary," I said as my shoulders drooped. How could I have been so wrong? My mortification took a backseat to my confusion.

"But you were sure they knew something." Elisa gaped at me.

"I guess I made a mistake; maybe we should go," I sighed.

"Come on," Cassie said walking up to us. "Thank you for your time." She smiled at our hosts and walked from the room.

Trish looked at me, confusion painting her face. She shook her head after seeing my expression, not what she hoped for, and followed Cassie.

"Come on, Britt." Elisa swung an arm around my shoulders as we walked from the room.

I shot a quick glance back at Allister as I exited. His eyes, sad, or maybe disappointed, turned away from my gaze. Angelina stared hard after me, forcing me to look away from her accusing eyes.

94

We reached the Jeep, Cassie and Trish were already inside waiting for us. Elisa stopped before getting in, spinning around and leaning her back against the side of the vehicle. The look on her face made me pull up short and take a step back.

"If I wanted to start my Saturday off looking like an ass, I could have run naked through the neighborhood and been less embarrassed," she shouted. Cassie and Trish nodded their agreement from the Jeep.

"I'm sorry, but I was wrong. I guess it was just a dream," I stammered, trying to make sense of it myself.

"Fine time to decide," Trish said from the driver's seat.

"I think we need to be alone right now," Cassie said.

"I agree." Elisa glanced over her shoulder at Trish and Cassie. "It's only a few blocks to your house from here. Maybe you should walk to clear your head of that *bad dream*."

"Fine, I will." I turned without another look, storming down the sidewalk. The Jeep's engine roared. None of them turned their heads as they sped past. I successfully alienated the only true friends I had, losing my mind and taking them with me. I shook my head in disgust.

By the time I reached home my cell had buzzed in my pocket over a dozen times. I didn't take it out to look at it, too embarrassed to speak with them right now.

I walked up our driveway and punched the code into the keypad and the door inched open. I walked through the empty parking spaces, closing the door behind me. Glancing out the back garage door window as I passed, I paused, taking a step back to look out again.

The little shed sat in the back corner of the yard, the windows dark and the narrow path calling to me. I walked out of the garage, down the path, stopping in front of my abandoned pottery shed. I reached out and turned the knob. The door swung open with a creak and I stepped inside the dimly lit room, moving over to sit down on the old recliner covered in a sheet and pulling my knees to my chest as I wrapped my arms around my legs. What was I going to do now?

Glancing over at the pile of papers awaiting recycling stacked next to the chair, the light coming in through the window lit up the headlines.

Couple Found Dead in Park

I froze, staring at the picture. Under the bold letters, it showed the empty bench where the lovers sat when I saw them in my vision. I pulled it from the stack and read frantically. The official report said heart attacks, although the coroner had his suspicions on such a strange occurrence and planned to look closer.

Could he tell that their souls were gone? What was I saying? No one knew the real reason they died except me, and whoever was doing this. Was there a telltale sign that might tip him off that a serial killer was on the loose?

I reached a shaky hand and pulled the previous edition from the pile. Reading it once already didn't stem the panic that built up reading it again.

Councilman Found Dead in Alley
Apparent Heart Attack.

The man's blank eyes staring at me from his picture made my skin crawl. I never really saw the face of the first woman I'd witnessed being killed by the nurse's assistant. The councilman and the couple happened in a public place and made headlines, but what about Jessica, who they believed succumbed to the stresses of her cancer? How about the man watching the baseball game? The woman alone in her living room? Their deaths may never even be mentioned except in the obituaries.

As the thought crossed my mind I tore through the pages in my hands and dropped to my knees, spreading the paper on the floor. I ran my finger from one obituary to another searching for a key word or phrase.

It seemed that the nurse's assistant went for younger, healthier victims as opposed to the old and dying. I thought of Jessica as being an exception and then realized, after healing her, she was no longer sick and dying. The pattern still held true.

In that first paper, three possible people met the criteria. They were between twenty and forty who died unexpectedly. Was the nurse's assistant killing more than what I saw?

I sat back on my haunches contemplating the unthinkable. Could he have killed more than those I witnessed? I wouldn't see anything if I awake, right? If I didn't walk in on him taking Jessica's angel, I would never have known about her.

He continued to kill with no one even aware of it but me. A shaky hand rose to my trembling lips as tears ran down my cheeks. My ability to heal felt insignificant compared to the overwhelming damage the killer wrought with no one to stop him.

I slid over on my side, laying my head down on the newspaper, and cried at the sheer magnitude of what I knew and my helplessness consumed me.

Chapter 9

I moped around the house the rest of the weekend ignoring phone calls from Trish, Cassie, and Elisa. Thankfully, the nightmares remained absent from my sleep. But the question remained: how could I be around anyone, especially my friends knowing I was linked with a killer or at least was an accomplice to a killer?
I waited for the Sunday edition of the Duluth Tribune to come out, dreading what the headlines might read. My worst fears came true when the apartment building appeared on the front cover with the headlines:

Another Suspicious Death Has Police Baffled

"Suspicious," I thought. So at least experts can tell *something* is off when they've had their souls or whatever sucked out.

Late Sunday night, all the amigos texted me they were sorry. I was too. Sorry for being so horrible. I ignored several more texts until Trish texted she would pick me up at the normal time the next morning for school.

What was I supposed to do to avoid harming anyone in my personal, waking world? I didn't recognize any of the locations or people until they were noted in the paper. Maybe the amigos were perfectly safe with me as long as I kept them close. I texted Trish "thanks" and hoped my reasoning was sound.

The next morning I climbed into the Jeep and sheepishly looked at Cassie and Elise in the back seat before looking to Trish in the driver's seat.

"Sorry," I said.

"Mistakes happen," Trish said with a curt nod and a smirk, stepping on the gas and sending the Jeep racing down the street.

I looked over my shoulder to the girls in the back seat and they nodded.

"You guys are awesome," I smiled.

"Don't you know it," Trish said laughing.

I found a note in my locker at school that morning.

Britt,

Meet me at my car in the parking lot after school.

Allister

Finally, maybe I'll get some answers.

The day dragged on and on as I anticipated the meeting with Allister. He didn't let on anything at lunch, sitting at a table with Angelina and a few other students while Trish, Cassie, Elisa, and I stared at them from a distance, entranced.

"Why don't you sit with them," Trish stated, "you're at their table anyway?"

"I'm sorry," I muttered, turning back to the three glaring at me.

"What is it about them?" Cassie asked.

"I don't know, they're rich and gorgeous? Maybe we're just jealous, but I can't stop thinking about them either," Elisa admitted.

I didn't share the news of the date with the amigos, but told Trish I didn't need a ride after school.

"Okay," she said, looking at me curiously.

I waited to see Allister walking out to his car before leaving the school, not wanting to look too anxious, though I doubt it worked. Once he cleared the main entrance, I exited the side doors and walked over to him as he stopped before his shiny, black Camaro. Cars didn't normally excite me, but this one, was kind of awesome. I finally pulled my eyes away to look up at him.

"I thought we could go for a drive," he smiled.

"Sure."

"We giving rides now?" asked a musical voice. Angelina walked up looking not too pleased.

"Not 'we.' I need to talk to Britt." Allister told her calmly, opening the passenger door so I could slide in.

"I have to drop my sister off first," Allister said, opening the other passenger door.

Angelina took hold of Allister's shirt sleeve and pulled him away from me, not quite out of earshot.

"Are you crazy?" she started.

"I need to talk to her, I owe her that," Allister argued.

"You *know* what you should be doing," she fumed.

"It wasn't her fault, it was my doing," he said, walking back to the car door before looking back at her.

Angelina paused. Staring at Allister, she sighed heavily and walked over to slide into the back seat.

I turned, questioning, to Allister and he merely shrugged. I slid into the seat and he closed the door after me. I could feel Angelina's eyes glaring at the back of my head.

We drove in silence, uncomfortable silence, until I stepped out of the car in front of their house. Angelina slid to the door, pausing to share a meaningful look with Allister, and then stepped out. We exchanged glances, her eyes filled with nothing but anger for me. I got back in and Allister pulled away from the curb. I caught a passing glimpse of Angelina on the porch. Not happy, not happy at all.

"Don't worry about Angelina," Allister said, reading my mind.

"Why doesn't she like me?"

"She doesn't know you like I do. Give her time."

"So I'll be around long enough to 'give her time'?"

"If I have my way," he grinned. "This is your town, where can we go?"

"What do you want to do?"

"Talk."

I felt a little uncomfortable, but knew just the place. Somewhere I went as a kid to get lost in my thoughts.

"Take a left here." I pointed as we approached an intersection.

We drove out of town, past the high school and around a small lake, heading to my spot. I directed Allister until we pulled into a gravel parking lot and swung up along the far side. As we rolled to a stop, Allister gasped. The area before us dropped off into a vast ore mining pit, thousands of feet across and nearly as deep, thick steel cables strung between large posts, the only thing separating us from the pit.

"This is incredible." He looked excitedly to me.

"My dad brought me here as a kid." I got out, walking to the covered observation platform; the metal floor clanked under my feet. I paused by the informational plaque.

Allister followed stopping next to me, reading the plaque quietly. "It must have been amazing when they were digging here."

"I'm too young to remember, but this was always a good place to think."

"What do you need to think about?"

"You," I said boldly, looking at him out of the corner of my eye.

"Me? What's so interesting about me?"

"You're different than anyone I've ever met."

"So are you," he grinned.

"I, I, I...I'm sorry about the other day. I'm afraid you think I'm crazy."

"No, I don't," he assured me.

I took a deep breath and spilled. "Not only do I think you and your sister saved me after I went over that waterfall, but I think you're angels and cured my cancer somehow." There, I'd gotten it out, my crazy thoughts hanging out there, exposed, for him to see. I couldn't look at him, staring out over the large pit, waiting for the laughter to start. It didn't. I cautiously glance over at him, expecting to see a frightened look on his face as he considered the crazy girl. Except the look wasn't there. Instead, he gazed at me with such compassion it brought tears to my eyes. I stared up at him, afraid to speak.

"Britt, there are a lot of things you don't and can't know about what's going," he said and then turned away. "I don't want you to believe in fantasies, but I can't lie to you either." He stared at the pit, avoiding my eyes.

"Are you saying it's true?"

"I can't."

"What do you mean, you can't?"

"I mean, I can't. There are things that should remain secret, and I messed up more than I thought. Meeting you at the hospital and telling you to stop healing people was a huge risk as well."

"So you're saying it *didn't* happen and at the same time you say it *did*?" I could feel the confusion twist my features.

"I'm saying you're not crazy, but I can't explain why." He turned to me, his eyes urging me to believe him, to trust him.

"That's fine for you, but you just messed me up even more." I wanted to believe him as I stared into his deep blue eyes, only something felt off, like there was more to the story. More that I wasn't going to like.

"I don't want to do that." He hesitated a moment and then turned to look out at the pit again. "I'm pretty sure you should stay away from me." He didn't look back at me.

"Why?"

"It's complicated."

"Ah." I threw my hands up. "You're talking in circles. So you don't want me around? Will you stop with the bullshit and come clean?"

I glared at him, my anger and frustrations rising.

"Britt, take it easy. I like you and know I can't avoid liking you. There's something about you that draws me to you. I feel it inside, attracting me to you, making me want…It's just, being around you is going to be very…difficult."

"I've never shied away from difficult," I said, putting my hands on my hips.

"I can see that, but this may test even you."

"I'll take my chances."

He gave me a nod and turned back to the pit.

I stared at him for a while and followed his gaze into the mine. The frustration drained from me and I felt my heart slow while I stared into the abyss, in awe of its sheer magnitude.

An arm slipped around my waist and my heart took off to the races again. I felt his warm body against me and the scent of his cologne filled my nose. I sighed, leaning my head against his shoulder. His head came down to rest on top of mine and we stood watching the birds swoop into the pit in search of food and nesting on the pit's walls.

I'm not sure how long we stood there, but the sun touched the tree tops before either of us moved. I looked up and straightened as a thought came to me; he stepped away and stretched.

"So you and Angelina are angels?" I tried again, more directly.

"Not exactly." He shook his head.

"But you brought me back. I was dead and you brought me back. If you're not angels, what are you?" My answers weren't coming as clearly as I had hoped.

"You were dead," Allister agreed. "I touched you and brought you back, only it was as something different than you were before."

"Uh, I kind of noticed," I said, waving my hands around my body like a model showing him the latest fashions. "And that little thing about being able to heal people is new. So what did you bring me back as?" The words came out and I wanted to catch them and shove them back into my mouth. Fear swelled within me as I realized I wasn't sure I wanted the truth…if it was bad.

"I want you to know it wasn't my intention. I had no idea this would happen if I touched you."

"So you go around touching dead people all the time?" I folded my arms across my chest.

"Not dead people. I've never touched a dead person…until you." He looked at me and read my confused expression. "I've touched people who were sick; healed them so they could get better. I've done that hundreds of times, but never has anything like this happened before."

"Cut to the chase, Allister," I said in a low, firm voice, only hesitating for a moment when hearing he healed people too.

"I'm an Eternal," he said. He looked at me like I should know what that meant.

"Okay, so you're an Eternal. Good for you. I'm a Scorpio. What is that supposed to mean?" My voice cracked as my frustration rose.

"My family and I are different from other people. There are things about us that no one else can know. It would change the way people view the world, and the afterlife."

106

"Allister." My tone turned hard as the need to know overwhelmed me.

"Some people are born without guardian angels because they are born without souls. That is what I am. That is what my family is. We don't have guardian angels and are destined to live soulless lives forever with no salvation or redemption. We are Eternals."

Now he had my attention. We were talking about something my Catholic educated brain could comprehend. Every person has a soul with a guardian angel to watch over it. Kind of like a personal bodyguard for your eternal spirit. I stared at him, trying to wrap my mind around what he was saying. He had no soul?

My eyes shot wide as I looked at him, the realization of why this information was pertinent to me becoming clear. "Allister, did you do something to my soul?" I asked slowly, the words coming out in a whisper.

"I'm so sorry..." he started, unable to hold my accusing gaze as his eyes looked to the floor.

"What do you mean, 'you're sorry?' What did you do to my soul? My eternal soul, the only thing that I hoped would bring me to a better place. You brought me back from the dead without a guardian angel, or a soul?" My voice continued to rise in volume until I screamed the last word.

"I didn't intend for that to happen," he defended.

"Then what *did* you intend to happen?" I flailed wildly as I spoke.

"I really didn't know what would happen." He turned from me, walking over to the railing to stare out over the pit, gripping the railing in his hands. "I saw you laying there, your life slipping away, and knew I couldn't let you go. That I had to try. I had no idea you would turn into an Eternal."

No. I shook my head as the idea of what Allister said sunk in. No. This wasn't possible. This wasn't how it worked. You lived, you died, and your soul went to heaven for an eternity of happiness.

"No," I said flatly.

Allister looked back to me from the pit, his expression confused. "No?"

"No," I said shaking my head.

"This isn't something you can just ignore and it will go away," Allister said.

"I don't buy it. What is an Eternal anyway? Why haven't I ever heard of Eternals before? No, I don't believe you."

"Britt, be reasonable…"

"Reasonable? Really?" I shouted. "You tell me this and expect me to just accept your word? Maybe you're some guy who gets a kick out of freaking people out."

"How would I have known about the waterfall?" he argued.

"Because I told you at your house. You could be a sick twisted person wanting to drive me insane so you're throwing it back at me now. My soul is safe and sound right here." I pointed to my chest. Even as my finger touched my chest, my doubts crept up. Did the dreams come from me being soulless? Somewhere deep down, did I know?

Allister moved closer, causing me to step back. He was beginning to scare me.

"What are you doing?" I threatened.

"I need to convince you I'm telling the truth." He moved forward, reaching to take hold of my arm.

"Let me go. Are you some kind of frea...?"

The last word never finished as we suddenly stood on the far side of the pit, looking back at the reviewing stand. I panicked and stumbled along the edge of loose, spent taconite tailings and Allister took hold of me, pulling me back from the edge and spinning his back to the pit.

"What was that?" I spoke in a whisper, shaking against his chest.

"Shimmering."

"Shimmering?"

"We can move over short distances with a thought. It's one of the perks of being an Eternal," his voice was lighter, almost amused.

Shaking my head, I pushed away from his chest, hard. "No."

The force caused him to stagger backwards a few paces. He teetered on the edge of the pit for a second as his eyes met mine and he toppled over backwards, surprise filling his eyes.

"Allister," I shouted in horror, dropping to my hands and knees and scrambling to the edge of the pit in time to see him splash into the lake below.

"Oh my God," I cried out.

"Humph."

I rolled over to see a drenched Allister standing behind me. He smiled deviously and moved over to extend a hand. I grasped it and he pulled me to my feet, covered in orange iron ore dust, staring at his confident gaze.

"You were surprised, but you weren't scared." I said, realizing it as I spoke.

"I can't die. There was nothing to be afraid of," he said smiling.

"No, this isn't real. This can't be real." I turned, threw my hands up in the air and walked away from the pit following the old road as it wound up over a hill and back towards the main road.

"Britt, wait, I'll take you back to the other side," Allister cried after me.

I didn't turn around, walking defiantly away from him and his bizarre claims. I froze in place as I realized something. If he could move across the pit like that, was the rest of his story also true? I shook my head, silly nonsense. I had my soul. His story was b.s. I needed to get out of here and sort this out. There had to be some reasonable explanation.

Allister appeared out of nowhere in front of me, his hands held up before him, trying to calm me down. "Britt, please, you need to listen to me."

I stopped a few paces from him, crossing my arms and glaring at him with my best daggered look. He cringed and I fought to keep a satisfied smile from my lips.

"I'm telling you the truth. You have to believe me."

I thought for a minute. "How old are you?"

"Eighteen," Allister answered.

"Ah ha," I exclaimed in triumph.

"What?"

"I thought you said you lived an eternity. How can you only be eighteen if you're immortal?" I said nodding with vindication.

"Eternals age ten times slower than normal people," Allister explained.

I did the math in my head. "No way." I stared at him with shock.

He nodded that it was true.

"A hundred and eighty? You've got to be kidding me."

"I'm not lying." He stared hard at me, his eyes pleading me to accept what he said.

I sat down heavily, adding to the orange marks the ore tailings left on my jeans. How could this be? How could I not have a soul and be oblivious to that fact? Allister sat down next to me, waiting patiently for me to look over at him, which I tried my hardest not to do. I stared back at the pit as birds dove below the edge, disappearing from sight, their calls echoing around us. When I finally turned to him, Allister looked calmly back, resignation on his face.

"How did I lose my soul?" I asked finding the strength to utter the words momentous.

"Angelina and I weren't the only Eternals on the riverbank that day." My eyebrow rose at what he implied. "A rogue Eternal has been tearing guardian angels from people and we followed him to that waterfall. He killed you before we got there. Your soul was gone before I touched you, except I didn't discover that until I touched you." Allister's words were hard to hear. He spoke them with such empathy, I almost felt sorry for him.

"Eternals don't usually take guardian angels from people?" I asked, still trying to digest the information.

"Not at all," he said vehemently. "We live quietly, trying to avoid unwanted attention from the angels. Taking guardians will bring the angels' wrath down upon us."

"Guardian angels' wrath?"

"No, these angels are more like the enforcers of the angel world. They ensure nothing happens to the guardian angel-human balance. Protectors seeing to it nothing interferes with the flow of nature."

I got to my feet, the idea of being an Eternal seeping into my reality, making me feel sick.

Allister looked up at me, questioning.

"Can you take me home? I don't feel too good."

"Sure," he said getting to his feet. He stepped closer, moving to take my arm again.

"No." I stopped him with a raised hand. "I'm not ready to do that again. Can we walk back to the car?"

"Sure." He nodded and stepped next to me as I walked along the path.

It was dark by the time we got back to the car. We didn't talk as I remained deep in thought. The silent car ride was nearly unbearable, though I didn't want any more information to digest, yet. My new reality loomed before me with no certainty I could deal with it. We pulled up in front of my house and he hopped out, running around to open my door. Allister leaned on the open door when I stopped to look at him.

"Can I die?" I asked, not knowing where the question came from.

"Not naturally, at least, none of us have yet," he clarified.

I nodded at his answer, more out of numbness than really registering it.

"Is it alright if I stop by later and check on you?"

"Yeah, I guess."

With a nod, he got back into his car and drove off as I watched the red taillights disappear around the corner over my shoulder. I turned to climb the porch steps and nearly ran over Angelina, standing in my way.

"We need to talk," she said, her expression hard.

I staggered back falling on my butt, stunned by her appearance out of nowhere.

"You need to stay away from my brother." She put her hands on her hips.

"What?" I gaped, getting to my feet and brushing the grass off my jeans before remembering they were already ruined by the iron ore stains.

"Are you hard of hearing as well as dumb? You need to stay away from Allister."

"Why?" I stammered, confused.

"You being around him isn't good for him."

"Why don't you tell your brother to stay away from me?" I frowned.

"I did, but he's too stubborn for his own good and I need you to stay away from him, no matter what he says."

"Why would I do that if he doesn't want me to stay away?"

"It's complicated and I'm not sure your small brain could comprehend it." She pointed to her head to emphasize her point.

"Hey, I'm getting a little tired of you referring to me as dumb and stupid." I took a step towards her and glared down at her standing a good head taller.

"If you care at all for Allister you need to stay as far away from him as possible." She crossed her arms in front of her and glared back.

I stared at this small, obstinate girl. She didn't look the least bit intimidated. I didn't know if I cared about Allister or not, but the way Angelina referred to his feelings about me, he seemed to care for me to the point he would ignore his sister's warnings.

"I don't know if I can do that," I admitted, surprising myself with my boldness.

"Ahh!" she spun away from me, throwing her arms up in disgust. "I knew I couldn't count on you to just do as I asked. Fine." She turned back and moved right up in front of me, pointing a finger in my face. "Allister did something that could get him killed. If you and he are seen together by the wrong people, both of you are in danger. Just stay away from him."

"You mean changing me into an Eternal can get Allister killed?"

She gave me an infuriated look, locking her eyes on mine for the longest moment. "So he went and told you everything. I might have guessed. The fool. Now we're all in danger and it's because he couldn't resist you." She considered me for a moment, and then put a finger in my chest. "If the Eternal Council finds out Allister touched someone when they were already gone, they can sentence him to death."

"What about the Eternal who took my guardian angel in the first place?" I argued and pushed her finger away. "Wouldn't they blame him for causing Allister to break their law first?"

"You don't get it, do you?" Angelina frowned. "What Allister did is strictly forbidden by the council. His crime is much more grievous and punishable by death. If another Eternal sees you, they will know instantly that you were created, not born."

I stood, staring at her, unable to fathom Allister being killed for saving my life.

"If you don't care about Allister's life, then maybe you'll save your own skinny neck. The council will kill you too, not to mention the Eternal who took your guardian will want you dead as well to cover up his crimes. Maybe you had better think about that." Angelina looked me up and down, and then vanished before my eyes.

I spun in place, looking around, but Angelina was gone.

Chapter 10

Flopping down on my bed I looked at my nightstand and reality turned bitter. I reached over, taking the picture of me with the amigos in my hand, wondering what to tell them.

"Nothing," I sighed.

After that whole fiasco at Allister's house, they would never believe anything like that again unless... Unless Allister told them. Why couldn't they know the truth? I would press the issue if given the chance.

Thinking about living forever it all became crystal clear. Everyone I loved would die and move on. I would watch loved one after loved one die and leave me, never to be with them again. No afterlife, no eternal happiness, the promise of reuniting with them someday taken from me, forever. Trish, Elisa, and Cassie would die and leave me. Mom and Dad, I expected to deal with someday, but anyone I cared about would eventually be gone and beyond me seeing ever again.

Except Allister. My family consisted of Allister now, and Angelina, I added with a grimace. You know what they say, you can't pick your family, but in this case, Allister had.

I didn't know how comfortable I felt with his ultimate decision. Time would tell. Time, the only thing I couldn't run out of anymore.

Lying in bed, thinking of the day's events, I couldn't get Allister out of my head. I still had so many unanswered questions, but like he said, there was no hurry.

I crawled out of bed and headed downstairs. I walked into the living room where Mom and Dad were watching the news. They looked up curiously as I entered.

"What's up?" Dad asked.

"Not much," I lied. "Can't sleep. Thought I would head out to the shed for a while."

Dad nodded with a smile.

"We hoped you'd feel like going out there again," Mom grinned knowingly.

"Yeah, guess I'm going to check it out and see if I feel it again." I shrugged and walked out the back door, following the lighted path to the shed adjacent to the fence that ran along the alley. I paused in front of the door, peering into the blackness inside through the window then reached for the door knob and gave it a turn. The door swung inward with a light creak. Searching the wall around the corner I flicked on the light and the shed lit up brightly.

White sheets covered nearly everything in the room except the shelves holding pots of different shapes, sizes, and colors. I walked over and pulled the sheet off the potter's wheel and chair, grinning with familiarity. I turned and pulled the remaining sheets into my arms and dropped them in a corner, turning back to look at the kiln, boxes of clay, and the large recliner set in the corner. I sat down in the chair in front of the wheel and flipped the power on, placing my foot on the pedal and tentatively pressed down. The wheel jumped to life. I grinned.

This was where I used to escape all the pain and harsh realities of my life. Creating something that would outlast me and maybe share some happiness with others when I was gone.

I lifted my foot from the pedal and the wheel ground to a stop while I spun in my chair to look up at the shelves holding my work. Each bore a label to the person it was meant for. Funny, I never thought I would outlast the people whose names claimed the pots, but if Allister was telling me the truth, that's exactly what was going to happen…unless Angelina was right and Allister and I were in mortal danger because of what he did.

I stood and walked to the recliner, flopping down in the comforting chair. How did all this happen? I stared at the wheel, trying to put the puzzle pieces in my head together to make sense of it all. Sliding down further in the chair, I pulled the blanket hanging over the back down and draped it over me. How could my life have become this?

I fell asleep, a whisper in my mind reminding me of the terrors waiting, just before drifting off. I recognized the setting; walking down the street to the school. A lone light shone in the gray cement building as I moved to a window and peered in. Mr. Kinsley worked at a desk, paging through papers, stopping every so often to take a drink of soda. I felt a strange tingling through my body and then stood in the classroom, facing my teacher.

He looked up with shock at my appearance. "Who are you?"

"Someone who needs something from you?" I said, my voice once again, not my own.

"You'll have to come back during school hours on Monday. I'm finishing up some grading and heading out

in a second. How did you get in here at this hour?" He glanced at his papers and then looked back with a frown.

"I can't wait until Monday. What I need from you I will take now," the voice said.

I moved beside Mr. Kinsley in an instant, placing a hand on the man before he could respond. His eyes went wide and his mouth opened to scream, but nothing came out. A familiar vapor rose from Mr. Kinsley, taking a vague shape as the hand grasped it before it could fully finish forming. The cries emitted by the vapor pierced my ears as it shrieked. It went silent and slipped into the extended arm, not my arm, a strangers arm, one I recognized from nights past.

I walked to the door, taking one last look at the lifeless body of Mr. Kinsley slumped back in his chair, eyes staring blankly at the ceiling, mouth open in one futile, final cry for help. I switched the lights off and the tingling feeling returned.

I jerked awake with Allister holding me, my sobs quieted into his chest, grabbing at him hysterically, wanting to hold something real, substantial, instead of the dream world tormenting me. I began to calm and think clearly again as the smell of lilac filled my senses. Then, I pushed him away as my anger built up in me. This was his fault. He did this to me and now no one was safe, even the amigos could be in danger.

"You can't just pop in anytime you want," I scolded.

"I'm sorry, but I didn't know you had dreams," he said.

"Nightmares, visions," I corrected, wiping the tears from my cheeks with the backs of my hands.

"What about?"

"Tonight Mr. Kinsley died. I went to his room at school and took something vapory out of his body and he died."

Allister looked at me, doubt and horror competing for control of his features.

"I'm sure it's real. I saw other people killed and then read about it in the newspaper." I stopped short, afraid of what Allister might think of my confession.

"I need to check something. Are you alright for a minute?" he asked.

I shrugged and he shimmered into nothingness. It felt longer than a minute as apprehension grew for what might come next. Then he reappeared and knelt down next to me. He looked at me, terror alone filling his eyes.

"What?" I whispered.

"Mr. Kinsley *is* dead."

"How is this possible? How am I killing all these people in my dreams?"

"You said you went to his classroom and took something from him?"

"I went to his classroom and killed him."

He shook his head, staring down at the floor. He looked at me, his eyes filled with compassion. "Britt, you aren't killing people. You're witnessing someone else killing them."

"But, I'm right there when they're killed. I'm as good as killing them myself."

"You're seeing through the eyes of the Eternal who took your guardian angel."

"What? How could this be happening? How am I seeing through the eyes of that monster?"

"I don't know, but I know someone who might," he said.

"Who?" I asked.

"My sister, Angelina."

"How would she know?"

"Angelina has the ability to sense a person who has been in a room before her or touched an object she touches. She may be able to touch you and see who this Eternal is."

"I thought you knew who he was?"

"We never identified him, though with Angelina's help, we might be able to sense where he plans to go next."

"You think the Eternal who killed Mr. Kinsley is connected to me after taking my guardian angel?" I couldn't wrap my head around this.

"Let's go find out," he said extending a hand to me.

I hesitated, not looking forward to the feeling of shimmering again, then placed my hand in his and had the same tingling feeling I felt in my dream. We now stood in a bedroom; a large four post bed with a silky, blue canopy took up a large portion of the generous space. Other ornate and luxurious furniture filled the space while the light smell of potpourri filled the room, nothing like the lilac I smell after witnessing the murders.

Angelina sat looking at us from the edge of her bed, no sign of surprise on her face. "Brother, we are now bringing the secret into our very house?" she said with disapproval.

"She dreamt of the Eternal we seek," Allister told her, causing Angelina's eyebrow to rise.

"She keeps surprising you, Allister. Soon you will need to test her for all her possible skills," she said, standing and moving over next to me.

She stopped before me and placed a hand on my head, a rush of energy dropping me to my knees and a flash of white across my vision. Seconds later, I knelt on the floor, blinking rapidly, trying to get my vision back. Allister knelt beside me, his arm around my shoulders, comforting me.

"Are you alright?" he asked.

"Yeah, fine, I enjoy being blinded," I said.

"You whine a lot," Angelina quipped.

"I'm still getting used to this Eternal stuff," I shot back. "So what did you find out? Or did you blind me just for fun?"

"I believe I would have done it just for fun anyway, but I discovered who the Eternal is. His name is Kendal Stratford. He has been in Europe prior to now, but decided to do his dirty deeds here so his family would avoid further scrutiny."

"You got all that from touching my head?" I gawked at her, her face still fuzzy in my vision.

"Indeed," she smiled.

"Wow," I gasped. "How do we stop him?"

"It is too early to speak in 'we,'" Angelina pointed out.

"But I'm in this up to my eyeballs. I need to stop him as much, maybe more, than you do." I let Allister help me to my feet. He stood next to me, still supporting most of my weight.

"We need to get you out of here first," Angelina said. "Before Mother or Father sense you. I'm surprised they haven't yet; you give off a strange, different vibe than I'm accustomed to."

"You feel it too, the pureness, the pull deep inside?" Allister asked eagerly.

She nodded, much more sedate than her brother.

"Come with us," Allister suggested. "We can discuss this at Britt's house," he said pulling me closer as the tingles swept through me and we stood in the pottery shed once more.

Angelina sparkled into existence off to one side and looked around.

"Can Kendal sense you and your family are here in Grand Rapids?" I asked.

"I believe it's the reason he chose this location for his behavior," Allister said.

"But, if you just moved here, how could he know already?" I pressed.

"He may have some foretelling ability similar to Angelina," Allister surmised.

"Not likely," Angelina snorted. "More likely he followed us here from New York."

"How many guardian angels has he destroyed?" I asked, now making the connection that was the true nature of the vapor in my visions.

"Six, including Mr. Kinsley tonight," Angelina said.

"Is that enough to alert the angels to you?"

"Plenty," Allister sighed. "They may not detect us, but they will come to investigate and, seeing how they can't sense us, it will identify what we are."

"Why aren't your parents involved in this?" I asked.

"They are," Allister answered quickly.

"But with you among us, Allister fears the repercussions of his actions. We must pursue Kendal alone, else make our parents aware of Allister's indiscretion," Angelina pointed out.

"Why is saving me so bad?"

"It isn't about you," Allister comforted. "We aren't allowed to touch people already gone with our powers. If we bring someone back who is already gone, we can create soulless monsters we will need to destroy; else they go on a rampage ravaging every guardian angel around."

"I could be one of those?" I asked.

"We're not sure, yet," Angelina said.

"How do you mean?"

"It can take up to a year before a soulless can turn destructive, until then, they can function like any other person with a soul," Allister explained.

"Then one day, snap." Angelina snapped her fingers. "The person turns into a crazed maniac."

"What?" I turned to Allister, fear and anger gripping me all at once. "I might be a monster?"

"No, you aren't." Allister glared at Angelina.

"How can you be so sure, Brother?"

"Feel her essence," he urged. "She is as pure as any Eternal I have sensed."

"It's true, I feel an attraction pulling me to her," Angelina agreed reluctantly, "Although one can never tell for certain."

Allister rolled his eyes and gave his sister a dirty look.

"We should go," Angelina pointed out again. "If Mother and Father discover us gone, they will question our whereabouts."

"I'll see you later," Allister told me, then vanished.

Angelina stood in the corner, still looking at me. "Don't hurt my brother," she warned. "He cares about you, but sometimes people want something bad for them. You won't like me if you hurt him."

I stared, mouth open, as she shimmered into thin air.

Not only did I not have a soul, now I had a protective sister warning me not to hurt her brother, another Eternal going around destroying angels, and possibly more angels on their way to kill Allister, his family, and me. How could my life go from horrible, to wonderful, back to horrible so quickly?

Chapter 11

I walked up to my room and dropped down on my bed. What a day. Found out I was soulless, witnessed Mr. Kinsley's murder, and got threatened by a protective Eternal. All in one day.

I pulled the blankets over me and thought of Allister. My stomach churned at the thought of his blue eyes, filled with regret and concern. Did I have feelings for him? I enjoyed the kiss in the school parking lot after he'd defended me. The concept felt so foreign, it didn't seem real. How could I feel for him when he made me a monster? I lay staring at the ceiling, hoping the dreams wouldn't return. My eyelids slowly inched closed, sleep drifting over me as fatigue won out.

The dream did return, but it felt subdued compared to the previous one. I walked along a street and then recognized Allister's house. I stopped outside and watched as shadows moved in an upstairs window. Angelina's window, I thought.

I could make out the outline of Allister and his sister through the window coverings and, after observing for a while longer, continued down the street.

I felt a tingling and woke the next morning as the sun shone through the windows into my eyes. I glanced at the clock. Nine o'clock.

Taking the cell phone off my nightstand, I read a text from Trish. Party at Cassie's today.

I got up, showered and got ready for the day. I had just slipped on my shirt when Allister appeared in the bathroom, causing me to jump and bang my head against the hook on the back of the door with a thud.

"Ouch."

He smirked.

"My bathroom, really?!" I placed my hands on my hips frowning at him.

A light knock tapped on the door. "Britt, are you alright?" Mom asked.

"Yeah, fine. Just slipped and banged my head against the door."

"Okay, but be careful."

I glared at Allister. "Okay, Mom."

"I'm sorry," he said, raising a calming hand.

"Give me your phone." I extended my hand. He gave me his phone and I punched my number in and handed it back. "There, make sure you call first from now on and no more bathroom or bedroom. The pottery shed only. My Dad would flip if he found you up here." I turned to gather my phone from the vanity and tucked it into my pocket. "I'll meet you there in a minute." He shimmered as I opened the bathroom door to find Mom standing there.

"Who are you talking to?" she asked, leaning in past me to look around the small bathroom.

"No one," I said, looking over my shoulder at the empty room.

"I swear I heard voices." Mom frowned, confused.

"Just talking to myself. I seem to be doing that a lot lately." I shrugged and walked past her and down the stairs without looking back, pausing briefly to grab a coat on my way out.

I hurried to the pottery shed, closing the door and peering out to be sure Mom wasn't following me. I turned around to find Allister sitting in the recliner.

"We tracked Kendal for a few hours last night."

"Did you see him?"

"No, he lost us in the woods north of here. Angelina and I decided to wait until he strikes again and see if we can get a fresh trail to follow."

"You're going to wait until he kills someone else before you look for him? That is so wrong."

"What do you expect us to do?"

"I don't know, get more Eternals to search for him or, I don't know, something besides waiting until he kills another person."

"He's very creative and hides his path well. I think he realizes we are searching for him. He will continue to be more cautious now he knows we're aware of him."

"But you need to stop him before he kills again."

"It isn't like he sends us a note to let us know where he is going to be next," Allister argued.

"Are you sure you and Angelina can handle this by yourselves?"

"We have to," he sighed.

"Not good enough. You need to stop him before another person dies. With me connected to him you should be able to pinpoint where he is. Maybe Angelina could somehow tap into my dream."

"I'll see if Angelina thinks that will work, but if it doesn't we have no choice other than tracking him after he kills again, I'm sorry."

"There has to be another way. How can we sit back and let another person die without trying? We need to step it up here."

"I understand how you feel, but there is only so much we can do."

"That sucks. It drives me crazy to know he's out there killing people and we can't do anything about it."

"We'll catch him as quickly as we can. I promise."

I stared back at him, realizing my misplaced anger did nothing but hurt our effort. "I know," I said sadly. Then I remembered the dream from last night. "I dreamt again last night and we were outside your house."

"Really, what did he do?" Allister sat up abruptly.

"He looked up at Angelina's window and watched your shadows for a short time and left."

"He's onto us. We have to be more diligent about watching our backs. Hold on." He shimmered and was gone only a minute before he shimmered back. "Angelina is looking into the possibility of tapping your dreams. I warned her about Kendal being suspicious of us. She will circle our house and look for any remnants of his presence."

Glancing at the clock, I grabbed a coat to head to Cassie's. Slipping it on, I pulled my hair out from under the collar.

"Where are you going?" Allister asked.

"Over to Cassie's," I said and then paused. "Want to come?"

"Is she the little one?" Allister asked.

"They all will be there, but yeah, Cassie is the small blonde."

"I suppose it's time we come out to your friends."

"There's nothing to come out about. There is nothing going on between us." Even as I said it, my stomach did a flip-flop. Was I kidding myself? "Besides, the three amigos will accept whatever I do, no matter what."

"Why do you call them the three amigos?"

"My dad gave them the nickname after watching that old movie with Steve Martin, Martin Short, and Chevy Chase," I laughed. "It stuck."

"You're lucky to have them," he smiled. "Ready to go?"

"Yeah, I'll ask Mom if I can borrow her car."

"I'll drive," he said.

I looked at him questioningly.

"My car is around the corner. Wait here until you hear me at the door. I'll pick you up in a second."

"I have to learn that," I said as he disappeared.

I went back to the house and waited in the kitchen. It felt like forever before the doorbell rang. I ran through the living room as Mom opened the door to Allister.

"Good afternoon Mrs. Anderson, my name is Allister Parks, I'm here to see Britt," Allister greeted her politely.

"Hello," Mom said, staring at him in shock.

"Britt and I are going to attend a party at one of her friend's this afternoon," he said.

I slid to a stop behind Mom as she turned to look at me, questioning. "Cassie is having a party today and Allister and I are going for a while. Is that okay?"

"Have fun," she said as I walked past her.

"I won't be too late, but don't wait supper." We walked out the door and down the sidewalk to his jet black Camaro.

"I could use a car," I sighed.

"What kind would you like? We kind of get what we want." He pressed his lips together and raised his eyebrows at my amazed look. "It's one of the perks of living so long. You can acquire a great deal of wealth over nearly two hundred years."

"No, you don't need to get me a car." I got into the front seat as he held the door open. I slid my legs in as he shut the door. I quickly flipped down the visor to check my hair in the mirror, pulling the thick mess of waves away from my face as he got into the driver's seat.

"You look great," he smiled, glancing over at me.

"Thanks, but I'm nervous how everyone will react."

"Don't worry. This is a much smaller group. We'll see a bigger crowd tomorrow at school."

"Great," I sighed. "Now I'm nervous about tomorrow too."

"You're so beautiful."

"Thanks to you," I pointed out.

He leaned back, frowning. "Where did you get that idea?"

"You changed me when you touched me."

"Britt, I can't create you or instill beauty on you any more than I can create a star or change the color of the moon. The beauty existed inside you before I came along." He held my doubtful gaze for a moment and then started the car with a roar.

I stared at him, contemplating his statement.

"It's true." He laughed and punched the gas, sending us racing down the street.

I turned away, embarrassed, in time to see Mom staring out the window as the car jumped into motion. We pulled alongside Cassie's house on the corner. All heads turned to watch as the sleek black car eased to a stop and Allister got out, walked around to my door, and helped me out.

I looked up hesitantly to see Trish and Elisa staring. Trish held my gaze and mouthed, OMG, her eyes open wide. I nodded and a huge smile spread across her face. Elisa raced over to give me a big hug and then looked up at Allister.

"Isn't this a nice surprise?" she smirked.

"Nice to see you again Allister," Trish said, coming up behind Elisa.

"Hello." Allister grinned. "Where is the third amigo?"

"Oh my God," someone shouted from the direction of the house.

We turned to see Cassie, a pile of buns at her feet as an empty plate tilted in her hands. Her face, a mix of excitement and shock, she dropped the plate on top of the buns and raced across the yard. I looked around, shifting my weight from one foot to another as all eyes locked on us.

Cassie nearly tackled me, whispering in my ear. "You have to be kidding me."

"Maybe we should speak later, your guests are preoccupied with us and I think Britt would prefer they weren't," Allister pointed out.

"Yeah, right," Cassie said. "Come on, Elisa. Help me get the burgers on the grill and the salads on the table." She pulled a reluctant Elisa after her, looking back over her shoulder and grinning at me.

"Sorry about that," I said with a grimace.

"Nothing to worry about," he smirked.

We walked with Trish to the deck and found some Diet Coke to drink. We stood on one side of the deck with Trish as everyone took turns whispering and staring at us.

"You two are a couple?" Trish asked.

"Uh, no, I don't know." I shrugged.

"You always date the girls that accuse you of being an angel?" Trish pressed.

"We talked it out and it was just a misunderstanding," Allister said. "She thought she saw something that day at the waterfall. I was impressed that she was brave enough to approach me."

I bit my lip as Trish looked at me with a raised eyebrow.

"I saw that she was a real person and liked that about her. She's genuine," Allister told her, smoothing over my friend's doubt with ease.

"Yes, yes she is that." Trish was smiling.

I exhaled, relieved as she looked at me with a 'you're so lucky' expression plastered on her face.

Cassie came over, took me by the hand, and pulled me with her. "I need to borrow Britt for a moment." She looked at Allister as he gave her a nod.

We went into the kitchen, Trish close behind, and Elisa waiting, leaning against a counter. Once the door closed behind us, they all began to talk at once.

"When did this happen?" Trish wanted to know.

"Did you kiss him yet, is he a good kisser?" Elisa asked, of course that would be most important to her.

"Is it serious?" Cassie asked.

"I'm not sure, nothing's 'happened' yet. No, we didn't kiss, and I don't think it's serious, that way, at least," I explained.

All three burst out with questions that I stopped with a raised hand. "You guys are the best friends ever." I smiled, reaching out to pull them into a hug.

"You better believe it," Trish agreed.

I forced another smile as the guilt of keeping the truth from them burned inside, threatening to eat away my soul. Oh, right, I didn't have to worry about a soul anymore, thanks to Allister.

My mood turned gloomy after that. The realization that Allister's change now forced me to be dishonest with my best friends grated on me. We went out to the deck with the rest of the guests where some of the girls already gathered around Allister. Noticing me coming, they scattered like a flock of birds on the side of the road taking flight when a car passed. I felt certain of the flock's return if I left him alone again.

I stood beside him, not looking at him, but taking in the rest of the party. Everyone except my three amigos now gave Allister and me a wide berth.

After a long time, Allister stepped around in front of me, looking down at me with concern.

"What?" I looked up at him and then away at the other guests.

"Something is on your mind," he said.

"No, I'm fine." I glanced over, then continued to look around the yard.

"You're upset about something," he pressed.

"Okay, if you want to know," I whispered. "I hate having to lie to my best friends. I can't stand avoiding the truth or only telling them half-truths. I've never lied to them before and it is killing me."

"Britt, you know you don't have any choice," he said.

"That's right, I don't have a choice. But you did. You chose to bring me back, like this." I motioned to my body with my hands, "Forced me to keep the truth from the only people I've ever trusted."

"Ah." Allister nodded. "So that is what this is all about."

"What do you mean by that?"

"It's typical to feel guilt for being what you are when your friends are not a part of it."

"You make no sense." I rolled my eyes.

"Britt, I'm truly sorry for being selfish and changing you without your consent; forcing you to be something you did not choose for yourself. Knowledge of our kind places your friends in grave danger."

"They wouldn't tell anyone," I whispered as two girls walked by, hopeful expression on their faces, seeing us fighting.

"It goes beyond us, and even my parents. We have a duty to all Eternals to keep our secret. The fewer people who know about us, the less likely the angels will bother with us."

"The Eternals would kill my friends if they knew?" I gasped.

"I can't say for certain, but are you willing to take that chance?"

I looked at him with horror, then lowered my eyes, shaking my head. No, I wouldn't put my three amigos in harm's way like that, ever.

The scent of lilac wafted to my nose and a shudder surged through my body causing me to stagger into the deck railing. My head spun, my vision turning blurry.

Allister wrapped his arms around me, supporting me as I teetered, trying to regain my balance.

"What is it?" he asked concern in his voice.

"I don't know, I feel dizzy," I gasped.

I looked across the back yard, not a lilac bush in sight. The glows I learned to ignore leapt into my vision. Why did the glows come back now? The thought didn't form completely until I saw him. He stood, talking to some girls and a guy by the back fence, listening to them, yet staring right at me. His dark brown hair and dark eyes shone brightly as his perfect skin failed to glow in the slightest to my vision.

I gathered my strength, lifting off the rail as Allister supported me with his hands on my waist. I never took my eyes from his and he held my gaze, studying me, tilting his head, looking at me curiously. It took all the strength and concentration I could gather to push the dizzying effects of being close to him to the furthest reaches of my mind.

I recognized him instantly, the nurse's assistant. The connection felt like a cable, linking us together. His eyes twinkled in amusement and a smile touched his lips, and I knew his name.

"Kendal," I whispered. "He's here."

"What?" Allister hissed. "Are you sure?"

"He's by the back fence, staring at me."

Allister looked across the yard and his hands flexed on my waist as his body went rigid.

"What do we do?" I asked.

"We're sunk," Allister sighed.

"How do you mean?"

"He knows what you are. He knows you're not a natural Eternal. He will betray us."

"Why would he do that when he's the one killing angels? Wouldn't he be punished for *his* crime?"

"It's his word against ours on that, but you, on the other hand, can be identified by any Eternal."

I turned to stare at him. "Why didn't you tell me this before?" I whispered.

"As long as Angelina and I kept your secret, it didn't matter. Now that another Eternal has seen you, my crime is going to be seen as greater than his, and more easily proven."

"What do we do?"

"We stop him," he answered.

Without waiting for him, I raced for the stairs, leaping down to the yard and running for the back fence.

Everyone turned and watched in shock as I ran through the people mingling in the yard.

Allister suddenly appeared behind a large pine tree and sped ahead of me.

Kendal stood motionless until Allister reached for him. Then he turned, jumped over the fence, and ran down the alley with Allister in close pursuit.

I ran to the fence, stopping against it with my hands in front of me as the fence rattled with my impact, trying to see down the alley as first Kendal, then Allister, shimmered out of sight.

A hush hung over the yard as the guests stared at the fence where Kendal and Allister disappeared. All eyes turned to me as I stood, balancing myself against the fence, my equilibrium returning once Kendal was gone. I looked at their harsh, questioning stares and then raced from the yard.

I ran to the front of the house, sliding to a stop in the middle of the street, uncertain where to go. A feeling filled me and I raced down the street, somehow knowing that it was the right direction. I couldn't tell for sure if I zeroed in on Allister or Kendal or both, but I felt them ahead of me.

As if on cue, Kendal bolted out in front of me onto the street and then ground to a stop as he faced me. He smiled as our eyes met, recognition filling his deep brown orbs.

Allister burst from the trees lining a yard and stopped, hesitating when he saw me and Kendal facing off.

Kendal smirked, gave me a wink, and then shimmered.

Allister sprinted to where Kendal stood, shimmering instantly out of sight when he reached the spot.

I stared at the empty space where two immortals holding my fate stood seconds ago. When they didn't reappear after a few moments, I walked, defeated, back to Cassie's house.

As I came up the front sidewalk six hands collected me, ushering me into the house.

I sat down on a chair in the kitchen as the girls looked at me, their faces filled with worry.

"What the hell was that?" Trish asked crouching down to look at me.

"Uh, I don't know." I shook my head.

"Bullshit," Cassie said sharply, out of character.

"You know more than you're telling us," Elisa said. "Spill it."

I looked from Elisa to Cassie and then back at Trish as she put her hands on my knees and stared hard into my eyes.

"Britt, we know something is up and your boyfriend just ran across Cassie's backyard like a gazelle, leaping a fence and chasing a guy I've never seen before. What's going on?"

"I can't tell you," I whispered.

"You can't or you won't?" Elisa accused.

"I want to, I really do, but if I tell, something bad might happen to you and I couldn't live with myself if it did." I looked to them all in turn. They weren't buying it.

"Come on Britt," Cassie shouted, throwing her hands up. "You show up at my house with Mr. Dreamy and he races off after some random guy and you can't tell us what's going on?" She spun away in disgust.

Allister said it was dangerous if they knew too much, and now with Kendal knowing about me, that knowledge could be even more dangerous.

The screen door slammed behind them as we looked up to see Allister standing in the kitchen, his expression so fierce, I gasped. He glared at the girls for an instant and then his features softened.

"Sorry to cause a scene," Allister said.

The girls stared at him in disbelief.

"Are you alright?" he asked me, causing my friends heads to spin my way.

"Yeah, you?"

"Couldn't catch up to Kendal." Allister sighed and then looked at Trish who stood nearest to him. "He used to date my sister. I told him the next time I saw him…"

"A protective brother excuse, at least you're original." Trish scowled.

"We're not buying it," Elisa said, putting her hands on her hips.

"Are you and Britt going to come clean, or are you going to insist on lying to us?" Cassie crossed her arms.

Allister looked at me, his eyes pleading me to call them off, but I held no power over them when they got like this.

"I'm sorry," Allister said, his words sounding sincere. "If I felt confident about the results of telling you the truth, I wouldn't have any problem doing so. It's too tenuous right now to take that chance."

"You make it sound so perilous." Trish made a face.

"It is," Allister assured her.

"Quit being so dramatic," Cassie chimed in. "It isn't like life or death."

"Is it?" Elisa asked, reading the expression on my face.

"It could be, let's leave it at that," Allister said, taking me by the hand and helping me to my feet. He swung his arm around my waist and ushered me towards the door.

The three girls sprung ahead of us, blocking our exit. Allister and I looked questioningly at them.

"We won't let you hurt our girl," Elisa said, glaring up at Allister.

"I will do everything in my power to see that no harm befalls her," he said.

"We don't know you, and I for one don't trust you." Trish stuck a finger in Allister's muscular chest.

"I understand your concern for Britt and let me assure you again, she is the most important thing in the world to me. I would never let any harm come to her."

"But a guy we don't know, that you felt compelled to chase, was only feet from her in my backyard. How is that protecting her?" Cassie pressed.

Allister raised his hands defensively before him as the girls hit him with their angry stares.

"You don't know the whole story, and we don't have time to go through it now." He backed away, pulling me with him around the corner, out of site.

He leaned down, whispering in my ear, "Hold on."

I tingled all over and we stood next to his car. Shouts erupted from inside the house and the screen door burst open as the girls raced onto the deck. Cassie saw us first as we climbed into the Camaro. She jumped from the bottom deck stairs, running and screaming across the yard with Elisa and Trish close behind.

"Stop," she cried, as the car squealed away from the curb and roared down the street.

I turned, watching the three amigos stagger into the middle of the road as they disappeared from my view.

Chapter 12

We raced across town, my thoughts so twisted up I couldn't form a coherent sentence. We screeched to a stop in front of Allister's house before I finally spoke. "What are we going to do about them?"

"Your friends are too smart for their own good. Let's hope they keep their mouths shut. We may be able to go back and make them agree to keep quiet. Otherwise, it won't be good."

I stared at Allister, fear for my friends making my heart pound and my blood race through my veins. How could I get them into something like this?

"We have to speak to my parents. I can't put it off any longer."

He got out, ran around the car and opened my door, extending his hand to help me out. We hurried up the sidewalk to his porch where I stopped. He took a couple more steps before realizing I wasn't right behind him.

"What is it?"

"This is the first time I'm meeting your parents, I'm kind of nervous. If they don't like me, it will be a long forever."

"How can they not like you?" he smiled.

"Uh, because you created me. Because you did something forbidden to create me. I could see how that might make them not like me." I looked at him, worried.

"Britt, they will understand this is my doing. They will know you are innocent in this just by seeing and sensing you," he reassured me, putting an arm around my shoulders.

"You keep saying that, but what is so different about me that you sense?" I shrugged his arm off.

"It's hard to describe. It's a kind of… purity, it's sweet to my senses. Your smell, your touch, the way you look, all set you apart from any Eternal I have ever met. Angelina can feel it too. It is almost like there is something about you that tugs at our inner emotions, our greatest desires."

"How is that possible?"

"I don't know, but Angelina and I tried to keep you away from our parents for that very reason. Unfortunately, now that Kendal saw you, we need to tell them and I need to face the consequences."

He pulled me into a reassuring hug, leaning down to touch his lips to mine. My heart raced and the fear disappeared for a second. When he held me I felt so safe, so at peace. He pulled back from our kiss, sucking the air from my lungs as his lips released mine. I gasped, breaking our kiss leaving me jerked from unadulterated bliss.

We turned together and he opened the door. Upon entering the foyer, a large man stood staring. He twisted the hair of his neatly trimmed beard, which matched the long dark hair on his head. His dark brown eyes held not judgment, merely mild curiosity.

"Your parents are waiting for you in the study." The man nodded, opening the door for us to enter.

I looked questioningly at Allister.

"I called Angelina after losing Kendal and told her to tell them we needed to speak to them.

"Thank you, Taylor," Allister said, pulling me after him as we slipped by him into the room.

I remembered the library from the morning the girls and I confronted Allister. That day felt so distant now. Shelves lined the walls, filled with books and a large wooden desk sat in front of the big bay window facing the street. Allister's car was visible on the street. They saw us coming.

The door closed behind us and we stood facing a tall, slender man with vibrant blue eyes like Allister's and thick, short, golden brown hair. He looked at me and an uneasy feeling of being exposed flowed through me. I looked away from his knowing stare only to meet the eyes of Allister's mother. I knew it had to be her. She looked like Angelina's twin. Her golden hair hung to her waist and her eyes swirled with a mix of turquoises. I felt like an ugly duckling compared to the four Eternals. Angelina sat in a chair off to one side, looking away from us, though I knew she observed us just the same.

"What have you done, Allister?" his father started.

"I couldn't help myself. She called to me, urged me to touch her, bring her back. Can't you feel it? Can't you feel her pureness? Surely what I've done can't be so wrong when this is the result." Allister held his father's gaze with an urgency in his eyes. Pleading for him to see what he saw in me. I'd never seen him like this.

"What she is is beside the point."

"The hell it is," Allister shot back.

"You know what you have done and you knew it to be wrong," his father insisted, unyielding.

"He is right," their mother spoke up. "Allister is right," she clarified when the two men looked to her. "He has created something that is a wonder and shouldn't be denied. I don't care how this girl came into existence in her current form, but she is truly an amazing creature."

I blushed, looking down at the floor as their eyes turned to me. I glanced at Angelina as she stared.

"Come here, my dear." The woman extended a gentle hand.

I looked at her and then moved closer. When I came within reach, she touched my cheek so delicately, it felt like nothing more than the kiss of a breeze.

"You are a wonder." She smiled. "I am Allister's mother, Jennavia."

"Britt Anderson," I whispered, awed.

"That brooding man over there is my husband, Victor." She lowered her head to look into my eyes as they turned back to the floor.

"Don't worry about him, he knows I'm right." She grinned. Jennavia placed her soft hands upon my cheeks and stared into my eyes, the turquoise seemed to ebb and flow in her own. She gazed for a long moment, and then let out a gasp, looking up at Victor with a start.

"What is it, what do you see?" Victor asked.

"Angelina, you say Allister touched her after she died?" Jennavia asked, not looking away from me.

"She was dead," Angelina insisted.

"This is strange," Jennavia whispered. "Allister, Angelina says you tracked the Eternal who took her guardian. Did you actually see him take her guardian?"

"Not physically, but Angelina sensed it and I could feel another Eternal's touch on her."

"May the spirits have mercy on us. Do you realize what this girl is?" Jennavia asked no one in particular. Her eyes opened wide as she faced me. "She still has

145

some of her guardian within her, only you fused it to her soul by touching her," Jennavia explained.

"So I'm not an Eternal?" I asked.

"Oh you are an Eternal, Allister saw to that, but you also have the essence of an angel still inside of you," she spoke with wonder.

"You can't be serious," Victor broke his silence.

"I most certainly am," Jennavia said defensively spinning on him.

"What am I?" I asked turning to Allister, my hands on my hips, desperately trying to understand.

"You are the first Eternal with a guardian angel," Allister said, worry heavy in his voice.

"Great, not only am I a freak, I'm the freak of the freaks now?" I threw my hands up in disgust.

"No, my dear." Jennavia brought my attention back to her. "It means there is no one else on this earth like you."

"I could have told you that," Allister said softly.

"It means she can be sensed by the angels, and by the Eternals. She will bring the wrath of both down upon us for doing such a thing," Victor said.

"It means, we're screwed," Angelina said as we spun to see her horrified look.

"We need to leave, get her away from here before anyone comes for her," Allister said, panic heavy in his words.

"At least neither side has discovered her existence," Jennavia sighed.

Allister stiffened and Victor noticed.

"No one has seen her, have they?"

"Kendal, the Eternal who took, partially took, her angel," Allister said.

"When," Victor asked.

"Just before we arrived. He appeared at Britt's friend's house and I pursued him, but he shimmered before I could reach him."

"This is bad." Victor lifted a hand to his chin, "Very bad."

"Why is it bad?" I whispered to Allister.

"Kendal will alert the council. All he knows is you are a created Eternal. He doesn't have mother's ability to see that you also have an angel. He will identify you and they will demand we come before them for judgment."

"Then don't go," I said, feeling fear coil inside me at the thought of him facing an angry council.

"We would have to be on the run forever if we refused a summons from the council." Allister shook his head.

"How long do we have?" I asked.

"A few weeks, a month at best," he said.

"Won't they just shimmer here?" I raised an eyebrow and frowned.

"Shimmering only works for short distances. We can't jump over and over again, it drains our strength. We can go back and forth to a close location, but something keeps us from going from one place to another, leap after leap, or over great distances." He shrugged at my confused stare. "I don't understand it myself, yet I must live by the rules."

"Kendal will travel back to Greece to inform the council about you. They will summon us and then give us

147

time to reach Greece before they send out a retrieval party to forcibly bring us to them," Victor explained.

"We should get away from here, now," Allister said.

"Where would we go?" I asked.

"We can head into Canada, hide out in the wilderness. We have a lodge on an isolated lake. No one will find us up there," he assured.

"No," I said.

Allister turned to me, his eyes wide and mouth hanging open.

"I can't leave my family, my friends, and my senior year with no explanation," I told him.

"Britt, this is about life and death, yours as well as mine." Allister took hold of my arms just below the shoulders. "If we don't leave, they will find us and eliminate every trace we were ever here."

I looked at him doubtful and unwavering.

"That includes your friends, your parents, and anyone in close contact with you since you changed." He turned away from my horrified gaze.

"It's true." Jennavia nodded. "If a retrieval party comes, they will have sweepers. Eternals able to sense close contact between you and others, similar to Angelina and myself, only much stronger. People who know too much will die."

My body began to shake, my legs weakened and I eased myself down into a nearby chair. My friends, my family, killed because I lived. Killed because of what I had become.

"Why did you have to change me?" I said, my whisper catching in my throat as I stared at my feet.

"Why couldn't you just let me die and be done with it?"

"I'm so sorry, Britt," Allister pleaded for my forgiveness. "I didn't know."

"You didn't know?" I repeated, coming to my feet in a rush, my fists clenched at my sides, anger raging to get out as I glared at him. Slapping him hard across his face, I cried out, "Then why did you do it?"

His head snapped to the side with the force of my blow and then he turned away bowing his head, but not touching the reddening handprint on his cheek.

"I understand your anger," Victor said, taking a step closer so he interrupted my glare at Allister. "I believe what Allister means to say is he didn't realize his touch would manifest itself in this manner. Kendal destroyed the natural transfer of your soul to the afterworld, thus leaving part of your angel inside you, very weakened by the attack. You should have become an empty husk destined for death, but Angelina and Allister stopped Kendal from finishing the job. When Allister touched you your angel fused with your soul, thus turning you into an Eternal with a soul unlike any other."

"He had no way of knowing the ramifications," Jennavia added.

It didn't matter. I lived at my loved ones' peril. No rationalizing could change that.

"What do we do now?" I looked from one puzzled face to the next, searching for a way out of this.

"Jennavia and I will try to find Kendal, hopefully we can catch him before he reaches Greece," Victor said.

"The three of you need to continue on until we

determine the extent of our predicament." He looked from one teen to the other, assuring we understood.

"Very well, Allister, make sure Britt gets home safely. Your mother and I will leave at once." He turned and strode from the room.

"Goodbye, my dears," Jennavia said, following him.

I looked over to Allister as he stood behind the desk staring out the window.

"I will see if I can get a fix on Kendal's direction to give Mother and Father an idea of where to start," Angelina said standing. She glanced my way with a wary look and then left the room.

I hesitantly walked over to Allister, feeling a mix of emotions. I wanted to hate him for what he did, except I didn't have the strength to do so. I stood next to him and placed my hand lightly on his shoulder.

"I am so sorry," he whispered.

"I know." The only words I could think of felt so inadequate.

"I need to take you home," he said, turning to me.

I nodded.

Chapter 13

We stepped onto the front porch when the Wrangler pulled up. Trish brought the Jeep screeching to a halt, pulling the parking brake while Elisa and Cassie jumped out before the vehicle completely stopped.

They raced up the walk, leapt up the steps and stood before us, their hands on their hips, anger sizzling in their eyes. In all the years we'd been friends, they never scared me like they did right then.

"You owe us an explanation," Trish ordered.

"I can't," I started, but Allister's hand on my shoulder stopped me and I turned to look up at him.

"They're already in this too deep. The truth may keep them from inadvertently getting in harm's way," Allister pointed out.

I nodded, turning back to the girls. I spotted the porch swing and some chairs off to the side and motioned for them to take a seat.

They looked warily at us, moving over to sit as Allister and I walked over and leaned against the railing facing them. Glancing at Allister, he motioned for me to go ahead.

"Humph." I cleared my throat. "I'm sorry we ran out. I'm sorry I lied to you. I'm sorry I've gotten you involved in something dangerous. I'm so sorry." I stared at their questioning faces, guilt pouring over me as I tried to explain they may have a death sentence imposed on them by being my friend.

"Okay." Cassie nodded. "So you're sorry. I followed the first two, but endangering us?"

"Remember the story I told you about the canoe trip?" I asked.

They nodded.

"It's true. Allister saved me." They waited expectantly for me to continue. "When he saved me, he changed me into something other than human."

"A vampire, I knew it. Allister is a vampire and he bit you; he changed you into an immortal," Elisa said wide eyed.

"No, no, Allister is not a vampire and he didn't bite me. You've been watching too many movies." I laughed, raising my hand to calm her.

Elisa blushed, glancing from Cassie to Trish with a shrug. "It could happen."

The girls rolled their eyes and then turned back to us.

"I'm an Eternal," Allister said, helping me. Observing the girl's lack of comprehension, he continued. "A very small number of people are born without souls so they live forever. I'm one of those people, as are my parents and Angelina…and now Britt."

The girls looked at each other, mouths hanging open and eyes wide.

"If you don't want to tell us the truth, just say so." Trish stood in a huff. "Don't feed us bullshit and expect us to say, yum, can we have some more."

"No, he's telling the truth," I assured. "How do you think we got out of Cassie's so quickly?"

Trish softened her stance as she thought. "There wasn't any way you could have done that," she admitted.

"But we did," Allister said and shimmered into nothingness before their eyes.

"We have powers that allow us to do many things that are beyond your comprehension," he continued as he shimmered next to a tree in the yard.

Elisa nearly fell to the wooden floor and Cassie jumped. Trish spun as she stood in front of me, staring at Allister in disbelief.

Allister vanished again and reappeared next to me once more.

The girls stared at him in shock, speechless.

"So what does the fact you and Allister are … Eternals, have to do with putting us in danger?" Cassie finally asked, frowning.

"You remember the guy I chased at your house?" Allister asked.

"Yeah, I never saw him before," Cassie nodded.

"He's an Eternal too?" Elisa gasped.

"Yes, he's an Eternal." Allister confirmed. "He's the same Eternal who tried to take Britt's guardian angel when Angelina and I interrupted him. He is somehow tied to her and she now sees him take other angels from people."

"Your dreams are actually what that freak is doing in real life?" Trish looked at me. "What does he mean angels?"

"Yeah," I grimaced, waiting for them to throw up their hands and run. "We have guardian angels inside us."

"Like a soul?"

I shook my head. "*And* a soul." Surprisingly, Trish said nothing, only appearing distinctly uncomfortable and blinking a few times before giving a quick nod.

"Okay. Weird, but okay."

"We shouldn't divulge any more right now, for your own safety," Allister interrupted. "We need you to promise not to say a word of this to anyone. You shouldn't even discuss this with each other for fear of being overheard."

"Why?" Elisa asked.

"If the wrong person hears you speak of this, it would be dangerous for you," Allister told her.

"You mean if the person happens to be another Eternal," Trish stated.

"Yes, touching Britt and bringing her back to life is forbidden in our world. She and my family are in danger because of my actions and now, unfortunately, so are you."

Elisa and Cassie stood up next to Trish, all three sharing the same shell-shocked expression from the information they struggled to process. They walked down the steps, entranced, as they moved to the Jeep.

Cassie turned back to where we stood on the porch and then took a few steps closer. "Does being an Eternal mean you don't age?" she asked. Trish and Elisa walked back to hear our answer.

"We do age." Allister nodded. "But we age much more slowly."

"How much slower?" Trish asked.

"About ten times slower, give or take," Allister replied.

"So if you say you're eighteen, then you're …a hundred and eighty?" Elisa calculated, her eyes opening wide.

"Around there," Allister agreed with a brief head nod.

"Wow," Cassie gasped.

"Remember to come over and study with me for history." Trish gave a feeble smirk.

"We'd better go." Allister took my hand.

I looked blankly down at our hands and then back to him. He let go as his eyes dropped from my gaze. I hadn't forgiven him for changing me and putting all of us in danger, not just yet.

We walked to the car as the girls drove off in the Jeep. Allister opened my door and I slid inside. He climbed in and started the engine, looking at me, the shame visible in his expression as well as his posture. We drove to my house without a word, each lost in thought, or at least I was. I got out, not giving him a chance to open my door and he stood, looking awkward as I shut the door behind me.

"I'll check on you later," he said.

"Call before you do and I'll meet you in the shed."

He nodded and I walked to the house, feeling his eyes on my back as I closed the door behind me. I leaned against the closed door, exhaling heavily. What do I do now?

I excused myself from supper, which they held even though I asked them not to, telling my parents I ate too much at the party and wanted to go to bed early. I didn't tell a total lie, I did want to go to bed early, feeling the strangest urge to try and dream of Kendal hoping to find him and end this quickly.

I got to my room and closed the door, sitting down heavily on my bed. My hand dropped between my legs and brushed the edge of the mattress and box spring, hitting the notebook I kept there with the names and descriptions of the people I needed to heal. I opened the book and looked at the last name I penciled in at the top that no longer needed my powers. Mr. Kingsley. He should have been my next happy ending, instead, he was the latest victim of the psycho I now took walks with in my dreams. My phone buzzed and I looked to see Allister's name flashed on the screen.

"Hello?"

"Britt, can you meet me in the shed?" Allister's tone was wary.

"Yeah, fine," I said, too harsh.

I slipped down the stairs, past the living room where Mom and Dad sat reading and watching TV, and hurried across the dark backyard to the shed, shutting the door softly behind me. I didn't bother to turn on the light. Only then did I realize I still held the notebook in my hands.

"What's that?" Allister asked pointing to the notebook.

"Nothing, just a list of people I was going to heal someday." I shrugged with indifference.

"We spoke of this. Your powers are so new and underdeveloped; you might kill them or injure yourself." He took the notebook from my hand and stepped to the light flowing in through the window from the streetlight. He paused at the first page and then paged through page after filled page. He glanced at me after a few pages in disbelief and then turned a few more pages before tossing the notebook onto the chair. "You need to be careful you don't push yourself too far. It takes years to master," he said condescendingly.

"I've got it under control," I said, a little insulted. "I healed three people with cancer a few weeks ago," I reminded him and then pulled away.

"Three? No wonder people were starting to get suspicious," he fumed. "Why didn't you just send up a flare or put up a sign?" Allister shouted.

"You weren't very quick at contacting me to tell me I shouldn't," I shot back.

"Okay, okay, you're right," he said raising a calming hand and turning away to look out the window. He stared out the window in thought for a moment and then turned back, nodding. "It should be fine. We can't heal cancer."

"You healed mine," I reminded him.

"Yes, but I changed you. Permanently healing cancer is impossible. If I hadn't changed you into an Eternal..." Allister attempted to reason.

"But I *did* heal them."

Allister stared at me hard for a moment then sighed, shaking his head. "If you say you did it, then you did, but that is amazing. I'm pretty advanced at healing, but I can't heal cancer...not completely."

"I only healed those three that day. I tried to heal four," I said, sadly recalling my failed attempt to heal the woman with the beaten and battered body.

"You did three in one day?" Allister exclaimed, shocked. "I knew about the one," he mumbled under his breath.

"Yes," I ignored his muttering, wanting to finish explaining, "but I couldn't heal the fourth one and then I passed out. When I woke up, this came back." I lifted my arm into the light and showed him the scar that returned after that failed attempt.

"You mustn't do that again," Allister cautioned, his eyes troubled.

"I understand I need to be more discreet," I said with a nod. "I stopped healing people after you warned me."

"Not only that," he added, "if you overexert yourself, it appears you bring back your mortal injuries. We don't want you to bring back the injuries you suffered when you went over the falls."

"But I wasn't injured when I went over the falls," I pointed out.

"Britt, you died. Your body suffered broken bones, head trauma, and internal injuries. You could not have survived those injuries even as an Eternal."

"You said you couldn't die unless your heart was torn out by an Eternal."

"Not unless you exceed your capacity for damage trying to heal someone and then suffering mortal damage on top of it. Even we have our limits," he paused.

"And what? There's more?"

"An angel can rip out your heart and kill you too." Allister held my stare for a minute as frustration and disbelief percolated to the surface and he turned away from my accusing eyes.

"Is there anything else you conveniently forgot to tell me?" I moved closer to him as he stood with his back to me.

"You've just progressed so fast with your powers and now everything is collapsing in on us. I thought I had more time. I don't know what to do next."

"I don't know what to believe anymore," I said as my determination to be mad at him wavered. Standing this close to him, seeing him so upset I faltered. "You made this choice for me and now I need to decide if I can live with it. The way it looks right now, I don't think I can."

Allister turned to me and I spun away from his hurt look.

"We need to get past this." Allister spoke gently to my back.

I looked over my shoulder, the dim light from the streetlight shining on his face. "That's pretty easy for you since you made all the decisions."

"Britt, don't you see what I did actually *saved* your soul?"

"But you didn't know that would happen when you touched me." Facing him, I pressed forward, making him take a step back. "You made the decision knowing I might have ended up a soulless monster. Now you put me in a position where my family and friends are in danger because I'm alive. I don't know if I can forgive you for that."

"I understand, but the thought of losing you wasn't an option then and isn't an option now." I felt the intensity of his stare even in the darkness.

"I just don't know what I should feel."

"I know I don't want to live without you," he said, turning to look out the window at the night.

My feelings for Allister were undeniable, yet my guilt over the danger to my loved ones overshadowed those feelings right now. If he let me die on that riverbank, none of this would be happening. Then again, three more people might be dead or dying of cancer if I didn't have the power and opportunity to heal them. How could something this wonderful turn into something so terrible?

I looked at Allister, tears blurred my vision as the stress and frustration became unbearable.

In a heartbeat, Allister had me in his arms, my head on his shoulder, my tears wetting his shirt.

"I have to stop doing this," I cried.

"It's fine, my shirts dry," Allister soothed.

I groaned a chuckle and lifted my head to look at him. "I mean, I need to accept my lot in life and keep my family and friends safe, not sit here and cry about it." I wiped my cheeks and eyes.

"I'll be by your side as will my parents and Angelina," Allister assured me.

"Angelina?" I raised an eyebrow.

"She'll come around. Give her time."

"I doubt that very much." I shook my head, and then paused, looking at him. "Did you say you don't want to live without me?"

"Yes," he said, becoming still, holding his breath.

"Wow." I leaned in and wrapped my arms around him as he exhaled. His strong arms encircled me and I sighed within their comfort.

"So are we okay?" He pulled back to look down at me as I turned my face up to his.

"I guess, but it's time for me to start deciding things for myself."

"Sure, no problem."

"I mean, I fought cancer head on and will fight this too." I frowned at the reference finding it hard to believe such a short time ago, I was going to die and now…

"What's wrong?"

"I guess I didn't actually beat cancer, but I'm going to protect my friends. I won't let anything happen to them."

"I know you won't." Allister smiled down at me. He lowered his lips to mine and my emotions surged, getting away from me. He pulled away but I leaned into him, keeping our lips together for as long as possible. Our lips separated at last, leaving me yearning for more.

"What?" I groaned in exasperation, looking at his confused expression.

"Nothing, I just remembered I should check on Angelina since Kendal was watching our house last night."

"Yeah, you should go." I was focused on breathing.

"Call me if you dream of him again tonight."

"Sure, now get going." I gave him a playful shove away from me, my foul mood gone.

He shimmered out of the shed, his white smile the last thing I saw.

I snuck back to my room just as my phone buzzed in my pocket as a text message came in from Allister.

Sleep well.

I cringed, feeling guilty. I knew sleeping well wasn't at the top of my list for tonight.

I climbed into bed, concentrating on the last image of Kendal I had; him standing in the middle of the street by Cassie's house right before he shimmered. A short time later, I felt myself drift and then the nightmare began.

I stared at the moon, full and bright overhead. I walked along a street I didn't recognize and past houses foreign to me. Understanding, I looked through Kendal's eyes; the scent of lilac came to me and I braced for anything.

This night was different. He walked into an isolated park and sat on a bench facing a swing set. The wind blew as the swings squeaked back and forth giving an eerie, scary movie feeling to the setting. My vision turned to the left as a man approached, a long black coat wrapped around him and a wool hat pulled down over his head obscured both his form and appearance. He sat next to Kendal and smiled, the moon glinting off a silver tooth in his mouth.

"Why did you want to see me?" I heard Kendal's familiar voice.

"I think we can help each other," the man replied.

"Don't need your help."

"Oh, I think you do." The man smiled again.

"How so?"

"We understand some rules are being broken around here and we mean to bring those who are perpetrating the crimes to justice."

"What kind of rules?"

"Come on, friend. We're aware of your taste for angels." The man raised a hand to silence Kendal's objections before they could be voiced. "Don't make this harder on yourself."

"Don't know nothing about that," Kendal said.

"I believe you do and that's the reason for my visit."

"Nope, you're talking to the wrong guy."

"I don't believe so. I have it from very good authority there is an Eternal in this area taking guardians. I'm confident that Eternal is you." He motioned with his hand and two men stepped out of the shadows.

"Wait." Kendal held up his hand.

The men stopped and turned to the man with the silver tooth, questioning. The man gave a nod and the men relaxed their aggressive stance only slightly.

"What if another crime has been committed, something forbidden by the council?" Kendal continued, a slight tremor in his voice.

"Then we'll investigate that allegation as well, although it doesn't diminish what you've been doing." The man shook his head.

"What if the crime involved the Parks family?"

The man turned, eyes narrowing as he studied Kendal for a moment. "What kind of crime?"

"The touching of the dead," Kendal watched the man closely for his reaction.

The man's eyes shot wide and a grin crept across his face as his tongue reached up to rub against his silver tooth reflexively.

In my dream world I felt a chill rush down my spine.

"If there is proof of said crime, I would be very interested in making a deal with whomever brings me sufficient evidence for a conviction with the council."

163

"You let me go and I'll get you evidence," Kendal assured him. He stood and walked away. I felt a tingle, and my dream with Kendal ended.

I sat up, reached over, clicked on my light, and then flopped back down on my pillow. My bedding was soaked with my sweat and my t-shirt stuck to my skin. Kendal planned to give proof to this man that Allister touched me. That alone terrified me. Then, I wondered what evidence that might be and felt another shudder rattle through me.

Chapter 14

I sat awake the rest of the night, recalling the man with the silver tooth. His manner made me uneasy. The way he grinned when Kendal told him the crime involved the Parks family. The information appeared to bring him joy, euphoria, like bringing the Parks down was personal.

I still stared at my ceiling when the alarm went off the next morning. I reached over and slapped the button with a moan, rolled out of bed, and headed to the shower.

I heard a car horn honk as I came down the stairs and rushed to the door, opening it to see Allister leaning against his car. Angelina stared out the passenger window with indifference. I closed the door behind me and walked to the car, texting feverishly to Trish I didn't need a ride.

"Morning." Allister smiled and leaned down to give me a light kiss on the lips.

"Morning." I blushed and then frowned at my own reaction.

"Please, do I have to be a witness to that?" Angelina sighed from the car.

"Yep," Allister said, opening the car door and ushering his sister out of the front seat.

Angelina sauntered out of the car and slid into the back seat, not looking at me as I got in. Allister eased behind the steering wheel and we rolled into the school parking lot a moment later, pulling up next to Trish's Jeep as she and the girls got out.

"Hey Britt," Elisa smiled.

"Hi," I said back, grateful she didn't seem upset after yesterday's information dump.

Trish and Cassie waved as they hurried into the school.

"What's up with them?" I asked Elisa as she pulled her backpack from the Wrangler.

She shrugged, unconcerned. "They had to meet the boyfriends this morning."

"What about you?"

"Tommy had an early practice today. No rush for me."

We walked into the school, students staring and whispering. I smiled, walking next to Allister as Angelina paced ahead, not looking back.

"What's her beef?" Elisa asked.

"She has her reasons for not liking me much," I said, understanding Angelina's resentment. My existence put her brother and family in danger as well as mine.

Sitting in Calculus later that morning, the cold reality slapped me in the face as a female substitute stood at the front of the class where Mr. Kinsley stood just a few days earlier. Kendal's existence now made a lasting impact on my life, along with every student in school. The sooner we stopped him, the better.

Lunch became a spectacle as my friends and I joined Allister and Angelina at their table. The other students stared as we ate our lunch, whispering between glances over at our table. Angelina's face showed nothing but distaste as we sat down, but Allister smiled and welcomed us.

"Hey," he said.

"Hi," I smiled back.

Elisa, Trish, and Cassie sat down, nodding to Allister while carefully avoiding Angelina's dirty looks.

To make matters worse, Jeb, Tommy, and Carl all sat down with us as well, turning Angelina's mere disgusted look into appalled. The boys looked at her for a moment and then turned their attention to the rest of the table, ignoring her disdain completely.

Allister visited with everyone, smiling and asking questions of the guys. Jeb, about his music, Tommy about the team's chances in the upcoming game, and Carl about the knowledge bowl competition he participated in.

I sat watching, fascinated how this appeared outwardly normal, recognizing the bizarreness of it all. Allister could be friendly with the guys, yet never friends on the level of the amigos and me. Knowing he would eventually watch them go into the ground. I couldn't help but feel sadness for him. Sorrow washed through me as I realized once the girls were gone, my friendships would also become much like that, merely superficial.

Angelina stormed off just before the bell and our heads turned to watch her leave. Her attitude remained pretty much the same when we met up at the car after school. She slid into the back seat without a word and remained silent the entire ride to my house.

Allister hurried around the car, helped me out, and walked me to the door. Angelina moved to the front seat and turned her back to us.

I stared at her as Allister and I stood by the porch.

"Don't worry about her." He looked back at his sister.

"I wish we could be friends," I sighed.

"She'll get over it."

"Yeah, right." I rolled my eyes.

Allister leaned down, gave me a kiss, and smiled as he pulled away. "See you later." He walked back to the car as I climbed the steps, looking over my shoulder as they drove off.

Dad worked late again so Mom and I ate a salad and I excused myself to my room to get my homework done. Walking through the living room, the local paper had an article on Mr. Kinsley. I lifted the pages and read how they found poor Mr. Kinsley at the school, correcting papers where he'd had a heart attack and died.

So they still thought Kendal's murders were heart attacks. No one suspected we had a mass murderer in Grand Rapids, just a rash of heart attacks. I set the paper down and headed to my room. We needed to stop him before he could hurt anyone else.

I crawled into bed around 10:00pm and tried to get to sleep.

I'm not sure when I fell asleep, but the dream came quickly. I walked down a dark alley, strangely familiar, yet too dark to identify. I looked from side to side, no one in sight. I stopped behind a house, the upstairs, completely dark, while a few lights shone on the bottom floor. I slipped into the yard, finding a dark corner behind a shed, hidden from prying eyes.

Just as the tingling began, panic gripped me. I recognized the yard and the house. Mine.

My room materialized before me as the smell of lilac came to me and I stared through Kendal's eyes at my bed as I slept. He crept closer even as my mind screamed for me to wake up, to just, wake up.

168

My eyes flew open and I sat up.

Kendal, only a step from me, jumped back in surprise. Regaining his composure he moved closer.

"Stop," I shouted, my heart racing.

He smiled, his teeth shining white in the dim light from the lamp on my desk and he kept coming.

"I'm warning you, stop," I said again, hearing the panic in my voice.

He put a raised finger to his lips, silencing me. "We wouldn't want Mommy or Daddy to come in and find me here, would we?"

Oh my God, I forgot. They couldn't help me when dealing with Eternals. They were more vulnerable than I was.

"I'm warning you," I whispered feebly.

"I'm just here to finish the job Allister and Angelina interrupted," he grinned.

"You can't hurt me," I bluffed.

"Is that what they told you?" he laughed. "All I have to do is pull your heart out. It's quite painful, from what I've witnessed, and very final." He raised his hand in front of him and came closer still until lilac pervaded my senses.

"Why? Why are you doing this?" I cried.

Coming up short, he blinked. "After I tried taking your angel I had strange feelings. At first, I didn't understand. Not until seeing you at that party. I was drawn there; it must have been because of you. I know we are linked somehow. The strange feeling is you, inside my head. That must end, you see, it interferers with my plans."

"Your plans to kill more angels?" I sneered.

My anger failed to affect him. "Angels are like a drug, giving us euphoria and strength. I like it too much to quit and, with other Eternals in this area, I can bring the blame down on the Parks and relocate somewhere else. I win either way."

"What about the man with the silver tooth?" I stalled, growing desperate.

"The man you are referring to said I could remain a free man if I bring him evidence of Allister's crime. You're evidence alive *or* dead. And with you dead, there is no witness to tell them I'm the one taking the guardians. As you can see I've given this a lot of thought." He smiled and lunged.

I caught his wrist, his hand hovering above my chest. I strained to keep him from touching me, grunting with exertion. He pressed his weight down over me and his hand inched closer. His fingertips touched my bare skin as my t-shirt slid down in the struggle. Pain erupted in my chest and I felt a jolt of searing pain. I screamed out then bit my lip, remembering Mom downstairs.

The taste of blood filled my mouth as I struggled to hold his hand at bay; I felt my teeth go through my lip.

I was weakening rapidly, Kendal's hand pressing even harder against my skin. Using my last ounce of strength, I kicked up against his stomach, pushing him up and off of me. Without warning, something flashed over my bed and collided with Kendal, hurtling him across the room, and smashing him into my dresser, toppling the lamp. The fallen light created gruesome shadows of their struggle on my pale bedroom walls.

I rolled over in time to see Kendal vanish and left Allister standing with his back to me, shoulders rising and falling as he panted from the exertion. He spun around, rushed to my bed, and knelt at my side.

"Are you alright?"

"Yeah, fine," I gasped, still feeling the burning on my skin. I looked down to see five red fingerprints on my chest, between my breasts.

"How'd you know?"

"I sensed something was wrong. When I got here I found Kendal over you." Allister couldn't contain the anger in his voice.

"You didn't call first." I touched the red marks on my skin and flinching at their tenderness.

"I save your life and you're worried I didn't call first?" he smirked.

"I guess it's okay this one time," I told him, blushing.

A knock at my door startled us. "Honey, are you okay?" Mom asked through the closed door.

"Yeah, fine."

"What was that noise?"

"I had a nightmare and knocked over my lamp," I replied, trying to exude nothing but calm in my voice.

"Do you want me to come in and help you clean it up?" The door knob turned as she started to come in.

I scurried to the door as Allister shimmered out of sight. Catching the door as it opened, I put my body in the opening to block her view of the trashed room.

"I've got it. Sorry to scare you." I spoke quickly.

She leaned to the side to look past me and I moved my head to obstruct her view. "That's okay, as long as you're okay." Though she appeared dubious, she let it go. Maybe it was the hour, regardless, I didn't question my good fortune.

"I'm good. Just want to get back to bed," I said easing the door closed, shrinking the opening.

"Good night," she replied, sounding uncertain, as I closed the door.

"Night."

I latched the lock and turned back to find Allister standing right behind me. I jumped and put a shocked hand to my chest, cringing as it brushed Kendal's fingerprints.

"I can heal you, if you'd like," he offered, nodding at the marks on my chest.

"Oh no. Remember the last time you healed me? Look at where that's gotten us." I walked past him and sat down on the bed.

"Not much more trouble I can get us into then, is there?" He raised an eyebrow.

I shrugged, laid back, and moved my hand as he sat next to me and eased his hands onto my injuries. His skin felt cool and soothing compared to the heat coming off Kendal's marks. The pain increased and I sucked air through my clenched teeth, and then, the pain disappeared.

I looked up at him as he leaned over me. He stared into my eyes, his hand still touching my chest. I could feel the edge of his hand touching either breast as it pressed against me and my heart quickened.

His incredible eyes, so full of passion, love and desire, all mixed together, seemed to transfer into me. I reached a hand up behind his head, weaving my fingers into his thick hair, grasping it in my fist as I pulled him down to me and pressed his lips to mine. My heart raced, the touch of his lips driving all thoughts of discomfort from my mind, my need for him overwhelmed me.

He tried to pull away but I pulled harder, keeping his lips pressed hard to mine. He gave in to it and his tongue darted into my mouth, flicking against mine, and drawing a moan from deep in my throat. After all too short a time, he forcefully pulled away, panting. I gasped at the sudden separation.

"I need to warn Angelina that Kendal is in the area and he's grown bolder," he said as he straightened, pulling his hand from me with some reluctance.

Pleased to see he seemed just as affected as I, I made my way to the dresser where I pulled out fleece pants and a sweatshirt to wear over my pajamas. "I'll come with you."

"Hurry, I don't know what he might try next, but we shouldn't leave her alone."

"When can I learn to shimmer so you don't have to be with me all the time?" I asked, taking his hand.

"Later. It takes years to learn the discipline needed to shimmer without putting yourself inside a wall or a something."

He grinned and I tingled. We instantly stood in his sister's room, the darkness felt oppressive with not a glimmer of light anywhere. I felt Allister stiffen as he wrapped a protective arm around my waist.

"She always keeps a light on," he whispered.

We eased to one side and he clicked on the light.

The room was disheveled; furniture overturned, bedding strewn about, pillows torn apart, the stuffing still floating in the air. Most alarming, the blood was everywhere.

"Angelina!" Allister rushed over to the corner by the bed where Angelina lay staring blankly at the ceiling; her blood painting the wall beside her.

My breath caught in my throat, squelching the scream waiting to escape as I stared at her.

She blinked. I pushed Allister aside when he appeared only able to gape at his sister in shock. I knelt next to her, placing my ear to her mouth. My hair fluttered and I looked up with excitement.

"She's alive, get over here, she's alive." I motioned to Allister.

He knelt beside me, placing his hand on her chest. Blood oozed out of five holes around his fingers and onto his hand. Her arm looked broken and her leg twisted the wrong way. Allister could heal her. He *would* heal her. He had to.

Allister closed his eyes as he pressed his hand against the source of her most threatening injury. His eyelids squeezed tight in concentration and then opened wide. His face turned to a mask of horror as he stared at his sister and then up at me.

"What, what is it?" I cried.

"She's too far gone, I can't bring her back," he whispered, his voice hoarse.

"You brought me back, what's the difference if you break the rules once or twice, save her," I shouted.

"No, it's not that, I don't have the power to bring her back. He might as well have ripped her heart out, he's severed the arteries," he cried, tears rolling down his cheeks.

"No, she can't go. I won't let her go," I shouted back.

In a panic I pushed his hands aside, replacing them with my own. Instantly I felt her pain. Her broken bones, her internal bleeding, and the deep wounds in her chest; I felt them all. I sensed something rising within me, something surging to the surface like at the hospital. At first I wanted to slow it, to try and control it; afraid of it taking control and burning me to ash. Then, the choice was taken from me as something burst free from within and took over.

I tilted my head back screaming, scorching my vocal chords with the intensity released through my throat. Anger erupted at the thought of losing her, of seeing Kendal get away. I let go; all my will power, all my thoughts of caution telling me I pushed the boundaries. I ignored them and let the energy do what it will. The pain manifested in a rush of white, hot, scalding light in my brain and then everything went black.

Chapter 15

I opened my eyes, more like pried them open, since they refused to listen to my commands. I struggled, forcing them to finally respond.

Allister sat next to me. I lay on a bed, the canopy partially hanging on the only post left intact of the four. Angelina's bed. The thought of Angelina brought her fate rushing back to me. I sat up so quickly my head wailed in protest. I put a hand to my spinning head and felt the pucker of the scar from my brain surgery against my fingertips. Allister's warning rang in my memory. I slid a hand to my side and sure enough, the appendix scar rubbed against my fingers. Then, I saw Angelina next to me her face at peace, content. It was all for nothing. I failed. Damn it, I failed. Tears filled my eyes as I looked upon Allister's sister.

Allister reached over, took me by the chin, and turned my head to face him. His tired smile confused me and I pulled free of his hand to look back at Angelina. I focused on her chest and saw the movement. I froze, not willing to accept until I saw another, and another.

I spun back to Allister, my tears spilling down my cheeks.

He smiled, his tears wetting his face.

"You did it," he whispered.

"I did it," I repeated, monotone.

"You did it," he said again, pulling me into his arms, burying his face in my hair.

I sobbed into his shoulder, unable to control the emotions pouring out of me. I shook in his arms and he held me close, not moving, but holding me tight until the spell passed.

When I moved a little he relaxed his hold, allowing me to lean back, his shirt wet with my tears.

"I'm sorry. I don't know what came over me," I sniffed.

"It doesn't matter," he grinned. "You saved my sister when I couldn't. I owe you my life. No matter what happens, you will always have my gratitude for what you did tonight."

He put his fingers on my chin and tenderly pulled my lips to his. I felt my heart race. Losing myself in his touch again, I didn't have the strength to fight it, not even if I wished to, which I didn't.

"Humph."

Allister and I jerked apart as Angelina sat staring with disapproval.

"Sister." Allister leaned across me to embrace her.

She hugged him back and then pushed him away, eyeing me curiously.

"You saved me?" she asked.

I nodded, unable to form words, still waiting for my heartbeat to slow.

"Why didn't you?" she turned to Allister looking stern.

"I couldn't. I tried, but I didn't have the power to do so."

"And *you* did?" she looked back at me.

"I don't know how, but yes." I shrugged, "I did."

"Thank you," she said with a hint of a smile.

"Sure, no problem."

"Does this mean I have to like her now?" she turned to Allister.

"Yes, it does." He nodded, unable to hold back his smirk.

"Damn," she sighed and looked at me, resigned.

I healed Angelina completely, the only remaining sign of her attack the five minor scars where Kendal touched her. I pulled my sweatshirt down, exposing my own scars from his attack to her and she met my eyes, another thing binding us together.

"He shimmered in out of nowhere," Angelina explained. "I didn't even sense him, and suddenly, he was in my room."

Nodding, I held my hand to my new scars. "I saw me through his eyes in my dream and woke just in time to slow him down. Allister arrived before he finished me off," I told her.

"Good thing, else I wouldn't be here either," she pointed out matter-of-factly.

"I swear he'll pay," Allister said through clenched teeth.

I saw the rage boiling within him. The image sent chills through me. I hoped his rage never sought me out.

"I better get you back home," he said, turning to me.

Fear pulsed through me, the thought of Kendal hunting me turning my blood cold.

Allister sensed my reticence. "Angelina and I will keep an eye on your house tonight," he said, turning to Angelina.

She nodded her agreement.

"He won't reach you again, I promise," Allister assured me.

"He could harm you too, or did you forget?" I reminded him.

"I'm a more dangerous adversary than either of you," he said.

I looked at him doubtful, but when I turned to Angelina, she nodded her agreement. The image of his rage filled eyes flashed through my mind and I believed them.

"Kendal would be lucky to leave with his life if he confronted Allister." She smiled. "And he won't catch me off guard again. The next time won't be so easy."

"A fighter *and* a healer?" I asked. "How'd that happen?"

"Just lucky I guess. I believe healing is a redeeming factor to any violence I need to exact. If I had a soul, I would say it is my redemption." He shrugged, downplaying the importance of his declaration.

I chuckled, shaking my head at his reasoning, realizing I used the same rationalization to excuse my connection to Kendal's killing.

I took his extended hand and still tingled after reaching my room. Angelina helped me neaten things up while Allister circled the house to assure Kendal didn't lurk in the shadows. He shimmered back in a moment after we put everything in its place.

"No sign of him," he said. "Can I borrow your cell phone?"

"Sure." I took it off the desk and handed it to him.

"I need to tell Mother and Father what's happened," he said, shimmering out of the room.

"I'll go see if I can pick up Kendal's trail. Don't worry, he'll not get by us," she declared. "See you tomorrow." She vanished.

Allister returned, handing my phone back as I looked at him, expectant.

"They're on the jet, nearly to Greece," he said. "They'll come straight back once they refuel."

"What'd they say about Kendal?"

"They've been doing some checking and Kendal is very connected with the council in Greece. They're suspicious this is a plot to eliminate our entire family."

"Why would anyone want to do that?" I asked.

"Victor once led the council and holds sway over them even now. If we're eliminated, other factions will have a greater chance of overthrowing the council, which Father supports."

"And then add me to the mix," I sighed, feeling even more a burden.

"You're the best thing that's happened to me in over a hundred and fifty years. I'll never regret breaking the law to keep you in this world." He leaned down and kissed me, shimmering the instant he pulled away.

I sat down on my bed, my head still spinning from his kiss. I didn't realize I still held my cell phone until it buzzed in my hand.

I glanced at the screen. Trish. "Hey."

"Can't sleep. You know that thing with Mr. Kinsley?" Trish asked.

The image of Mr. Kinsley's guardian angel being pulled from his body flashed across my mind. His dead eyes, hauntingly staring into nothingness still made me sick to my stomach.

"Yeah, crazy huh?"

"You know who did that?" Trish asked.

"Yeah."

"Thought so. Kind of creepy," she sighed.

"Try being there."

"I can't imagine, Britt."

"Really sucks."

"What's up? You don't sound too good." Concern warmed her voice.

"I think I'm really falling for Allister," I confided, changing the subject to something more enjoyable.

"Who wouldn't?" she laughed. "He's gorgeous."

"I suppose you're right," I giggled.

"Does he feel the same about you?"

"I think so." I felt my insides warm at the thought.

"Britt, if you're going to live forever, why not be happy with someone like Allister?" Trish was surprisingly reasonable.

"I know, but I'll outlive everyone I care about," I told her the source of my unhappiness. "You, Elise, Cassie, Mom and Dad."

"Except Allister," she reminded. "Don't over think this like you always do. Being normal, you might already be dead. Being an Eternal, you'll outlive everyone, except other Eternals, one of which happens to be in love with you. Don't make this a bad thing, cause it isn't."

"Thanks Trish," I smiled.

"For what?"

"For being the friend who can see the good in everything."

"That's what I'm here for." She laughed. "See you tomorrow. Night."

"Night." I ended the call and set the phone on my dresser.

I curled up in my blankets, feeling better about being an Eternal for the first time.

Mom knocked on the door the next morning to wake me up. I scrambled to unlock the door, realizing I forgot to plug my alarm clock in after the attack last night.

I rushed to get ready, pulling a shirt over my head as a car honked out front. I glanced out my window overlooking the street. Allister stood beside his Camaro, arms folded, waiting for me as Angelina leaned against the black car's trunk, giving me a nod when I looked out.

I warmed at the simple gesture from Angelina as I grabbed my backpack and headed downstairs. At least we might be able to be in the same car without me getting frostbite from her now.

Mom stood in the entry.

"Where are the girls?" she asked.

"They knew Allister and his sister were picking me up," I told her.

"Don't let having a boyfriend pull you away from your friends," she cautioned.

"Don't worry, they like Allister too." I grinned, giving her a kiss on the cheek as I walked past and headed out the door.

Angelina hopped in back as I slid into the front and Allister got behind the wheel. The rumble of the engine still excited me as we pulled away from the curb.

"Did you guys get any sleep?" I asked, first looking at Allister and then turning to look at Angelina.

"Some," she replied. "Kendal looks long gone."

"Good, I think. Shouldn't we be searching for him? Doesn't he have to pay for what he did to those innocent people, and what he tried to do to us last night?" I asked.

Allister's eyes narrowed. "I promise you, he will."

His words made me shudder. Their intensity left no doubt; Allister would see that Kendal paid for trying to kill Angelina and me.

We pulled into the parking lot as the other students milled around the building entrance. It seemed to me, nearly everyone stopped and stared as Allister opened my door and helped first me and then Angelina out. I wondered when the novelty of us being together would wear off.

"Don't they have anything better to do than ogle us?" Angelina mumbled under her breath as we headed for class.

"Let them look," Allister grinned. "They're jealous I have the two hottest girls in my car."

"The car doesn't hurt either," I smiled back.

Only a few steps away from our parking spot, the Wrangler pulled up and the three amigos piled out.

"Morning," Elisa greeted us warmly.

"Hey." I nodded back.

Angelina gave a slight smirk and walked ahead.

"Does this mean Angelina is warming up to us?" Cassie asked, looking at me and then back to Angelina.

"A bit, maybe, as long as you can keep a secret." Angelina gave Cassie a cautionary look.

"Sure, sure, no problem," Cassie said raising her hands defensively in front of her.

"How's our girl?" Trish asked, swinging an arm around my shoulders.

"Good. Thanks again for the talk last night," I whispered.

"No problem." She winked at me.

We split up once we got inside and headed to our respective classes.

When I walked into my history class before lunch, I stopped, stunned as Allister sat in the seat next to mine. With a raised eyebrow I slid in next to him, staring at him until he turned to me.

"I needed to get this class in before graduation," he grinned. "Might as well take it with you."

I nodded as the teacher started the lecture. I stared most of the hour at Allister, the teacher so enthralled in early American politics he never noticed.

After the bell we walked together to lunch. The girls already sat with Angelina at a table saving our seats. We got our food and sat down with them.

"Ladies," Allister greeted.

The girls laughed, saying hello and Cassie blushed.

"I want you to know, I understand the relationship you have with Britt and I respect it, but what is said at this table must remain at this table, understood?"

The girls nodded enthusiastic, thrilled by their inclusion at last.

Allister turned to Angelina and me. "We speak of nothing specific in front of them, only vague generalities, agreed?"

"Agreed," I said.

"Fine." Angelina tipped her head.

"I will patrol around Britt's house tonight," Allister said. "Trevor came home from Greece ahead of Mother and Father to stay with Angelina," he added, seeing my concern at her being left alone.

"That guy with the pony tail and all the muscles at your house?" I questioned.

"He's one of our private security team," he explained.

"Where were they last night?" I asked.

"We believed Kendal was headed to Greece and thought the security would be better used with Mother and Father. We won't underestimate him again."

"What happened last night?" Elisa asked and then put a hand to her mouth as our eyes swung to her. "Err, sorry."

"You can know Kendal tried to hurt Britt and Angelina last night. By being around us, you may endanger yourselves as well. You must decide if it's worth the risk." Allister looked to each of them.

"If being with Britt is dangerous, I'm willing to risk it. I won't abandon a friend when times get tough," Trish said proudly.

Cassie and Elisa nodded.

"But I thought you couldn't die?" Cassie spoke up, confused.

"Only another Eternal can hurt us," Angelina explained. "In order to kill us straight away, they need to tear out our hearts."

The girls gasped.

"We'll usually heal from any other wound," Angelina added.

I unconsciously raised my hand to my chest and the the prints Kendal left behind, still burning.

The bell rang and we scattered to our classes again, meeting up outside by the cars afterwards. The girls looking questioning to Allister, Angelina, and me as we reached our car.

"You should spend some time with your friends." Allister turned to me. "What would you normally do now?"

"We need to go shopping," Elisa said.

"Then go shopping," he said mildly. "Angelina and I will go back to the house and see if anything has developed. I'll stop by later."

I nodded and stepped next to him, stretching up expectantly.

He smirked, glancing at the audience and shrugged. Leaning down, he kissed me softly.

"Ooh," Elisa sighed, envious.

He pulled away, leaving me as breathless as always.

I turned and hopped into the Jeep.
Trish started the Jeep and we sped off, destined for a girl's day like we use to have before everything changed.

Chapter 16

The Jeep pulled into the parking lot of the mall and we piled out, all except Trish. She sat behind the wheel, the motor still idling. We stopped, waiting for her, but she stared straight ahead, deep in thought.

We walked back, waiting for her to snap out of it.

"What are you doing?" Elisa asked as she pulled her auburn hair back into a ponytail and secured it with a scrunchy.

"I'm bored with Grand Rapids shopping." She blinked at us.

"So, what do you want to do?" Cassie asked.

"Let's go to Duluth," Trish suggested.

"Duluth, on a school night? I don't think mom..." Cassie objected.

"We're eighteen. We're old enough to spend an evening in Duluth shopping," Trish insisted.

"Let's do it." Elisa smiled and jumped into the back.

"We better call our parents and let them know," Cassie said.

We nodded, pulling our cell phones out and dialing. None of our parents had a problem with it and we were soon speeding along the highway to Duluth.

Curving down the large hill leading to the port city we could see out into Lake Superior as it disappeared along the horizon. We moved our jaws to relieve the air-lock in our ears at the sudden change in pressure the steep incline caused. I realized I forgot to call Allister and quickly dialed him, getting his voicemail.

"Allister, its Britt. We're in Duluth for the evening. I'll call when we're heading back." I slipped the phone into my pocket and noticed the girls smirking.

"What?"

"Like a little married couple," Trish teased.

"With Kendal after me he needs to know where I am," I defended myself.

"You never said he was after you," Elisa exclaimed, eyes wide.

"What did you think when Allister said Kendal tried to hurt me and Angelina?"

"I don't know, I guess I didn't think 'psycho stalker' type of hurt," Elisa admitted, frowning.

We pulled to a stop in the parking lot of the large mall. The girls stared at me, concerned at this new information. I turned in my seat to face them and pulled my shirt down at the collar to expose the five finger marks on my chest between my breasts.

"Holy shit," Cassie cursed and I looked at her, surprised. She never swore.

"You said it," Trish murmured.

"He tried to rip your heart out?" Elisa gasped.

"Yeah, he would have done it too if Allister hadn't shown up in time."

The girls gave a collective gasp.

"Maybe we should get you home," Trish suggested. "This wasn't such a bright idea."

"We're here now, we might as well shop," I said with a brief smile.

"Okay, but everyone needs to keep their eyes peeled for stalker Kendal, right?" Trish instructed.

We all agreed, piling out of the Jeep and racing into the mall. People milled around everywhere, the mall was packed. We hit our favorite clothing stores first, finding something for each of us, and then we looked in some trinket shops. I was searching for something small but sentimental for the two Eternals linked to me forever. I found the perfect gifts and we hit a restaurant for dinner.

We ate and laughed, forgetting about the dangers possibly lurking outside the mall, at least for a while.

Then my cell buzzed in my pocket. I pulled it out, and Allister's name showed on the screen. I hit the answer button with a wide smile on my face.

"Hello?"

"Britt, what are you doing in Duluth?" Allister sounded panicked.

"Just shopping, don't worry. We're surrounded by people," I assured him.

"We found Kendal's trail. He's headed right for you!" he shouted into the phone.

My eyes shot up as the girl's faces turned pale. They'd heard Allister's voice through the phone.

"Get out of there now!" he ordered. "If he finds you, he'll get to you. A crowd won't stop him if he's as desperate as I think he is."

"Okay, okay," I tried to stay calm.

"And Britt," Allister brought me back, his voice much quieter. "Keep the girls close. I think he knows how important they are to you. They'll be targets as well."

"Allister," I whimpered, feeling panic threaten to shut down my ability to think or even move. "What should I do?" The thought of Kendal hurting the amigos devastated me.

"Get on the road," he advised, "maybe he'll pass by without noticing. Angelina, Trevor, and I are on our way. We'll meet you on the road and escort you the rest of the way, but you have to leave now. And Britt, don't let the girls out of your sight."

"Yeah, okay," I whispered, ending the call.

I stared down at my phone. What had I done? I looked up at the girls, studying me in silence.

"We have to go. Kendal's on his way here," I told them flatly.

We threw money on the table for the food, not bothering to count it, and raced out with our bags. Like maniacs, we ran through the mall as people around us turned and stared. We burst out of the mall and sprinted to the Jeep.

We sped up the long winding hill leading out of Duluth, reaching the top as a silver Mercedes on the other side of the two lanes screeched to a stop and did a U-turn through the grass median spraying dirt and grass behind it. The cars around it veered off into the ditches on both sides of the road.

"That's him!" I shouted, not so much seeing him as sensing him. The eerie feeling it gave me was undeniable.

Trish punched the gas and we roared through a red light, cars honking and swerving to avoid us. Cassie and Elisa looked back as the wind blew their hair around their faces in the open Jeep. Elisa's ponytail all but pulled free of the band, flailing back and forth across her face.

"He's gaining on us," Elisa shouted over the deafening wind as she gripped the frazzled ponytail in her hand and pulled at it nervously.

"We can't out run him with this!" Trish shouted back.

I frantically dialed Allister. He answered on the first ring.

"He's after us and we can't lose him!" I shouted into the phone.

"Where are you?"

"Just outside of Duluth."

"We're still thirty miles away," his voice sounded strained. "Do what you have to do and we'll be there as soon as we can."

"Okay," I cried, adding needlessly, "hurry."

The phone went silent and I grasped it tightly as Kendal pulled in close behind us, slamming into our rear bumper. Trish struggled to keep the Jeep on the road, the vehicle swerving uncontrollably for a minute and then pulled away from the Mercedes slightly.

"I can't let him do that anymore!" Trish shouted. "I almost lost it."

"Here he comes again!" Elisa shouted over the wind.

Cassie sat with her head in her hands, her knees pulled up tight to her chest.

I turned around as Kendal crept closer.

Without warning, Trish jerked to the right and we sped down a gravel road. The Mercedes screeched to a halt on the highway, laid rubber in reverse, and came after us.

Gripping the Jeep's support bar, I looked at Trish, surprised by her maneuver.

"I have to use the advantage the Jeep gives me," she cried over the sound of churning gravel. "Call Allister and tell him where we are."

"Where are we?" I shouted.

Coming out of her coma from fear, Cassie shouted the mile marker number listed before we'd gone off the road.

"Right." I nodded.

I dialed Allister as Trish took a steep incline, rocks on either side, forcing Kendal to circle around for another path.

"Yeah, we're almost there," Allister answered.

"We're off road now, keeping ahead of Kendal. Can you find us?"

Allister paused.

"Hello, hello?" I shouted into the phone.

"Yeah, I'm here. Angelina has you, we're on our way."

The phone went silent. Oddly the fact that Angelina could sense my whereabouts didn't creep me out under the circumstances.

Trish took a path with deep ruts up over a ridge and a steep hill on the other side sending us plummeting into a large pond before she could avoid it. Water rose up in a huge rolling wave and splashed over the top of the Jeep, soaking us and stalling the engine.

The Mercedes roared into the clearing, grinding to a halt on the far side of the pond not more than twenty feet away.

Kendal stepped out, his dark hair blowing around his face in the wind and his black eyes zeroing in on me. The smell of lilac reached my nose as I sat drenched in the front passenger seat of the water logged Wrangler. He smiled the same smile he'd flashed before putting his mark on me last night. He stepped to the edge of the pond, his hand on his hips, assessing the situation.

"I only want you, Britt!" he shouted to be heard across the distance. "The others mean nothing to me. Come here and I'll spare them."

"He's lying," Trish cried, grabbing my arm and bringing my eyes to hers. "Don't listen to him, Allister will be here."

"He won't get here in time," Kendal warned. "I can kill you all in seconds and you know it. But if you come with me I'll spare your friends. You have my word."

"What good is his word?" Elisa whispered, eyes filled with terror.

"It's all she has," Kendal said.

"How'd he hear that?" Cassie gasped.

I looked down at my phone, Allister's name flashing on the screen. What if he couldn't find us? I panicked, looking back at Kendal.

I tucked the phone in my pocket and slipped a foot out of the Jeep, Trish grabbed my arm. "What the hell are you doing?"

"I can't let him hurt you, any of you," I said, looking hard at her.

The resolve in her eyes wavered as I pulled away. I gave Cassie and Elisa one last glance and stepped from the Jeep into the water, waist deep, cringing as my phone plunged beneath the water. I trudged to the bank and Kendal. He didn't touch me, but moved over to open the passenger door of the car and motioned me in.

"You tell everyone that you lost Britt at the mall and couldn't find her. Understand? You mention me and I will kill her." Kendal shouted at the girls.

I stepped to the door, pausing to glance at the girls sitting in the Jeep, stranded, desperation plain on their faces, and then slid into the black leather interior before Kendal slammed the door shut. He eased behind the wheel in an instant and we sped away, leaving my friends safely behind.

We reached the highway, spinning onto the pavement and racing back towards Duluth. Not far away, Allister rushed off the road towards the pond with no clue how bad things had turned. Meanwhile I rode with Kendal, certain this was how it would end.

Chapter 17

"Here's the deal." Kendal leaned closer, snapping closed a thin silver bracelet on my wrist. "I changed my mind about killing you, for now. I have bigger plans for us, but if you give me trouble, I can always revert back to my original plan and eliminate you at any time. Do we understand each other?"

I looked down at the bracelet, nodded, and then glared back at him.

"This will keep Angelina from finding you too easily and keep you from shimmering in case you get any bright ideas of escaping. And remember, I know where your girlfriends live and they would be delicious to dispose of." He reflexively licked his lips.

"If you touch them," I hissed.

"You can't stop me, or haven't you figured that out yet?" he laughed at my feeble threat.

I stared down and the plain silver bracelet. I knew Allister wouldn't give up on me, I had to believe that. He would follow me to the ends of the earth. I needed Kendal to keep me alive until Allister came.

But what was he planning and where were we headed?

We drove north, though I couldn't tell for how long. I watched the signs, keeping track as we went. I felt the lump the cell made in my wet pocket, probably ruined; worthless. No way to reach Allister. Hopefully, Angelina could still sense us and catch up.

It turned dark, the only light now coming from the headlights and an occasional house along the road, its yard light glowing dull yellow in the pitch darkness. No moon lit the way, only blackness mirroring the blackness threatening to take over my heart.

A sign indicating the US/Canadian Border lit up in the headlights. Canada?

I considered making a scene at the border, except Kendal read my mind, giving me a cautionary look as we slowed and pulled up to the border patrol station. He held my gaze for a moment longer as the guard stood impatient at the closed window.

Kendal turned on the smile and rolled down the window with a whir. "Evening sir."

"Headed to Canada on business or pleasure?" the officer asked.

"Pleasure. Visiting some historic sights and such," Kendal answered easily.

"Passports."

My hopes soared. I didn't have a passport, the guard would turn us back. I restrained my victorious grin as Kendal looked over to me, leaned in, and popped the glove box. The door dropped open and two passports slid across the cover. I stared in shock as he retrieved the passports from the storage space, pausing to give me a devious grin and turn back to the guard, handing him the documents.

"This looks in order." The officer nodded, handing them back. "Have a nice stay in Canada," he smiled, motioning us through.

"Thank you, I'm sure we will," Kendal said with a chuckle, pulling the car through the checkpoint and onto the road into Canada.

"Don't ever underestimate me," he warned with a smirk, underlying the seriousness of his words. "It could cost you your life."

I turned away in a huff, staring out the window and the blackness still threatening to seep into my heart as the hope of Allister reaching me became bleaker by the mile.

I fell asleep at some point, the effort of keeping my eyes open to read any sign of where we were becoming too much. I woke as the sun shone in through my window, still headed north, I surmised from it's position.

Kendal glanced over as I sat up, straightening my clothes, their dampness chilling me and my teeth began to chatter.

"We can pull over at the next town to get you some dry stuff as long as you behave," he cautioned.

I nodded.

"This isn't personal, you know," he started.

I stared at him, incredulous.

"No, really." He shook his head. "I didn't realize Allister would save you that day at the waterfall. I knew you wouldn't need your guardian angel since you committed suicide, so I took it, well tried to take it." He snorted, making light of my life changing day. "It didn't want to come out of you, it kind of hung on." He paused, staring out at the road as he remembered. "Never saw anything like it before. Your angel willed you to live, it fought to hold on."

I looked at him opening my mouth to respond, but I had nothing. I turned away, looking out the window as the trees rushed by.

"Why were you up there at all?" I asked, "In the middle of nowhere."

"Your essence drew me in, like a predator to a fresh kill. I could taste your guardian; irresistible." He licked his lips.

"How can you do that to people?" I said clenching my jaw out of anger and to stop my teeth from chattering.

"You should try it, it's such a rush." He grinned with pleasure.

I turned away, sick to my stomach at the mere thought of doing something so heinous, the memory of the dreams enough to leave distaste in my mouth.

He pulled into a gas station, turned off the key, and got out. He leaned down, peering through his open door at me as he slipped the keys into his pocket.

"Go inside and get what you need. I'll come in and pay for it with the gas. Behave," he added before slamming the door.

I got out of the car, watching him push a button on the pump and begin to fill the tank. I walked to the front of the store, going inside and looking around for any clothing they might have.

"You look like you've seen better mornings," a woman said with a smile from behind the counter over the top of a newspaper, "Tough night honey?"

"Huh, yeah, I guess," I mumbled, tempted to confide my plight to her, but realizing she could end up a hollowed out husk like my teacher. "You have any clothes? I fell in a creek and need something dry."

"Down the aisle behind you," she said pointing. "Sorry, but we don't carry much, especially undergarments."

"That's okay, thanks."

I meandered down the aisle, picking out a red, I Love Canada, t-shirt, a pair of gray sweat pants with a red maple leaf on it, and some white sweat socks with Canada across the tops. I took them up to the counter as she looked up from her paper.

"He'll pay for them." I motioned to Kendal at the car. "Is there a place I can change?"

"The restrooms are around the corner." She smiled, motioning to her right.

She pulled the tags off the clothes and I scooped them up and walked down the hall to the bathroom, hesitating to stare at the gray back door only a few more steps further. The image of Kendal pulling the angels out of the amigos squelched that thought and I pushed into the bathroom door.

I stripped off my stuff, pulling my phone out of my pocket. I held it up and droplets of water showed under the screen. I pressed the power button, but nothing happened. Like I thought, ruined.

I dried my underwear and bra with the hand dryer and put them back on. I pulled the shirt on over my head and hiked the sweat pants up. As I slipped my socks on, my phone began to shake on the counter next to the sink.

I grabbed it from the counter, hitting the answer button as I put it to my ear. "Hello?" I whispered in case Kendal lurked outside the door. Nothing. I pulled it from my ear, staring at the water logged screen, and then put it to my ear again. "Hello, hello," I whispered urgently. Still nothing.

I stuck it into the pocket of the sweats and straightened my hair the best I could with my fingers. It would have to do. I unlocked the door and walked out of the room carrying my damp clothes.

Kendal leaned against the wall across from the bathroom, nodding as I stepped out.

"Need something to eat?"

"I'm fine."

"Don't be a martyr," he condescended. "Get something. You need to eat."

I lowered my eyes. I did need to eat. "Okay." I nodded.

I grabbed a packaged sandwich and a container of milk, placing it on the counter for the woman to ring up. Kendal paid for it, handed my food to me, and walked out ahead of me without a word to the cashier.

"You seem like a nice girl." The woman smiled and then it slipped from her face as she leaned across the counter. "Dump the zero." She winked pulling a strand of gray hair from her thin face.

"I would if I could," I sighed. "Thank you."

I trudged out after Kendal, getting into the car, and tossing my clothes into the back seat. The woman stared out the window as we drove away, worry visible in her eyes. I hoped she remembered us when Allister stopped and asked. She would put him on the right path, if he got this far.

We drove another hour and then turned off the main road onto a gravel path grown over with weeds and grass. It wove through the tall trees that blotted out the sunlight until stopping at a large log cabin next to a sparkling lake.

"Welcome to your new home," he said getting out.

I opened the door, the scent of pine filling my nose as a light breeze blew in off the lake. The setting took my breath away and, under different circumstances, was easily tranquil. With the murderer holding me captive, the beauty felt oppressive.

I followed him to the door as he unlocked it, swinging it inward until it stopped with a thud against the wall. He gestured for me to enter and I walked in, quickly scanning the room for anything I might use to my advantage in making my escape.

Metal poker, fireplace shovel next to the hearth, pole used to open the uppermost windows on the wall of windows opposite the lake side, pots, pans, many other things giving me a weapon choice with which to assail Kendal.

He stepped up behind me, leaning close as I cringed at his breath in my ear. "We are going to get to know each other very well," he rasped. "We have plenty of time before my friends arrive."

I turned my eyes his way, keeping my head steady. Friends? The man with the silver tooth? Now my timeline for escape began narrowing in my mind.

He closed the door and motioned me in further as I moved into the living room. Wooden furniture with blue denim upholstered cushions filled the space, the log walls remained unadorned.

Kendal moved over and began to stack wood in the fireplace. I watched from behind him, eyeing the metal poker, yearning to take it in my hands and end this now. However, I knew better. My experience with Kendal made me cautious. The marks on my chest burned with the memory of his touch. I could not match his physical strength. He promised to harm my friends if I fought him and I did not doubt him. I nervously spun the silver bracelet declaring my captivity around my wrist.

He glanced back at me, showing no worry or caution at turning his back to me as he returned to his task.

The fire soon crackled in the hearth. He stood, walked over to a chair and sat down stretching his legs out upon the wooden coffee table. He motioned for me to sit in the chair next to him and I moved over and sat down.

"Why are you doing this?" I asked.

"It started as fun, and then turned into a job. Now it's a matter of survival."

"How do you mean?" I frowned.

"You wouldn't understand."

"Try me."

He looked at me and his features softened as he sighed.

"I enjoy taking angels. It makes me feel…alive. The only problem is, it's frowned upon. So I must be very cautious and move around a lot."

I grimaced at the idea of killing someone for their angel. His taking my angel grated on me and the images I witnessed while riding along in my dreams made me nauseous. I stared back at his amused expression blankly and his face went emotionless.

"Why did you take my angel?"

"I spotted you in the community." He nodded. "I found you an easy target, besides, your angel felt so… irresistible, I had to have it."

"Why is that?"

202

"I've found when a person has struggled to survive, their angel becomes more pure with the torment they've endured. I couldn't help myself."

"So you followed us?"

"I followed you. I had no interest in your parents. Allister and his sister followed my trail. They are more clever than I gave them credit. They arrived before I had a chance to get all the angel's essence out of you." He frowned as if the memory disturbed him.

"That's when Allister touched me," I breathed.

He nodded. "Yeah, you were pretty much dead by then and the angel didn't have enough strength to hold on. He should never have touched you. It's forbidden."

"So I've heard, but that isn't worth much coming from a guy who goes around taking angels," I growled, hoping he hadn't guessed the full extent of what happened to my angel and soul that day.

"Hey, even I know better than to cross that line," he said putting his hands defensively before him.

"So after you tried to kill me and Angelina, something changed to make you decide to kidnap me instead?"

"Old Silver Tooth suggested I keep you alive," he nodded.

I ventured a guess. "The Eternals from Greece?" I remembered hearing the Parks talk about them.

"Yeah, they want you alive to take before the council. They'll use you to condemn Allister and disgrace Victor and his wife."

I felt my heart clench. "How could my existence do that?"

"You are considered an abomination," he said.

"A what?" I stood up.

"Hold on." He held out a hand to placate me. "I said they consider you an abomination. I don't necessarily agree."

"You don't?" Surprised, I sat down.

"At first, yes, but the way you protected your friends back there takes guts. And how you healed Angelina; no one should have been able to bring her back from what I did to her. And the way you…"

I stared at him as he searched for the words. "The way I what?"

"The way you…feel." His eyes got a faraway, vacant look in them.

"Hey, watch it," I raised my voice as my anger threatened to boil over. I didn't like this twist; him being interested in my "feel."

"There's this pull whenever I'm close to you. Like desire, it has me yearning to be near you. I want to touch you, to hold onto you."

The way he'd spoken of hurting Angelina, like talking about the weather, pissed me off. I wanted to hurt him, hurt him bad. I bit my lip, forcing back the urge to lay into him. I needed to think things through. And then when he started to describe how he felt when I was close, it gave me the creeps. I stood abruptly.

"Where am I going to sleep?" I asked.

"Right through there." He motioned to the door off the living room, still dazed from his musings about me.

I got up and walked into the bedroom, closing the door behind me. I sat on the bed, pulling the phone from my pocket, flipping it open and praying it worked. The screen lit up and my heart soared.

"I'm sorry I made you feel uncomfortable," Kendal said as he walked in and then stood with his hands on his hips, staring with disbelief at the phone in my hand. He strode over, took the phone and threw it against the wall sending pieces scattering everywhere. He looked back at me with a hurt expression and walked out again, slamming the door behind him.

I threw myself back onto the bed with a hopeless groan. My only chance to contact Allister, gone.

Chapter 18

I lay in bed the rest of the day and into the night, staring at the plank ceiling and contemplating my next move. I came back to the same realization over and again. I didn't have a next move. My options consisted of nil, nada, and nothing. Kendal held all the cards and he wasn't dealing me in.

Would the Eternals coming from Greece be a better option? I doubted it. They wanted Allister and the Parks destroyed with me being the final nail in their coffin.

The sun shone in the window the next morning and I pulled myself from the bed. I opened the door and Kendal looked up from staring at the fire.

"Hungry?" he asked.

"Yeah," I conceded.

"Some food on the table." He motioned to the next room and turned back to the fire.

He didn't seem too worried about me running. Guess I didn't have anywhere to run.

I walked into the room to find an assortment of fruits and pastries. I pulled a banana from a bunch and peeled it, looking out the window at the lake as the sun shimmered off its rippled surface. I glanced at Kendal with his back to me and then walked out the door. I walked casually down the path to the dock, feeling Kendal's eyes on my back, and then out onto the wooden planks as the structure shook under my weight.

Reaching the end I plopped down, hanging my feet over the edge, dangling them just above the water. I took a bite of banana and moaned. It tasted so good. I took another before finishing the first, my cheek puffing out with the fruit stuffed into it.

The dock shook and I looked back to see Kendal coming my way. He stopped next to me, looking out over the water as I stared up at him. He then looked down and sat next to me. Turning his eyes to the water once more, he sighed.

"I'm sorry you have to be in the middle of this," he said, still looking out across the lake.

"Uh huh," I mumbled with my mouth still full. I took another bite, not wanting to converse with my captor.

"You seem like a really nice person," he said, looking down at his hands folded in his lap and then up at me.

I stopped chewing, my mouth hanging open, filled with banana. I stared at him in disbelief.

"I know, I know. I don't believe it either, but if things were different, I would like to get to know you." He turned away from my gaze.

I choked on the soft fruit, forcing it down. "I, I…" I stammered.

"I want you to know, I'm sorry," he said. He got to his feet, glanced down at my upturned face, and walked back to the cabin.

I stared out at the lake. "Holy shit." I looked back at the cabin. Did that actually happen? Kendal? No…no way. He didn't say he…

I took the last bite of banana and sat chewing it shaking my head trying to process what just happened, grasping the hint of a chance to get out of this mess. Swallowing the banana, I got to my feet and hurried back to the cabin. I tossed the peel into the woods near the door and strode into the cabin.

Kendal sat in front of the fire, not looking up when I came in and sat in a chair.

"Kendal," I drew his attention back to me. "I don't know what you want me to say. The only thing you've shown me is evil. How am I supposed to think anything other than that of you?"

"I understand," he said turning away, his expression looked like he just tasted something bitter. "I don't match up to someone like Allister. Never did. But if someone like you got to know the real me, maybe, just maybe, there'd be a chance."

I hesitated as my initial feelings of repulsiveness threatened to leap out and rant on him. I clamped my mouth shut until the urge passed. "I guess stranger things have happened. But until you try, how would you know?"

He looked at me, shock registering on his face, my response taking him aback.

"Can we start over?" he asked, hope, begging in his eyes.

"I…suppose we could try," I forced out trying to keep the disgust out of my voice and off my face.

A grin twisted his lips and he turned back to the fire. His humming broke the uneasy silence.

We sat and talked the rest of the day. Kendal explained the history of the Eternals and I told him about me, as much as I trusted him to know. By evening I understood how the council, once controlled by Victor, now saw him as a threat. Certain members and their supporters searched for any way to take his power.

My existence gave Victor's rivals the opportunity they needed to disgrace the entire Parks family forever. Over the years, Allister's status had risen steadily in the Eternal world, being known as a great healer and a great fighter. Many of the younger Eternals, if you can call two hundred year olds younger, turned to Allister as the leader of the future. This troubled the traditional Eternals and they plotted the entire family's demise.

Kendal wasn't happy about the role they forced him into, but his sense of self-preservation drove him to comply.

"I'm not strong enough to resist them," he sighed. "I'm only one and they are many."

"But you could leave, hide, avoid contact like you did for so many years until now," I told him.

"They have my family." He put his head in his hands. "If I don't cooperate they'll kill my entire family; all my uncles, aunts, cousins, brother, sister, parents and grandparents. They said they'd erase my family's existence as if we never were."

I tried to feel sympathy only it wouldn't come. The images of him killing people forced all other feelings aside. I sat silently looking at him.

"I'm sorry," the words came hard.

He looked at me with gratitude in his eyes. He gave a little smile and reached for my hand. I drew back defensively and he turned back to the fire.

Mentally exhausted, I stood and walked to the bedroom, pausing in the doorway to turn back to him. "Good night, Kendal."

"Good night, Britt." He glanced up at me briefly.

I closed the door, leaning my back against it, letting out a heavy breath. I didn't realize acting took so much energy. Climbing into bed, staring at the dark ceiling, wondering if Allister still searched for me. Two days since Duluth, and I didn't have any idea how much time before the other Eternals arrived. My thoughts turned to the three amigos and, despite the potential danger I'd put them in, fell asleep with a smile as their memories filled me with happiness.

The next morning I showered, getting into my own clothes and out of the horrendous tourist-wear purchased from the convenience store.

I walked into the living room. Kendal sat in the same place as last night. He looked up as the door opened. Sadness rimmed his eyes and it appeared he hadn't slept.

I stared for a moment, and then moved to the kitchen. More fruit and pastries covered the table, he'd replaced what I consumed yesterday. I grabbed a danish today, figuring one wouldn't hurt and took the walk out to the dock again and sat down. Ducks swam nearby and water bugs strode across the glassy smooth surface.

The dock began to rock and Kendal sat down beside me without a word. I didn't look over, concentrating on the activity of wildlife on the water. I felt his eyes on me, but refused to look up. I gathered the resolve to begin another day of pretending, not sure I possessed the strength.

I forced a smile to my lips and turned to him. He frowned as my eyes met his.

"You really love him, don't you?" he asked.

I hesitated, caught off guard by the directness.
"Uh, yeah, yeah I do." I nodded.

"Is it because he created you?"

I stopped to think, staring out at the sun glistening
on the calm lake. Was that why I loved Allister so much?
Because he saved me? Numerous times? Could it be as
simple as that?

"No, well, yes maybe partly. And because he
loves me so completely. And I feel something when I'm
with him I've never felt before. And I yearn for him when
we're apart." I stopped, realizing I rambled on, and
looked back at Kendal.

His face went slack, even more than before, and
he looked down at his hands in his lap. A sour grin curled
his lips as he looked back at me. "So a guy like me
doesn't stand a chance. No matter how hard I try, no
matter how much I care. I don't stand a chance as long as
you have Allister Parks in your life."

Chills ran up my spine and the hair on the back of
my neck tingled. His words, a statement of sad fact,
resigned.

"Kendal, what are you thinking?" I whispered,
realization dawning I might have done something terrible.

"As long as you have Allister, you will never be
mine." He looked at me, his expression blank.

"Kendal." I stared intensely into his eyes hoping
to project the strength of my emotions. I wasn't sure what
would come of it, but I needed to try. One thing I knew
for certain; I couldn't forsake my love for Allister even to
help me escape Kendal. "I love Allister. If he were
beyond my reach, gone from me forever, I would still

love him. My heart belongs to him and nothing will ever change that."

"Thank you for being honest." He nodded slow and deliberate as he got to his feet.

"What are you going to do?" My eyes followed him.

"I think I have feelings for you, Britt. I don't know when it happened, but you have this power over me, drawing me to you like a moth to a flame. No, maybe love is too weak a word. I need you. I don't want to live without you. That pull you have on me is driving me crazy. I think about you every minute of every day and, for an Eternal, that is a damn long time. Since your heart belongs and will always belong to Allister Parks, you leave me no choice." He sighed and began walking down the dock, shoulders slumped from the weight of his decision.

I sprang to my feet, racing to catch up with him. "What choice, what are you going to do?"

"What I've been told to do." He stopped and stared down at me. "Hand you over to condemn Allister."

Fear flickered in my guts. "You were considering something else?"

"I considered running away; just you and I leaving all of this behind, letting Allister live in peace as long as I had you."

"We still can. We can go right now before the others come. I'll do it, Kendal. Let's leave and not look back," I pleaded for Allister's life, willing to sacrifice my own happiness to be with Kendal in order to save his.

"No, not now." His smile was tinged with disgust. "Now I know the truth that the only way you may come to love me is if Allister is gone from your life."

"But if we go now he'll never find us," I cried, trying to reason with him.

"You would always have the hope that he might come back to you." He shook his head, a twisted smile on his lips. "If the council takes care of him, you will some day realize I'm worthy of your love."

He strode off as I stood watching, tears blurring my vision, realizing my love for Allister had just condemned him.

I ran back to the cabin, rushing past Kendal as he walked through the door, running into the bedroom and slamming the door behind me. I threw myself on the bed, sobbing into the pillows.

"Allister, I love you," I gasped into the pillows. "I'm so sorry."

I lay in bed, the hours passing unnoticed in the small bedroom. Light faded outside and soon shadows filled the space.

My eyes popped open at the sound of slamming car doors. My heart stuttered. They're here. I jumped from bed, creeping to the door and opening it just enough to peer through the crack.

Several men stood in the living room, movement behind them alerted me to others in the kitchen. A small man, no taller than Angelina, with his back to me exposing a black pony tail reaching his waist, stood in front of Kendal.

"She's here?" the man asked.

"Yes." Kendal nodded towards the door I peered out of.

"Excellent," the man said. He turned and his silver tooth shone as he smiled and ran his tongue over it. "You have done well my vile friend."

"What are you going to do with her?" Kendal asked.

"She will stand as evidence of Allister's crime," the man said.

"After, what will happen to her after?" Kendal pressed.

"Her fate will be at the discretion of the council. I, for one, hope they dispose of her," the man replied coolly.

"What if she escaped capture?" Kendal asked.

"The order stood at capture, dead or alive. Her corpse will serve the same function as her breathing body. In some ways, I'd prefer if she were a corpse; fewer complications. If she gives us any trouble, we will kill her to ease the transport."

Kendal's body tensed.

"I will get her ready to leave." Kendal nodded.

The man stepped aside and Kendal moved towards the door. I slipped back, leaning against the bed; the knowledge of my fate slowing my thinking as panic overwhelmed me.

Kendal opened the door, stepped into the room, and shut it behind him. He leaned against the door, staring at me without saying a word as I looked back at him, fear coursing through my body.

"You must run," he said coming over to me, taking me by my shoulders and leading me to the window. He slid the window open and turned to me,

unsnapped the bracelet from my wrist and handed me
something small and black.

My passport. I looked up in shock. "Where?" I
whispered slipping the passport into my jeans pocket.

"I don't know, but you mustn't let them catch you.
You heard Bastion. They'll kill you. Run, and keep
running until you're safe. I'll try to slow them, but you
must stay ahead of them."

I slipped a leg out the window and stopped,
turning back to him, wanting to thank him, but the words
wouldn't come.

He looked at me, curious for a moment, and then
pushed me out the rest of the way. I landed in a heap on
the ground covered in leaves and sticks. I pulled myself
to my feet and leaned into the window as he slid it closed.

"Thank you," I whispered as he stopped to look.

He nodded, pushed me out of the way, and then
shut the window and pulled the shade.

Chapter 19

I ran. What direction, where, it didn't matter. I ran to get as far away from Bastion as I could, as quickly as I could. I ran through brush, thick and clinging at my legs and waist. I ran around trees, dense and compact, sometimes needing to slip sideways to get through. The woods here, untouched by humans, impeded my progress yet I pressed on.

Darkness fell on the forest and soon I couldn't see my hand before my face. I never knew what that meant until now. I stopped, listening for pursuit for the first time since fleeing. Nothing. Not a sound. Odd. Shouldn't there be animals out here?

Out of nowhere, a loud engine roared and light lit up the blackness. The light shone maybe thirty yards away; too close for my liking. I dove to the ground, sliding under a fallen log and digging myself into the soft, rotting debris, covering up completely so that each breath brought with it the stench of decaying matter.

The light shone around, searching, looking for me. I felt positive Bastion was behind the search. Only a small tickle in my mind for an instant gave me doubt. For the briefest moment I thought it might be Allister looking for me, but the risk of exposing myself was too great to chance.

I stayed buried, listening to the engine of a helicopter roar overhead. Even as it faded into the distance, I lay in my bed of rotting organic matter. The prickling of insects, crawling across my skin, made me want to scream, but I lay there, not willing to expose myself. I bit my lip as other creepy-crawlies moved across my exposed skin, some even getting under my clothing, still I kept out of sight.

I don't know how long I stayed hidden. I knew I needed to get moving again to stay ahead of them. I understood their desire to have me, to bring the Parks down, was too great for them to ever stop.

I decided to stay put until first light. There was no point in stumbling through the darkness, possibly injuring myself, and making little progress besides. I closed my eyes and steadied myself against the insects moving around in the darkness. Nothing out here was poisonous, right?

When it was time to go I stood, brushed myself off, and picked as many bugs from me as I could find. After the last uncontrollable shudder from plucking a sizable insect from my hair and dropping it on the ground, I headed out. At least, I started to. Then I stopped, looking at the landmarks. They all appeared the same, and completely different from last night.

I turned back to the log where I spent the night. Noted the side I hid beneath, guessing my bed lay on the side of the log from the direction I came from. I grinned and stepped over the log and headed out, confident I moved away from the cabin, and certain capture.

I pushed through the thick woods for hours, often finding my path blocked by a thick growth of trees too dense to push through or a marshy low-lying area with mud that waited to suck me under the surface of the water. Several times I was forced to backtrack and find another way around. Nearing exhaustion, I broke out of the dense foliage unexpectedly, tumbling down a steep incline and rolling to a stop next to a gravel road.

I picked myself up, wiped the dirt from my face, and looked first one way and then the other at the road disappearing in either direction. I sat down, smiling to myself, proud to have found civilization again. Now I needed to find some people.

After resting a short time, I stood and contemplated my next choice. Left or right? It sounded easy enough, but the wrong choice could wind me back around to where I started. I felt confident heading south, back to the states; the best option. I looked up at the sun sitting low in the sky already, sunset must be close. I turned and began to walk, taking the southern direction the road offered.

I didn't stop as darkness fell. The moon rose high and bright in the sky, lighting the road well enough to continue on. Deer, raccoons, and even a bear startled me as I walked, though they didn't show much interest in me other than a passing glance or a brief pause. I walked alone most of the night.

Once, something large and on four legs strode out ahead of me. I paused, waiting for it to clear my way. It looked at me, the eyes glowing in the moonlight, and then loped off into the woods. I continued on, but soon felt someone behind me. Glancing over my shoulder, the glowing eyes and lurking form padded silently behind me, never gaining, but maintaining an even distance between us.

I glanced back every so often as the yellow eyes stayed there. I felt a strange kinship with my escort, confident it intended me no harm and feeling less alone.

The animal I identified as a wolf, stayed with me until predawn and then, with a yip of goodbye, disappeared into the forest. In the dim before dawn I felt a pang for my companion, even being just an animal, its presence comforted me.

After another day of walking, not meeting any vehicles or seeing any signs of humans, I feared I might walk forever without coming across anyone. Just as hope waned, the gravel road intersected blacktop. I stared at the surface filled with disbelief and relief. Tears rolled down my cheeks and I scolded myself for being so foolish, but knowing I stood closer to rescue than before, I cried openly.

I followed the road, seeing nothing but trees and rocks all morning, and ready to jump into the roadside lined with high, uncut grasses at any sign of life. It was in this heightened state of anxiety when something recognizable crept into view. The longer I walked, the surer I felt the convenience store where Kendal and I stopped for gas and clothes lay ahead. I quickened my pace, my spirit lifting. I hurried to the door, swinging it in as the bell on the handle sounded. I rushed to the counter, the same lady sat on a stool, looking out the window.

"I'm so glad I found you," I gasped, knowing the tattered image I must be.

The feeling started small, an itching just below the surface then it grew, becoming harder to ignore as I stared at the woman sitting motionless on her stool.

"Hello?" I said.

The woman didn't move.

"Excuse me, I came in the other day," I tried again.

The woman stared out the window as if I didn't exist.

I inched around the counter moving next to her, studying her and seeing something unnatural about her posture, her stillness. I reached up, touching her shoulder with a finger. Her body moved under my touch then sprang back, stiff.

Terror rose up as I took a step closer to see her face looking out the window at the pumps. Her eyes stared, glassy, while her mouth hung open, slack and empty.

I leapt back, banging into the shelving holding the cigarettes and they tumbled down over me in an avalanche of white packages. A ping on the air hose by the pumps spun my attention outside. A small man with a long ponytail stepped out of the back seat of a large, black Mercedes. A dozen or more men hovered around two other cars and scanned the surroundings.

Bastion. My mind raced yet I stood frozen in place staring at the man as he slowly turned to look at the store. I ducked down behind the counter. Had he seen me?

I crawled along the counter and into the back room. Scrambling to my feet, I ran for the gray door leading out the back. I pulled the door open and burst out in a full sprint only to slam into someone so solid and hard, the wind shot from my lungs and I crumbled to the ground.

The man grabbed me by my forearms, pulling me to my feet as I gasped for air. He turned with me, his ponytail swinging around and brushing against my shoulder. I opened my mouth to scream, but his hand clamped down before even a whisper escaped.

He pulled me along, hand over my mouth, around the back of the store to a waiting car. He opened the door, threw me inside, and the car roared into motion before I could right myself.

I felt someone in the back seat next to me and I looked up, expecting to see Bastion. Angelina's worried face met my gaze and I flung myself at her, hugging her tightly, my eyes clenched shut and the tears dripping down my cheek.

"You found me," I sobbed. "You found me."

The reunion, cut short as the Camaro squealed out of the parking lot amidst cries of protest from the men standing by the pumps. The sounds of pursuit and the ensuing roar of engines cut into my embrace and I righted myself in the seat to look out the back window as three black cars raced after us.

"How is she?" Allister shouted from the driver's seat.

"Battered, bruised, and stinky, but she appears alright," Angelina said.

"I'm okay," I yelled over the engine noise, overjoyed to see his beautiful face again.

"We're not out of this yet," Taylor, the owner of the not-Bastion ponytail pointed out.

"We can't outrun them," Allister admitted, glancing back in his side mirror at the gaining caravan of Mercedes.

"They won't be alone," Taylor reminded him. "I'm sure they'll call ahead for help."

"We can't let that happen," Allister countered. "We have to take them out."

"Take them out?" I shouted. "There's at least a dozen of them and only four of us."

"Fifteen, actually," Taylor corrected, shrugging as I gave him a TMI look.

"Angelina, can you handle two?" Allister asked, glancing back at her in his rearview mirror.

"Two, maybe more." She nodded.

"That leaves six for you and me." He turned to Taylor.

"Got it." Taylor nodded.

"What about me?" I asked. "How can I help?"

"You stay in the car, no matter what happens. Kick and hit anyone who tries to get to you. We'll defend you the best we can." Allister glanced over his shoulder, catching my eye and pausing for a split second. His determination and worry for me showed on his face.

"We have to do it now," Taylor reminded.

Allister nodded, turning onto a side road running parallel to the main road, racing down the gravel surface with rocks pinging off the bottom of the car as we sped along.

The black cars followed close behind. The trees on either side of the road widened into meadow and Allister hit the brakes turning the wheel quickly, sliding along the grass to a stop.

Allister, Taylor, and Angelina exploded out the doors, advancing on the speeding cars before they could completely stop. I watched from my vantage point in the back seat, leaning forward to lock the doors and peer back at the three.

Allister raced full speed at one of the cars. He leapt at the last second dipping his shoulder and turning in midair. The grill and hood just missed him as he drove his leg through the windshield and into the driver. The car skidded to a stop as Allister scrambled across the hood and braced himself for the men hurrying to get out. Allister took each advancing man head on, rendering them unconscious one by one, smoothly and efficiently, with fluid punches and kicks.

I shook nervously at the chaotic scene, spotting Angelina grappling with a man twice her size. She used her greater speed to avoid his attempts to pluck out her heart.

She jumped over his outstretched arm, wrapping her arms around his neck as her body flew over his head and tossed him to the ground. In his dazed state, she struck him across his face, knocking him out.

Taylor stood surrounded by four men, all nearly as large as he. His expression bore no emotion as he stood rotating in place while the men tried to find an opening in his defenses. One took the offensive and fell to the ground after a well-placed strike to the head. Taylor turned to the other men in the shrinking circle.

The passenger side window shattered, shards of glass spraying me as I jumped away from an arm reaching in the open window.

"You're mine." Bastion sneered, reaching for me and catching a piece of my shirt.

I pushed my feet against the passenger side flexing my legs, holding my body against the driver's side. The pulling on my shirt bent my body in half as my legs held firm, but my back and waist couldn't resist his tugging. Reaching out, I slapped at his arm and hand, trying to break free of his iron grip.

Bastion's face leaned in the back seat of the Camaro, grimacing with effort, his eyes wild with fury and vengeance.

I reached back as I clenched my hand and drove my fist into his face with all my strength, sending him rocking backwards as his hands came up to cup his crushed nose. Blood gushed from between his fingers.

"Ah, you bitch," he screamed furiously. He took a step towards the car, unwilling to admit defeat, then stopped as he realized his men were losing the larger battle raging around him.

I glanced out the back window to see many men lying motionless on the ground while Angelina, Allister and Taylor still stood.

Men raced back to the cars and Bastion retreated as well, holding a hand to his bleeding face. The Mercedes sped away with four men in them. Eleven lay helpless upon the ground.

I unlocked the doors and slid out the driver's door, running to leap into Allister's arms. He held me tight, his face buried in the side of my neck, his vice-like arms pressing me close.

"I thought I lost you," he whispered.

"Me too." Tears made my voice hoarse.

He leaned back to look at me, his nose scrunched up.

"I know, I know." I rolled my eyes.

"Sorry, but you smell like rotten leaves and sweat." He frowned.

We stood for a moment longer, silence hanging heavily over the incapacitated Eternals in the meadow.

Taylor hung his head, shaking it slowly.

"What is it?"

"A sad day when an Eternal must fight one of his own," he sighed.

I lowered my gaze, nodding.

"Let's get out of here," Angelina spoke for the first time.

I looked at them. It was unclear where their blood started and their adversaries' began.

Bastion's blood covered my forearm and sleeve of my shirt. I guess everyone drew an Eternal's blood today.

We swept the glass off the back seat the best we could and headed to the closest town.

Chapter 20

A small motel with plenty of vacancies in the next town filled our current needs. I went in to get some rooms; my appearance, even after two days in the wilderness, the least offensive.

We each showered and changed into the clean clothes bought at a local store. We sat in the room eating pizza ordered in from the one pizzeria, and talked. I missed plenty while Kendal's prisoner and Angelina filled me in while Allister and Taylor verified Bastion's retreat.

"Your friends are all fine, as are your parents," she informed me.

"My parents," I cried. "I bet they're going crazy with me disappearing like that."

"They went to Duluth after your friends told them what Kendal instructed. The police searched the mall and all the surrounding areas for you for days. They even sent divers down in the harbor looking for you." Angelina's somber mood reflected the severity of the situation.

"They must be frantic," I moaned.

"There is speculation that you may have wandered off, given the changes in your health. Some are thinking you may be suffering from temporary amnesia."

"Amnesia? Really? And they bought that?"

Angelina gave me a "get real" look and I nodded. Things around me were very strange; amnesia was a more feasible explanation of what occurred in the past few months than reality. I nodded acceptance.

"How did you escape Kendal?" Angelina broke into my thoughts.

"He let me go."

Angelina's head snapped up from pulling a piece of pizza from its box. "What? That doesn't sound like Kendal, especially with what Bastion had over him. Why would he let you go?"

"I think he likes me," I answered quietly, averting my eyes.

"That's sick," she hissed. "He took your angel and left you for dead. Now he has feelings for you?"

"Guess so, please, don't tell Allister," I urged.

She looked at me for a moment, unblinking, then nodded.

"Thank you," I whispered as the door to the room opened admitting Allister and Taylor.

"What'd you find?" Angelina asked.

"They're gone, for now," Taylor said.

"I'm sure not for good," Allister added, glancing awkwardly at Taylor, avoiding my eyes.

"What?" I asked.

"They took Kendal," he said.

"So, they got a killer out of Grand Rapids. Good for them," I said, maybe a little too enthusiastically.

"But not necessarily good for Grand Rapids, or us," Allister added.

"What do you mean?" I failed to understand how Kendal not killing more people was a bad thing.

"Bastion didn't know where you lived. He used Kendal to get you and now he needs to extract the whereabouts of your home from him so he can come and get you himself," Taylor explained.

"What if Kendal won't tell him?" I asked hopefully.

"Why would he do that?" Allister asked.

227

I looked to Angelina as she bit her lip and kept her mouth closed, the effort it took showed in her eyes. She flicked her eyes from me to Allister over and over again.

Subtly I shook my head, not wanting to do as she asked.

"Tell him," she cried out at last.

"No." I shook my head.

"I will if you don't." She folded her arms across her chest.

"You promised. Only seconds ago, you promised," I argued.

"Tell me what?" Allister interrupted, brow furrowed.

"Why Kendal won't tell Bastion where Britt lives," Angelina sighed.

I glared hard at her, but she rolled her eyes, smiled, and turned back to Allister.

"Fine, I'll tell him," I blurted. "Kendal thinks he has feelings for me. He let me go when he heard Bastion say the council would kill me once I helped the council prove you guilty."

Allister's expression was dazed, then hardened. "Do you have feelings for him?" His voice wavered with controlled anger.

"No, how could I, no, never!" I stammered.

"Do you think he cares enough to keep your secret?" Taylor asked, matter of fact.

Allister gave Taylor a dirty look and Taylor merely shrugged.

"I don't know," I admitted.

"That's not our only problem," Allister pointed out. "With Bastion still in the area, he'll try to stop us from getting back into the US. He'll follow us to Grand Rapids unless we destroy him first."

Bastion still posed a threat to my family and friends; the victory in the meadow, short lived.

"What do we do?" I asked.

"I will go to Greece and face the council." Allister squared his shoulders.

"What?" Taylor, Angelina and I exclaimed in unison.

"This is my fault. I need to go to the council and face them, take what punishment I'm given."

"That could be death," Taylor hissed.

"If the council so decides." Allister nodded.

"No, you can't. It's my fault, I should be the one to go before the council." I stood up.

"Don't be ridiculous. The council will kill you on sight. You're considered an abomination." Allister moved to pull me into his arms. "You didn't choose to be touched. I had the choice and made it." He kissed the top of my head. "I'll never regret touching you that day. Creating you is the most wonderful thing I've done in all my 180 years."

A cell phone rang and Angelina answered, walking out of the room to talk. Allister leaned down as I looked up, giving me a light kiss and then followed her.

"What are his chances?" I asked Taylor.

"Britt, I don't know if it's my place to say," he frowned.

"Please," I pressed.

"Creating you is the greatest offense an Eternal can commit. I don't know if leniency will be shown."

I put a shaking hand to my mouth. How could this be happening?

"If it's any consolation, I think you are far from an abomination," Taylor comforted.

His words did little to assure me though. I'd stood on the brink of death only a short time ago and now had so much to live for. All of it hung in the balance now.

Angelina came in followed by Allister, their faces grim.

"What?" I asked.

They looked at Taylor and then to me, their eyes filled with sadness.

"They're holding Mother and Father responsible for my indiscretions," Allister began, the words coming out hard. "Unless I come before them in a week's time my judgment will be their judgment."

"Father said an ally informed him Bastion already knows this and will try anything to assure Allister doesn't make it to Greece in time," Angelina added.

Taylor drew in a hissing breath and I gasped. This was what Bastion wanted all along, to discredit and bring down Victor. Allister was his means of doing it, but now Victor would stand trial in Allister's stead. Bastion only needed to keep Allister away from Greece.

"We have to get to Greece," I said, bringing all eyes to me.

"No, Britt, Taylor and I need to get to Greece," Allister said. "Angelina and you are going home."

"I'm going to Greece." Angelina stole my response.

"Sister, think about it. You need to stay safe to carry on the Parks name. You need to stay to protect Britt and the people we've endangered in Grand Rapids."

Angelina opened her mouth to retort, then snapped it shut with a click. She nodded.

Allister reached out a hand to me and I looked at it curiously.

"Come take a walk with me," he said.

I slid my hand in his and we went out the door into the parking lot. Together, we walked past the building and into the forest up along a rise above the motel a slight distance before he stopped.

He turned to me, still holding my one hand and then taking my other in his. He looked into my eyes and held my gaze. I gazed up at him motionless, mesmerized.

"I want you to promise me you won't follow us to Greece."

I opened my mouth to speak, but he squeezed my hand and shook his head.

"Please Britt, promise me you'll stay in Grand Rapids and stay safe."

"I can't make that promise; what if you need me?"

"I have all the help I need and Angelina will come if we need more. Please, no matter what, you must promise to stay away."

"You're asking too much. I'll come if you need me."

"You don't understand. Going to Greece is a death sentence for you. You must not risk it. I can't go on thinking you may follow me to your death. I need you to promise me you will stay away, no matter what."

I stared into his eyes. The pain overwhelmed me, hurting me just to look at them. Pressing my eyes shut I leaned into his chest, willing this to all be a bad dream; for it to end, for it all to be over. I looked back up at him.

"Alright, I promise," I whispered. The words taking all the effort I could summon.

He pressed his lips to mine, his desire surging into me as he swept me up in it. The feeling filled me so completely, I lost track of everything but his touch, his lips. His body against mine became everything.

He pulled away abruptly without warning and my eyes opened wide in surprise. Allister sagged unconscious, blood dripping down from a wound on his forehead and supported by two men as Bastion stood by holding a bloodied club. His broken nose swollen and his eyes black and blue, he stared at me with an amused look on his face; the silver tooth glistening under his swiping tongue.

"Well, well, isn't this romantic," he sneered.

"Stop it! Allister," I shouted lunging towards him.

Bastion stepped between us, halting my advance. "Come with me and the circle will close, Britt. First Victor Parks will pay for Allister's crimes in his absence, and *then* we will present Allister to pay for his own crimes. We will bring you along to finish the triad. The council enjoys neat endings and your destruction will end the existence of an abomination as well as close the chapter on the Parks's history."

"You forgot about one thing," a high melodic voice drifted from a nearby hill. "The Parks women are just as deadly as the men."

Angelina and Taylor rushed the group, setting everyone into motion. The men holding Allister shimmered out of sight. The four standing behind Bastion split and two each met Angelina and Taylor.

"No," I cried.

Bastion charged me, striking down towards my head with his fist. I dove away from him, rolling, and coming to my feet.

I didn't know what to do except evade. I couldn't fight, but used my quickness to stay a step ahead of him. He began another charge, then blinked out of sight without warning.

I looked around to find myself alone. Allister, Angelina, and Taylor, were nowhere in sight. I spun in a full circle, looking for any signs of them. Confused, I moved up to higher ground, searching for a clue, finding none. After several attempts to discern their whereabouts, I gave up and returned to the motel room.

I waited, and waited, and waited, looking out the window every few minutes at any sound, at any perceived noise; anything announcing their return or indicating their whereabouts.

I jumped at the few cars driving into and through the parking lot as day gave way to the night. I shivered not at the cold, but the feeling of abandonment and isolation I felt at losing the only thing I finally accepted would be forever.

On the evening of the next day, I decided to do something; anything was better than nothing. I found the keys to the Camaro along with some money on the dresser. I checked to see I wasn't leaving anything behind and pulled the door closed behind me. I walked to the car looking expectantly in the direction of the nearby forest where they disappeared. I unlocked the car and slid behind the wheel. Allister had the window repaired the first day in town and looked out the clean window up the hill where he left me.

Starting the car, I backed out of the parking spot and slid into first before pulling away, willing them to come running out of the woods, jumping in before I left. They never came. I continued slowly out of town, wondering if I did the right thing, not knowing what else to do.

I bought a map at a store on the edge of town, plotted my path back to Duluth, and jumped on the highway taking me back to the states. The drive, as lonely as I've ever experienced, dragged on forever.

Reaching the boarder, I pulled the passport out of my back pocket, looking down at it as the realization that even the Eternal who gave me this, was now gone, perhaps forever. An uneasy feeling came over me as I acknowledged the sense of loss even for Kendal's bizarre form of companionship.

No, I thought. No way. I pushed the thought of missing that Eternal from my mind. I pulled up to the checkpoint, rolled down my window, and gave the guard a smile.

"Evening Miss," he said with a nod. "Passport please."

"Evening." I handed him my papers.

"Why did you visit Canada?"

"I was doing a little hiking," I answered. Not a complete lie, I couldn't help but grin.

"Everything appears in order." He handed the passport back. "Have a nice night."

"Thank you." I rolled up my window and breathed a sigh of relief as I pulled out of the border station.

A weight lifted from me as I relaxed, thankful to be in the US again. I set the cruise and settled in for the couple hour drive to Duluth. I planned to stop, gas up, and get something to eat there.

The sun slipped behind the trees as I pulled up to a gas pump in Duluth. My teeth began to chatter as a cool breeze blew in off the lake. I stood by the pump, looking over the bay and wondering where my Eternal friends were. I pumped the gas and paid for it inside.

I didn't feel too hungry so I grabbed some pop and licorice for the last ninety miles home. Switching on the heat as the temperature dropped, I set the cruise and scanned for deer; a problem in this part of Minnesota.

Anxious to get home, the trip seemed to take twice as long. I pulled up in front of our house, the outside garage lights on and a light shining through the living room window.

I braced myself and set the story straight in my mind. It took only a moment; I'd been preparing since leaving the motel in Canada. Allister found me at the north shore and I couldn't remember how I got there. He loaned me his car since he and Angelina needed to fly out east to meet their parents.

I took a deep, settling breath, opened the car door, and strode up the walk. Opening the door hesitantly, I walked into my house.

Chapter 21

"Britt?" Mom's anxious voice drifted to the entry.

"Yeah, it's me," I answered.

I could hear hurried footsteps as Mom and Dad rushed into the entry, wrapping me in their arms and holding me tight. We hugged in silence, each grateful to be reunited. Dad stepped back, took a deep breath, and I braced myself.

"Where have you been?" Anger and worry had aged him these past few days.

"We've been worried sick," Mom added, new lines creasing her forehead as well.

"I don't know what happened," I stammered. "One minute I was in the mall with the amigos and then the next Allister found me in Grand Marais." Saying it out loud, my story felt thin.

"Grand Marais?" Mom exclaimed.

We stared at each other for an uneasy moment.

"They said this could've been a case of amnesia brought on by your sudden medical changes," Dad offered, his tone hinting that he wasn't so sure.

"So how do you feel?" Mom asked, seemingly more willing to circumvent her doubt in favor of a believable explanation.

"I feel fine, just really tired," I said as a well-timed yawn stretched my jaw, slurring my words.

"No more out of town excursions for a while," Dad ordered, holding my gaze until I nodded.

"Deal," I said, relieved at the simple solution.

"Night, Britt." Dad moved back in to take me into a one armed hug and kiss the top of my head.

"Night," I said as Mom hugged me again and gave me a kiss on the cheek. I climbed the stairs, pausing to look back at them as they turned to each other still in a palpable state of shock.

I flipped the light on in my room, shut the door, and flopped down on my bed rolling my eyes. I wasn't sure they bought that entirely. Still, they hadn't questioned me too heavily; they wanted easy. Who wouldn't after their years of fear and stress spent worrying over my well-being.

I rolled over and it hit me. Hit me hard. Tears streamed down my face as my loss finally hit home. Allister, Angelina, and even Taylor, gone. There one minute and the next, vanished.

I reached for the house phone on my night stand, dialing quickly. "Come on, come on, pick up, pick up." I willed.

"Hello?" the voice I needed to hear.

"Trish," I cried into the phone.

"Britt, oh my God, are you okay?"

"Yeah, but I need to see you. Can you…?"

"I'll be right there," she said.

"Elisa and Cassie?" I questioned.

"I'll call and pick them up on the way, bye."

My parents took little convincing to allow the girls to run up to my room and check on me and, minutes later, true to her word, Trish, Cassie, and Elisa walked into my room. We all instantly fell into a giant group hug then sat down on the bed so they could hear all about my nightmare. This time, the nightmare hadn't come in a dream, but while I was wide awake, every second of it.

I shared everything. Kendal's twisted proclamation of feelings for me, his letting me go, the dead convenience store attendant, the battle, and the Eternals disappearing and not coming back. Everything.

They listened intently, gasping, moaning at all the appropriate places, their faces animated. When I finished they stared, at a loss; something I never witnessed from them before.

I glanced from face to face searching for some answers; some explanations. Desperately, I hoped for some suggested course of action, yet got nothing but blank stares.

"What do I do now?" I pleaded. "Throw me a bone, girls."

Trish shrugged. "I've got nothing."

"Me either," Cassie sighed.

We turned to Elisa, our last hope for some glorious revelation showing us a way to right this wrong.

"He made you promise not to put yourself in harm's way or follow him to Greece?" she gaped at me.

"Yeah," I replied.

"You agreed to this?" she asked, dumbfounded.

"Yeah, but," I began and she raised her hand, stopping me.

"We need to think this through," she said. "There is still a chance this Bastion will try to find you and kill you?"

"Right," I sighed.

"And if he does find you, the three of us and your parents might be in danger as well?" She met my eyes steadily.

"Right," I moaned, dropping my head to my hands.

"That leaves very few options." She sat up straighter as we all looked at her. "We need to prepare for a trip to Greece on a moment's notice." She pressed her lips together and nodded with resolve.

"What?" I frowned as Trish and Cassie stared in shock.

"If Bastion comes here we need to be prepared to flee to Greece. It's the only way to keep Grand Rapids safe, possibly save Allister and his parents, and clear your name as an abomination." She finished her summary and suggestion for a simple course of action with a nod.

We looked back at her, eyes wide in amazement. Her logic sounded reasonable; it even made sense.

"I'd say we go with that." I nodded.

We all agreed and the girls headed home for the night. They wanted to take shifts staying with me, but I made them all go home, assuring them of my safety.

"My parents are right downstairs. I'll be fine," I told them closing my bedroom door behind them and they showed themselves out.

I slipped between the covers of my bed...my bed. That sounded good and felt even better. I couldn't help smiling just a little at the thought.

I flicked off the light and my thoughts turned grim. Images of Allister having his heart ripped out of his chest played over and over in my mind. The thought of losing him tore my own heart apart.

And worse, I imagined Angelina being tortured to reveal my location; threatened with her life if she didn't give me up. How I longed to see her smile at me in her disapproving way. To have her tell me I caused all of this like she did in the beginning. But she followed me when Kendal took me to Canada. She came with Allister and Taylor to save me. I cried for them, for the entire Parks family. They showed me nothing but kindness, and now they might all die because I existed. I rolled over, burying my head in my pillows, sobbing myself to sleep.

I didn't dream. Oddly, I yearned to see through Kendal's demented eyes just to have a connection to an Eternal. Having failed, I woke the next morning feeling the loss, realizing the twisted reality I lived in.

I got ready for school and the girls picked me up. I left the Camaro parked on the street out front, not having the heart or the will to drive it. I turned and stared at its black sleekness as we drove away.

I sat in Calculus staring out the window, thinking about bumping into Allister in the hallway on our way to the next class. The substitute for Mr. Kinsley didn't have any luck keeping my attention and my mind wandered all class.

Lunch depressed me most of all. The girls and I sat at the table we'd shared with them and the boys slid in beside us. We told the boys Allister and Angelina had to go back to New York for a while and they joined us in our silent salute to their absence, not uttering a word just eating their lunch in silence.

I was grateful for the company. The loneliness didn't feel so oppressive when I shared it with them.

We spent the evening together at one of our houses, googling Greece, finding out as much as possible about our next destination, should the need arise.

On one such evening, Cassie Googled "greek gods" instead of Greece by mistake. She moved the mouse to click the back button and I froze where I stood behind her.

"Oh my God get over here you have to see this," I shouted. Trish and Elisa rushed up to peer at the images on the screen over our shoulders: pictures of sculptures in Greece depicting the Greek Gods.

I began to shake, a chill running down my back as I stared at the pictures. I leaned heavily on the back of Cassie's chair. Trish and then Elisa put a supportive arm around my waist.

On the screen, the spitting images of Victor and Jennavia stared back at us. Under the pictures were the names Zeus and Hera.

I lost all strength to my legs as Trish and Elisa eased me to a sitting position on the floor. They sat down next to me, still looking up at the screen on either side of Cassie's chair.

"Is it true?" I asked in a breathy whisper. "Are they gods?"

"Do you really think Victor and Jennavia are the gods Zeus and Hera?" Cassie asked.

"I don't know what to think anymore," I admitted.

"Anything is possible with them," Trish said.

"Yeah, except coming back, it seems," I sighed. Trish and Elisa put an arm across my shoulders.

Trish dropped me off out front of my house and I slunk through the door. Dad stood in the doorway leading to the living room, leaning against the frame.

"Still no Allister?" he asked, no hint of malice.

"No."

"It's nice you have your friends to keep your mind off him." He nodded.

"Yeah, they're great."

"Honey, I didn't approve of you seeing Allister, but I want you to know, I hope he comes back. I understand how much he means to you and I want you to be happy."

"Thanks Dad." I walked over and wrapped my arms around him.

He returned my hug and kissed the top of my head.

I gave him another squeeze and turned to the stairs, climbing them heavily.

Slipping into bed, I looked at the clock assuring I'd set the alarm. I closed my eyes, trying to picture Allister's perfect face; sad when I realized the exact details eluded me.

The images sprung bright and clear in my dream; I walked down a familiar street, close to the park by our house. I moved purposefully to my goal: a garage door open, the light on and the noise of someone working with power tools. I stayed clear of the light spilling out of the open door, keeping hidden in the shadows. I stepped back to assure my concealment when a twig snapped under my foot. I froze as the man's head came up and looked my way.

Mr. Geffre? The man who taught me piano lessons years ago. His hunched shoulders lifted as he scanned the shadows for the origin of the sound. Satisfied with his inspection, he turned back to the project on his wooden work bench.

I slipped closer to the opening, still deep in the shadows. Sliding up along the siding of the garage, I peered around the corner.

At that point I was fully aware of the dream's origin. I saw through Kendal's eyes again. Screaming with all my might for him to stop, "Don't kill Mr. Geffre.'" I watched in horror as he moved forward without hearing. I tried to force myself awake, like the night Kendal attacked me, but my effort proved futile. I screamed within the prison of my dream, trying to connect to the Eternal planning to kill someone I knew. Someone I cared about. Someone close to me. Guilt weighed on me at the thought. Should I be more appalled if the victim was someone I knew rather than someone I didn't? Had I become that callous?

Kendal's hand reached out of the darkness, touching Mr. Geffre on the shoulder. The man's face turned pale, his spirit drawn out, his scream forming, but never escaping his throat. He fell to the cement floor, dead before he rolled to a stop.

I sat up in my bed, tears rolling down my face as I cried hysterically. Mr. Geffre, gone. Then, something bigger hit me. Kendal was back.

I rested my face in my hands, my sobs coming so hard my body shook, the spasms racking me. Then I stopped; I realized what I must do. Find Kendal and convince him to stop killing people. I understood it bordered on impossible, like trying to stop a meth addict from his addiction. Yet, if we held interventions for human addicts, why not Eternal addicts? I don't know why, but the thought sounded reasonable at that moment. If Kendal really had feelings for me, wouldn't he want to impress me? I smiled with confidence; I could do this. I curled up in my blankets and forced myself to close my eyes even though I feared what I would find there.

In the light of day, the idea to have an intervention for an Eternal hooked on human spirits, seemed ludicrous. I packed my things in my backpack for school and headed out the door, gloomy over the possibility of Kendal killing more people in my small town. The girls told me each victim of Kendal's had shown symptoms of heart attacks and they were ruled natural deaths. It gave me little comfort his crimes continued to go unnoticed.

The horn of the Jeep sounded and I walked out the door, pulled it closed after me, and hurried to the Jeep. I slowed as I passed the black Camaro, abandoned at the curb since the day I returned from Canada. The memory of my time spent with the three Eternals, now AWOL, stung like a dagger to my heart. They had to be in Greece by now. Gone from my life, possibly for good.

I hopped into the front seat of the Wrangler with a nod to Trish while Cassie and Elisa talked in the back. Both gave me a tap on the shoulder in greeting as we drove to school, the wind too noisy for us to talk when Trish had the top off. The weather, an Indian summer, was warmer than usual this year. Trish pulled the Jeep into a parking spot, we gathered our things, and walked in the main entrance.

"Did you hear." Cassie turned to look at us as we walked. "They're going to start bussing the Calculus classes to the community college for the rest of the year."

"Great," I sighed. "Now I have to endure a bus ride every morning."

"You might find a cute college guy," Elisa said, quickly putting a hand to her mouth, her eyes opened wide.

"Yeah, like I need that," I shot back, offended she would even say such a thing.

"I'm sorry," Elisa apologized and placed a hand on my arm.

"Forget it." I shrugged, trying to brush it off, but the thought of someone taking Allister's place tasted bitter in my mouth. I walked away as Trish scolded Elisa. It didn't matter. Allister faced an angry council, over me. His fate hung in the balance. The thought of him not coming back to me hurt more than I ever imagined; an ache deep inside chewed me up.

I walked into Calculus as the rest of the students stood by the door with their bags.

"Get in line please," the substitute instructed. "We'll be boarding the bus in a minute."

I fell in at the back of the line, wanting nothing more than to go home and hide in my room away from all of this. I trudged along with the group like first graders going to lunch on first day of school. We boarded the bus and rumbled through town to the local community college, Itasca Community College, ICC.

The substitute led us into a building, up the stairs, and pointed us into a classroom. We walked in, taking the available seats as the college kids smiled knowingly. Being at the end of the line only one desk remained by the time I entered. Not looking up but staring at my backpack I set on the desk, I slipped into the seat at the back of the room.

I prided myself with being able to see the glows around people only when I chose to, but when I looked over at the person next to me, the glow around him came unbidden, blinding me. I put my hand in front of my eyes, squinting at the radiant light flowing from all around him.

Glancing around to see if anyone noticed, I proceeded to push the glow out as it tried to creep in around my efforts to block it. When I turned to the student next to me again the light shone back painfully.

"Hi." He turned to me after scanning the other newcomers' faces. He didn't seem to notice my discomfort. "My name is Gabe…" he faltered when his green eyes met mine. He stared for an uncomfortably long time and then forced himself to turn away.

"I'd like to welcome all of you from the high school to our Calculus class," the tall skinny teacher with a long beard and deep, monotone voice said from the front. "I am Mr. Brunson and I'll be available outside of class to help you from 8am to 4pm. If you need further assistance outside those times, we have a student tutor at your disposal in the tutor room off the campus library. Gabe, would you please stand up."

Mr. Brunson motioned to the back of the room. Heads turned as the student next to me stood up. I turned as well and looked up at Gabe as he ran a nervous hand through his long brown hair and glowed brightly despite my efforts.

I watched, my curiosity aroused by this college kid who shone brighter than a spotlight. I may need to stop by after school for some help, I smiled. Yes, indeed.

After bussing back to the high school I steeled myself to go by and see Gabe that night. In my classes for the rest of the day I daydreamed about the reason for his intense aura, but the only reason I could fathom didn't make any sense: he was an angel.

I sat with the girls at lunch, lost in concentration as they took turns staring at me with worried expressions.

"What?" I turned to them when I couldn't take it any longer.

"Are you alright?" Cassie spoke up.

"Yeah, fine." I tried to sound confident. The words came out feeble.

"Don't bullshit us." Trish leaned closer. "You've been getting more depressed every day and ..."

"And we're concerned," Elisa finished for her.

"Thanks."

"You have to realize they may not come back," Trish started.

I closed my eyes, desperately holding back the barrage of anxiety trying to burst forth. I opened my eyes, raising them to my worried amigos as I felt the pain tearing through me.

"Britt, you have to snap out of it," Cassie urged.

"Not knowing anything is driving me crazy," I muttered quietly.

"We know, and you have to get a grip," Elisa said gently.

I glared at her, causing her to lean back in her chair with her hands raised defensively before her. Get a grip, what the hell did that mean anyway? The person I loved had vanished. His sister, vanished. His parents, vanished. Even the bodyguard who I didn't feel any real connection to, vanished. I couldn't wrap my head around it all, but the pain of loss didn't have any problem messing with me.

"What Elisa meant to say, is you need to keep talking, letting us in, and dealing with your feelings." Cassie reached over to put a hand on my arm.

I looked down at her hand and she slowly pulled it back.

"You want in, fine. Kendal is back in my head, I saw him kill Mr. Geffre last night. I have such a void in my chest it feels like it's going to crush me from the inside, and the college math tutor's spirit glows so bright, I think I'll go blind if I look at him again. There you have it, do you like to be inside my head?" I looked to each of them, my jaw set and determined.

"I had no idea," Cassie said, her eyes wide.

"No wonder you're going crazy," Elisa whispered.

"Doesn't it feel better to let it out?" Trish asked flatly, her arms crossed over her chest.

I stared at her. Yeah, I did feel better. I nodded with a slight smile.

"Good." She grinned, leaning over to put an arm across my shoulders. "Don't lock us out anymore. We're here for you."

I nodded again, thankful I had them, feeling better with a little relief from the isolation.

"So what do you think is up with the tutor?" Cassie asked.

"Gabe? I don't know." I shrugged.

"Wait, you can see spirits?" Elisa leaned forward.

"Yeah, sort of," I sighed, resigned to revealing another reminder of my difference.

"How does that work?" Trish asked.

"I see a glow around everyone, everyone except an Eternal that is. The dimmer the glow, the closer to death the person is. The brighter, the healthier they are."

"So this Gabe must be really healthy." Cassie concluded with a nod.

"I'm not so sure," I frowned.

"Why?" Elisa asked.

"His glow is different somehow. I've never seen anything like it before."

"Maybe he's something different." Trish pressed her lips together in thought.

"How do you mean?" I asked.

"If Eternals have no glow because they don't have a guardian angel's spirit in them, then an incredibly bright glow might mean…" Trish paused, eyes going wide as she looked at me.

"He might be an angel," I agreed, nodding at the revelation.

"An angel," Trish repeated, shaking her head.

"Come on," Elisa laughed. "He's not an angel. That's ridiculous."

"Is it?" Trish raised an eyebrow.

"We didn't believe in Eternals until we met some." Cassie shrugged.

"Exactly," Trish exclaimed, causing several people at nearby tables to turn and stare.

"Until we discover them." Trish leaned closer to the table, lowering her voice, "We have no idea these things exist." She sat back in her chair, folded her arms across her chest, and gave a satisfied nod.

Elisa, Cassie, and I exchanged glances, the feasibility of Trish's hypothesis sinking in. That there might be other beings we didn't know about only by lack of exposure was life-changing. One by one we nodded, agreeing to the plausibility of it.

The bell rang and we stood to go to class. As we dropped our garbage in the trash cans. We stopped, huddling at the end of a hall.

"I'm going to see Gabe after school," I told them.

"We should come with you," Trish said.

"None of you have Calc; it would look odd," I argued.

"Then what should we do?" Cassie asked.

"Drop me off and wait for me at the Jeep. It shouldn't take me too long," I said.

The looks on their faces turned disapproving.

"What would he do to me in the school where anyone could walk in?" I pointed out the obvious, ignoring my mind's flash to the hospital and Kendal's brazenness. "I'll be fine."

We turned and headed our separate ways to class. I'll be fine, I repeated in my head. I hope.

Chapter 22

My resolve to go see Gabe dwindled throughout the day to near nothing as the final bell rang. The thought of exposing myself to an angel becoming less and less appealing as the day went on. The word abomination came to mind. The words Bastion chose to describe me hung in my ears. If Bastion thought of me in that manner, then what would an angel feel? Allister said angels didn't care for his kind and wasn't I, at least partially, his kind?

I steeled myself, walking down the hallway to the library after the girls drove me to the college. I rounded the corner to the room off the library. I planned on walking by, looking in, and reassessing the glow around him, that was all.

I felt the plan a sound one, striding confidently along, cruising to the doorway with no intention of slowing down. The plan would have gone off without a hitch, except Gabe stepped out of the room, his attention focused on something behind him, and I ran smack dab into him.

We both tumbled to the floor, sprawling across the hallway, my backpack falling from my shoulder and sliding across the tile. Gabe tumbled over me, the armful of papers he held scattering everywhere, floating down over us as we lay in a jumble of arms and legs on the ground.

"Ow," I moaned. I had to stop running into supernatural boys, I thought cringing and wishing I could disappear.

"Oh, I'm so sorry." He pushed himself off the floor and subsequently, off of me.

He looked down and our eyes met, his green irises reflecting my startled face back at me, his pupils dilating in surprise.

I squinted back at him, my eyes stinging as his glow blazed bright, my concentration gone, not allowing me to dim it sufficiently. I took a deep breath, focusing hard as his glow dimmed to a tolerable level.

"It's my fault," I said, trying to get to my feet only to fall again and trip over his leg.

"Oh, sorry again," he mumbled, taking my arm and lifting me to my feet.

"No, that's okay," I said, looking around for my backpack, locating it across the hall. I walked over, picked it up, and swung it onto my shoulder. I flinched as a twinge of pain pierced my back, causing me to stop and grimace.

"Are you alright?" he asked as he stooped to collect his paperwork.

"Fine," I said, the pain causing my voice to waver.

"No, you're not." He frowned. "You better come in here and sit down."

He took me by the arm and pulled me into the small classroom. Walking over to the desk chair, he sat me down, pulling the backpack from my shoulder, and placing it on the floor.

"Rest a minute and see if it gets any better," he smiled. "Britt, isn't it?"

"Yeah." I nodded.

"Where does it hurt?" he asked, appearing genuinely concerned.

"I'm fine." I started to get up, but pain stabbed in my back again, making me gasp and I dropped back into the seat again.

"You don't sound fine," he said. "Where does it hurt?"

"My back, just above my tail bone," I said mortified and blushing. "Between my shoulders too," I added in a rush.

"Nothing to be embarrassed about." He dismissed my pink cheeks. "I stepped in front of you, it's my fault."

I stretched backwards, trying to pull free the knots forming in my muscles. "Ah," I gasped as it knifed again.

"You should go to the nurse's office," he suggested.

"No, I'll be fine," I said with a painful exhale, feeling my muscles spasm.

"Stubborn one, aren't you?" he smirked.

I nodded, unable to say anything as another rush of pain grabbed my back.

"Lean forward then," he instructed.

I spun my head in surprise and paid the price as my neck kinked painfully. I clenched my eyes against the pain and then looked up at him suspiciously.

"Trust me, I know what I'm doing," he assured. "Now lean forward on the desk and relax."

I gave him another questioning look and he nodded to me. With a shrug that I regretted, I leaned onto the desk, still sitting in the chair.

He placed his hands on my neck first, finding the kink straight away and gently rubbed the knot out.

An unexpected moan escaped my lips. I felt my face get hot and bit my lip to prevent it from happening again.

He chuckled softly and continued to move his hands in small circles as he rubbed the stiffness out of my muscles. He eased down to right above my tail bone and I gasped when he touched the second knot. It hurt so good as he rubbed and pressed evenly on the injured muscle. I let my eyes close as the pain began to subside.

Just as my body started relaxing, I heard a gasp at the door.

Gabe stopped massaging and I looked up to see Trish, Cassie, and Elisa staring at us in disbelief.

"Oh my God," Cassie cried out.

"What are you doing to her?" Trish accused him, glaring.

"Nothing," Gabe and I said at once.

"Looks like more than nothing to me." Elisa had her hands planted on her hips. "And I should know," she added with a nod.

"Uh, we collided in the hall," I stammered.

"She hurt her back and I'm trying to massage the knots out," Gabe said.

"Looks like inappropriate behavior for a tutor with a student." Cassie frowned.

"Cassie," I warned. "Don't start."

"She's right." Gabe caused me to turn and look up at him as he stood over me.

"It wasn't inappropriate," I pointed out. "I wouldn't go to the nurse like he suggested so he rubbed my back to stop the pain, which it did," I said, somewhat surprised realizing it was true. I stood and stretched, amazed at the absence of pain.

"I told you I knew what I was doing," he smirked.

The girls were not amused. They stared, disapproving and waited for me to gather my backpack and walk over to them.

"Maybe we should report this to the dean," Cassie suggested. "I'm sure he won't approve of tutors using their time to hit on high school students."

"Report what?" I said. "Nothing happened. I was sitting at the desk while he showed me how to do an assignment I had trouble with."

"That's your story?" Trish huffed.

"And I'm sticking to it," I said with a curt nod.

"Fine," Trish sighed. "Can we go now?"

"Yeah, good idea." I pushed past them as they stood in the doorway.

I glanced back at Gabe who wore a knowing smile and then strode down the hall. The girls hesitated a moment longer and hurried after. I didn't have to look back to know Gabe watched us walk down the hall and turn the corner, confident he stared until he couldn't see us any longer.

"I knew we should have come with you," Trish groused as we walked down the hall.

"And what would you have done differently?" I asked.

"I, I …I don't know, but I sure as hell wouldn't be lying across his desk getting a massage," she shot back.

"I'm not making it up. I planned to walk by and look at him as I passed. Just when I got to his door, he stepped in front of me and we ran into each other."

"How convenient," Elisa snarked.

"Really?" I glared at her.

"And you hurt your back," Cassie kept us on track.

"Yes, and I hurt my back," I said, stretching my back at the waist and smiling at the absence of pain.

"That's it?" Trish sounding less doubtful.

"Sorry to disappoint." I shrugged. "But I did discover one thing."

The girls stopped and I took two more steps before stopping and turning back to their questioning stares.

"What's that?" Elisa asked. "Is he an angel?"

I shook my head and shrugged.

"Is he an Eternal?" Cassie asked.

I indicated no again.

"Then what?" Trish said, exacerbated.

"He has great hands." I grinned, liking the rise I got out of them.

"Ah." Elisa threw up her hands.

"Oh my God." Cassie rolled her eyes.

"You suck." Trish gave me a shove.

I stumbled a few steps before catching my balance, laughing at them.

We walked out of the building to the parking lot and jumped in the Jeep, still laughing. We cruised past Allister's place the way we did every day, just to be sure. Seeing it, I felt the familiar tug at my heart. As we pulled past the house, I spotted someone moving alongside.

"Stop," I shouted and Trish slammed on the brakes.

"What?" she looked at me, wild-eyed.

"Back up, back up," I hollered.

She put the Jeep into reverse and squealed backward. A tall shape moved along the house and my blood went cold. I hopped out as the girls stared at me, not moving.

"Get out of here, now," I ordered.

"Who is it?" Elisa asked.

"Just go, now," I said.

"Britt, who is it?" Cassie cried.

"Kendal." I watched Trish's eyes light up with understanding.

"What about you?" Trish shouted as I ran towards the house.

"I'll be fine, get out of here," I hollered over my shoulder.

The Jeep's engine revved and the big tires threw rocks as Trish punched the gas. I watched it disappear around the corner and then crept closer to the house. I slid my back against the front of the house, peeking around the corner as Kendal peered in a window. He turned my way and I pressed myself against the siding, the ridges digging into my tender back. I leaned forward again and saw Kendal moving to the back, obviously not getting in. Not getting in? He's an Eternal. All he has to do was shimmer into the house. Why was he trying to break in?

I eased nearer, looking his way as he vanished around the corner. I crept quickly after, keeping low and close to the house for cover. I stepped around the corner, peering ahead to see where he went and his hands grabbed hold of me, throwing me down to the ground. His weight pressing on my lungs as he sat on me, holding my arms up against the grass. My sore back began to spasm.

"Well, well, lookie what we have here," he sneered.

"Kendal, get off," I gasped.

"Why you sneaking up on me?"

"Why are you skulking around the Parks's?" I countered.

"Checking to see if they came back."

"Why, are they coming back?" My voice brightened with excitement.

"Easy, easy, I don't know. They were still in Greece when I left. At least Victor and Jennavia were. Hard to say where your boyfriend and his sister are."

"Allister wasn't in Greece?"

"Nope, still missing."

"Get off, I can hardly breathe." I struggled to push him off me.

He rolled to his side leaning on his elbow, resting his head in his hand as he stared down at me.

"Still as beautiful and feisty as ever," he grinned.

I ignored him. "Why are you back?"

"I missed you and besides, this place has some really juicy angels just ripe for the taking." His smile gave me goosebumps.

"Like Mr. Geffre last night?" I shot back angrily.

"The old guy? Yeah his angel felt so good." He shrugged and then his pleased expression turned sour. "You watching me again?"

"Like I have a choice."

"Come on, give a guy a break. It's not like I can just quit."

"Why don't you?"

"We went over this before. I can't help myself."

"It's wrong."

He gave me a hard look and then turned away, getting to his feet.

"Where is Allister if he isn't in Greece?"

"Don't know, don't care." He shrugged and shimmered to nothing.

"Ah!" I slammed my fists against the ground. I didn't have a chance to ask him how he got away from Bastion or why he didn't just shimmer into the house. Our encounter had left me with more questions than before.

Allister said Bastion took Kendal with plans to extract my location from him. I stared at the sky above me, the fluffy white clouds and the clear blue space between, as fear raced through me, like ice taking over my veins.

What if Bastion 'let' Kendal escape with the hopes of following him here to me? I jumped to my feet.

"Kendal, Kendal," I shouted, hoping he had shimmered close by and might hear me. I ran to the front of the house. "Kendal, Kendal," I cried.

"Why all the noise?" Kendal's voice spoke from behind me.

"Holy shit!" I jumped, turning to him, my hand to my chest to keep my racing heart from bursting through.

"What?" he looked at me, suspicious.

When I gave him an exacerbated look, he frowned.

"You called me," he reminded.

"How did you get away from Bastion?" I asked.

"I'm kind of good at getting out of tough situations, if I do say so myself." He smiled. "I slipped away when they went after Allister in Toronto."

"Allister was in Toronto?" I brightened at mention of him.

"I thought you were asking about me and how I escaped." He frowned with a hurt expression.

"No, you're right. How'd you get away?" I wiped away all traces of eagerness.

"I slipped the bracelet off. They didn't have it on very tight. And I shimmered away down the street. I jumped a train and headed back here." He puffed up with pride at his accomplishment.

"The one you put on me was pretty tight, why would they put yours on so loose? Is that normal?" I asked.

"I'm not sure," he said slowly, the realization of what I asked making more sense now. "So you think Bastion let me escape on purpose? Why?"

"To get to me."

"Makes sense." He shrugged. "Except no one can track me," he boasted. "No really," he said, seeing the doubt on my face. "How do you think I've managed to stay alive and out of prison all these years?"

"Just lucky?" I raised an eyebrow.

"After all the angels I've taken, I'm the top priority to the Eternals and the Avenging Angels. None can stop me."

"About that," I started and then hesitated.

"What?"

"Back at the cabin you said you felt something for me," I said, treading lightly on this dangerous subject.

"Yeah, so?"

"Were you lying?"

"No." His eyes narrowed with suspicion. "Why?"

"If you have feelings for me, you need to stop taking angels," I blurted out.

He spun away from me though his hand came to his chin in thought. "Are you saying you might have feelings for me...now that Allister is out of the picture?"

"He isn't out of the picture," I argued.

"Sure, sure, but if he were..."

"I would be more likely to see you in a positive light if you stopped taking angels," I spoke honestly.

He looked over his shoulder at me, doubt heavy in his eyes.

I tried to put as much sincerity into my eyes as I could as I pleaded for him to believe me.

"I suppose I could try," he said with a slight nod.

"It would also lessen the attention we might draw from the angels and Bastion," I added.

"I told you," he said smugly, "I can't be tracked."

"Let's hope in Bastion's case, you're right," I said.

"Let's." He nodded and vanished.

I liked Kendal. The thought surprising as it came to me. Even being so cruel and unfeeling about the people he took angels from, he made no bones about what he was. What you saw was what you got with Kendal. But if I could give him hope he might have a chance with me if he stopped taking angels, I would lead him on to save lives. The only question that lingered was how far would I go to keep up the charade? Would I kiss him? I pushed the thought from my mind with a firm shake of my head as I started walking home. The only feeling I had for Kendal was revulsion. My misdirection had limits.

Trish and the girls pulled up alongside me about a block from the Parks's house.

"What happened? Did you talk to him?" Trish spoke first.

"Yeah." I nodded.

"And." Elisa watched me, curious.

"Allister and Angelina were in Toronto, but Kendal doesn't know where they are now."

"Why is he back?" Cassie wanted to know.

I gave her a flat stare and she nodded with realization.

"He's back because of you," she answered her own question.

"He made it sound like the easy pickings motivated his return, but I doubt it," I sighed, knowing as I spoke that I was right.

"I can tell you're not too happy about a psychotic Eternal having a thing for you, but what aren't you telling us?" Trish read me like a book.

"I think Bastion let Kendal escape so he could find me," I told her.

The girls sat speechless, a rare thing for them, at least all at the same time anyway.

"Don't worry." I did my best to put confidence behind my words. "He assured me not even Bastion could track him back here."

They nodded, visibly relieved, something I couldn't afford to feel.

Chapter 23

I hopped out of the Jeep in front of my house, the sleek black reminder still parked at the curb. I glanced at it in passing and pulled my eyes away reluctantly as I walked up the porch steps.

"Mom, I'm home," I called. Nothing. I walked into the kitchen noticing a note on a yellow legal pad sitting on the island.

"Britt, we have dinner plans with the Hastings. Leftovers in the fridge. Won't be too late. Love, Mom."

I turned from the island, opening the fridge door, staring at the Tupperware labeled with tape. Meatloaf-Monday. Lasagna-Sunday. Chili-Saturday. I spun away, swinging the door shut on the menu of Minnesota standards. The only thing missing: Tater Tot Hot Dish. Oh there it was, behind Saturday's Chili; Tuesday's delicacy.

Realizing my lack of appetite, much less after seeing what waited in the fridge, I climbed the stairs to my room, dropped on my bed, and rolled onto my back. A twinge between my shoulders reminded me of the collision with Gabe and the subsequent back rub. I smiled at the memory.

I glanced at my dresser as I turned to flick on the light on my nightstand. A red and black box sat on the dresser and I leapt to my feet, realizing its contents. My new phone. My waterlogged one from my jaunt to Canada, later shattered by Kendal had left me without my most used communication device. I tore into the packaging, pulling the shiny touch screen phone out of the plastic. I unwound the charging cord and plugged it in with great anticipation.

I pulled homework out of my backpack and paged through the notes and textbooks. Every so often, I checked the progress of the charging phone and then dropped back down on the bed in disgust.

Unwilling, or more like unable to wait for the charge to finish, I pulled the plug and powered the phone up. It took forever for the phone to cycle through the startup and I tapped anxiously on the dresser as the little hour glass spun on the screen, infuriating me every time it I checked only to see it still spinning. I looked yet again just as the spinning hour glass flashed off and the red connection arrow blinked over and over again, the little message symbol adding numbers in front of it, one after another. By the time all the messages were downloaded on the phone, it read 43 text messages.

I opened the first message, from Angelina.

Going after Bastion and Allister, hope you get home safely. Will text later.

For the next hour I paged through the texts, a random voicemail mixed in, from Angelina, telling me they were doing everything to stop Bastion and get Allister to Greece.

Around text message number thirty-eight, the messages got shorter and more worrisome.

Britt, we landed in Athens. Bastion and Allister within our reach.

Still looking for Allister, Bastion has gone underground with him.

Saw Mother and Father today. They are being held until
Allister comes forward.

Father went on trial today for Allister's crime of creating,
will write more, later.

I stopped reading, letting my hand holding the
phone drop into my lap. Angelina meant me. Victor was
on trial because Allister created me. I steeled myself and
lifted the phone to keep reading.

Good news. Father found not responsible for Allister's
actions. Still haven't located Allister and Bastion.

Bastion turned Allister over to the Greek Eternal Council
today. Allister looks defeated before trial even begins.

Trial halted today until more evidence of Allister's crime
can be brought forward. Britt, be careful. I think Bastion
intends to search for you as evidence. If Bastion brings
you to Athens, Allister could be sentenced to death. If no
other evidence is found, maybe life in prison.

I dropped the phone this time. It bounced off the
carpeting and slid against the dresser. Did she know
Kendal came back to Grand Rapids? That Bastion might
be on his way here searching for Kendal?
I crouched to the floor and crawled over to
retrieve my phone. I tapped out a message on my keypad.

Kendal is in Grand Rapids. Will Bastion be able to find
him here?

I pressed Send.

I hoped for an answer right away, but none came. I stared at the phone, willing it to chime with a text from Angelina, but nothing.

I sat on my bed, leaning against the headboard, horrified at the possibilities facing Allister. Prison or death? When given those two choices, what would Allister want? For me, an everlasting lifetime without Allister seemed too overwhelming. Give me death.

I'd started to doze off when a chime from my phone woke me with a start. I jerked the phone up and opened the text from Angelina.

Britt, Kendal is good at avoiding detection. Chances are Bastion won't get within 300 miles of you. Don't worry.
Angelina.

Don't worry. Yeah, right. Questions and thoughts rolled through my mind. I didn't know where to begin, so I typed the first one I caught.

Tell Allister I love him. Send.

I felt exhausted. I set the phone on my night stand and slid down so my head rested on my pillow. I didn't even have the strength to get under the covers. I curled up on my comforter and fell into a deep, fitful sleep.

I should have known better. Should have reminded myself where I would end up; in Kendal's mind. Luckily I never had to hear his thoughts, but everything else played through my vision like a movie in HD.

He stood, or should I say, we stood outside a nice brick home with black shutters and a large porch. No, I screamed. Not this house. Kendal, no, not this house. He walked up the stairs onto the porch, looking in a dark window. I felt a tingling sensation and then we looked at a bed, covers pulled up on the person sleeping so only the her blond head showed.

I knew the bed, I knew that blond head. Kendal! Kendal! I screamed frantically. Get out, don't you dare! I never knew if he heard me or not, but I did everything I could to reach his mind. You sick sadistic bastard, not this house! Not this bedroom! Not, Cassie!

Cassie rolled over, restless in her sleep. She cracked her eyes a sliver, and then they flew open. Her mouth stretched wide to scream and then she stopped. Recognition and resignation mixed in her expression. She knew Kendal, had witnessed him up close when he kidnapped me on the way back from Duluth. She knew what he did and what he was about.

She sat up, staring right at him; not turning away in fear even though I could see her body shaking with terror.

"Kendal." She spoke and I actually felt him flinch. "Kendal," she repeated, this time without a reaction from him. "If you hurt me, you'll hurt Britt."

Kendal stopped. Not moving one way or another, standing as if in thought. Consideration.

"Why would I care?" he whispered.

"I know you don't want to hurt Britt." Her voice shook. "You don't want to hurt the person you love."

"I don't love her," Kendal shouted.

267

Good, maybe Cassie's parents will hear and scare him off. I closed my eyes and urged her parents to wake up.

"Of course you love her," *Cassie, gaining control of her voice, spoke more confidently.*

"It doesn't matter. She loves Allister," *Kendal said evenly.*

"Allister may not come back," *Cassie countered.*

Good girl, I thought. Keep him thinking. The longer you delay the more chance we have of saving you.

"No, he may not," *Kendal agreed, his voice softer, lighter.*

"All you need to do is not hurt her and when Allister doesn't come back," *she stopped, letting Kendal's imagination do the rest.*

"You're right," *Kendal said, hope in his voice.*

I felt tingling and we were out in the street once more and then I sat upright in my bed, my hair matted to my head with sweat and my clothes damp with perspiration. Grabbing my phone I hit C for Cassie on my speed dial.

"Hello?" Cassie answered on the first ring.

"Cassie, are you alright?" I shouted into the phone.

"How'd you...you were with him?" Cassie gasped, her fear audible.

"I screamed my lungs out trying to get him to stop."

"I was so scared." Cassie began to cry. "I thought I was dead."

"You were friggin' awesome," I praised. "The way you remembered he loved me, brilliant!"

"I didn't think it'd work," she sobbed, her emotions getting the better of her.

"But it did, girl, it did."

We stayed on the phone the rest of the night. We mostly listened to the other breathe, yet neither of us could hang up until dawn lit the morning sky.

"Bye Cassie," I whispered, exhausted, into the phone.

"See you in a bit." Cassie chuckled weakly.

I hit the end button and felt relief for the first time since Kendal stood on Cassie's front porch.

I got up from bed, resolving to speak with him and letting him know my unhappiness with him if he hurt my girls, or their family. Maybe I'd give it another shot at making him stop. Play on his feelings for me. Him quit? Not likely, I sighed heading to the shower.

The Jeep's horn sounded way too soon and I threw my clothes on and ran down the steps, only to run back up to gather my backpack and race down again. I jumped into the seat and noticed Cassie missing.

I looked to Elisa and Trish, my mouth hanging open and eyes wide.

"She's okay, just exhausted," Elisa explained quickly.

"Surprised you look as good as you do." Trish nodded.

"She told you?" I asked.

"Called to tell me she wouldn't need a ride," Trish said. "Spilled the entire story in two seconds flat."

"So it's true, Kendal went to kill her?" Elisa gasped.

"Yeah, and I came along for the ride." I nodded. "I have to hand it to the girl, she thought fast. Told him if he hurt her, he'd hurt me and lose any chance he had at being with me."

"But she lied." Elisa leaned forward between the seats as Trish pulled away from the curb.

"Totally." I smiled at her. "Like I would love a murderer like Kendal." I shook my head, smiling fondly, "It'll always be Allister for me."

A roar of pain ripped through the morning air and Trish trounced on the brakes as a figure jumped out in front of the Jeep.

Chapter 24

Kendal slammed his hands on the hood of the Wrangler, crumpling the metal as if it were tin foil. His eyes met mine and I knew he'd heard me. His face twisted in rage as his dark eyes threw daggers through me. He held my stare and, ever so slowly, his wrath filled face softened and a little smile spread across his lips.

It sent a shiver down my back and the hairs on my arm stood on end. In a blink, he vanished. I knew where he headed and I screamed to Trish as she tore out, laying a patch of rubber and sending smoke from all four tires. We squealed around corners and accelerated to nearly sixty miles an hour on the straight stretches.

I leapt from the Jeep before Trish came to a complete stop, tumbling on the pavement and tearing up my hands, arms, and knees through my jeans as the material shredded on impact with the abrasive surface. I sprinted up the front porch steps, burst through the front door and raced up the stairs. Throwing open Cassie's bedroom door, I came upon Kendal. He stood, holding her above the floor with one hand around her neck.

I cried out, furious, hurling myself into Kendal with all my strength. I bounced off him, not budging him in the slightest as I collided with Cassie's desk on the rebound.

"You think you can trick me?" Kendal shouted. "I'll show you what happens when you try to make a fool out of me."

"No," I cried out as I scrambled to my feet, lowered my shoulder and rammed his stomach.

Air rushed out of Kendal's lungs at the impact, doubling him over, though he didn't relinquish his hold on Cassie, now beginning to turn white.

I picked myself up off the floor again, bracing for another charge when Kendal backhanded me across the face. My head exploded in pain, my back hitting the wall and dresser as I crumpled to the floor. I watched through blurry eyes, watering uncontrollably from the pain radiating through my back and legs.

Kendal stood tall, holding Cassie away from his body with an extended arm. The telltale mist began to drift from Cassie's limp body as I tried in vain to get up.

A flash of light blinded me, leaving nothing but spots where objects should be. Kendal roared in agony and then anger. Then there was nothing. Silence. The only the sound, my sobbing.

Gentle hands eased me off the floor and lay me on Cassie's bed. I felt myself rub against someone else in the bed and I looked, blinking wildly to clear my vision. I reached over, feeling Cassie's long, soft hair. I touched her cheek, pulling back convulsively. Her skin was cold to my touch.

The room erupted with activity as people rushed in to where we lay on the bed. I tried to focus, but only vague images dominated my vision.

"Britt, my name's Eric, I'm here to help you," the man said. "Where are you hurt?"

"Back, legs," I gasped. The pain was so overwhelming, my thoughts burst like bubbles as soon as they formed. I felt the bed move and Cassie's cool flesh disappeared from my fingertips.

"No, wait," I cried, hearing the bodies rush from the room and down the stairs.

"Don't worry, you're going to be alright," Eric told me.

"Cassie?" I asked.

"They're doing everything they can for her."

But I knew from experience, Kendal didn't leave anything to heal. His touch was complete; final.

They strapped me to a backboard, lifted me on a gurney, and carried me downstairs, my eyes finally starting to focus. We hurried out the front door and I heard Trish and Elisa cry my name.

I raised my hand in their direction, not yet able to see that far clearly. A hand clasped mine and another touched my shoulder.

"It'll be okay, Britt," Trish said. I heard the tears in her voice.

"Cassie?" I asked, focusing on her face.

She shook her head.

"No."

"She's alive," Elisa whispered. "They said she's still alive."

I nodded, hopeful. Kendal never left a victim alive before. I wondered why now?

As they slid me into the ambulance I caught sight of a bright glow to one side. I put my hand on the paramedic sliding me in and he stopped, glancing down at me curiously.

"Wait a minute," I whispered, trying to see the source of the light. I pointed at the light and it moved closer. I concentrated through the pain as I pushed the intensity of the aura down. A gentle hand took hold of mine and the face moved closer. My eyes opened wide and I saw Gabe, concern heavy in his features. He smiled down at me, holding my hand.

"It's okay, Britt," he whispered, leaning close. "I'm here to protect you now."

I stared at him in shock as he released my hand and the men slid me into the ambulance. As the doors swung shut I felt a surge of panic race through me. If Gabe came to protect me, did he know what I was?

The ambulance ride brought back memories of a life I thought I'd left behind. They rushed me into a curtained area and began cutting my tattered clothing from me. They hooked me up to monitors and my heart beat sounded strong and steady. Not dying today, I thought with a grimace.

Once they verified my stability they left me to concentrate on the person in the area next to me. The curtain pulled closed didn't allow me a view of the patient, but I knew it was Cassie. I closed my eyes, listening to the heart monitor over the buzz of activity around her.

Her heartbeat, steady, but weak, never skipped a beat or changed its pace.

The curtain around me flew open and Mom stood, tears running down her cheeks, staring at me in horror. She took two quick steps to my bedside and placed a hand on my arm.

"Britt, what happened?" She asked and then her eyes narrowed and she looked me up and down.

"What?" the rapid change in her expression making me curious.

"You don't look … hurt." She stared, her eyes filled with surprise.

"Huh?" I pushed myself up to lean on my elbows. My clothes, cut away to expose my injuries, showed me nothing. A little dried blood here and there, but I didn't have any injuries at all.

"How can this be?" Mom stepped back.

"Mom, Mom," I said drawing her eyes to mine. "I'm fine. I can't explain right now, but please, don't freak."

"Britt, they told me you were seriously injured, maybe paralyzed."

"Please, just trust me. I need to check on Cassie, okay?" I pushed my legs over the edge of the bed as I sat up, testing my balance.

"I, I, don't know what to think." She looked at my legs and then back at me, unable to argue with the evidence of my well-being she could see with her own eyes.

"Please, go home. I'm fine. I'll explain later." Like I even could, I thought.

She nodded, still in a daze, and walked out without a word.

I set my feet on the floor easing my weight off the bed to balance over them. I moved to the curtain and peered around the edge as a nurse took Cassie's vitals. She spun and rushed through the curtain on the other side. I guessed Cassie's mom and dad were on their way here so it was now or never.

I stepped next to Cassie. Her face pale, her eyes staring straight ahead vacantly. I put a hand tentatively on her cheek, prepared for the sudden coldness her skin transferred to me. I hesitated, remembering Allister's warning, and ignored it. I never thought I would have an opportunity to bring back one of Kendal's victims besides Angelina, that I was destined to watch helplessly, useless as the killings continued.

I felt the familiar energy surge inside me, rush to my arms and then into my hands. The force of it flowed stronger and more controlled than the first time I healed someone. Everything around me slowed, the beeping of the monitor, the pulsing of the ventilator, the dripping of the IV monitor doling out fluid and medicine into Cassie's arm.

My energy streamed through my arms and entered Cassie. My will to bring her back urged me on, telling me I could do this; I could save her. But the energy continued to flow, taking much longer than the others. My confidence wavered as my strength began to falter. Doubt tickled my mind, warning me to be aware. Too much energy passed to another might not leave enough for me.

A movement caught my attention though I didn't look away from Cassie. A figure stepped to the other side of Cassie and stood very still, watching.

Ignoring the newcomer, I kept my focus on my objective, pushing every ounce of power into her to bring her back. Just when I thought it useless, my flow surged, increasing in the rate it entered Cassie. Without warning, the excess energy backlashed into me and sent me sprawling across the floor.

I slid into the cabinets with a bang, shaking my head to clear the sparkling fireworks before my eyes.

Gingerly, I got to my feet and looked over at Cassie, not feeling the least bit confident I'd accomplished my goal. I froze as my eyes touched on Gabe, the intruder, standing over Cassie. He looked up from her face, smiled at me, and then turned back to look at Cassie again. I followed his gaze to see Cassie grinning at me, her eyes bright and alive. Alive.

I rushed over, taking her hand and holding it tightly between mine.

"I thought we lost you for a minute." I smiled, tears rolling down my cheeks.

"I did too." Her smile was tired. "Thanks to you two, I guess you'll be putting up with me for a while longer."

I looked over at Gabe, his expression torn. "We need to talk." He motioned to the hall with a lean of his head.

"I'll be right back." I inched closer and whispered to Cassie.

She nodded, letting go of my hand as I walked around the bed, following Gabe through the curtain.

I opened my mouth to speak and Gabe put a finger to his lips, silencing me. I stopped, raising an eyebrow in question. He motioned to a room across from Cassie's bed and we stepped inside as he closed the door behind us.

Racks lined the walls with supplies and I realized we were standing in a storage room. I turned to him, crossing my arms in preparation for what he was going to say.

"You shouldn't have tried to heal her without more experience," he frowned.

What did he know about me healing people? I clenched my jaw tightly.

"Did you hear me?" he whispered, an edge to his voice.

"Yeah, I heard you."

"If I didn't come in when I did, you might be lying in the bed next to her, both of you dead."

"Right." I shook my head. "I've done this before."

"You shouldn't have." He glared.

"What do you know about what I can and can't do?"

"Britt, listen, I know you're a half angel and you want to help your friends when you can, but you don't have enough power to heal someone who just got touched by a soulless."

"Half angel?"

"Yes, half angel. Don't you know what you are?"

"I thought I did."

"Ha, yeah, right. I've seen plenty of you 'h-a's'."

"So how do you make an 'h-a'?"

"You don't make an h-a, they're born. We call them half angels because they're part angel, and also part human."

"I was made," I told him stubbornly, determined to shake the confidence from his expression.

His eyes narrowed. "No." He shook his head. "Not possible."

"I'm telling you it is."

"Who made you then?" He folded his arms across his chest.

"An Eternal."

His eyes shot wide and his mouth dropped open. He tried to talk, his mouth moved but nothing came out.

"It's true." I nodded.

"How?"

"First off, are you an angel?" I asked.

"Yes, an Avenging Angel." He nodded.

"A what?" Panic raced through me as Allister's warning about Avenging Angels surged into my mind and I kicked myself for my stupidity.

"Avenging Angel. I show up when something, or in this case, someone is disrupting the natural flow of things. This Eternal going around taking Guardian Angels is messing up the natural balance and I'm here to put a stop to it."

"Oh." I chose my next words carefully. "So you're here to kill Kendal."

"Kendal, who's Kendal?"

"The Eternal who hurt Cassie."

"You know him?" Gabe gasped.

"Unfortunately." I shrugged.

"Is he the Eternal who changed you?"

"No, another Eternal did." I looked away, trying not to give anything away.

"There's more than one Eternal in Grand Rapids?"

"Not now, but at one time, there were …five."

"Five," he shouted, then remembered where we were and whispered, "Where are they now?"

"I'm not sure I should tell you. I don't want you to hurt them."

"Why do you think I would hurt them?"

"Don't you kill all Eternals you find?"

"Who told you that?" he laughed, his features softening.

"Uh, one of them."

"I'm here to remove the Eternal doing the harm. If the others are functioning within the boundaries set by the council, I have no interest in them." He looked at me, his expression unaccusing, and then it began to shift the longer he stared at me. "How did this Eternal 'create' you?"

"Kendal took my guardian angel and the other Eternal tried to heal me. He did, but this is the result." I shrugged, downplaying Allister's infraction.

"Can I place my hands on you?" he asked.

"Didn't ask before." I frowned, not feeling playful.

"That was just a massage. This is a little more intimate."

"Whoa, I'm not sure I like the sound of that." I put my hands up defensively, backing away.

"Nothing like that," he blushed. "I need to touch you to see what you really are. Your aura says h-a, but if you speak the truth..."

"I do," I said evenly, knowing there was no way of hiding what I was.

"This will show me." He looked at me expectantly.

"Fine," I sighed, putting my hands to my side.

He took a step closer, placing one hand on my forehead and the other to my heart. I jumped a little when he placed his hand on my chest, then stood as still as possible.

He concentrated, eyes closed, lips pressed together, his breath blowing steady against my hair.

I stared up at his face. Did I want to know if I was this new mix, or had I accepted that I was an Eternal?

He gasped slightly and I studied his face for a reaction, but his expression stayed the same. He exhaled heavily, pulling away, turning from me to lean against a shelf of sheets.

"What?" I stepped closer, putting a hand on his shoulder.

"I've never felt anything like it," he whispered, not looking at me.

"What, what is it? You can't just study me and not tell me what you found."

"Nothing."

"Don't keep the truth from me. I demand you tell me."

"Nothing," he repeated.

"I heard that, now tell me what I am."

He turned around, his normally glowing face, dull and pale. "Britt, you have no sign of either a guardian angel or a soul as separate entities like they should be. They're combined somehow. It's as if you have no soul or guardian angel, but a combined essence of both," he said, looking into my eyes with sympathy.

"I knew that." I shrugged.

"You did?"

"Yeah, Alli...the other Eternals told me I didn't have a soul, like them."

"But you still have some of the guardian angel's essence in you too."

"What does that mean?"

"It means you are part Eternal, soulless and destined to walk the earth forever and..."

"And what?" I grabbed his arm.

"You have a guardian angel within you."

"I can't, can I?"

"Not normally," he agreed.

"I'm not normal. No part of this is normal."

"Britt, you are definitely not normal. I sense the angel side in you, but when I look closer, you have the Eternal side as well. I have never encountered something like this before."

"Is it bad?"

"I can't say. I doubt the Eternal Council will approve and I'm not willing to say the Angel Senate will like it either."

"Angel Senate, you mean the leaders of the angels?"

He nodded.

"Does that mean I'm damned on both sides of the line?"

"Kind of," he laughed.

"I'm glad you find this so amusing." I glared.

"I'm sorry." He sobered. "But seeing you, I understand you pose no threat to our side. I advise you live your life…"

"Which is forever, now," I interrupted angrily.

"Yes, live your everlasting life as quietly as possible. Don't draw the attention of either side."

"You're not going to tell?"

"I see no need." His soft expression begged confidence.

"Thank you." I wrapped my arms around him, squeezing him as tightly as I could.

"You're welcome." He gasped at the exuberant squeeze.

"Now, you say you know this Kendal who tried to kill your friend?" he said, pulling away from my embrace.

"He kidnapped me once."

"He what? No, never mind. I don't want to know." He raised a hand to stop my response.

"He's in love with me. He attacked her to hurt me when he realized I could never love him back."

"You have the strangest acquaintances," he sighed.

"Tell me about it."

"I think we need to keep an eye on your other two girlfriends while you and I hunt him down. Do you have any idea where he is or where he might strike again?"

"I thought you were the expert here?" I questioned.

"I am, I mean, I can handle this, but I thought you might know his tendencies so I can pin point where he might be."

"I might be able to help with that," I said, biting my lip.

"And how would you do that?"

"When I dream, I see through Kendal's eyes."

"Oh no you don't," Gabe gasped in horror.

"Yep, unfortunately true." I shrugged, shaking my head.

"We can use that to find him tonight and you'll be rid of us all."

I nodded, agreeing with what he said in principle, but knowing I had many more issues to deal with than just Kendal. Bastion still lurked out there, somewhere, looking to bring me to Greece and condemn Allister to death. I don't know how Gabe would react to that, so I pressed my lips together and went along with the plan to eliminate at least one of my tormentors. It was a start.

Chapter 25

After checking to be sure Cassie continued to recover with her parents around her, we left to find the other girls. We didn't need to go far. They sat worrying in the waiting area off the emergency room.

As Gabe and I walked in, Trish and Elisa leapt to their feet and threw their arms around my neck.

"Britt, you scared us to death," Elisa cried.

"Are you alright?" Trish said, pulling back to look at me, my tattered clothing draped over me, covering me the best they could. She looked questioningly over at Gabe.

"Yeah, fine," I sighed.

"How's Cassie?" Elisa asked.

"She's going to be okay." I looked at Gabe as he pursed his lips. I didn't let on that he had saved her. "We need to stay together tonight, hopefully keep Kendal from coming after either of you."

Elisa and Trish exchanged scared looks and then turned back to me and Gabe.

"What's your story?" Trish asked Gabe.

"Just here to help."

She turned back to me with a curious look.

"Gabe is a …friend. He can help," I explained.

"Fine, if you don't want to fill us in, fine." Trish gave a curt nod.

"Where are we going to do this?" Elisa asked.

"My house, I guess," I said.

"Let's go." Trish motioned with her hand.

We walked out the emergency door past the ambulances and into the parking lot where the Jeep sat. I climbed in, noticing Kendal's handprints on the hood. I'd forgotten how strong Eternals were. The memory of Allister attacking the black Mercedes in Canada came to me and I shuttered. Kendal could have easily killed me this morning.

I looked up at the sun already beginning to drop low in the western sky. "How long have we been here?"

"All day," Elisa said.

I turned, looking for Gabe as he climbed into an old Ford Focus, rusted and dented.

"I'll meet you there in a few minutes." He closed the door. The car shook as the engine turned over and he chugged out of the parking lot accompanied by a cloud of blue smoke.

"Kind of cozy with him, aren't you?" Trish said.

"Not like that, but if we want to stop Kendal, we need him," I said, looking at her.

"For what?" Elisa asked.

"You better ask him." I shrugged.

Trish started the Jeep and we sped out of the lot towards the girls' houses to collect their things and then make our way over to my house.

Gabe sat parked behind Allister's black Camaro. His car looked pretty lame next to the muscle car.

He stepped out as we pulled up, grabbed some of the girl's bags and carried them towards the house.

"What about my parents?" I asked, having temporarily forgotten about them.

"Taken care of," Gabe smiled.

"What did you do?" I gasped, assuming the worst.

"Nothing bad," he chuckled. "Your Dad has some issues at the plant. Something to do with machinery mysteriously not working." He smiled, holding up a large bolt in his hand.

"And Mom?"

"Cousin Hazel happened to need a ride to bridge club tonight," he grinned.

"She lives in Keewatin," I breathed in amazement.

"I bet Mom will be spending the night then."

"You're devious." I laughed, suddenly feeling light.

"Whatever it takes," he said, shrugging.

We hauled the bags into the house and up to my room. I pulled out some air mattresses and we inflated them, spreading them out on the floor. By the time the beds for Elisa and Trish had blankets and pillows piled on them the sun had dipped behind the trees.

"So, what's up with you?" Trish said to Gabe. She'd been stewing about it as we got things organized. I'd felt it.

"I'm here to help," he shrugged again.

"But what are you?" she pressed, needing answers.

"What do you mean?"

"Don't play dumb." Trish put her hands on her hips. "Are you an Eternal, an angel, what?"

Gabe stared at me aghast. "Don't you keep anything secret?"

"I didn't say a word, really."

"Hey, leave Britt out of this." Trish stepped towards him defiantly. "We know about her, we know about Kendal, we know about Allister, Angelina and their parents…"

As Trish started down that road, I rushed across the room towards her, my words trying to come out fast enough, but arriving too late to salvage the situation.

"No, Trish stop," I cried, falling over one of the air mattresses before I could reach her. I rolled over onto my back, resigned that the proverbial cat was out of the bag.

"Allister, Angelina, the Parks?" Gabe looked down at me in shock.

I nodded looking up at him, upside down, from the mattress.

"Why didn't you tell me?"

"Need to know; I didn't think you needed." I pursed my lip and raised my eyebrows.

"Ah." He threw his hands up and stormed from the room.

"What's his problem?" Trish asked as Elise stared in silence.

"Gabe is an Avenging Angel sent here to eliminate Kendal for disrupting the natural balance of things." I raced out the door after Gabe.

I found him sitting on the deck out back. He stared up at the night's sky, entranced in thought, as I slid into a chair next to him.

"I'm sorry for keeping it from you," I whispered.

"A little late now." He frowned down at me.

"It should never be too late to admit I'm wrong."

"True, but did you have to blurt out those last facts to your girlfriends?"

"You heard that?"

"We hear very well."

"What's the big deal about the Parks?"

"They are something like royalty in the supernatural world," he sighed.

"Like king and queen type royalty?"

"Yeah, like king and queen type royalty," he mocked.

"How am I supposed to know that? They never said anything about being royalty."

"Britt, Victor and Jennavia are the oldest Eternals in existence and have maintained excellent relations with our kind for millennia."

"Good to know, so why is there a problem?"

"Victor and Jennavia are being held in Greece, along with Allister, for doing something forbidden of all Eternals."

"I did know that," I mumbled, looking away.

"Then you should know, we have been ordered to capture the 'indiscretion' Allister created if we encounter it."

"Oh," I said, everything becoming clear, crystal clear.

"Yeah, 'oh.'"

"So, are you taking me in marshal?" I tried to joke, putting my hands out for him to handcuff me.

"Britt, it's not funny." Gabe wasn't playing.

"I know, but if I don't laugh about it, I'd cry."

"I'm in a serious predicament," he moaned, rubbing his face.

"And to think, I'm only worried about my own fate. How self-centered of me."

He blinked at me for a few seconds then slapped his hands on his legs. "First things first." He stood. "We need to stop Kendal. I'll decide what to do with you later."

"I'm right here. I wish you wouldn't talk about deciding my fate as if I was a chair or some other piece of furniture you need to rearrange at your convenience."

"Sorry." He appeared contrite. "Habit from working alone."

We walked back upstairs, the girls staring at Gabe dubiously until he threw up his hands.

"What? What? Ask your questions, but stop staring at me like I have two heads."

"Nothing," Trish said, turning away.

"You're really an angel?" Elisa asked.

"Yep, and here to stop Kendal. That's all I can share really."

The girls nodded and looked to me to elaborate.

"Gabe is going to track Kendal when I make a connection with him in my dream tonight," I explained.

"Then why are we here?" Trish asked.

"For your safety," Gabe stated and the girls turned to him. "Kendal is angry with Britt. He exposed himself in daylight. That was both reckless and very careless. It proves he is not thinking clearly when it comes to her."

"So he might go nuts again and come after Trish or me," Elisa said her eyes lighting up with understanding.

"Exactly," Gabe agreed. "We will use it to our advantage."

"So just hang out here, stay out of the way, and let me and Gabe stop Kendal," I said.

"I guess we can handle that." Trish shrugged.

"Good, let's get started." Gabe motioned for me to get into bed.

I climbed between the covers and pulled the blankets up to my chin. I looked at three sets of eyes staring back at me, making it nearly impossible to relax.

"Humph," I grunted.

"Oh, yeah, right," Trish laughed, reaching over to turn off the light and get into her bed.

I heard Elisa scrunch on her mattress for a while and then go silent.

I lay staring at the dark ceiling, feeling Gabe's eyes on me, not able to shake the questions running through my mind. Would he turn me in? The thought kept rolling through my mind.

After several minutes, I let out a big sigh. "I'm sorry. I can't get to sleep with you looking at me."

"I can help with that." He moved closer, his shadow easing over in the darkness.

"What, so now you're part sandman?"

"Sort of. Didn't you know we're all related?"

I could hear the smile in his voice and smiled as well. I felt his warm hand touch my forehead and gasped at the sudden contact.

"Sorry," he whispered.

"It's okay."

His hand soothed my thoughts, sending all the doubts to the deep recesses, leaving only the happy feelings I had. Strangely, they were mostly of Gabe. His smile, his touch, his protectiveness, and his attempt at loyalty as well.

I fell asleep and searched a neighborhood through Kendal's eyes instantly. Like always, he didn't seem to sense me with him, but I suspected he knew I'd be with him sooner or later. The houses didn't appear familiar and I felt relief even though I knew his intent. Again, the uneasy feeling of guilt filled me as I felt relief because he would kill a stranger as opposed to someone I knew. I couldn't help it, I considered myself lucky I wouldn't witness a friend's death.

We passed house after house, we were in Duluth. I recognized a park I played baseball at during the summer. He sat down on a bench in the park, leaned back and my view of the surroundings skewed upwards.

"Nice of you to meet me." A voice spun our vision to a dark figure standing next to a tree, blending in with the dark shadows of the trunk.

"You said it was imperative we talk," Kendal replied.

"Indeed it is," the vaguely familiar voice said.

"You came alone?"

"You said to, else you wouldn't show." Bastion stepped from the shadows.

My blood ran cold. Bastion was only 90 miles from here. I wanted to scream, although I knew from previous experience no one would hear me.

"So, what do you want?" Kendal asked rudely.

"Always were a cut to the chase kind of guy, huh Kendal?"

"Yeah, short and sweet, that's my motto. What do you want?"

"You know what I want."

"Britt," Kendal whispered my name.

292

"Is that her name? Doesn't matter. Once I get her back to Greece, she'll cease to exist in short succession to Allister."

"Why must she be killed?" Kendal asked.

I found myself surprised by the sadness in his voice.

"She's not natural. She was never meant to be. She is an abomination."

"You don't know her," Kendal defended. "She is beautiful, honorable, and loyal..." his thoughts trailed off.

"Now I see why you let her escape. You're in love with her."

"I don't deny it."

"You should, for your family's sake."

"Your threats are useless against me now."

"So you think you've gotten your loved ones out of my reach, do you?"

"Being aware of you is all they needed. They are quite adept at protecting themselves. They need no coddling from me."

"Very well, let's not talk threats. Let's talk duty; responsibility."

"I feel none of it. I go where I want, do what I want. That is my way. You can go your own way now. I'm done talking."

My view of Bastion changed as Kendal stood.

"No, I'm not done talking." Bastion motioned with his arms.

Two large men walked up on either side of Kendal, standing ready for any movement.

"Why do you have such hatred for the Parks?" Kendal asked.

"My reasons are my own," Bastion spat. *"Where is she?"*

"I don't know."

One of the men swung. The hit landed with a thud as Kendal gasped and my view lurched to the ground. Kendal looked up and I saw Bastion standing over us, his arms folded across his chest.

"I will ask you again, and you will tell me where she is. Else this can go on all night."

I felt the telltale tingling of Kendal shimmering, but pain racked me as the ground rushed up to my eyes. I couldn't see anything but darkness.

"You think we didn't prepare for that?" Bastion laughed. *"We placed shimmer sentries to prevent you from leaving too soon. Again, where is she?"*

"Thank you gentlemen." A voice came from the darkness and Kendal turned his eyes towards it.

A tickle of recognition touched my mind. That voice, whose voice, why did I know it?
Gabe stepped into the dull glow from the security lighting surrounding the field. I wanted to scream for him to leave, to get out of there. He planned to meet up with Kendal, not Bastion and two of his henchmen.

"This doesn't concern you," Bastion growled.

"Oh, but it does." Gabe sauntered forward. *"This Eternal has violated many people and must answer for his crimes."*

"That is but minor compared to the information he possesses. We will leave him to you after we extract what we need."

"Sorry, but I need to be sure he is alive to link all the crimes to him. We wouldn't want another Eternal running around breaking the law and not know it."

"I assure you, he will not be causing any more problems for you. We will see to it," Bastion said through clenched teeth.

"Again I must apologize for disagreeing. My law comes first and foremost. You may wish to contact the senate to ask for a meeting with him while he is in our custody." Gabe didn't back down.

"No," Bastion shouted, sensing he was losing.

One of the men hurled himself at Gabe, but the angel moved so quickly the man landed on the ground in a heap where Gabe once stood.

The other man jumped from behind Gabe, ending up in the same jumbled pile the first had landed in.

Bastion attacked head on, following Gabe as he backpedaled easily and then stopped abruptly for some unknown reason. Bastion's collision with him took Gabe by surprise, making for an awkward impact. The Eternal veered to one side, stumbled to the ground, and rolled into a metallic box sitting on the ground.

Gabe approached Kendal as I watched through the Eternal's eyes. The tingling started again, but this time the pain didn't come. This time after it passed, we lay in a parking lot. I could see tires and Kendal stood next to his silver Mercedes. He slipped behind the steering wheel and we soon raced along the road as a green sign announced "Grand Rapids 75 miles."

I woke to find Gabe sitting on the edge of my bed, looking down at me, disgust furrowing his forehead.

"Are you alright?" I asked, sitting up.

"Fine, you?"

"Yeah, but Bastion and those other two, they're so close." I said. The name changed his expression to disgust.

"You know him too?" his voice rose until he shouted the last word.

Trish and Elisa woke at Gabe's raised voice. Trish clicked on the light and they turned to look at our confrontation on my bed.

"He had Kendal kidnap me. Only Kendal couldn't hand me over. Bastion's looking for me. He needs me to prove what Allister did. They intend to kill Allister for creating me."

Trish and Elisa gasped in their beds, their eyes wide as they stared at me.

Gabe glared at me, his eyes seeing something in the distance, something not in this room. He focused on me as his face turned glum.

"Britt, there is no happy ending here, I'm afraid." He pursed his lips. "I believe Allister is lost to you."

"Don't say that." I slapped him across the face.

His head snapped back from the blow and the girls gasped, still he kept staring into my eyes.

"I don't want to hurt you, but you must see Allister will never return to you, and you can never go to him, else they kill him due to your existence."

I slid my knees to my chin, wrapping my arms around my shins, and leaning my head against the tops of my knees. I needed Allister. More than I'd ever needed anyone in my life. The hope of him returning, the only reason I was able to keep going.

I looked up at Gabe, my eyes blurring with tears.

"I'm sorry." he bowed his head and walked out of the room.

I leaned my head down against my knees, my crying turning into uncontrollable sobs. I felt two sets of arms wrap around my shoulders, comforting me. I still had them, my three amigos. Although I nearly lost one today, they would always be there for me.

Chapter 26

After crying myself out I went looking for Gabe. For some reason I knew he wouldn't be far. I found him on the deck again, sitting in a chair, staring up at the stars. I sat down next to him and looked up at the early morning sky. We sat together, not speaking. I felt comforted by his presence.

"What do I do now?" I asked.

"Only you can decide that."

"But how?"

"You must decide what you want more: to see Allister again or to keep him alive."

"That's a no-brainer. I want him alive."

"You've already decided then."

"I guess I have."

We sat in silence for a long while, the pain in my heart building as I sat, pushing, trying to spill out of me.

"Why didn't you tell me you were in love with him?" Gabe broke the silence and the surge of pain and guilt building inside me as well.

"Would it matter?"

"Maybe, a little?"

"How?"

"Then I wouldn't have allowed myself to develop an attachment to you."

I pulled my gaze from the sky to him with a jerk. "What?"

"Britt, there is something about you. Something drawing love to you. I felt the tug the first time we met."

I blushed, not knowing what to say.

"You know I have to eliminate Kendal."

"Yes," I nodded.

"If I can do it before Bastion catches up with him, you may be able to stay here and live a happy life."

"Humph," I grunted with a shrug. Happy? Happy without Allister? Not a likely scenario.

"But if he discovers your location, you must flee or risk being brought to Greece ensuring Allister's and your own destruction as well as everyone around you." He looked over at me and our eyes met. His anguish at his mission filled me with sadness. I believed my death would bring Gabe pain.

"I want you to live, Britt," he said, confirming my suspicion.

"I'm not sure I can without Allister," I admitted honestly.

"Please, for your friends' sake, your parents' sake, and for," he paused, "my sake."

There, he said it. He wanted me to live for him. I felt guilty. Guilty over wanting to live. A small part of me wanted to live for Gabe. Wondered what life would be like with him in it. Being taken care of by an angel intrigued me until I pulled myself out of it. He barely knew me, I barely knew him. How could feelings be building already? Was I that fickle? Maybe this affection thing worked both ways? Maybe my feelings developed for those who deeply cared about me as well? What else would explain my desire to help Kendal break his addiction to angels?

"What about the order to capture me if given the opportunity?" I asked.

"More of a suggestion than an order." He lifted a shoulder. "Once Allister is sentenced, the desire to find you will become less urgent."

"Then what?"

"I rid us of Kendal and you can go about your life as before."

I put my head in my hands; the thought of Allister being alive and in prison a much better option than gone for eternity.

"Do we try to find Kendal again tonight?"

"I feel it is our best option."

We went back inside to explain our plan to the girls. With Kendal still out there, we needed to stay together until Gabe had the opportunity to eliminate him as a threat.

To our amazement, Mom called home to tell me she was staying in Keewatin with Hazel for a few more days. Just as I hung up with her, Dad called and said he'd been called away for a meeting in Chicago so he'd be gone for a few days as well. Something had told him to bring a bag to the plant the night before and he planned to leave by corporate jet from the airport without coming home.

Trish, Elisa and I ran up to the hospital while Gabe saw to other matters. Cassie perked up when she saw us and she looked very well.

"Did you get him?" she asked.

"Who?" Trish said.

"Kendal, weren't you going after him last night?"

The three of us looked at each other, confused, and then back at Cassie.

"Gabe stopped by last night and told me I wouldn't have to worry about Kendal again," Cassie explained.

"You know about Gabe?" I asked.

"Britt, when you're touched by an angel, you know it," she smiled.

"Yeah, I guess you do." I grinned at her.

"So, did you get him?" Cassie raised her brows.

"No, afraid not." I shrugged.

"We're, uh, they're going to try again tonight," Elisa said.

"I hope you get him." Cassie shivered. "Knowing firsthand what it feels like to have Kendal touch you makes me sad for all the people who had their angels taken by him."

"Yeah," I sighed, recalling every guardian angel Kendal pulled from a person while I watched, helpless, through his eyes.

We headed back home after lunch and pulled up as Gabe stepped out of his car. He came over to the Jeep, looking down at Kendal's handprints on the hood. Reaching up, he put his hands on the dents and they popped out.

"Thanks." Trish smiled, getting out of the Jeep and walking towards the house with Elisa as I hung back, waiting for Gabe.

"So now you're a body man?" I smirked.

"I have many talents you don't know about," he flirted.

"So it seems."

"Have you given much thought to what we discussed last night?" he asked as we walked up the sidewalk.

"Yeah." I nodded.

"And?"

"I won't do anything to put Allister in danger. If I have to live without him…," my voice cracked.

"You will have to," he said as we walked up to the house.

"Then I will do whatever it takes to keep him alive."

"Fair enough."

He opened the door for me and we went inside. We all sat around watching TV the rest of the day, waiting for night to come. When it finally arrived, we took our places in my room and I let Gabe put me to sleep again.

I went to Kendal immediately, seeing the houses and the trees pass by as he walked quickly through the neighborhood. I tried to read any sign telling me where he hunted, nothing stood out.

A movement off to our left drew Kendal's attention and he turned. I could see a man heading down an alley between two older office buildings. I still couldn't place the neighborhood as Kendal followed the man into the alley. As we came closer, Kendal froze and then he flattened himself against the wall of the building.

The man turned abruptly and Bastion's face smiled back at us, the streetlight reflecting off his silver tooth.

"I'm getting closer," Bastion sneered.

I felt the tingling and we shimmered to another location. I lost contact with Kendal and woke in my bed, screaming.

"You're okay, you're okay." Gabe held me in his comforting arms as Trish and Elisa looked on curiously.

"No, I'm not." I pushed him away. "Bastion found Kendal again, right away."

"Did they capture him?" Gabe sat up straighter.

"No, he shimmered and then I woke up."

"Did you recognize Kendal's location?"

"No, but I think it might be another town nearby." I looked at Gabe with fear pulsing through me.

"Not good." Gabe turned away.

"What do we do now?" I asked.

"We need to get to Kendal before Bastion," he stated the obvious as he paced, hand to his chin in thought.

I looked at Trish and Elisa, their faces full of worry. If Bastion found me I felt certain he would try to eliminate anyone who knew about him, about Eternals. Allister told me their kind demanded secrecy. Bastion would kill off my friends to keep his secrets.

As I stared at Trish and Elisa, I decided what I needed to do. I didn't have a choice. I needed to protect them.

"What are you thinking?" Gabe said, leaning down so he could look into my eyes.

"Nothing."

"You're not a good liar, Britt," he sighed.

"I'm tired." I turned away and pulled the covers up over me as I lay down.

303

The next morning Trish, Elisa, and I headed off to school. At least we wanted Gabe to think that. As we got ready in the bathroom, I filled the girls in on what I needed to do today. Find Kendal.

They looked at me like I'd lost my mind. I insisted I hadn't, that this was a good idea.

"I need to find him and see if he can disappear."

"What about Gabe?" Trish asked.

"Why don't you let him take care of Kendal?" Elisa agreed.

"Because he hasn't so far," I said. "And Bastion is getting closer. If he finds me, he'll take me to Greece so they can sentence Allister to death."

"And you too," Trish added.

Elisa put a hand to her mouth, her eyes open wide.

"Who told you that?" I asked.

"So it's true?" Trish said.

"Yes." I shook my head knowing Gabe must have filled them in.

They didn't have any more air in their lungs to make additional sounds and they didn't need it; their expressions of horror said it all.

We headed out, driving around in the Jeep to every location in town I'd seen through Kendal's eyes over the last month. We cruised by Allister's house on a hunch, it being the last place I saw him.

We drove past, slowing so I could look between the houses. Nothing. I motioned for Trish to take the side road by the house and we crept past. Nothing. I noticed the alley and I pointed. She gave a nod and pulled down the dusty road. We passed the detached garage, nearly as large as my house, when I noticed movement in a window over the garage.

"Stop," I shouted.

Trish jerked the Jeep to a stop, looking at me questioningly.

"I saw something up there." I pointed to one of the windows over the garage.

"Shouldn't we get Gabe?" Elisa questioned.

"No, I need to do this myself," I said.

Elisa and Trish began to get out, but I put a hand on each of their arms, stopping them.

"Stay here. He hasn't hurt me yet. I can't say that about my friends." I stared at each until they nodded. "I'll be right back."

I hopped out of the Jeep moving around to a side door. I grabbed the handle and gave it a twist, locked. I pressed against it with my shoulder. No good. I stepped back, looking up at the window where I noticed the movement.

"Kendal," I shouted. "I know you're up there. I need to talk to you."

I heard a click of the lock and walked over to try the door again. The handle turned and the door swung in. I stepped into the darkness broken up by beams of light filtering in through the garage door windows. Taking the stairs leading to the second level I stumbled slightly as my eyes adjusted to the darkness. Finally reaching the door at the top of the stairs standing ajar, I pushed it in and it squeaked under my touch.

Kendal stood looking out a window as I entered, not bothering to look at me. "To what do I owe this pleasure?" he asked.

"I need to talk to you."

"So you said. Then talk."

"I need a favor," I said, the word catching in my throat.

"Oh really?" He turned to glare at me. "Why should I do anything for you?"

"Because you love me." I played the only card I had up my sleeve, maybe not the best opening move.

"Ha, I think that approach is a bit worn out, don't you?"

"I guess." I shrugged. "But have your feelings for me changed?" Touché.

He glared at me hard, his lip curling up cynically. "What's the favor?"

"I want you to kill me."

His face lost all muscle control and went slack. His mouth gaped open and his eyes stared so wide I could see the red sockets around them.

"You what?" he whispered.

"I. Want. You. To. Kill. Me."

He put a hand over his eyes and then ran it down his entire face, his mouth still hanging open when he finished. "No, no you don't."

"Yes, I do. I don't want to live without Allister anymore and I don't want to be the reason Allister is killed." I tried to sound confident.

"Then come away with me," he pleaded.

"What about Bastion?"

"Screw Bastion."

I pressed my lips together and exhaled heavily through my nose.

"We can keep ahead of Bastion," Kendal offered.

"Like you've been doing?"

"You eavesdropping again, Britt?"

"Not by choice."

"So you know he's getting closer."

"That's why I'm here. Sooner or later he'll get you to tell him or he'll find me some other way. Either way, it can't happen."

"I'll go away, lead him off far away from here," Kendal reasoned.

"Do you really think he'll give up, even if you're gone? He already knows the general area to look. It's just a matter of time."

"But Britt, to kill you, you're asking too much."

"Am I? Am I really? You took part of my guardian angel from me and started this. I'm offering you the rest. Doesn't that appeal to you?"

He licked his lips. "I can't lie, it does, but ..."

"I know you're not as bad as you seem." The sincerity behind my statement surprised me. "You're out of control, but now you can do something good. You can make a difference."

"By saving Allister?" he hissed.

"Yes, by saving Allister. For me."

He spun back to the window, shaking his head. "When?" he asked, not turning back.

"Tonight, at my house."

"What about your angel friend?"

"I will be alone. You kill me and run. Don't stop running because I know Gabe will come after you... forever."

"Got him wrapped around your finger too, huh?" Kendal glanced over his shoulder at me.

"I need you to do this and then be gone so Bastion has no reason to come to Grand Rapids, ever," I continued, ignoring his jibe.

"I will do it, but I do it for you, not Allister."

"I know." I walked to the door, stopping as he started to speak.

"You must love him a lot." He looked at me, sadness in his eyes.

"More than I can explain." I nodded. I walked down the stairs as my cell phone vibrated. I opened it up, seeing a text from Angelina, the only one I'd gotten in days.

Allister wants me to tell you he loves you, no matter what happens. If you wouldn't be in peril, he would sacrifice his life to see you one more time.

I stopped on the stairs, contemplating going back and telling Kendal it was off. The thought of seeing Allister one more time before I died appealed to me, but I couldn't let my desires outweigh my love for him. With me gone he could live on and I would be where I should have been since that day on the river's edge, dead.

"Is he leaving?" Trish asked as I jumped into the Jeep.

"Yeah."

"For good, he's leaving for good?" Elisa couldn't hide her enthusiasm.

"For good. You don't need to sleep over anymore, unless you want to." I forced a smile. "Can you drop me off at home, I'm kind of tired?"

Gabe sat waiting on the hood of his car as we pulled up. He slid down and walked over as I jumped out. Trish pulled away and I waved.

"Not staying here tonight?" he asked.

"No, no need." I walked past him without stopping.

"Why is that?"

"I told Kendal to leave Grand Rapids."

"You what?"

"I told him to leave."

"And he listened to you?"

"Yep, sorry but you'll have to hunt him down on your own now."

"No problem, although I'm a little surprised he'd listen to you. Even if he is in love with you," he added when he caught my expression.

"So that's it." I stopped at the base of our porch steps and turned to him, extending my hand.

"What's it?" he looked at my hand as if it was some hideous tentacle.

"You can go and chase down Kendal on your own. I'm done with it."

"You don't care he nearly killed Cassie?"

"Of course I do, but I have to get him out of here so Bastion doesn't find me and hurt everyone I love."

He stared at me, incredulous, then turned and stormed off. He slammed his car door and sped, as much as a Focus can speed, down the street.

Chapter 27

I rushed inside. Details, details, I needed to get the details for tonight set so I didn't forget anything. I started by taking out some paper and sitting down at my desk.

Dear Three Amigos,
I know you will be upset with my decision, but I hope someday you will understand I do this for love. Love of you and Allister. Bastion is closing in and if he finds me, he will surely want to eliminate you three to keep his secrets.
I do this for Allister, to keep him alive, not giving Bastion any evidence to use against Allister to put him to death. He created me out of love and I am giving up my life out of love as well. I don't regret the past months he allowed me to feel alive again. I treasure every minute the three of us spent together, time I never could have had without Allister's gift. So please, don't cry for me, my life is what I always hoped for. I have the love of someone I love with all my heart and I have the love and friendship of the best friends any girl could wish for.

Eternally yours,
Britt.

I wiped the tears from my eyes and cheeks, dabbed them off the paper, and folded it in half. I planned to ask Kendal to leave this at Trish's house afterwards.

The rest of the evening I gathered some things together, placing them out for easy discovery. Lockets, rings, and other jewelry I deemed precious. I held the locket I picked out for Angelina on that fateful shopping trip to Duluth, in front of my face. The intertwined hearts with the words *sisters forever* gleamed back at me. I sadly set it on my dresser. I took the ring I bought for Allister and rubbed my thumb against the shiny surface of the black onyx stone set in gold. On the back it said: *Eternally Yours, Britt.* I set the ring next to Angelina's necklace and turned away, not wanting to feel the agony looking at them brought me anymore.

I stared out my window waiting for Kendal as the sun set, bringing my last day to a close. Much calmer than I thought I'd be.

"So you're really going to go through with it?" Kendal's voice came from behind me.

I jumped out of my chair, spinning to face him. "Yes."

"Allister is a lucky man to have you love him so deeply you're willing to sacrifice your own life to preserve his."

"I'm the lucky one," I said truthfully.

"Are you ready for this?"

"One thing." I held up my letter to the girls. "Could you leave this at Trish's house once it's over?"

"Now I'm a delivery boy?" he raised an eyebrow.

I looked at him, unblinking.

"Fine." He took it and shoved it into the front pocket of his jeans.

"Okay." I stood, inhaling deeply.

"I need one thing first," he said.

I looked up at him, my nerves creeping closer to the surface, threatening to break free and shatter my stoic facade. "What?"

"I want a kiss."

"Huh?"

"A kiss. I want you to kiss me first. Then I'll do it."

I looked away from his expectant gaze. Did I want the last lips I touched to be those of a killer? My killer?

"If you don't, I won't." He sensed my hesitation.

"Fine," I sighed. "But just a little one. Don't get any big ideas." I narrowed my eyes at him and he nodded.

Uneasy, I stepped close to him. His breath brushed against my forehead as he stared down at me. I looked up. His eyes were dark and hard, nothing like Allister's brilliant blue. I closed my eyes, trying to push away the reality of who I kissed, thinking only of Allister. His lips touched mine, soft and gentle, not like I expected. They pressed harder against mine, his passion pushing into me; his desire washing over me. If it were anyone else maybe it would be pleasant, enjoyable, but the knowledge that the lips pressing mine belonged to Kendal sent any hints of those feelings into an empty abyss inside of me, never to have meaning or purpose.

After long enough, I opened my eyes and pulled away. Kendal stood motionless, eyes still closed, not willing to come out of his moment. He finally opened his eyes to look sadly at me.

He nodded. "Are you ready?"

"Yes," I whispered. I closed my eyes as Kendal drew his hand back to plunge into my chest and rip my heart from me. "I love you Allister," I whispered my last words to him.

"No," a voice cried out.

My eyes flew open in time to see Gabe shoot a bolt of energy from his hand into Kendal's chest. The Eternal convulsed and staggered backwards. Kendal regained his balance, lunging for me where I stood frozen in shock. As his thrusting hand grew closer to my chest another blast of energy hit him, driving him into the closet doors. The doors pulled off their hinges on impact and toppled to the floor with Kendal.

Gabe shoved me out of the way, rushing to the fallen Eternal as he struggled to get up. Gabe raised his fist over his head and it glowed with energy. With incredible force he sent it down, plunging it into Kendal's chest. Instead of pulling Kendal's heart out like I expected, Gabe kept his fist inside the man's chest. Kendal looked at me with eyes filled with sorrow. Even as he faced his end, I somehow knew he sympathized for me and what I needed to face now that he could no longer help me. I watched energy glowing within Kendal and then he shimmered and was gone, though not before a glowing mist-like vapor rose from him.

The vapor from the Eternal rose above me, settling over me as my back arched convulsively, my toes coming off the floor as I floated above the ground. The mist hovered above me for a moment and then drove straight into me violently. I screamed in pain. Slowly my body lowered back to the floor and I lay panting for air as the pain echoed through me.

Gabe knelt by my side. "Britt, what's wrong, did he hurt you?"

I couldn't respond, the pain so enveloped me my thoughts couldn't form into whole words. I gasped for air, my lungs burning. My breath came in short siphons instead of the large gulps I needed. A flash of light blinded me and then the room went dark. I lay still, the pain gone, but afraid I'd bring it back with any sudden movement. I looked around, trying to discern any identifiable shapes. A moan came from across the room and I saw a figure rise up. I knew Kendal was gone; it had to be Gabe.

Gabe inched closer on his hands and knees until he reached me. Putting a hand on my arm he leaned close enough I could see his face in the pale light filtering in through the window from the street below.

"What did you do?" I was crying.

"What?"

"Why did you stop him?" I sobbed. "He was my last chance to save Allister."

"What are you saying?" He leaned away from me.

"I *wanted* him to kill me, to keep Bastion from taking me to Greece and sentencing Allister to death," I said between jagged sobs.

Gabe didn't make a sound. Not a sigh, not a gasp, nothing to indicate he still sat there.

"Gabe?" I said when my cries subsided.

"I'm here," he answered.

"I'm sorry I disappointed you," I whispered.

"Is that what you think?" he inched closer to me so I could see his face again. Pain etched his features.

"Then what?"

"I'm saddened you would rather die to preserve Allister's life, than perhaps eventually live a life with me."

"Gabe," I started. He put a finger to my lips.

"I pray someday I will find a love as pure as Allister has."

I reached up, put a hand behind his head and pulled him down to me. Placing my head next to his, I wrapped my arms around him and held him tight.

When he pulled away there was a curious expression on his face.

"What?"

"Britt, you've changed."

"Changed?"

"Can I touch you?"

"Yeah." I gave him a "duh," look. Like he hadn't just been doing that very thing.

He reached over, touching my face and my chest as before. I couldn't see his face in the shadows as he leaned forward in concentration, but his body went rigid next to me. He pulled back, obscured in the darkness while I waited.

"Well," I prompted when he didn't volunteer any information.

"I don't know what to say."

"Just tell me the truth."

"I don't know the truth," he whispered.

Fear grabbed me, threatening to suffocate me. If an angel didn't know what I was, then who did? "I'm not an Eternal anymore?"

"Yes Britt, I still sense the Eternal in you, but..."

"But what?" I clenched my eyes closed, bracing for what was to follow.

"Your soul and your guardian angel are inside you again."

"My what?" My eyes flew open with shock.

"I sense your soul and guardian angel have fused into one like before, only now their parts are equal. You have the essence of the angel, though not the angel itself. And you still have the traits of the Eternal you were while your soul is intact."

"So what kind of freak does that make me?"

"An Eternal and an angel, I guess," Gabe spoke softly.

I couldn't speak. My attempt to protect Allister had backfired, changing me into the thing the Eternals condemned. A monstrosity, an abomination; something that never should be.

"Kill me," I pleaded.

"What?" Gabe said, his voice wavering.

"Kill me, I need to be gone from this world so Allister can live."

"I can't," Gabe answered, his voice hoarse.

"Just do it, for me. If you have any feelings for me, do this, please. I'm begging you."

"I didn't say I wouldn't kill you, though I definitely will not. What I said is I can't kill you."

"That makes absolutely no sense."

"Even if I was willing, I don't have the power to kill you."

"You killed Kendal and he's an Eternal. I'm part Eternal, so kill me," I argued.

"The way I killed Kendal won't work on you. My power enters an Eternal and fills the empty space where his soul should be. It expands and destroys him, from the inside out. That's how we kill Eternals."

"So, go ahead, do it to me," I pressured him.

316

"Britt, aren't you hearing anything I'm saying? You have a soul *and* the essence of a guardian angel. I can't kill you like other Eternals because there is no void. And in your case, you are also an angel. The only thing more impossible to kill than an Eternal, is an angel."

"But Kendal killed guardian angels," I argued.

"Eternals absorb guardian angels and, as you saw, when the Eternal is killed the angels are released."

"So all those people Kendal killed, their guardian angels are back to guide their souls to eternity?"

"That's right. All those lost souls are no longer lost. They will be guided by their guardian angels to the afterlife now, as it is meant to be."

"So you're saying I'm indestructible now?"

"No, but pretty near." Gabe shrugged.

"Aw," I moaned. My only chance and I blew it, no, more than blew it. I just became an indestructible piece of evidence where before I was merely a piece of evidence. I'd just condemned Allister to certain death.

"I know you wanted to save Allister, and you still can by staying ahead of Bastion. Draw him away from here to protect your family and friends," Gabe suggested.

Right. The most important thing now is to protect my friends and family. Plan one didn't work out the way I'd wanted, but plan two could still work. Even if it meant I needed to leave and never come back.

"What if Bastion finds out and still comes here when I'm gone?"

"We need him to see you and then give chase while we lead him away from here," Gabe explained.

"We?" I frowned.

"You didn't think I would leave you to face this alone, did you?"

"I guess I don't know the schedule of an Avenging Angel." I sniffed.

"I'm pretty busy, but I'll make time for you." He forced a grin.

"Okay then," I sighed laying back, collecting what rational thoughts I could. Maybe Gabe would show me what I could do as an angel before I left.

Chapter 28

I slept like a baby that night. With Kendal gone the nightmares of seeing angels sucked out of people stopped. I woke the next morning refreshed and happier than I'd been in a long time. My room showed no signs of the battle from the night before, thanks to Gabe. Saying a silent thank you, I strolled down to the kitchen as Mom and Dad sat at the kitchen table.

"Hey." I greeted them, happy to see their faces after I'd mentally said good bye.

"Don't you look happy this morning." Mom smiled.

"It seems you're looking forward to the weekend?" Dad asked.

"Yeah, sure." I grinned. Maybe it could have something to do with being whole again.

"What do you have planned?"

"I'm hanging out with a guy I met at ICC in Calculus class last week. His name is Gabe."

"It's good to see you moving on," Dad said and drew a glare from Mom. "Oh, I mean I like Allister and all, but if he isn't around, you shouldn't sit in your room and pine for him either."

"Yeah, thanks Dad. Gabe is just a friend."

"Sure, friends are good. Go hang out, have fun." He turned red as he struggled to dig himself out of the hole he'd dug.

"Have a good day." Mom's smile disappeared as she turned to Dad.

I walked out the door, laughing despite myself as I heard Mom rip into him. Poor Dad.

Gabe sat on the hood of his car and slid off when I stepped outside. He smiled and my insides turned over. What? I needed to focus. I needed to get away from Grand Rapids and draw Bastion with me. For Allister. Focus. Focus.

"Hey," Gabe said.

"Uh, hi."

"I think I found them."

He looked at me when I spun on him.

"Already?"

"They're in a little town about thirty miles from here, Nashwauk."

"Yeah, I know it." I nodded. I walked around to the passenger side of his car and stopped, waiting for him to get in. I looked at him questioningly.

"What?" he asked.

"We going?"

"I thought we might see if you could 'travel.'"

"If we get in the car, we can travel a lot faster." I replied sarcastically.

"No, I mean *travel*," he repeated. "The way angels go from place to place."

"Like shimmering?"

"What the Eternals do is much more limited. They only jump from one place to another. We can go anywhere we want." He smiled at my amazed expression.

"Do you think I can?"

"Only one way to know. Try."

He disappeared and then appeared next to me. I jumped with a start.

"How did you do that?"

"Think of where you want to go, and you go." He shrugged.

No big deal, for him. I still didn't know how the Eternals shimmered, even though I'd ridden along with Allister a few times. I stood there, not sure I could do this.

"Okay, let's try," I sighed.

"I will ride with you. Tell me where we're going, and then I'll help if you stray." He placed his hands on my shoulders and I tensed under his touch. "Relax. You'll do fine."

It wasn't the traveling I worried about. His touch made me feel safe, comfortable. My mind, still loyal to Allister, rebelled.

"Picture the sign outside the town."

"I'm thinking of the sign outside of Nashwauk. Now what?"

"Concentrate on it and you'll be there."

I closed my eyes, picturing the sign in my mind and telling myself I wanted to go there and touch the sign. I wanted to be in Nashwauk. No tingling, no fluttering, just one second we stood beside Gabe's car and the next we stood in front of the sign.

"Oh my God," I gasped, lurching forward before I caught myself.

"Cool, huh?" Gabe grinned.

"I can go anywhere like that?"

"Anywhere as long as you can picture it."

"What if I picture a field that is a building now? Will I end up in the wall or something?"

"You watch too many movies." He laughed. "You will not be able to appear in a wall or anything like that. You will move to the next available space, that's all."

"Good to know," I said.

"Bastion and his goons are staying at a little motel on the north edge of town. We could just kill them."

"Would they send more?" I asked, not liking the idea of killing anyone...even Bastion.

"More than likely."

"Then we need to be sure they follow us out of the area and keep them coming after us until the council decides to pass judgment on Allister. Without me as evidence ..." I looked at Gabe.

"They should sentence him to life in prison." He nodded.

"That's my goal then," I said.

He extended his hand and I looked down at it, not taking it.

"I know the location. You wouldn't want to appear in the middle of their room, would you?"

"No, that wouldn't be good."

I took his hand and we instantly stood on a hill of ore filings overlooking a small motel. Three black Mercedes sat in the lot and a few men stood around smoking cigarettes. I suppose, if you could never die, why wouldn't you smoke?

"I counted a dozen including Bastion," Gabe said.

"What do you suggest?"

"Pull your car in at that entrance." He pointed to the entrance furthest from our position. "Then drive by like you're looking for someone. Once they see you, act surprised and make a run for it."

322

"Then what?"

"We take them north, towards Canada. We get across the line and dump the car and travel somewhere they will never look, like Mexico." He grinned, proud of his plan.

"Canada again?" I groaned.

"Something wrong with Canada?" Gabe asked raising an eyebrow.

"Kendal took me to Canada when he kidnapped me for Bastion. What is it with you people and Canada?"

"Don't lump me into 'you people,' but the wilderness in Canada gives our kind freedom of doing what we want without being seen. Plus it's close."

"Sorry…makes sense," I said ashamed I included him with the likes of Kendal and Bastion.

"Forgiven, but we need to act fast."

"Let's get ready and do it tomorrow then," I said.

"It has to be tonight," he said. "We know where they are and the location is perfect."

"I wanted to say goodbye to everyone," I argued.

"Tell your parents you're leaving, but tell the girls you're leading Bastion away. How long could that take?"

"Fine."

"See you back at your place," he said and disappeared.

"Great," I sighed. Now I have to race an angel; I rolled my eyes.

I concentrated on my house and it appeared before me. Or did I appear before it? Hard to tell.

Gabe's Focus already sputtered down the street and I turned to the one thing I didn't relish. Not in the least. I stood looking at the house, knowing what followed wasn't going to be pleasant. I walked into the kitchen, my parents still sitting at the table drinking coffee.

They looked up at me as I walked in the kitchen.

"What's up, Britt?" Dad asked.

"I'm going away for a while." I braced for their reaction, raising astonished eyebrows as they both nodded.

"We knew you would eventually want to go after Allister," Mom said, a little sad.

"It was just a matter of time," Dad agreed with a tired smile.

"But, how?"

"We've noticed something different about you since the accident," Mom explained. "And then when you and Cassie were attacked, you going from near death to not a scratch just confirmed it for us."

"Confirmed what?"

"You're something beyond us," Dad said, pain in his voice. "We understand there are things in this world we will never fully comprehend and we're guessing you're a part of something bigger than us. It explains how we got you back when we were losing you. Before the accident."

Tears warmed my eyes. "I wish I could explain, but that would only put you and Mom in danger."

"Allister is in the center of all of this, isn't he?" Dad questioned. "And you love him?"

"Yes, I love him and he is smack dab in the center." I nodded.

"Your Father and I know what it's like to be in love, Britt," Mom said, surprising me.

"We don't approve, but we do understand." Dad nodded. "Just try to be safe and call us when you can."

"I will."

"Gabe going with you?" Dad asked.

"Yeah, for a while at least."

"Good, it's safer than traveling alone," he said.

I went over and hugged them both, shocked by their understanding and calmness. I guess the last few months had changed more than me. After giving them one last squeeze, I ran upstairs and gathered my things. Throwing them into a duffle bag, I carried them downstairs and dished out another round of hugs.

"Got your phone?" Mom asked.

I raised my hand holding the phone and she nodded.

"Here." Dad handed me some money in a roll bound by a rubber band. "Call if you need more. We'll see what we can spare."

I hugged him tightly around his neck and stepped back as he wiped tears from his eyes.

"I guess my watch is over," he said sadly. "I hope Gabe knows what he's doing."

"He does, trust me, he does," I said, wiping my own cheeks.

I pulled them both into one last hug and whispered, "I love you both." Then stepped back.

"We love you too," they said in unison.

I rushed out the door, hoping the pain I felt would be left behind as the door closed after me, but no such luck. The sick feeling in my gut hung there like a lead burrito. I went to Gabe's waiting Focus as he popped the trunk and hopped out. Before I threw my bag into the trunk I stopped, looking over my shoulder at Allister's Camaro.

Changing directions, I pulled the keys out of my pocket and unlocked it with a beep of the security system. I popped the trunk and moved around to drop my bag in. Slamming the trunk shut, I saw Gabe staring at me, a shocked expression on his face.

"If you think I'm going to run for my life in that piece of shit, you're nuts. We wouldn't stay ahead of them for a mile."

He grinned and walked over to the passenger side of the car while I went around to the driver's side and slid in. The engine popped off right away, surprising me after sitting for so long, and we drove over to Elisa's house.

Elisa opened the door, surprise on her face seeing me and Gabe standing there.

"What, is it Kendal again?"

"No, Kendal is gone, but we have to leave." I turned my eyes so I didn't have to see the pain fill hers.

"You're leaving, Britt?"

"We have to lead Bastion away from here," Gabe said when I couldn't speak.

"When are you coming back?"

"I, I…don't know if I am." My eyes met hers and they locked, unable to move away. Tears blurred my view of her face and I saw her wipe her own cheeks.

"So this is it? Goodbye and maybe we'll meet up again someday?" Elisa sniffled.

"I guess so," I said with a jerky sob.

Elisa threw herself at me, wrapping her arms tightly around my neck and squeezing me until I thought

I would burst. "I love you Britt Anderson," she whispered in my ear.

"I love you too."

We leaned back, still with our arms around each other, looking deeply into the other's eyes and seeing the resolve to never forget.

I gave a nod which she returned and we stepped apart. I hesitated for a moment, turned awkwardly, and walked down the steps to the waiting car. Gabe stood on the steps for a moment longer, nodding as Elisa spoke to him and then he turned and walked back to climb into the Camaro as I sat waiting.

We went to the hospital next to see Cassie. She smiled brightly as we walked in, but she picked up on my mood and looked at me worried.

"What's wrong?" she asked.

"We have to leave Grand Rapids," I told her.

"Why?"

"To keep all of you safe."

"Is it Kendal?"

"No," Gabe said. "Kendal's dead. He won't hurt anyone anymore."

"Then why?" Cassie whispered.

"Bastion is trying to find me and we need to keep him from coming here and hurting anyone." I hoped getting Elisa out of the way would make Cassie easier, but a lump formed in my throat as I spoke.

"Are you coming back?"

"I don't know, but I hope so, someday."

Cassie reached up and pulled me into a hug. She let me go and kissed me on the cheek as I pulled away.

"Remember me," she said.

"Always." I said, the tears flowing again.

"Take care of her Gabe." Cassie wiped tears from her eyes.

"I will. You have my word," Gabe said and gave her a nod.

"I guess I can't ask for more. To have the word of an angel is worth something." She forced a grin.

"I would like to think so." Gabe reached over and kissed her forehead.

"Bye Britt." Cassie took my hand and squeezed. "I love you."

"I love you to, Cass." I squeezed back and she let me go. The symbolism not lost to me as her fingertips slipped from my hand and I walked out without turning back.

I fought the tears the entire drive to Trish's house, feeling my heart being torn apart with every beat. A part of me wished I could have taken the easy way out and had Kendal do the job instead of facing my friends' sorrow in person.

I pulled the car up to the curb in front of Trish's house and she sat on her front steps waiting. Gabe began to get out, but I put a hand on his arm to stop him. He looked at me questioningly.

"I need to do this alone," I said.

He nodded and took his hand from the door handle with a nod.

I stepped out, took a deep breath, and walked around the car not looking at Trish but down at the ground. I didn't look up, walking with my head down, following the sidewalk until I saw her feet before me. I looked up and she stared at me, the streaks of wet from her tears already leaving red marks and lines down her face.

My tears, I'd thought my ducts had dried up by now, streamed down my face, dripping from my chin as I looked at her. Trish was the first friend I ever had. She stood beside me through everything; giving me comfort, support, and a kick in the ass if I needed one. Now I needed to say goodbye, possibly for the last time, and the thought of it wrenched my insides apart.

"I hear you're leaving," she said when I didn't speak.

"Uh huh."

"Playing the martyr again?"

"Guess so."

"Shit, why do you always step in it like this?"

"I don't do it on purpose."

"I never met anyone who has such god-awful luck, Britt."

"Not my fault," I said, getting a little pissed.

"I know, I know." She nodded her head. "I just wish it didn't happen like this."

"Me too." I looked at her as we shared our miserable moment together.

"Could you do me a favor?"

"Yeah, sure, anything," I said, confused by the request.

"Could you kick this Bastion in the balls for me when you finally get the chance?"

"You got it."

"They do have balls, don't they, I mean, I guess I never really thought about it, but they must if they have kids, right?" She looked up at me, her tears mixing with her confusion.

"I'm pretty sure they do," I said, forcing back a snicker.

She stood abruptly and gave me a big hug, turning her head to kiss me for a long moment on the cheek.

"I love you Britt girl," she whispered in my ear. "You come back to me. Damn it, you'd better come back to me."

"I will," I lied. "I promise." I resolved to try. To keep my promise and at least try. I kissed her cheek and stepped back as she reluctantly released me.

"Bye Britt," she said, her eyes overflowing with her sadness.

"Bye Trish." I turned to walk away. I got two steps and her arms surrounded me again as she lay her head against my back.

"I believe in you," she whispered and let go.

I wanted to look back, but my strength was fading fast and I held onto what resolve I still had. To leave before it evaporated completely. I strode purposefully to the car, got in and squealed away, putting as much distance between me and my overwhelming sorrow standing on that sidewalk.

Chapter 29

We motored out of town, heading north to Nashwauk. We didn't speak, my words used up earlier and my desire to form others distant.

It didn't take long to arrive. I took the lone highway heading north through the small mining town. As we approached the motel, I slowed to get my bearings and then stopped just out of sight of the motel.

"I'll travel back to the car once you get their attention and start heading for Canada," he said.

"We can do that?"

He smiled and then disappeared.

I put the car in first and let out the clutch, easing it into motion, confident Bastion would remember the distinctive vehicle on sight. I pulled into the parking lot and cruised through, actively looking at the room numbers, but keeping a watchful eye on the black Mercedes.

As I pulled even with the first one, a man walked out of the room and lit a cigarette. I let my foot off the gas and the engine rumbled as it slowed down. His eyes met mine and Bastion recognized me at once. His mouth opened to shout out orders as his silver tooth glittered. I didn't wait, gunning the Camaro and squealing out of the parking lot, spraying the black cars with rocks as I went. Not part of the plan, but gravy, I thought.

I raced by the parking lot on the road heading north as men scrambled to their cars and the black German beasts lurched into motion. I shifted and punched the gas, spinning the tires again and rocketing out of sight.

"Easy, you don't want to lose them," Gabe said. I jumped at his silent, sudden arrival.

I slowed, watching my rearview mirror until I spotted the first pursuit car and then punched it again. Shifting smoothly, my memory of Dad teaching me to drive stick in the field just outside of town coming unbidden to me. We raced towards the border, hoping to stay ahead of them until we hit the patrol checkpoint.

We hurtled towards International Falls some 120 miles away, pushing our speed close to 100 mph to keep ahead of our pursuers. I slowed as we approached the border. Pulling up to the guard station, I rolled down my window.

"Passports please," the guard asked.

I handed mine over and then Gabe reached across to hand his to the agent.

"What's the purpose of your visit?" The guard asked.

I wanted to scream, "escape" or "To get away from the guys following us," but I pushed the urge down and smiled. "Just heading up so we can sightsee in the morning."

"Thank you," he said benignly. He handed the passports back and stepped away from the car.

I saw the headlights move closer as our pursuers eased in behind us. The agent waved us to move along and I put the car in first, slowly pulling away. As soon as I turned a bend in the road, I punched the accelerator and shifted rapidly, speeding down the road.

Gabe reached over, putting a hand on my arm and I glanced over. "We can slow down now." He turned to look out the back window.

"We want them to think we headed deeper into Canada. If we lose them, they might think we doubled back."

I nodded at the logic.

"We need to keep them after us for some time in order to assure they feel we, or should I say you, are on the run permanently."

The reality of this life hit me hard. This plan meant I'd be running from them until the council sentenced Allister. How long it would take, I didn't have a clue.

"Pull in here," Gabe directed. He motioned to a small roadside diner as we approached and then vanished.

I shook my head. I didn't think I'd ever get used to that. I pulled into a parking spot and turned the car off. Getting out, I stretched, feeling the kinks from the other night. I waited for a moment and prepared to go inside when the car shook and Gabe stepped out of the passenger seat.

"Well?"

"They stopped just inside the border," he said.

"Why would they do that?"

"I think they suspect we'll try to double back. Remember, they have all the time in the world. Allister is in custody; he won't be going anywhere. They can take their time and present you anytime they catch you."

"What?" I cried. "No, if they sentence Allister to life they can't come back and sentence him to death if Bastion brings me in. That's double jeopardy, they can't do that."

"Britt, you're thinking human still. The Eternal Council can do anything they want.

"Now you tell me," I shouted, the injustice making my head hurt.

"I thought you knew."

"No, I didn't." I turned and stormed away from him, folding my arms in disgust.

I strode behind the diner, walking down a path into the woods that flanked the property. I walked in the dark, following the light colored path and mulling it all over in my head. On the run forever? And I mean, forever. Being immortal definitely had its down side. If I wanted Allister to live I needed to stay away from Bastion or anyone else the council sent after me forever.

I sat down on a stump next to the trail, the frustration pushing to the surface in the form of tears. I leaned down, setting my head in my hands and sobbed. This sucked. I already lost Allister, now I lost everything I loved for good. As if on cue, Gabe appeared next to me.

"Would you quit that."

"Sorry."

"No." I took a deep breath. "I'm sorry. You've done nothing but help me."

"I understand your pain. I wish I could make it better, but I can't."

"Then what good is being an angel?" I asked, more of myself than of him.

"We get to help people. There is that." He shrugged.

"Maybe you, but I'm some freaky hybrid between an Eternal and an angel. I'm not good for anything."

"Not true."

I stared at him. In the darkness he gave off a glow when I let myself see it. His beauty undeniable. I sighed at my shortcomings compared to his radiance.

"I will never be anything like you, or like Allister." I closed my eyes and images of Allister's perfect face, his amazing smile flickered into focus. The memory of his easy laugh brought more tears to my eyes.

"But you already are, Britt. You have the best of both."

"No, the Eternals are damned to walk the earth forever, never to know the wonder of the afterlife."

"What are you talking about?" Gabe stepped in front of me, his eyes staring at me in horror.

"Eternals don't have souls and are damned to walk the earth forever," I repeated what I'd been told.

"Britt, Eternals don't need souls." Gabe leaned closer to me. "Where did you get this nonsense?"

"Allister and his family."

"Their kind might feel that way, but somewhere they went astray of what they are. They have already gotten their salvation."

"They don't have guardian angels," I pointed out.

"True, that is very true, but it isn't because they're damned or not going to heaven. They don't have angels because they don't need angels. They can find their way to heaven on their own."

"Even though they never die?" Gabe had me spinning in circles. I didn't know what to believe anymore.

"None have, so far."

"How is that possible?"

335

"Eternals are here for a specific purpose; a specific event. And that event hasn't happened yet."

"What event?" I asked, not sure I wanted to know.

"That isn't for me to say, but I do know that Eternals have been created perfectly to defend mankind when this foretold event comes."

I glared at him, pissed he'd told me just enough to get my mind running wild with crazy images of Armageddon and all the biblical stuff drilled into my head over the years.

"Hey, don't shoot the messenger," he said raising his hands defensively.

"Then why tell me this?" I began.

"To make you realize you're special and have a purpose. We all do, and you may be destined for something bigger than any of us."

"Yeah, right." I rolled my eyes. "I'm the *one*."

"Let's go get something to eat, I'm starving." He flashed his brilliant smile, visible even in the dim lighting, and extended a hand.

I grinned in spite of my bad mood, taking his hand, and walked back to the diner.

We took a booth next to the high bank of windows facing the road. The décor was right out of the sixties, from the checkered tile flooring to the vintage jukebox spinning records in the corner. We ordered from the waitress dressed in a poodle skirt and a big bouffant hairdo and then contemplated our next move.

"Where do we go now?"

"The closest major city is Winnipeg," he answered. "If we lead them there, we might be able to keep them busy for a while."

The plan sounded like a good one. I nodded my approval. Then, a question lingering in my mind for a while pushed itself to the surface, and I looked at Gabe.

"Are you the Archangel Gabriel?" Six years of Catholic school and I couldn't help but wonder if he was the same angel who came to Mary two thousand years ago.

"I go by many titles." He stared at me flatly.

"Nice try. Quit dodging, answer the question."

"Yes, I've been known as an Archangel, though my role now is as an Avenging Angel."

"And what does that entail?"

"Kendal isn't the only problem I need to find. There are others out there interfering with the natural order. My job is to ensure they stop."

"Stop by killing them?"

"Stop one way or another." He didn't elaborate.

A thought came to me. One I wasn't sure I wanted to know the truth about. I looked up at Gabe again and hesitated a moment, biting my lower lip.

"Britt, if you want to ask me something, just ask."

"You say there's no one else like me; that I'm unique, a hybrid. Would you consider *me* someone interfering with the natural order?"

I expected him to laugh, to tell me I thought too much, worried too much. He didn't. Instead, he stared at me hard for a moment, his deep green eyes holding my gaze. They softened and he turned away, looking out the window.

I gasped, still staring at him. His lack of an answer said it all. He came along because he felt I could interfere with the natural order of things. He came along in case I caused problems and he needed to take me out.

"Why don't you just kill me now and be done with it, like I asked back in Grand Rapids?" I whispered heavily.

He turned back to me, his eyes glossy with tears as he searched for the right words.

"I don't see anything about you indicating you could ever do anything I need to kill you for."

"But?" I waited for the but, there was always a but.

"You're one of a kind. Angel and Eternal. I can't be sure what abilities you might have and what you might do with them. I needed to come to be sure it was... safe."

"*It* was safe?"

"The world, Britt. I have a responsibility to the world."

"So now I'm a threat not only to my hometown, my friends and family, to the Eternals I care about, but the entire world?"

"Don't put words in my mouth."

"They may not be in your mouth, but they *are* in your head." I glared at him, using my anger to mask the pain and hurt I felt.

Gabe dropped his eyes.

The perky waitress in the poodle skirt delivered our meals, eyeing us nervously. Sensing our moods, she hurried away after setting the plates in front of us.

"You're taking my words out of context," Gabe spoke soothingly.

"I don't know. It seems to suck no matter what context it's in. So you're not here to help me, just to chaperone me and make sure I don't turn into some crazed monster out to destroy the world?"

"Britt," he sighed.

I looked down at my food and began to eat. I didn't look at him the rest of the meal. I still seethed when we were walking to the car, refusing to make eye contact.

"We could head to a motel down the road a ways and wait for them to come looking for us in the morning," Gabe said.

"Whatever." I still didn't look at him as I ducked into the car.

He got in as the engine turned over. I felt his eyes on me, even though I stared straight ahead. We drove the few miles in silence and pulled into the gravel parking lot of the Moonlight Motel.

The clerk checked us in, raising an eyebrow as I gave the name of Mr. and Mrs. Anderson and showed him my ID. He nodded and gave me a key. Gabe and I walked along the sidewalk to the room's door. I opened the door, swinging it inward as he collected my bag from the car. He walked past me and tossed the bag down on the bed. Turning, he walked back out and I finally looked at him.

"What are you doing?" I asked.

"I'll sleep in the car," he said, a little sharp. He took a few more steps towards the Camaro.

"There are two beds in here."

"I wouldn't want you to misunderstand my intentions," he said, the sarcasm heavy in his voice.

"Don't be a jerk." I folded my arms across my chest.

"Oh, it's fine for you to overreact and get all snippy about my intentions, which might I remind you, you took out of context, but I can't get upset you don't trust me enough to listen to my reasons for being here?" He threw up his arms in disgust. "I'll sleep in the car."

I stared at him, my mouth going dry as I tried to say something. The right words wouldn't come.

"Britt, I care about you. You. I'm not here out of fear of what you might become. I'm here because of what might become of you. I want you to live. I don't think I've wanted anything so much in my entire existence."

"You want me to live?"

"Very much."

I walked over to sit on the bumper of the car, at a loss. How could someone like Gabe, Gabriel, the Archangel Gabriel, care so much about me when he barely knew me?

Gabe sat next to me, placing his arm over my shoulder and pulling me into his chest. It was warm and felt comfortable being in his arms. The arms of an angel, I laughed softly to myself.

"What's so funny?"

"Uh, nothing." I grinned into his chest.

"Can we get past all this?"

I leaned back to look at him as he concentrated on my reaction. I liked Gabe a lot, and he also scared me to death. The way he'd destroyed Kendal…

"I'm sorry," I whispered. I stood and took a few steps towards the room, stopping to turn back to him. "Now come in here and use the other bed."

"Okay." He shrugged and walked over next to me.

"Good." I grinned.

"Ladies first." He motioned with a flamboyant bow.

"Does that actually work with the ladies?" I asked.

"Don't know." He smirked. "You're the first I've tried it on. Did it?"

"Not really." I gave him a playful shove and strode past him into the room.

"I'll make a note of that." He laughed, closing the door behind him.

Chapter 30

Gabe woke me the next morning with a start, his eyes wide and his face pale with anguish. I'd never seen him that way before.

"What? What is it?" I asked, sitting up in bed.

"They're on their way. We only have a few minutes before they get here."

I leapt from bed, throwing my things into my bag, and rushing out the door behind Gabe, just in my t-shirt and underwear. He jumped behind the wheel and I threw my bag in the back seat before I climbed in and slammed the door.

Gabe had the Camaro throwing rocks as he burned out of the parking lot just ahead of the first black Mercedes. They spotted us and kept coming, racing up on our bumper as we fishtailed out of the gravel parking lot onto the blacktop.

Gabe shifted adeptly, putting the engine through its paces, and soon had the muscle car roaring down the road, the Mercedes hot on our tail. I pulled some jeans from my open bag and tugged them on. Gabe hit the top end of fourth gear and shifted to fifth, squealing rubber on asphalt as he went, pulling away from our pursuers. He inched his lead out by the second until we had nearly a few blocks on them.

"We didn't decide; Winnipeg?" He glanced over.

"Yeah, what other choice do we have?"

"Whatever choice you want, but Winnipeg's a good start." He nodded for emphasis.

"Go for it," I shouted over the roar of the engine.

We approached a crossroads. "Hang on," he cried.

I gripped the 'oh shit' handle over my door as he downshifted, pulled the parking break, and skidded into the intersection, turning to the left. He dropped the break down again, hit the gas to pull us out of our slide, and quickly shifted to get us back up to fifth gear.

I watched out the back window as the first Mercedes tried the same maneuver and slid into the ditch across the road. The second fared a little better, then caught a wheel on the soft shoulder and sank up to its axel. Only the third car made the turn and raced after us.

"We lost two," I shouted.

"Good. Now they have to stay close, but can't try anything drastic for fear of losing us." Gabe nodded.

We sped towards Winnipeg, hoping to lose them in the city and buy us and Allister some time to get lost.

As we drove I texted Angelina, hoping to inform her of our plans and waited impatiently for her reply. It didn't come.

Gabe slowed, managing to come within a reasonable range of the speed limit as the Mercedes, still on our tail, slowed as well, giving us some room.

After driving for another hour, my cell pinged that a message had come in. It was Angelina.

The trial is still on hold waiting for Bastion to bring you in. He sent word he has you in his sights and capture is inevitable. Keep going, we all believe in you.

Tears came to my eyes as I read. Marveling at the faith these Eternals placed in me; totally unfounded. I lowered the phone to my lap staring out at the desolate road.

"Good news?"

"The trial is waiting for Bastion to bring me in."

"That will be some time if we have anything to say about it." Gabe said, his eyes narrowing in determination.

We sped into Winnipeg after dark, the lights of the Eternal's car right behind us. Another set of lights joined the first not long after dark. I assumed the third car would arrive in short order.

"What now. How do we lose them?" I asked as we slowed down for the city limits.

Gabe gave me a smirk and took a hard right, hit the gas and propelled us down a side street before turning another right and then a quick left. He moved through the streets like it was second nature, not slowing or stopping for any traffic lights. Incredibly, they all went our way. As he came up to traffic, he veered and maneuvered like he knew what the drivers were thinking and kept going without ever touching the brakes.

We pulled into the underground parking ramp of a large hotel and jerked to a stop in an open spot. Gabe turned the car off and got out quickly, pulling me after as I snatched the handle of my bag and dragged it along.

We went to the front desk and checked in. This time Gabe did all the talking as the people called him by his first name and smiled knowingly. He took the key to his "usual" room and we climbed in the elevator a matter of minutes after pulling into the ramp.

While the elevator bell dinged at each floor, I looked over at him curiously. "Been here before?" I asked.

"I like Winnipeg. Not too big to be friendly and not too small to be overly noticed." He grinned.

The elevator opened to a large suite, walls of windows overlooking a river and the city as the lights sparkled in the darkness. The spacious room had an enormous living room and two bedrooms off of it. I nearly jumped out of my skin when a man stepped forward out of the bar/kitchen area, handing Gabe a drink and waiting patiently.

"Would the lady care for a drink?" he asked, looking at Gabe more than me.

"What would you like to drink?" Gabe looked to me, expectant.

"I could go for a beer." I blew through pursed lips.

The man began turning back to the bar, when Gabe intervened. "The lady would like a Diet Coke?" He raised an eyebrow at me.

"Yeah, fine." I frowned.

The man went to get my drink and I glared at Gabe.

"Doesn't being an Eternal-slash-Angel eliminate the need for a drinking age? If I'm going to live forever, what's the point?"

"I need you fresh and sharp. No need to muddy your thoughts."

"Fine," I sighed, too tired to argue, as the man returned with my Diet Coke.

"Will that be all, Sir?" The man asked.

"Yes Kurt. Thank you." Gabe smiled.

The man disappeared through the kitchen and we were alone.

"Don't you think they'll find us here?" I asked, taking a sip of my Coke.

"Eventually, but by then we might get lucky and they'll be less determined to find you."

I wasn't sure I agreed. "So what now?"

"We go about living. The chance of them coming across us is slim. We need to be careful, but we can see the sights, maybe take in a play, and enjoy ourselves for a while."

"What if they think we ducked back into the states? Won't they start searching for me where they left off? Nashwauk is only 30 miles from Grand Rapids."

"I'll keep an eye on them. I can find them and make sure they're still here." His confidence was comforting.

"Okay. I'm beat. Which room is mine?"

"Take your pick. Either is fine." He motioned to one and then the other bedroom in the suite.

"Thanks." I smiled at him. "Goodnight Gabe."

"Goodnight Britt." He grinned as I turned away and went into a bedroom.

A king-size bed greeted me and I rolled the sliding doors closed behind me before diving onto the soft, welcoming mattress. I tossed my arms up over my head and got a whiff of my armpits. Whew. I didn't have a chance to shower today and I could tell.

I slid off the bed and went into the bathroom, turning on the six, count them, six shower heads and basked in the soothing steam and spray until my muscles turned to noodles.

I crawled into the bed with my hair still wet, not caring what kind of bird's nest resulted the next morning.

I was just beginning to drift off when I noticed the message light on my phone flashing from its perch on the nightstand. I picked it up and opened the text from Angelina.

Britt, the trial will continue in a few days. If you can stay hidden for at least that long, we might be able to get Allister released or a jail sentence. Victor thinks he might be able to convince some of the council members to show mercy on Allister. He might be able to keep them from changing the sentence even if you are captured at a later date. So please, *please*, stay hidden 3-4 more days.
Angelina.

I set down the phone again. Hope dared enter my mind for the first time in so long, I barely recognized it. I may be able to live with myself after all. Allister may be allowed to live. Jail wasn't the most ideal way to live, but maybe Eternal prison was like the kind they send politicians to when they take a bribe or Wall Street execs when they swindled people.

My eyes slid shut, the stress and excitement of the day catching up with me. I felt a smile curling my lips as I drifted off. Maybe I could see Allister again, someday. Now at least there was a glimmer of possibility.

The next morning I woke to loud music coming from the other room. I got up, pulling down my t-shirt, and slid the doors to my bedroom apart. At that moment, I witnessed something I thought I would never see in my lifetime; Gabe rocking out to AC/DC. He sang 'Dirty Deeds' at the top of his lungs, playing air guitar and head banging like an old pro.

I couldn't help myself giggling in the doorway. He turned toward the sound and changed a dozen shades of red, then hit the mute on the remote in his hand.

"Uh, yeah, good morning Britt," he stammered.

"Gabe, you never told me angels can rock," I said laughing.

"You still have a lot to learn about us," he smiled, laughing as well. "I can only speak for myself, but being on earth as often as I am, I do find rock and roll enjoyable. A worthy stress reliever."

"Good to know." I nodded, still smirking.

"Hear any more from Greece?" he asked, sweeping back his hair with one hand.

"Yeah." I wondered if he could read my mind. "Angelina said if we can avoid Bastion for the next few days Victor may be able to work something out and keep Allister from being sentenced to death...ever."

"That's wonderful."

I think he truly meant it. Even though Gabe wanted me to be with him, I think he wanted me to be happy too. "Maybe we should hole up here instead of going out, at least for a few days," I suggested.

"Nonsense. Bastion won't find us in Winnipeg too easily. It's like finding a needle in a haystack."

"Well...if you think it's safe."

"Trust me. We'll be fine. I already have tickets for us to see Les Miserables tonight."

"Theatre, really?"

"If you're going to live forever, it won't hurt you to get a little culture along the way." Gabe frowned at my reaction.

"Alright." I nodded, conceding the point.

"But today, you need some new clothes."

"I don't have money to buy clothes," I informed him, a little embarrassed. "I only have enough to keep me going for a short time."

"No worries," Gabe grinned. "Being immortal gives you time to save up for a rainy day." He winked at me.

"Save up? Like how much have you saved up?"

"I don't like to talk about money." He turned towards the windows.

"Come on. Give me a hint."

"Britt," he sighed, still not looking at me.

"Hundreds of thousands?"

Gabe didn't respond.

"Millions?"

Gabe kept his back to me, watching the city below.

"Billions?"

He smirked over his shoulder at me as my mouth dropped, eyes wide.

"You have to be joking," I said, short of breath.

"Like I said, money tends to make people nervous."

"So shopping it is?"

"As soon as you're ready."

I raced off to take a shower and get dressed. Thirty minutes later we were driving through downtown Winnipeg in the hotel's limousine, stopping in front of a very swanky looking boutique.

"Are you sure?" I gazed up at the shiny sign over the door.

"Anything you want." Gabe smiled.

We went in. I tried on different outfits not only for the night of theatre, but also everyday clothing with prices three times what they would cost in a normal store. Gabe didn't bat an eye as we bought a trunk load of clothing and hauled it back for the poor bellhops to lug up to our room.

When we arrived back at our room, lunch waited under silver covers. We sat in front of the high windows eating lobster and shrimp. Gabe asked me about my life before meeting Allister and I fought hard to steer away from the cancer stories and stick to the happier times; the times with Trish, Elisa, and Cassie. I went quiet after saying their names, missing them terribly.

"So what would you like to do with your life?" Gabe changed the subject, "If you didn't have Eternals chasing you?"

"I'm sorry." I looked at Gabe as he frowned, confused.

"What would you need to be sorry for?"

"If I could do anything right now…"

"Go on Britt," Gabe urged.

"I'd like to be with Allister, just the two of us. It's been so long since we've spent time together where we could feel more of what we had before this all went crazy."

Gabe's face turned red and he stood, wiping his lips with a napkin and tossed it down on his plate.

"I'm sorry." Sensing that I'd wrecked the mood, I felt like a heel.

"Not your fault." He looked at me, his eyes filled with hurt. "I hoped you could find your way to considering me romantically."

I didn't have anything to say. I stared at him, my mouth gaping uselessly.

"I need to get ready for tonight. I suggest you do the same." Gabe paced off, not turning back as he slid the door to his bedroom closed.

Chapter 31

I felt bad, really bad, but I'd never intended to lead Gabe on. I never told him I would choose him over Allister. Don't get me wrong. Gabe was incredible in his own right, but when your heart makes a choice it rarely is logical or controllable. My connection to Allister couldn't be ignored; even with thousands of miles separating us, my feelings for him never lessened.

I walked into my room, the dress for this evening laid out by the suite's butler. Dark green satin, cinched at the waist, fairly low neckline; nothing I could imagine wearing in Grand Rapids, ever.

I took a long shower, the warmth relaxing my tense muscles and lessening the strain on my nerves. Only a few more days and Allister's life would be safe again. A life in prison didn't seem much like a victory to me, still, it left the possibility of seeing him again as opposed to the finality of the alternative.

I entered my bedroom and noticed a small black box sitting above my dress laid out on the bed. I moved over and sat on the edge of the bed, my towel wrapped around me. I lifted the box, my hands trembling as I considered its contents. Easing the cover open, I watched the light above reflect off the contents; a necklace, emeralds and diamonds to match my dress were surrounded by elegant strands of silver and gold.

I lifted the jewelry from the case letting the gems sparkle and glimmer as I turned my hand, examining it from every angle. I gasped, the beauty of it causing me to hold my breath while I admired it. A small piece of paper sat in the box, my name neatly scrolled across it. I unfolded the paper, reading the words written on it.

Dearest Britt,
I wanted you to feel special tonight. Please do me the honor of wearing this, although it will pale next to your beauty.
Gabe

I smiled while tears welled up. I did feel special with Gabe. He made me feel very special. My heart hurt as I wished I could give him more of it. Yet how could I give him something someone already possessed? I dried my tears and turned back to the bathroom to get ready.

An hour later I slid the bedroom doors open. Gabe waited before a fire burning in the fireplace. He wore a beautiful tux, cut to fit perfectly. The dark fabric shimmered with faint pinstripes and his cuff links bore diamonds nearly as big as a nickel.

"You're ravishing," Gabe smiled at me with sad eyes. He walked over to take my hand, helping me down the stairs to the sunken living room where he'd waited.

"Thank you." I blushed. "You're very sharp yourself."

"If you live forever you find out what works for you and what doesn't." He grinned, flashing stunningly white teeth at my compliment.

"Good to know I can get better at this."

"You nailed it the first time, I'd say. Shall we go?" He held his arm up so I could lace mine through his and we walked to the private elevator. As the door slid open to the garage, a limousine waited for us, door open, chauffeur standing by ready to receive us.

"This is crazy." I couldn't help giggling.

"This is the way it could be every day," Gabe said simply. Both of us hearing what he wasn't saying. *If I was with him this would be our life.*

I averted my eyes, getting into the limo and sliding over. He slid in next to me, glancing at me, expectant. Not wanting to take this away from him, I looked out the far window and said nothing. We rode through Winnipeg in strained silence. I kept staring out the window trying to feign interest in the sights, really not wanting to look into Gabe's hurt eyes again.

The car stopped in front of a grand old theatre, lit up for the evening. Gabe stepped out first, taking my hand and helping me from the limo. We walked arm in arm up to the entrance where the doorman bowed and pulled the door open for us to enter. An usher checked our tickets and led us upstairs to the balcony level. He then turned down an isolated hallway to a row of doors. Stopping at the very end, he nodded to Gabe.

Gabe smiled and placed some money in the man's outstretched hand.

The usher stepped back bowing his head and opened the door for us to enter.

Inside, the scene from countless movies lay before me. The curtains, fine silks; luxurious upholsteries covered everything. The ornate carvings along the walls and outlining the stage with its acres of fabric overwhelmed me. I stood gawking, taking it all until Gabe chuckled behind me.

"All very impressive, huh?" he whispered.

I nodded dumbly, unable to speak as my eyes scanned the huge theatre, trying hard not to miss even the slightest detail. Our seats were incredible, just off the stage but far enough back to see the entire panorama clearly.

"These seats are awesome." I turned to Gabe, my eyes shining with excitement.

"Nothing but the best." Though he downplayed it, his pride at my reaction was evident.

The lights flickered and I looked to Gabe, confused.

"They're about to start, we should sit down." He motioned me towards the chairs and I stepped over, sliding my hands along the back of my legs to smooth my dress before sitting.

Gabe moved next to me, taking his seat gracefully. Leaning on the arm rest between us, he unbuttoned his jacket as he edged closer.

The lights went dim and the curtain came up. I turned to Gabe, my mouth opening with delight. His face was mere inches from mine and he stared at me, ignoring the production getting underway.

I forced myself to turn away from him and concentrate on the play. It proved harder than I expected. The play was wonderful, exhilarating beyond anything I might have imagined, but Gabe's attention to me made me feel self-conscious. I shifted my weight nervously, trying to keep his glimmering eyes, reflecting the lights from the stage, out of my mind.

When I finally started to relax, I glanced into the crowd scanning the faces all turned to the stage enjoying the show. I smiled at the expressions of enjoyment, the enthralled looks as they peered at the actors, whisking them away to another place, an escape from their burdensome lives.

As I perused the audience I skimmed over faces not watching the stage, but focused on me. I stopped, frowning at such an absurd thought, then, when I went back, the glaring eyes of Bastion and his men stared back at me.

My heart didn't skip a beat; it stopped completely. I watched Bastion, my recognition seemed to bring him pleasure and he slowly came to his feet. He moved to the aisle, his men sliding in front of the disturbed audience members right after him. The group rushed up the aisle to the rear exits and disappeared into the lobby.

I turned to Gabe, my heart stuttering to gain its rhythm again. He stared at me, ignoring all else.

"They're here," I whispered frantically.

"What?" Gabe eyes flew open wide.

"Bastion," I repeated. "They're heading up here now."

Gabe took hold of my arm, pulling me along as we hurried to the exit. He swung the door open and we burst into the hallway. Taking two steps back the way we entered, Bastion and his men rumbled into the hall as well, the old theatre structure echoing under their footfalls.

We jerked to a stop staring at the only other people not inside, watching the production.

"We should have guessed you had help Britt...but an angel, very impressive." Bastion said.

"She is under my protection," Gabe stated definitely, taking a step in front of me.

"That matters little, angel," Bastion replied unaffected. "We have orders and the authority to take her to Greece for questioning."

"What crime has she committed to warrant Eternals sending their bounty hunter to retrieve her?" Gabe asked, not politely.

"Her very existence is a crime," Bastion hissed.

"Surely you can do better than that." Gabe chuckled.

"She was created by an Eternal from a person already gone. It is the highest crime an Eternal can commit. She is to be taken to Greece as evidence to the Eternal's crimes and then destroyed."

"Hmm." Gabe placed his hand to his mouth in thought. "But if she is under my protection now, I guess you must defer to my authority."

"Your authority does not have any jurisdiction over Eternals, angel. Now go before we are forced to destroy you and take the girl." Bastion took two steps towards us, his men right at his heels.

Gabe raised his hand, halting their advance. "I guess if you feel you need to threaten me, you should know who you threaten." Even standing behind Gabe, I could feel his smile spread across his face as he finished speaking.

"And what angel are we to rid ourselves of tonight?" Bastion laughed.

"I am Gabriel," Gabe told them calmly and the Eternals began muttering behind Bastion, whose face turned ghastly white.

As the Eternals hesitated Gabe reached back, taking my hand, and the theatre changed to the living room in our hotel suite.

"Oh my God," I shouted, dropping to a knee on the carpeting.

"Are you alright?" Gabe turned and knelt beside me, his concern for me almost painful.

"I thought we were dead," I gasped, struggling to regain control over my breathing.

"They had us, but their hesitation gave me the time to visualize and get us out of there."

"You need time to travel?" I asked, still confused at how it worked.

"Concentration is the key. Remember, we always concentrate first and *then* travel. If they had rushed us without giving me time to concentrate on this suite, we could have been in trouble."

"They seemed like they're afraid of you." I looked over at him as he stood up and moved towards the mantle, the fire was still burning in the fireplace.

"Being an Archangel does give one some street credit." He turned, smiling down at me.

"And...?" I knew there was more. There was always more with him.

"During a battle with some rebellious Eternals many years ago, I might have taken out an entire regiment myself." He shrugged nonchalantly, blushing a little.

"They must consider you the Eternal slayer then." I got up and sat on the couch.

"Why do you think they charged me with eliminating Kendal?"

"Makes sense." I nodded.

"Would you care for some wine?" He asked.

"Sure, I think I earned a drink," I sighed.

He poured two glasses of wine out of a decanter sitting on the coffee table, handing me one as he took a long drink.

A buzzing in my clutch purse made me scurry for my phone inside. I pulled it out and looked at the text, from Angelina.

Trial starts up again tomorrow. Life sentence likely, we did it.

I smiled, unable to contain the joy at having saved Allister's life. I looked to Gabe, his eyes turned down to me, glazed and staring.

"Gabe." I jumped to my feet just as he fell into my arms. I eased him down to the floor and knelt beside him, his head resting on my lap.

"Poison," he whispered, barely audible.

"What?" I stared down at him, confused. I didn't think you could kill an angel so easily. "Gabe," I cried as the elevator doors slid open.

Bastion strode out of the elevator. The butler, Kurt walked alongside with another half dozen men. I quickly grabbed my phone and tucked it under my dress, into my underwear.

"You were right." Bastion shot a glance at Kurt, "the first thing he likes to do is have a good glass of wine."

He moved over to me as I cradled Gabe's head and gave a nod to one of his men. The man, as huge a man as ever I saw, strode over to me and raised his hand above me. The last thing I remember is that enormous hand coming down and then black.

Chapter 32

I woke rocking back and forth between two men in the back of a limo. I suddenly had an enormous dislike for limos. I kept my eyes open as slits to avoid alerting them of my consciousness. What should I do? My mind, still cloudy from the blow to my head, didn't make it easier to concentrate on my options. 'Concentrate' echoed in my head as Gabe explained the need when trying to travel.

Gabe. I forced back the tears at the thought of my loss. He did nothing but try to protect me from all of this and now he was gone too.

Allister. I needed to find a way to escape. Otherwise I sentenced him to death. I focused on the one thing I could with all my heart. The interior of the car blurred and I sat on Trish's bed.

I turned just as Trish came awake. Seeing me sitting on the edge of her bed she let out a scream. I screamed back at her reaction and we sat screaming at each other for another second or two.

Finally regaining our wits, we looked at each other in shock and flung ourselves into a tight embrace.

"Where the hell did you come from?" Trish gasped.

"Winnipeg," I said, hesitant to tell her too much.

"Britt, I mean how did you get here?"

"I can do a few things now," I said with a shrug.

"You don't say," Trish sighed and glanced down at the floor. "Britt, what's that?"

I followed Trish's gaze down to the floor and then to my foot resting on the carpet. A soft green light blinked every few seconds in the dark around the vicinity of my foot.

Trish clicked her nightstand light on and we stared with surprise at the clunky black box attached to my ankle.

"Tracking device." Trish stated.

"I screwed up," I cried, lowering my head into my hands.

"It'll be okay." Trish pulled me into her arms.

"How could you think that?" I pulled away to look at her. "I just lead Bastion to all of you."

My phone pinged as a text came in and I dug it out from under my dress. I lifted it and opened the message from Angelina.

Court back in session, think Allister will get life, not death. Angelina.

"Who was that?" Trish scrunched up her brows.

"Angelina." My relief at having Allister's life spared was tempered by the blinking green light on my ankle. "I think I stayed away from Bastion long enough to save his life at least.

"That's great, isn't that what you wanted?" Trish asked, seeing my tears.

"Yeah," I cried. "But the reality of never seeing him again just hit me."

Trish pulled me into her arms, holding me tight as I sobbed.

A ping sounded on my phone and I pulled away to read another message from Angelina.

Bastion sent video evidence. The council sentenced
Allister to death.

I sat frozen on Trish's bed as the phone fell from
my hands, clattering to the floor.

"What, what is it?" Trish asked, then leaned over
to retrieve the phone when I didn't. I could only stare off
into space. She read the message, gasped, then typed
back.

I heard another ping on my phone as Angelina
responded to Trish's message. "Britt," she said her voice
low. "Britt," she repeated when I didn't respond the first
time.

"What?" I turned to her, my eyes unable to focus
on her face, still staring at something distant.

"They're going to execute him…now." Even
though she whispered, the words drove into my mind
with such force, I snapped back to reality as jarring as if
I'd been thrown. I stared at her and she leaned back, her
fear clear on her face.

"No," I whispered, the sound echoing hollow in
my brain. "No, no, no, no," I shouted, coming to my feet.

I concentrated on Allister with every cell in my
body; focusing on his face, his smile, his hair, his touch,
his smell, his kiss. I pulled his image and memories to me
bringing them to life, bringing them to the here and now;
insisting they come to me and demanding they obey.

Trish's room melted in front of me as stone,
granite, and marble took its place. I knelt on the hard
white floor on one knee. My hands touched the cold
surface next to my feet as my head bowed and steam rose
from my body. My dress smoked, some had burned away

exposing skin underneath while other parts still survived. The tracking device on my ankle fell away, smoking

A gasp rose around me as I raised my head, the smoke dissipating and my eyes clearing. Not more than a few feet in front of me stood Allister, hands bound behind his back as a man held each of his arms at the elbow. A third man stood in front of Allister, his arm pulled back as if to punch him.

The three men stared at me in disbelief as I got to my feet, easing myself to my full height. The man in front of Allister lowered his arm. Anger enveloped me as I surveyed the room, causing my vision to blur pure red.

Seven people, men and women, sat at the large stone table Allister faced. My rage rose; the council, I sneered. Galleries on either side of us and also behind caught my glance as I searched for other threats to Allister and myself.

I noted Victor, Jennavia, and Angelina, phone still in her hand, staring at me in astonishment. I turned my gaze upon the men beginning to gather around us, closing a circle cautiously. I held out both arms, hands up, stopping their approach, as I looked to the front table.

"So…the vile creation has come forward to face judgment."

I turned my gaze to the man standing near the table who broke the silence and he shrank back.

"How dare you intrude on these proceedings," a man seated at the table spoke up. "How did she shimmer in here, the chambers are blocked from shimmering?"

"No matter," the woman beside him said, "we can close this matter completely now."

"Who do you think you are?" I heard my voice coming in an unfamiliar deep, gravely tone. "None of you has the authority to condemn me." The memory of Gabe's words resounded clearly in my thoughts.

"Wait your turn." The man standing by the table tried again. "We will take care of you in a minute."

My eyes sought him out again, but this time, he only shook and didn't retreat. He looked to one side of me and two men move forward.

With the slightest thought, a bright energy burst from my hands, hitting the men and throwing them across the room. They landed, smoking in a heap. I sensed they still lived, a part of me was relieved, but the larger part remained focused on the council.

Cries of shock rose from the galleries and the looks on the council members' faces turned to terror.

"I come here to speak for Allister Parks and demand his release." I glanced at Allister as he looked over his shoulder; his face white.

"He has already been sentenced for his crime," the man standing at the table advised haughtily.

"How can he be sentenced when more evidence can be presented?" I rasped.

"Your existence is more evidence of his guilt, it will do no good if your hope is to stay his execution," the man replied.

"Aw, but you seem to be missing the point." I smiled unpleasantly sending a rumble of murmurs through the gallery.

"And what would that be?" another woman on the council queried.

"I'm not just an Eternal, I'm more."

"We feel you are an Eternal," the woman replied. "That's all that matters to this council."

"Is it?" I raised an eyebrow.

The galleries and the council began whispering amongst each other and finally the woman spoke again. "What are you getting at?"

"Your law states an Eternal cannot touch someone whose soul has left them." I stated, crossing my arms.

The woman nodded an affirmative.

"Then how do you explain my soul?"

The crowd began murmuring again and the woman council member stood, hushing them with raised hands.

"I can see that you are confused." She stared down at me. "You have no soul." Her words were measured, deliberately slow for effect.

"Don't you have someone here who can see souls or guardian angels?" I asked, knowing Jennavia had such powers, though I doubted they would allow her to attest to the presence of my soul.

"Yes, we do," the woman acknowledged, glancing down the table to a slender woman with long dark hair staring at me with horror filled eyes. The woman turned to the speaker, who nodded.

Bowing her head slightly, the woman rose, coming out from behind the table and walked cautiously in front of me.

"I will not harm you," she told me.

"Me either," I replied with a brief nod.

The woman, much smaller than I, reached up to place her hands on my face. Her fingers spread wide as she leaned her head close and closed her eyes in concentration. The hall became still as all eyes fell on the two of us.

The woman let out a small gasp, her eyes opening wide as she leaned back. Still holding my face in her hands, she gazed at me, amazement distorting her face. She stepped back, letting her hands lower as she turned to face the council.

"She has a soul…" her words echoed through the chamber.

The entire room burst into chaos as cheers and protests arose from every direction.

"And an angel's essence." She finished, barely audible over the noise.

"Order, order," a male council member shouted and the room quieted. "I'm not sure I heard that last part Celia," the man frowned.

"She has a soul *and* an angel's essence," Celia repeated, looking uncomfortable.

This time, not a sound echoed in the chambers. Not a gasp, not a breath, nothing. All eyes locked on me.

"Celia, we can sense her as an Eternal," the man pointed out.

"Tis true." She nodded. "Yet the more overwhelming part of her is angel."

"Then what are we to conclude?" the man asked, concerned. First looking at Celia, then down first one side of the table and then the other at the members of the council he clearly was assessing the possible fallout of this complication.

No answer came to break the silence.

"I place myself as evidence in Allister's defense." I said again. "He touched me while I still lived." They had no way to disprove it now.

"Impossible," the man by the table shouted, his face turning red.

"May I speak." A deep voice came from the gallery as Victor stepped forward.

"The council recognizes Victor Parks," a council man spoke up.

"I believe the reason for this anomaly is that the Eternal, Kendal, attacked the girl's guardian angel. My son interrupted Kendal's attempt on the angel and thus the angel only partially separated from the girl. With the angel present, the girl's soul still survived, albeit not strong enough to keep the transformation into an Eternal from occurring completely." Victor stopped, eyeing me curiously.

"May I?" I raised my hand.

The council nodded in unison.

"When Gabe killed Kendal…" I started.

"Who is Gabe?" A council man interrupted.

"Gabriel, an Avenging Angel," I said, drawing gasps from the chamber.

"They sent an Avenging Angel to kill the Eternal Kendal?" A council woman asked.

"Yes, and when Gabe killed Kendal, the remaining portion of my angel returned to me, turning me into what you see before you now." I extended my arms out from my sides.

"Amazing," the council woman gasped.

"You see." Victor stepped forward, "Allister didn't commit a crime here. He is merely another victim of Kendal as much as this girl."

"No," the man by the table shouted. "Allister's intent says he didn't care about the law and acted in violation of that law. It doesn't matter what else happened; he believed her dead."

"Did he?" I asked.

"Of course he did," the man screamed, his face turning red.

I looked at Allister as he stared at me. My eyes urged him to speak in his own defense. Seeing hope at last, he nodded and turned to the council for the first time since I'd arrived.

"May I speak?" Allister asked humbly.

"The council recognizes the accused, Allister Parks," a council woman said.

"I found Britt on the riverbank, no sign of life and a shell of a human being. Something about her spoke to me, urging me to reach out and touch her. I had to save her." He turned back to me as the men holding him let go. "I didn't care if she was here, or gone. I only knew I wanted her, no, needed her with me, more than I'd needed anything before. So if you say I am guilty for touching her knowing she may be dead, then I am guilty."

A roar of outrage erupted from the chamber.

"No," I cried in shock.

It took a moment, before the noise finally ceased and Allister, still holding my gaze, continued. "I saw the beauty in her and knew that if by my touch I could bring back something to this world as glorious as she, it was worth any price."

369

Tears ran down my cheeks as he spoke, the words touching deep within me.

"He's guilty," the haughty man repeated. "He admitted it, he is guilty. Carry out the sentence." He motioned to the men flanking Allister. The two men grabbed his arms once more and the third reared back to remove Allister's heart.

"No," I screamed, leaping between Allister and the Eternal poised to kill him.

Cries flew up around us, although I couldn't tell if they were in protest or approval. The hand, seeming to move in slow motion, drove forward as I stood in front of Allister. The executioner couldn't or wouldn't stay his strike and hit my chest with his full force, driving the air from me and pushing me back into Allister and the two men holding him. We tumbled backwards to the floor as I landed on top of Allister with him safely behind me.

The other men were upon us at once, pulling us apart and lifting us to our feet. They stared in shock as I stood between them with the two holding my arms, not a scratch on me.

Another group of men surrounding Victor jostled with the others for better vantage points.

"This is outrageous," Victor shouted over the chaos. "The council needs to rule based on the new findings and not allow Prosecutor Hamlin to act as both judge and executioner."

"Agreed," a voice said from the vicinity of the council though I couldn't see over the mass of Eternals now surrounding us.

"No," Hamlin shouted. "It is time for the council to realize they are no longer ruling in the best interests of the Eternals. Cowering before Victor Parks is no way to govern. Now is the time for a new order to take control. Men!" His last was spoken as an order.

A rush of hundreds erupted from the gallery thrusting the Eternals into a coup, a full blown coup.

"Victor, Angelina, Jennavia," I shouted as I sidled up and took hold of Allister.

The three Parks pushed through the crowd as Eternal fought Eternal; those who supported the council and Victor against Hamlin's Eternals supporting the coup.

Victor pressed Angelina and Jennavia next to me. "Take them to safety," he ordered.

"I need to stay and fight," I protested wanting to use my new strength.

"This is not your fight," Victor pointed out. "Please, take them out of here. You're the only one who can travel through these walls."

Allister stood next to me, his hands freed from their constraints and wrapped his arms around me. Without any sort of ceremony he kissed me hard and passionate, then stepped back, beaming.

"Please, take them out, Britt," he shouted over the chaos. "We'll catch up with you later."

I leaned in and kissed him hard then pulled away with a nod. I extended my hands and each woman took hold of one. Everything before me blurred and pain erupted in my head. I tilted my face to the sky and screamed as I thought my head would burst from the pressure. I forced my mind to concentrate on the study even as my arms and legs began to burn.

"Britt, Britt don't go. Stay here with us, fight Britt. We love you, don't go," Jennavia and Angelina's words reached me from far away.

"Britt, please, my love. Stay with me forever, stay with me," Allister pleaded.

I couldn't open my eyes to see him. The pain, so intense, I begged for it to end. Nothing hurt like this before and I just wanted it over.

It did end, but not the way I'd hoped. I eased my eyes open, seeing the sterile walls of a hospital room; the sounds, muffled at first, slurred into clarity as the whirring and beeping of machines and monitors brought back all too familiar memories.

I glanced to one side as a nurse checked my IV. The room was familiar, yet confusing. This wasn't Grand Rapids. This wasn't Rochester Mayo. This was...

"Where am I?" I whispered, the effort burning my throat.

"Oh, you scared me." The nurse jumped, putting a hand to her chest. "You're just fine. You're going to be just fine."

"What happened, where am I?"

"You're at the Ely Hospital; they found you by a river."

I tried to sit up only my arms and legs wouldn't work. I hurt all over. Did I dream it all? I panicked, unable to wrap my head around it. Ely was the nearest hospital to the BWCA. And the waterfall.

"Easy, you'll pull your IV out," a soft voice cautioned.

I turned my head and he sat looking at me. His bright smile not as bright, his normally sparkling eyes clouded with concern. Allister stood up and moved over to my bed, and sat down on the edge.

"Oh my God," I gasped, feeling the tears threatening. "I thought it was all a dream."

"A nightmare, you mean." Allister frowned.

"As long as I have you, it'll be a dream." I smiled through wet eyes. "What are we doing here?"

"You must have lost your focus because you traveled to the edge of the very river where we first found you."

"Why am I here?"

"The traveling with Angelina and Jennavia pushed you to your limits. You were badly burned and they needed to get you here to treat you."

"Why didn't Angelina or you just heal me?" I frowned.

"Britt, you're more angel than Eternal now. We can't heal you like we once could. I guess our abilities are limited to humans and Eternals. You're something entirely different."

"Bastion," I gasped, remembering the Eternal now knew where I lived.

"Don't worry. I think Bastion will have more important things to worry about. The Eternal Council survived the coup and all Eternals involved with the attempt will be hunted down and imprisoned. Bastion is in league with Hamlin. He should be on the run for a long time."

"Let's hope so." I felt my tension ebb. My friends and family were safe.

"There is going to be a lot of trouble over all this. They asked Victor to take control of the council again."

"And?"

"He's thinking about it."

"What about us?" I asked the question foremost in my mind.

"I think my family wants to stay in Grand Rapids for a while, if that's okay?"

"Okay? It's more than okay." I sat up, ignoring the pain in my damaged, shifting skin as I wrapped my arms around his neck.

Allister sensed my discomfort and looked at me with concern. "Sore?" he asked.

"Yeah. Can't I heal like before?"

"Angels are actually a lot more resilient than we are, but you pushed it. Even immortals can push too far."

"Then don't make me come save you again, okay?" I smirked and gave him a kiss. This forever thing might turn out yet.

THE END

Epilogue

Trish's Jeep sat alongside the road just before the 'Welcome to Grand Rapids' sign as Elise and Trish worked at changing the large off road tire. They'd struggled to get the spare off the back and now worked to jack up the back side of the Jeep.

"You'd think with all this racing around with Kendal,it would have gone flat then," Trish grumbled. "Not now."

"Quit complaining and let's get this thing changed. Cassie is waiting for us to pick her up at the hospital."

A sleek black Mercedes pulled up, the windows tinted too dark to see who was inside. The window hummed down partway and the girls turned to see the nose and jaw of the driver inside illuminated by the fading sunlight.

"Need some help ladies?" the driver asked them.

"I think we got it," Trish called out and turned back to changing the tire.

"Maybe we can catch a ride to the hospital and have the boys come out and get this?" Elise hated manual labor.

Trish straightened with a hand to her back as she considered the comfort of the black Mercedes. She nodded, "Alright, thanks mister."

"No problem, no problem at all." The man smiled and ran his tongue over his shiny silver tooth.

Stay tuned for book two of
The Angel Crusades
Summer 2014

ACKNOWLEDGEMENTS

I would like to thank my wife for her patient support of my writing. My four children, Ruth and Dale who are constantly cheering me on. My Roseville writing group, (Celia, John, Quinette, Cathy, and Michelle) who helped me wade through uncharted waters. And to Heather. Without her insight and input, this book would definitely be lacking. And to Sheri and Mike for the support an author can only dream about. You guys are awesome!

About the Author

C.S. Yelle was born and raised in Grand Rapids, MN, the "almost" middle child of six. He attended Grand Rapids Senior High School where he enjoyed music and sports. He received his BS in Chemistry from Mayville State University, Mayville, ND in 1987. He taught 7-12 Science and coached for six years in several North Dakota schools and currently works as an Executive Account Manager in the Water Treatment Industry where he has been for over eighteen years. He is the father of four and grandfather of one. He writes novels, screenplays, and an occasional short story. He has been writing seriously for over 15 years and plans to continue until his fingers are unable, maybe longer. He currently resides in a Minneapolis, MN suburb with his wife Jennifer.

Other titles published previously:

Reclaiming Ter Chadain
Black Stones of Ter Chadain

Follow CS Yelle on Facebook or go to his website:
http://p8.hostingprod.com/@csyelle.com/